Preface

This book draws substantially on the period 1979–2012 when I worked for the Australian Foreign Service. Over this time I spent an aggregated twenty-one years abroad from Australia, where I was witness to many memorable happenings and a raft of different cultures. Despite this, when it came to writing a novel it was soon obvious that a work of non-fiction faithfully reflecting my experiences would be all too bland. I chose, therefore, a Cold War spy fiction book, a retrospective narrative around which, loosely fashioned and highly embellished, I wrapped a human interest story based on my personal and professional experiences. Those who know and love me will recognize the human interest passages most apt to describe me, and those that do not!

Strictly speaking, the book's narrative spans fifty years, from the main character Lambert's birth on 14 March 1940 until 14 March 1990. The first twenty-five years, however, get scant treatment as they are designed only to prime the novel for Lambert's twenty-five-year career with the British Secret Intelligence Service, the SIS.

I chose the SIS for two reasons. One was as a government organization with representatives based overseas reporting to a home capital head office, it allowed me to superimpose my own experiences of working in a similar hub and spokes arrangement. The other was my unabashed admiration for John Le Carré and, in terms of my reading history, before him Len Deighton. Both are wonderful writers and both sources of inspiration. At the same time, I was very conscious of avoiding a knock-off of either. I am confident my novel achieves this through its multifaceted narrative, turning as it does on the axis of Lambert's story. Put it this way, any meaningful resemblance in what I have written and any of the works of the great masters is purely coincidental.

Memory of course is far from perfect and I am grateful for modern technology and the refreshing facility it offered. Yet no doubt there will be unintended factual errors. These are regretted and I fervently hope they do not detract substantially from any account provided. The novel has also demanded regular use of acronyms. A glossary is placed at the end of the book for ease of reference as required.

Finally, I need emphasize I have never been an employee of any Australian Government intelligence agency. But I have been a consumer of intelligence product and hence carry with me for life certain obligations under Australian law. It was the need to steer clear of any legal pitfall that convinced me to cast Lambert as an Englishman and apply my experiences to a UK institution of state, namely the SIS for reasons as noted above.

John Michell
Brisbane
May 2018

Disclaimer

This book is a work of fiction. Save for myself, no one fictitious character in it constitutes an attempt to refer in identifiable portion, much less totality, to any actual person living or dead. Any fictitious character's specific resemblance, therefore, to any individual living or dead other than me is purely coincidental.

I have never worked for or have been a client of any UK agency, intelligence or otherwise. I have signed no undertaking committing me to observe the provisions of the UK Official Secrets Act or any ancillary legislation. I have no inkling as to the procedural operations or internal structures of any UK Government agency, or agencies of any other country, and any reference to such in the book is entirely contrived.

Relations or exchanges described in the book between officials of any government agency or entity; or private entities; or individual persons with any other government agency or entity; or private entities; or individual persons, be any party depicted as from the UK or any other country, have no factual basis. They are entirely fictitious accounts.

Certain historical events are recounted. These do not pretend to be summaries of academic quality or of accuracy or balance. The purpose they serve is simply to establish a framework within which the book's fictitious narrative takes place.

Any remarks or assessments the book attributes to political figures, be they living or dead, or political parties or other public figures, in the UK or elsewhere, are not informed observations. They are again simply framework setting devices, baseless inventions for the carriage of the aforementioned fictitious narrative.

John Michell
Brisbane
May 2018

'Don't depend too much on anyone in this world because even your own shadow leaves you when you're in darkness.'

Ibn Taymiyyah 1263-1328

Chapter 1 – Konrad

It's Berlin. Monday 19 December 1966. East Berlin, actually. At
dusk. I was standing on the corner of Warschauer Strasse and
Stralauer Alle, just across from the forbidding darkness of the River
Spree and the lights of West Berlin on the other side. The wind was
whipping off the river. It was freezing, bloody freezing. I was
hanging around trying to link up with a person I'd never met before
and knew of only as Konrad. That was not his real name; it was his
work name. It was all part of Operation Skyman, an undertaking by
the British Secret Intelligence Service, the SIS, to exfiltrate Konrad
to the West. My small role in this was to provide Konrad with
papers, a forged exit visa valid for forty-eight hours from the
previous midnight permitting him to make a single visit to the
Western sector for work purposes.

The plan was for Konrad to walk past me towards the Café
Tagtraum on Warschauer Strasse. The café was a shitty bolt-hole in
the wall serving cheap East Berlin beer. It was not well frequented
on Monday nights and had been chosen for this reason. I had been
briefed that Konrad is in his mid-forties and will wear a distinctive
full-length brown overcoat with large side pockets. He was to carry
with him in his left hand a cheap satchel of the type favoured by
low-level East German bureaucrats. If Konrad carried the satchel in
his right hand the mission was to be aborted.

Inside the café Konrad was to hang his coat on a peg in the vestibule area separating the café's entrance from its main area. He was then to order a beer and repair to a bench to drink it. I was undercover as a Moscow-based British Foreign Office courier, freshly arrived in East Berlin earlier in the day. I was at a loose end and checking out the sights. That night I had decided to experience the gritty end of East Berlin life. I was to enter the café a few minutes after Konrad and hang my jacket in the vestibule. While there, I was to slip the slim sealed package of forged papers into one of the voluminous pockets of his overcoat. I was then to have a couple of drinks in order to confirm that having finished his beer, Konrad had reclaimed his overcoat and made off into the gloom.

I was nervous. After months of waiting, and only recently activated, this was my first foray as an SIS intelligence officer. Fortunately, a man I judged to be in his forties soon emerged from the haze and turned into Warschauer Strasse. There were not a lot of people about and none bar the man were wearing a heavy brown overcoat and carrying a briefcase satchel in their left hand. I studiously ignored Konrad as he passed. After forcing myself to count slowly to a hundred, I made my way up to the café.

I entered the Café Tagtraum vestibule. For a moment I was unable see much in the dim light. As my eyes adjusted, I anxiously scanned the hung garments for Konrad's coat. The document was in my front trouser pocket but first I had to wrestle off my thick jacket and stow my hat and gloves in it. Then, holding the jacket in my right hand, I fished out the package with my left. As I leant forward to hang my jacket, I was simultaneously to deposit the drop in Konrad's coat from behind the protective screen of my body.

At that instant the café entrance door opened with an enormous crash and in poured four very drunk and loud Russian soldiers. I stared at them like a rabbit in a spotlight. The noise alerted the café owner. A formidable German woman entered the vestibule from inside the café. She quickly established she had little time for inebriated Russians and, right then, similar feelings for transfixed imbeciles with idiotic smiles on their faces. 'Raus hier, raus hier,' she screamed as she waved the five of us into the street. I stumbled out onto the footpath, hands shaking and heart pounding. The Russians were vodka-charged and insouciant. They disappeared into the night laughing loudly without so much as a backward glance at me. I stood there uncertain what to do. The woman's scowling face glaring out of the window from inside the café forbade me from re-attempting the drop.

My composure slowly returned. I thought about fallback arrangements. If the drop could not be made, Konrad was to finish his drink and thirty minutes later position himself at the first tram stop north of the Bersarinplatz roundabout linking the southern and northern stretches of Petersburger Strasse. The walk to Bersarinplatz took about thirty minutes and was deliberately designed to keep Konrad moving lest a nosy policeman ask him why he is loitering.

Once at the tram stop, Konrad was to place his satchel on the ground and stand astride it to signal he was comfortable to be approached for a brush-by pass. He was to wait there no more than ten minutes. Reckoning that Konrad would take an additional ten minutes to finish his beer, I calculated I had fifty minutes to complete the job. I headed north up Warschauer Strasse.

It wasn't my night. Upon reaching the junction where Warschauer Strasse becomes the southern stretch of Petersburger Strasse, I found the road cordoned off for overnight resealing of its bitumen surface. *Fucking hell*, I thought, *what else can go wrong?* With growing agitation, I headed off looking for a parallel street from which I could backtrack to Bersarinplatz. All of a sudden there seemed to be people everywhere. I was reluctant to cut through the lines of apartment buildings; if someone spoke to me I would be revealed as a foreigner and with a pocket full of forged documents that was the last thing I wanted. On and on I went, until finally I managed to make my way back to Bersarinplatz.

My detour had caused me to take over an hour to arrive at the tram stop. But I reasoned Konrad would have run into the same problems with the road works. There were about six people in the shelter. A tram arrived and they all boarded. I hung about feeling increasingly awkward. Other people arrived and stared at me sensing my discomfort. A second tram came and went. After twenty minutes, I concluded Konrad had been and gone or wasn't coming. He would have to wait for another day.

Soaked in sweat, I slowly made my way back to my hotel in Alexanderplatz. Along the way I had rationalized my situation. *Konrad can't be that important otherwise why would they leave it to a novice like me to deliver his papers? There will be other opportunities to get him out.* Once in my room I felt sufficiently assuaged to take a shower. Then I rang the number I'd been given for Gloria Mytleford. Gloria was attached to the SIS station at the British Embassy in East Berlin, operating under cover as a political section typist. Her role primarily was to support the SIS field officers attached to the embassy under diplomatic cover.

The phone line was scratchy when Gloria answered. It was assumed the East German secret police, the Stasi, were listening. 'Hello Gloria,' I said, trying to sound relaxed and breezy, 'it's Joe Lambert the diplomatic courier from Moscow who got into town earlier today. I was wondering if you would like to come out for a drink?' The bit about having a drink was a pre-arranged code advising I'd not connected with Konrad. Had I made the drop my invitation would have been for a meal. I will never be sure what, if anything, those listening made of Gloria's sharp intake of breath.

But it sent a chill up my spine. I knew then my masters would not treat lightly my missing Konrad.

'Sorry, Joe,' Gloria said, giving the pre-planned response regardless of which message I used, 'I've just washed my hair. I'll have to take a rain check.' We bantered some more and then hung up. I spent the night staring at the ceiling. My anxiety was well founded.

I had barely set foot in the embassy the next morning when I was told to get down to the secure area, *toot sweet*. The SIS station head was a pompous individual called Stephen Maunder-Roberts. He had not paid me much attention the day before except to ask as I prepared to leave for my rendezvous with Konrad, 'Are you set?' At best, he gave the impression he preferred not to spend too much time with me. Now any semblance of nicety had disappeared. 'You fucking rank amateur,' he bellowed, his physical bulk belied by his curiously feminine habit of crossing and uncrossing his legs. 'I simply don't need useless cunts like you coming in here and making our difficult job impossible. I hope you're happy with yourself. If I have my way… MATE … you'll be drummed out of the Service. Now get the fuck out of my sight.'

I couldn't really argue and even if I could he wouldn't have listened. I had a 3 pm flight back to Moscow. With as much dignity as I could muster, I sealed my diplomatic bags and prepared the *laissez passé* and other paperwork necessary. No one else from the station spoke to me. I was not very communicative with the garrulous embassy security officer who accompanied me to the airport to watch over the diplomatic bags in the hold of the aircraft as I boarded, in case prying eyes decided the Vienna Convention on Diplomatic Relations need not apply. He soon worked out something was on my mind and thankfully shut up.

On reaching the embassy in Moscow, I sought out the station chief. He was already briefed. James Sim was a kindly enough man, a former academic in Russian and Far Eastern studies. All the same, he was transparently relieved I had messed up on someone else's patch and not his own.

'James,' I said, starting to try and explain what had happened. But he quickly shut me down.

'Joe,' he said, 'I can't sugar-coat it. All hell's broken loose in London. The target you missed was a big deal. The KGB pulled him in at some ungodly hour this morning. Maunder-Roberts has advised headquarters the agent planned to go over directly after last night's drop, had he received his papers.' Sim paused. 'You're being recalled,' he said. 'Permanently. The story for Russian and unindoctrinated UK staff is you have an urgent family illness. Go home and pack. They want you back in London by the weekend.'

Chapter 2 – Recruitment

My recruitment into the SIS – or the Service as I came to call it – owed much to a quirk of UK political history and a constitutional convention bearing on it. At the October 1964 general election Harold Wilson's Labour Party had fallen over the line with a four-seat majority. Patrick Gordon-Walker had been Wilson's shadow Foreign Secretary in the run up to the election. But Gordon-Walker failed to win his seat. Constitutionally, however, Ministers of State could hold office for up to three months without being members of parliament. Wilson, therefore, installed Gordon-Walker as Foreign Secretary even though he was not an elected MP, whereupon he assumed portfolio responsibility for the SIS. An effort to shoehorn Gordon-Walker into the parliament via a by-election in January 1965 was derailed when he also lost that election.

The upshot was that Gordon-Walker's lack of parliamentary legitimacy politically constrained him from making major policy decisions during his three-month ministerial tenure. Labour, however, regarded the SIS as a bastion of conservatism and thought it closeted, underperforming and insecure. So while he briefly held political oversight of the SIS, Gordon-Walker occupied himself by beginning to reform the organization, away from the public glare.

I later saw the transcript of Gordon-Walker's initial meeting with the SIS head of the day, Sir Dick White. 'Labour is concerned,' Gordon-Walker had said, 'the agency has become inbred. It is time the SIS began looking for recruits from further afield than Oxford and Cambridge universities. Get some people with dirt under their finger nails,' he instructed White, 'people who have experienced something of what the real world is about.'

White was renowned as a savvy bureaucrat. 'We'll get right on it, Minister,' was his recorded response.

The transcript I saw was also annotated by White's handwriting. This I knew because the added comments were signed as *C,* the Service chief's traditional sign off. White's instruction to his administrators was blunt and candid. *Let's pull in a few people from further afield*, he wrote. *Don't go overboard. The Government's majority is very slim; there's sure to be another election soon.*

I was born on 14 March 1940 in London. My mother liked to boast I shared a birthdate with Albert Einstein. I suspect there the similarities end. I lived only a matter of months in London. In November 1940 the family – comprising my parents, sister Elsie two years my senior and me – relocated to Bootle near Liverpool. My father worked in a reserved occupation as a wharf labourer and Bootle was the docking point for the trans-Atlantic convoys from the

United States keeping Britain afloat during the dark days of the Battle of Britain. That's where he was needed. Unfortunately, the strategic value of the Bootle docks did not escape Adolf Hitler. In the May blitz of 1941 my father was one of the 410 inhabitants of Bootle who lost their lives. The port authorities took pity on us after my father's death; we remained the tenants of our Knowsley Road, Bootle docks-owned house until my mother's death in 1959.

In the meantime the war ended and I began school. Our Bootle home was across from North Park, where I happily spent many summer days playing cricket and generally doing the things young boys do. School was another thing. Elsie was an exemplary student but I was the polar opposite. I just wasn't interested and never got into stride at any stage. Eventually, at age sixteen, I took up a labouring position on the docks.

My co-workers were not sainted warriors of the working class. Like any other group of people there was the good, the average, and the mad and bad. Being young and green, I attracted the attention of the mad and bad. I quickly grew street-smart enabling me to talk the talk while largely avoiding physical altercations. This was fortunate. I may have been just short of six feet tall and, as I matured, of reasonably solid build. But I genuinely feared violence. And unlike many others, I also had little natural inclination to dish it out. Half a lifetime later this aversion to violence would suddenly revisit me, in the most extraordinary of circumstances.

My mother's death from lung cancer, courtesy of her life-long smoking habit, apart from being a harrowing time coincided with the worst of my adolescent immaturity. At nineteen and wanting to show everyone how tough I was, I didn't stay with my mother to her end. Instead I left a couple of hours before she died, and went drinking with my mates. I continued the pretence in public. But in the wee hours of the night after my mother's funeral I woke to sounds of a howling animal, only to discover I was that animal. It was then the shame of my behaviour sheeted home. The guilt I felt over this failing in my duty became a life-long burden.

We were given a month to vacate our house. I moved into rooms off Marsh Lane. Everything I owned fitted into two suitcases. Elsie and I had never been close and we soon lost contact when she shifted to Manchester. I continued to work at the docks but became withdrawn. I copped some hostility from colleagues who apparently took umbrage at this but managed to talk my way out of the more threatening situations. My mother's dying plea imploring me to make something of myself haunted me. Even though I had pledged to heed her wish, at the time of its making my promise was not made sincerely. I said what I thought I needed to say. Now with my conscience rendered increasingly fragile by the recall of my dereliction of duty, I knew I had to do something. In 1961 I began night classes at the Bootle Polytechnic.

I had no real idea what I wanted to do but decided to learn about business, whatever that meant. I took a course in basic business administration. It was hardly rocket science yet I was pleased when I did quite well. On the advice of the college, I applied for an assisted place at the Liverpool Metropolitan University. Eventually, a letter arrived advising I had qualified for university entrance and that a place had been reserved for me subject to completion of enrolment formalities. The offer included accommodation for a small weekly fee at the University's Kingston Hall residential college. With all the precision of throwing a dart, I settled on an application for a Bachelor of Commerce.

By 1962 Liverpool was on its way to becoming the centre of the Universe for young people. Music was the catalyst. Live bands played the city's many makeshift clubs. When the Beatles released *Love Me Do*, the place exploded. I of course joined in, abandoning my crew cut hairstyle for a Beatles *mop-top*. Or at least I tried; my wavy fair hair and clear blue eyes were not conducive to the look, even if my pale complexion, a by-product of my father's Cornish origins, matched the Fab Four's sun-denied visages.

Being four or so years older than the bulk of my student intake meant I didn't form many friendships with male classmates. Most were typical eighteen-year-olds and daunted by the age difference, added to which I felt no particular inclination to befriend other males. As for the female students, the situation was a little more complicated. Before university my sex life had involved a few instances of slap and tickle, mostly when both parties were very drunk, and a visit to a prostitute as an eighteenth birthday present from my workmates. But by the time I got to Liverpool I was ready for a steady relationship. There was some trial and error as my first year progressed. Despite a putative free love mentality on campus, many young women I encountered already had one eye on marriage. Most were idealistic. The Prince Charming whom they imagined would walk them down the aisle never actually existed.

Nonetheless, being a little older than most female students seemed to give me a natural advantage. Opportunities arose for more appealing relationships. I entered into each with eyes firmly on the long term, which at age twenty-two probably meant at least a year. But coincidentally I experienced a noticeable blooming of the loner instincts that had first emerged in the aftermath of my mother's death. No sooner was I in a sought-after relationship than without exception the initially strong spark evaporated. I had a sense of being trapped. The instinct to take flight and be alone was overpowering. Try as I might, I couldn't resist it. And afterwards came feelings of depression and regret, slight at first then stronger. The insult to injury was I gained a reputation as a philanderer. Many female students, especially the more mature and confident, grew disdainful of me. In private, I felt their rejection keenly.

My self-analysis led me to conclude that my dysfunctional personal life somehow related to my appalling abandonment of my mother at her time of need. As a young man, I was unable to condense the swirling thoughts inside my head into anything more coherent. Maybe if I had sought professional help I might have saved myself a lot of subsequent heartache. But I never even considered it. It wasn't the right era; seeking counselling was to admit weakness and a serious compromise of the image young men were expected to project. The only psychiatric tests I ever did were for the Service. And they were so orientated to finding closet communists that issues of sexuality were never addressed.

One of the tutors in my final year was a man called Bernie Odgers. Bernie had history in a family printing business and tutored in an intensely boring elective I took called *Business Theory*. Bernie was past his best. Alcoholic fumes radiated from his dark-puce, weathered face. But he and I got on well. He found young students too irritating and liked that I had some grip on the world. Bernie had seen action in North Africa during the war before being taken prisoner in February 1941. After two years in captivity, he was repatriated as part of an exchange of British and Italian POWs. Bernie said he became ill after he returned home. From what I could deduce he had suffered a nervous breakdown. But Bernie had paid his dues and was entitled to some dignity. The University acknowledged this by allowing him to tutor once a week, with the practical bonus that Bernie filled a slot no one else would.

Deep in the bowels of the SIS personnel section Bernie's war service was also remembered. Nigel Shuttleworth had been Bernie's company commander in North Africa. Unlike his redoubtable subaltern, Major Shuttleworth had avoided capture. His Brigadier uncle had landed him an administrative position in SIS headquarters after the war. But Shuttleworth was not a strong performer. Although of sober habits and a good family man, his propensity to talk rather than work and predilection for shortcuts was legendary. The Service old hands reasoned he would be the ideal person to scour the country in search of a few token provincial recruits; God knows you'd never give him anything important to do.

In early December 1964, while waiting for final exam results, I received a note from Bernie asking if I could meet him at 9 am the next morning at Allerton Cemetery. The request did not surprise me; Bernie was eccentric and no stranger to unusual ideas. But this time when I arrived I was amazed to find him dressed to the nines, the erect collar of his dark blue trench coat around his ears. 'Important we're discreet old boy,' he said, 'don't want to blow our cover.' Oblivious to the fact he stood out like a beacon, Bernie told me in hushed tones, 'A Mr Sheppard in London would like to have a word with you.' If I were interested he would let Sheppard know. A return train ticket from Liverpool Lime Street to London Euston would be provided and on production of receipts, Bernie said, 'You will also get a few bob for a feed on the way.'

I asked the obvious question. 'How would I know if I'm interested or not? I haven't got the faintest idea what this is about.'

Bernie seemed stumped, momentarily torn between telling me enough and telling me too much. Finally, he said, 'Joe, what are you going to do with your degree? There's not many jobs around here; you will likely end up in London working in some civil service backwater. Dead boring. This is sort of civil service but mainly isn't. If nothing else you'll get a free run down to London.'

The idea of a day trip to London appealed. Mostly I didn't want to disappoint Bernie who was obviously keen for me to go. *Why not?* I thought. 'OK Bernie, tell this fellow I'll go to London and talk to him. But please tell him no guarantees. If I don't like what's on offer I'm walking.'

So it was that lazy Nigel Shuttleworth, aware of Bernie's tenuous link to the Liverpool Metropolitan University, had asked Bernie to talent spot for him. Paying scant regard to any objective criteria, least of all academic excellence, Bernie had nominated me.

I met Shuttleworth, whom I knew then as Sheppard, and another person calling himself Watts in a spartan office off Hampstead Road. Watts I later learned was a low-level pen pusher, real name of Middleton.

After preliminaries, Shuttleworth took the lead. 'Have you ever travelled out of England?' he asked.

'No I have not.'

'Would you like to live abroad doing work for government?

Missing the cue, I replied as might any nearly twenty-five-year-old asked whether he wanted an overseas holiday. 'How fabulous,' I said naively, 'I would love to see the Great Wall of China.'

Suddenly red of face, Middleton jumped from his chair with such force I thought he was going to assault me. 'It's not all beer and skittles, you know,' he snarled, as if he had twenty-five years of field experience to draw on.

A few more questions on my preparedness to work abroad, which I now negotiated very cautiously, and the interview moved to general matters.

'What do you think is the biggest political challenge facing the UK?' Middleton asked, calm again.

Here's a chance to impress, I thought, recalling a lecturer once mentioning Lenin's theory of imperialism, something to do with the concentration of capital. 'The concentration of capital among the few creates inequality,' I said confidently.

'And?' Middleton said, his right eyebrow raised.

My mind went blank. I now wished I'd paid more attention in class. My confidence evaporated and I panicked. 'Well, that results in no money being left over for others.' A pause as my nonsensical response was noted. I couldn't know it then but my botched attempt at sophistication was the answer Middleton was looking for – confirmation I had no ideological leanings.

Shuttleworth took over. 'What do you think about Soviet conduct in Hungary in '56?' I stared blankly, remembering only of all things once reading about the Russian and Hungarian water polo teams brawling at the 1956 Olympics. But at least I had the wit to understand the question ran deeper than this.

When I didn't answer, Shuttleworth asked, 'Have you read any of Graham Greene's books?'

Graham who? I thought. Inside my head the wheels were spinning but there was no traction. All I could do was to continue to stare blankly.

Perfect non-answers as it turns out. More notes.

Finally, Shuttleworth asked, 'Would you agree to psychiatric testing should the job offer progress?'

I eagerly agreed, happy at last to be able to answer a question.

'Go home and wait to be contacted by mail,' Shuttleworth said. 'Under no circumstances are you to breathe a word of our discussions to anyone.'

On the return trip I reflected on the interview. My interrogators had told me that competition for positions was intense and I'd clearly upset Middleton – who I then thought was Watts. But the way they spoke as the interview concluded had the air of a *fait accompli*. I resolved there and then I would take the job were it offered. I had no family or friends in Bootle and taking the job, I reasoned, would also honour my belatedly acted on pledge to my dying mother to make something of myself. On arrival, there was a letter from the University waiting advising I had passed my final exams – just. *Joe Walter Lambert B.Comm, servant of Her Majesty's Government*, had a nice ring to it I decided.

Chapter 3 – Initiation

In early January 1965 a letter in a Foreign Office crested envelope arrived. The message was terse: I had been selected for probationary employment in the Foreign Office research unit located at 54 Broadway opposite St James Park tube station. I was to report for duty in London on 25 January. My worldly possessions now filled three suitcases, leaving me forego the removal assistance on offer. Accommodation for a maximum of three weeks would be provided at the Strand Castle Hotel. And 300 quid a year to boot!

On the night of 24 January I arrived at my hotel. The sombre reception clerk informed me Winston Churchill had died earlier in the day. My abiding memory of arriving the next day at SIS headquarters was that the security guards, later known to me as janitors, all wore black armbands.

The first week passed in a blur of briefings and form signing. It slowly dawned on me I had joined the Secret Service. I could scarcely believe it. But I was young and robust and just rode the wave. From the outset the paramount importance of good security, principally the NTK or *need to know* principle, was rammed down the throats of me and my four other fellow inductees.

The other newcomers, all males, were roughly my age. I didn't have much in common with them. From day one they wore a variety of smart suits; until I received my first pay and was able to buy a cheap suit on the *never, never*, I was forced to rely on the threadbare best of my student wardrobe. Each of my colleagues was London-based and, as their Windsor-knotted ties testified, from well-heeled families. Two of them, whose names I can no longer recall, left the Service not long after completing basic training. The other two, Rupert Heneshaw and Frederick Ladler, were destined to become my sworn enemies. Both urbane young men, Rupert was slightly shorter, more thickset and of darker complexion than Frederick.

Heneshaw and Ladler first raised my hackles when it was emphasized at one of the induction briefings the Service should always have an up to date home address and telephone number for its officers should urgent contact be necessary. I didn't have a strong Liverpudlian accent, or Scouse accent as it was known among the working classes, primarily because at home my mother spoke in her native London accent. But I did have the habit of occasionally ending sentences with *like*, which was a dead giveaway as to my Merseyside, struggle-town background. 'I've only arrived in London,' I said, 'and still have to find somewhere to live.' With memories of my rooms in Bootle still fresh in my mind I added, 'When I do there's a possibility I might not have access to a telephone, *like*.'

Heneshaw and Ladler both sniggered at this unheard of revelation. 'No telephone?' Ladler said, feigning amazement.

Heneshaw responded in mock horror. 'I do believe we've a randy Scouse git in our midst.'

Ladler was highly amused by this reference to a popular television program of the day and the derogatory phrase used by one of the key protagonists to describe his Liverpudlian son-in-law. 'I hope he's not a bolshie as well,' he said, in reference to the son-in-law's ascribed socialist leanings.

Heneshaw and Ladler spent the next ten minutes exchanging looks and suppressing giggles. I harboured delusions of conflict resolution Bootle docks-style, but instead sat there in simmering humiliation for the rest of the day. Rupert and Freddie made little subsequent effort to disguise their regard of me as a social inferior.

A silver lining, however, was that the briefer introduced me to a Mrs Brooks who apparently administered Service property in and around London. She put me on to a retired Service couple living in Kentish Town. There I soon took up residence in a two-room granny flat in the garden of their Gatcombe Road home. It was a long haul into the office each day – the daily walk to Tufnell Park Road underground station and the crowded tube rides on to St James Park – and, seemingly, an even longer haul home. I also had the feeling the couple was watching me. Old habits die hard, I guess. But at least my watchers understood the business. I was chuffed to be told with knowing smiles no rent would be necessary when I informed them I was going away for basic training.

In April 1965 our five-strong intake arrived at Fort Monckton, the SIS training centre in Gosport, Hampshire. It was spring and the air was clear. From my accommodation block you could see the Portsmouth-Fishborne ferry steam by; on a good day the Isle of Wight was clear. It was an exciting time. But spring soon turned to winter and our workload increased. We were given all sorts of courses: in communications; secret writing; tailing people; protecting against tails; and in unarmed combat, or *one-armed wombat* as our Special Air Services instructor called it. At times we were sent to the nearby towns of Wallington and Portchester to practise aspects of our craft, such as dead drops and the like.

Life at the fort was generally harmonious, although Heneshaw did take the opportunity of one of the *wombat* sessions to sit me on my backside with a lot more vigour than was necessary, while all the while Ladler looked on in gleeful encouragement. The incident erased any doubt I might have had that in Heneshaw and Ladler I had made enemies for life. Back in London six months later, I resumed my austere existence.

The Service had sixteen operational branches and hence sixteen branch heads. Branches were paired together into eight divisions. A First Assistant Director General, known colloquially as an FADG, headed each division. The eight divisions were in turn paired and supervised by one of four Deputy Director Generals, or DDGs, answering to the Director General. A fifth DDG supervised one large administrative division, that DDG going by the acronym ADDG. Immediately subordinate to the ADDG was the Head of Personnel, a FADG-equivalent position known in abbreviated form as Personnel.

Awaiting my return was a letter from Personnel informing me I would be assigned to SPB, standing for Soviet Political Branch. Little did I know I was being attached to SPB over the branch's dead body, when Personnel finally prevailed in a bureaucratic arm-wrestle. SPB did not exactly welcome me with open arms, but nonetheless I ended up on reasonable terms with the branch head, a man called Martin Mumford. Mumford was a brilliant Russian linguist. He had lived and worked in Russia as a businessman, where no doubt he had come to the Service's attention. He went on to have a stellar career, deservedly rising to the rank of DDG. A tall and wiry man about a decade my senior and decent to his core, he was to have a profound effect on my life.

Like all other branches, SPB split into two sections. Moscow Affairs Section, MAS, focused on Soviet operations. It worked closely with its sister section Soviet Satellites Section, SSS, which dealt with those communist countries sharing land borders with the USSR; Poland, Czechoslovakia, Hungary, and Romania. But for all the branch's cohesiveness, MAS was decidedly the glamour section. Needless to say, I was attached to SSS.

Directors headed each section. My director was what the Service called a generalist. He spoke no Russian and, unlike most in the branch, had not served in Russia or elsewhere in Eastern Europe. This lack of in-theatre experience meant he relied heavily on his deputy, a willowy Hungarian woman called Katalin, or Kat as we used to call her. She took the surname of Phillips from a defunct marriage hastily entered into not long after her arrival in the UK in the wake of the 1956 Hungarian uprising. Kat was in her late forties. I found her enormously attractive, not helped by the fact I'd been living like a monk for nearly a year. The cloak of world-weariness in which she shrouded herself enhanced her attractiveness. It aroused my male protective instincts.

I think Kat was aware of my feelings for her; occasionally when we were working on a document she'd allow her breasts to brush my arm. The Service tacitly encouraged intra-service liaisons because they reduced the risk of pillow talk problems, albeit with some diminution to the ubiquitous NTK principle. At the branch Christmas party of 1965 I contemplated testing the waters. But I was simply not up to it; too scared I had misread the signals and anxious not to blot my copybook. Kat left the Service some years later. I never saw her again – but memory of her lingered.

SPB had a total of twelve staff. The others were mostly young and a mix of men and women, a couple of whom were civil towards me in a guarded sort of way. The entire place reeked of ambition. I quickly learned it was important to be seen when praise was in the offing and well below the parapet when it was not. My colleagues were very different to those in Bootle. The latter, for all their shortcomings, were by far the warmer and sincerer human beings.

I settled into a work routine blissfully unaware of the debate going on behind closed doors about what to do with me. In January 1966, as the first anniversary of my joining the Service approached, Mumford called me to his office. 'Joe,' he said, 'we've been giving consideration to posting you to Moscow under a deep cover arrangement.'

Naively, I thought this represented acceptance at last. I was also so heartily sick of living at Kentish Town that had a posting to Mars been suggested I would have jumped at it. 'I would like that very much, Martin,' I replied, not stopping to think how I might become operational in Moscow without speaking Russian.

'Good,' Mumford said. 'Tell you what, why don't we go up and see Personnel this afternoon?'

'The Sovs,' Personnel said to me, 'have been putting a lot of recent effort into identifying SIS officers in our Eastern Bloc embassies. Every time one of our diplomats leaves the building they have teams of watchers on their backs. No staffing thresholds to worry about for the bloody Russkies. They're starting to sort the wheat from the chaff if you get my drift. The added complication is we just can't drop people into Eastern Europe at whim. Visas take an eternity and we need in each instance to come up with plausible cover. This is causing us problems providing the various bibs and bobs that certain assets need from time to time, often at short notice. We've had discussions with the Foreign Office and it's prepared to create a position in Moscow, at our expense mind, which will involve you working in the embassy administration and every couple of weeks doing a courier run of diplomatic bags an FO courier will deposit at the post. You'll be going to places like Budapest, East Berlin, Warsaw, etcetera; you know, all the benighteds. As you'll already be in Moscow, you'll be able to obtain a multiple entry visa for any of the Eastern Bloc countries.'

Looking to Mumford for confirmation his sales pitch remained on course, Personnel went on. 'We're playing a long game on this. You won't be doing anything operational for quite a while. The reason being that the Russians will have a look at you after you arrive, especially when you're travelling. Most of the FO couriers like to get themselves pissed. It's not compulsory, is it?' he asked, turning to Mumford who smiled weakly. 'So for however long necessary, drop the bags off nice and secure wherever you're visiting and then get out among the fleshpots and on the swill. If you get the jack, the umbrella up the eye of your John Thomas is not a cost the Service will meet.' Mumford and I politely joined with Personnel in appreciating his joke. 'Provided you're sufficiently decadent, the Sovs will conclude over time you're nobody to worry about. We can ease you into a bit of work thereafter.'

I still cringe when recalling how thankful I was for this opportunity. In truth, I'd just witnessed a piece of bureaucratic mastery. I was still officially an SIS resource but to all practical effect had just been shunted off indefinitely to the Foreign Office. More to the point, I had been shunted off not to the prestigious diplomatic reaches of the FO but to its administrative wasteland.

Chapter 4 – Moscow

Unlike more benign postings, where the host government is friendlier, all British staff posted to Moscow have diplomatic status, regardless of agency or position. But as I soon found out when I arrived in February 1966, there were unofficially *A*-list and *B*-list diplomats. I was squarely a *B*-lister; the result being demotion in the pecking order when it came to embassy car parks, inferior office accommodation and often the incurrence of *A*-list disdain.

My courier work provided a reason periodically to access the embassy's secure area. There was not much moral support forthcoming from my SIS colleagues whose offices were located within. In fact, James Sim pointedly told me to avoid unnecessary contact with any of his people. He needn't have bothered; the nine others in the station ignored me as one. Time rolled by. I slaved away organizing the delivery of furniture lots from Denmark for use in the apartments allocated to UK staff by the Russian Diplomatic Services Bureau. In between, on average every fortnight, I travelled to most Eastern European capitals carting my diplomatic bags. Out on the road, I was diligent in building cover. Exploring the nightlife was also a convenient bulwark against the boredom and loneliness I experienced when in those drab cities.

After nearly six months *en-poste*, I started a relationship with a secretary from the American embassy called Patsy. In Moscow's repressive atmosphere romances among Westerners bloomed easily. I was no different. I keenly felt the need for female succour. Patsy was an engaging Minnesotan and my affection for her sprouted in the environment. But once into the involvement my instinct to escape soon took hold. In six weeks we were done. Patsy wasn't much pleased; in her own American vernacular she felt she had been treated eponymously.

I became frustrated at yet again my inability to tie down a relationship and harboured feelings of guilt. Loneliness and depression engulfed me. For a time afterwards I drank heavily, until the all too familiar ache of break-up had receded. Fortunately, the embassy caste system was such that no one who mattered was likely to drop in and witness my maudlin behaviour night after night in the darkened confines of my hateful Prospekt Mira apartment. That was a secret between me and the microphones buried deep in the apartment walls.

How long I might have been left *building cover* is anyone's guess. The Service's strategy, I later reflected, had been to coerce me into resignation through a combination of boredom and disillusionment. But political fate again intervened. In March 1966, not long after I arrived in Moscow, UK voters had returned to the polls. Those predicting an early election had been vindicated but few had anticipated the outcome. Harold Wilson was returned with a thumping majority. Six months later he reshuffled his ministry and appointed George Brown as Foreign Secretary.

In late September 1966, during the dark period following the demise of my liaison with Patsy, and as I was beginning to understand the Service had duped me, Brown had his initial meeting with the Service Director General, Sir Dick White. Brown had an expressed interest in the politics of class. After other discussions, he had turned to this topic. 'How much progress has been made in expanding the Service's social breadth?' he asked the DG.

White's briefing notes made no reference to the matter. 'Progress has been satisfactory, I believe,' he had extemporized.

Brown pounced, seeming to perceive evasion. 'I would like to know the current situation.'

White volunteered he didn't have the information with him. He proposed to take the question on notice.

'A response by this afternoon will be fine,' was Brown's reply.

White reacted with alacrity. No doubt Brown's political menace was not lost on him. The DG had a note to the Minister's office by lunchtime; I later saw it and the date and time stamp on it.

To his apparent consternation, White had discovered on return to the office that of the five yokels recruited, to use one insider's derogatory term, three had resigned and another, unable or unwilling to live abroad, had taken a position in the Service's communications unit. Only I was in the field. I say *apparent consternation* because later that day a *Top Secret* message *Personal for Sim from White* was flashed to Moscow: *As soon as feasible Lambert is to be given an operational task. Ready him.*

The Russian winter came early in 1966–67. One night towards the end of September I was hurrying to my car anxious to beat the evening chill. A member of the SIS station sidled up to me, 'Joe, how are you doing?'

I looked at him warily. This fellow was an *A*-lister and had never spoken to me before. I thought he was an arrogant shit. 'Yes?' I said as coldly as I could.

'Old Jimmy wants an audience with you first thing tomorrow morning. As soon as you get free, would you mind ducking in?' I recognized the technique. By speaking disrespectfully of the station chief he was establishing a little bond between us designed to build rapport. Before I had a chance to answer he added, 'No dramas. All good news. Cheers.' And then he was gone.

James Sim at least had the decency to look embarrassed. He licked his lips nervously. 'Ah, ah Joe come in,' he said. To his assistant sitting outside his office he shouted, 'Let's have some coffee down the back.' Down the back referred to a windowless room deeper in the already windowless secure area, where sensitive conversations were held. I knew of it but had never set foot in it. 'I've been watching your progress, Joe and I'm quite impressed,' Sim began. With this lie he was no longer able to hold my gaze. 'I've decided you're just about ready to get into something a bit meatier,' he said to the classified waste container off to one side. 'How do you feel your cover build has come along?'

'Well,' I said, 'every hooker in the lounge bar at the Forum Hotel in Warsaw knows me by name.' Sim looked at me as if I had just said something distasteful but otherwise let the sarcasm pass.

'Good,' he said, without conviction. 'I'll recommend back to London that Operations cable all Eastern Bloc station heads advising you are now an asset to be utilized.'

That awkward moment over, Sim relaxed and smiled a fatherly smile. 'Big moment for you, Joe. Selina's having a dinner party this Friday night. Real reason is to celebrate your activation and welcome you into the fold. But with us spooks of course cover is everything. It'll be a pretend birthday party for some lassie at the Dutch Embassy. None of those wearing clogs will be in the know.

So mum's the word. Don't wear your tails; it's going to be very informal.'

Selina was Sim's right-hand woman, the one who had made us coffee. Beyond a cursory nod, she had never before acknowledged my existence. She came cavorting up to me as I left the secure area and placed a manicured hand on my forearm. 'Hope you can make it Friday night, Joe,' she gushed. 'I'll leave an invitation in your pigeon hole in the Registry.'

'B-b-be pleased,' I stammered. And with a conspiratorial wink and flashing smile she sent me on my way.

What did I make of all this? Well, I knew my time in spying Siberia had not been a figment of my imagination. Evidently something had changed but as to what I was clueless. Where some of the young males in the station had developed close friendships, I had no male contemporaries, partly because I was an outsider and partly because as usual I felt no compulsion to make male friends. Unsurprisingly, therefore, efforts to coax a reason for my rehabilitation out of my Service colleagues were not fruitful. It was not until many years later, when I had climbed the Service's greasy pole and gained access to files dating back to 1966, that I saw the record of the DG's conversation with George Brown, attached to which was his follow-up note to the Minister's office and his subsequent instruction to

Sim. But at the time I ultimately gave up wondering and gratefully embarked on my new career direction.

A *Secret* cable from East Berlin station arrived in early December asking if *Leonard*, the code name given to my floating resource role in Eastern Europe, could be released to do a live drop in East Berlin on 19 December. Briefing to be provided on arrival. I was thrilled but tried not to show it. We dashed back a response, noting flight details and accommodation requirements would be provided through open channels. In other words, an unclassified communication would be sent to the embassy in East Berlin detailing the administrative aspects of my latest courier run. That information would find its way into the hands of the embassy's East German employee responsible for making hotel bookings. As a matter of course, the employee would pass this on to the Stasi. By now, so the theory ran, the Stasi was inured to my comings and goings and would not give my intended travel a second's thought.

The excitement of my launch into operational work was just a distant memory as I jetted back to London with my tail between my legs. I resisted the urge to drown my sorrows with a few whiskies. The inquest into what went wrong in East Berlin would be bad enough without someone trumping up a story I was out of control on the sauce. It was the Friday night before a Sunday Christmas when I landed. The Christmas lights in Knightsbridge cheered me temporarily. Booking into the Strand Castle Hotel, my cheeriness vanished. I reflected on my high hopes nearly two years ago. *What an awful fucking mess*, I thought. Sleep proved elusive. I was resigned to dismissal and sought refuge in that fatalism.

Head of Personnel, Martin Mumford and a senior officer called Petr Klaus were waiting for me when I arrived at headquarters on the Saturday morning, Christmas Eve. Personnel's smouldering silence made clear his general unhappiness at being dragged into the office when he should be on holidays. It was Mumford who spoke first, addressing me. 'You may know,' he said, 'that Mr Klaus is the FADG responsible for East German affairs. His supervising DDG has tasked him to conduct an in-house enquiry into the Konrad matter and report in early January.' Preamble over, Mumford moved to specifics. 'Konrad,' he said, 'was a low-level registry clerk in an East German Government agency.' He did not name which one. 'His job was to maintain up to date agency files. This meant he had access to an extraordinary range of sensitive documents. The loss of this unimpeachable intelligence is highly damaging to the Service's domestic standing and its relations with United States intelligence agencies.' With that, Mumford paused waiting for Klaus to speak.

I did know something of Klaus. He was of Czech background and had come to England in early adolescence with his family, who had the good sense to leave Czechoslovakia after Hitler annexed the Sudetenland. His father had apparently become a member of the RAF's vaunted all-Czech No. 310 Squadron. The Service picked up

Petr while still a student at Oxford University. Naturally skilled in the hand-to-hand combat characterizing British bureaucracy, Klaus had only to open his mouth to establish his intellectual superiority, no matter with whom he was speaking. His career inevitably skyrocketed. A small man with a round face, he stared unblinkingly at colleagues when conversing. This was a natural trait but it unnerved his *confrères* all the same. Klaus stared briefly at me. 'Perhaps we should hear Joe's version of events,' he said, signalling my interrogation was about to begin.

Wanting to remain strong and alert, I stared down the temptation to buy myself a bottle of whisky for Christmas. Time passed slowly. I read and dozed and periodically braved the elements to take walks along the Strand. I had declined the offer of leave, figuring I could do with the payout of leave credits when eventually I was sacked. On the two working days between Christmas and New Year I spent my time in the so-called transit lounge, a staging area within head office equipped with desks and other office paraphernalia where, as necessary, returning officers sat before taking up allocated head office appointments. I had some money but not much. I found a small flat off unfashionable Albany Road in South London. I moved in on 3 January 1967, the first working day of the year.

I never formally heard another word about East Berlin. Many years later my access to the files, and by dint of that Klaus's report, revealed Klaus had declined to scapegoat me. No doubt to the chagrin of Stephen Maunder-Roberts, the East Berlin station head, who maintained Konrad had intended to go West the night he was to receive his papers. Instead Klaus determined that Konrad's cover of a work visit to West Berlin dictated a less-conspicuous morning crossing at least three hours later than the time of his pre-dawn arrest. This led him ultimately to conclude that Operation Skyman's failure was immaterial. Klaus had also somehow divined that East Berlin station knew suspicions about Konrad were emerging. Yet neither London nor Konrad was alerted. *As a result*, Klaus wrote, *Konrad was left in place far too long, possibly to enhance the career prospects of some in East Berlin station.* Klaus's report attached all blame for Konrad's detection to this. Konrad was shot just six hours after his arrest. I never did find out why he had spied for us.

I had noticed in an internal placements circular some years earlier that Maunder-Roberts had been sent to New Zealand in a backwater liaison job. On reading the report, I came to understand this was his punishment for mishandling Konrad. Klaus died prematurely, at age forty-five, almost five years to the day from the date of his report. Prostate cancer. He was not in the business of doing favours for anyone. But I owe a lot to him and his unstintingly objective enquiry. I shudder to think what might have happened had any of the other Johnnies around the place conducted the review, imbued in class prejudice as most of them were.

Chapter 5 – Konfrontasi

Sitting in the transit lounge in the first week of January 1967 I had no inkling as to the conclusions Klaus would draw. I'd long given up any pretence of working and spent my time drinking cups of coffee and reading Harold Robbins's *The Carpetbaggers*. Then on the Thursday of the following week, Head of Personnel suddenly manifested in front of me. 'Wotcha reading, battlecruiser?' he asked, addressing me using the cockney rhyming slang for *boozer* and gibbering like the East End barrow boy he certainly was not. Without waiting for my answer, he said, 'You got a minute?'

I thought, *Mate, I've got the rest of my life* but simply said, 'Sure.' On the way to his office, Personnel talked about football and his love for Tottenham Hotspur. I was mightily confused by this time. I'd expected a summons and a curt sign this, get out of here and don't come back. Instead Personnel was treating me like we were long lost buddies. On reaching his office, Personnel settled in one of his comfortable visitor chairs and invited me to sit in another.

'Joe,' he said, 'you've been good enough to come home early from Moscow to assist us with some pressing matters. We need to recognize this. Unfortunately, the cover for your departure from the post was so definite you're unable to go back.' I opened my mouth to speak. Personnel held up a hand like a policeman stopping traffic.

'Past events are exactly that,' he said. 'There is no further need to revisit them.' With that, I shut up. I was beginning to wonder if these bewildering direction changes were more commonplace within the Service than I had thought.

'Now as I was saying,' Personnel continued, 'there was a promotion round you might ordinarily have contested that closed just before Christmas. The lazy sods on the committee are all on holidays and won't report until the end of January. If you wanted to make an application it will be considered. Freehand writing is fine. No need to submit it through channels. Return it to me and I will process it. In writing the application just make reference to the fact you've served in difficult cover circumstances in our highest interest post; also served in the supervising operational branch in headquarters; and that you're a mature man of good judgement and excellent interpersonal skills. I'll take care of reports from supervisors. A couple of paragraphs will suffice. Get it to me before we finish tomorrow afternoon, there's a good chap.'

Personnel paused for breath and smiled at me. I noticed his teeth at the extremities of his mouth were yellow from cigarette smoking. I wondered if I was the Service's only non-smoker – my mother's death had delivered me a stark warning about the evils of tobacco. Personnel's announcement he wanted to *look to the immediate future* withdrew me from my reverie. 'Have you ever been to Asia, Joe?' he asked, knowing full well I hadn't. 'Lots going on out there these days, especially in Dutch Indonesia. Seems the commies tried a coup, failed and are now getting their collective arse kicked by the army.'

He stopped abruptly, jumped up and moved to the telephone on his desk, where he dialled three times indicating a call to an internal number and spoke quietly into the mouthpiece. In a matter of seconds a tall, bespectacled woman entered the office. She had lank hair and wore a mien of intensity. 'Joe,' he said, 'I'd like you to meet Beverley Brittingham. Bev heads up our South East Asia Branch.' Brittingham shook my hand forcefully, her body twisting as a result of the energy she expended. 'We'd like you to take a position in the branch working on Dutch Indonesia,' Personnel said.

'Actually Cam,' Brittingham interjected, abbreviating Personnel's first name of Campbell, 'it's not been Dutch Indonesia since 1949. It's now the Republic of Indonesia.'

Personnel seemed to regard this as a mere technicality. 'Whatever it's called, Joe, we'd like you to work in the area.' Looking at Brittingham but talking to me he added, 'We think you should spend about six months there to familiarize yourself. Then we'll probably give you another six months to learn a bit of the lingo. By that stage you should be ready in the New Year to take up a posting with Jakarta station. What say you?'

'Yes ... yes, that should be fine,' was all I could get out.

'Excellent,' Personnel said. 'That's settled.' He never spoke warmly to me again.

Indonesia section, INS in the Service's shorthand, was of course one of two sections making up Brittingham's fiefdom. The other focused on the newly independent states of Malaysia and Singapore. MSS was accommodated some distance from us; we rarely saw its three denizens. A lanky, prematurely balding man called Hanson Scott headed INS. His stock joke was to call himself Handsome Scott. Hanson had been a journalist in Indonesia and spoke the language well. He was good to me and made sure I was allocated a decent desk. I was granted access to reams of highly classified reports detailing Indonesia's turbulent past, as well as the cables from Jakarta station that arrived overnight while we were sleeping.

There were four others in the section. We had in addition a Canadian exchange officer, who shortly after my arrival completed a three-month placement in INS as part of her two-year attachment to the SIS. Like Soviet Political Branch, the INS environment was thick with ambition. But no matter how hard they tried, the INS people could not quite match the perceived self-importance of their SPB colleagues. Accordingly, relations with my co-workers were warmer. They were not so good that we'd spend Friday nights in the pub together but there was some *esprit de corps*; particularly when

Brittingham was on the warpath, as telegraphed by the exaggerated swaying of her hips as she charged down the corridor to berate some unfortunate miscreant.

The Borneo confrontation, or Konfrontasi as the Indonesians termed it, was an armed conflict between Indonesia and Malaysia running from January 1963 until August 1966. Indonesia's President Sukarno regarded Malaysia's creation, first when a proposal and then from September 1963 as an existing entity, as a security threat to Indonesia's provinces on the island of Borneo – Kalimantan to the Indonesians. Malaysia's formation involved the incorporation of Britain's former colonial territories on Kalimantan and Sukarno perceived ongoing British influence. Malaysia and its proponents, the UK in the vanguard, interpreted Indonesian efforts to unravel Malaysia as a sign of design on those very same colonial territories.

The prevailing fear and misunderstanding was yet another opportunity too good to miss for the Cold War antagonists to square off against each other while safely avoiding direct confrontation. The Soviets supplied armaments to Sukarno's Indonesia. The British Commonwealth – notionally the UK, Australia and New Zealand – militarily backed fledgling Malaysia. The United States, fearful of the spread of Soviet influence, provided the Commonwealth with intelligence and diplomatic support.

In February 1966 Sukarno signed a decree giving army strongman General Suharto unlimited powers to enforce domestic security. This followed a coup attempt against Sukarno in October 1965 – the one to which Personnel had earlier referred – by Indonesian troops holding communist sympathies. Events moved quickly. Suharto was virulently anti-communist, ruthless and extremely influential. He quickly marginalized Sukarno, who remained president in name only before eventually resigning. Suharto took open control. The upshot of his rise to power was Indonesia's abandonment of the Soviets for the West, Konfrontasi's end and Indonesian recognition of Malaysia as a sovereign state. For the Service, Konfrontasi's end also meant a reordering of priorities. It was back to core business. Its best and brightest people were again directed to countering Soviet activities closer to home.

Notwithstanding Konfrontasi's end, South East Asia was still important to the Soviets; warm water ports in the region high on their list of priorities. Indonesia was South East Asia's largest country and decisively influential within regional councils. It stood between the Soviets and their ambitions. The Soviets knew Suharto would be there for the long run. They appreciated the urgent need to repair relations with him in the post-Konfrontasi era. Service interests in Indonesia, therefore, focused on Soviet plans for getting into Suharto's good books – about how the Bear intended ingratiation with the regional colossus.

Chapter 6 – Sarah

I stayed in INS for six months as Personnel had promised. Towards the end of that time, while lunching with a couple of section members in the staff cafeteria, our former Canadian exchange colleague joined us. Sarah Sutherland was about my age. She had grown her light brown hair long and it suited her. For the first time I noticed her beautiful hazel eyes. As would happen with me, some days I was more socially outgoing than others. On this day for no good reason I had the wind beneath my wings. Our lunch turned into a laugh-fest, with me the lead funny man. I suggested to Sarah as we left the cafeteria we take in a film at the weekend. 'That'd be great,' she said in her soft Vancouver drawl.

Sarah lived in Cottesmore Gardens in upmarket Kensington. We went to see *Doctor Zhivago* at a cinema not far from there. I had spent only ten months in Moscow and, apart from two or three weekend trips, had never been elsewhere in Russia. Sarah let me impress her by telling her how nostalgic the film made me, although she was too smart not to recognize the licence I was taking. Afterwards we ate supper at a trattoria in High Street Kensington, while sharing a bottle of chianti, much conversation and many laughs. Sarah was an adult woman mature beyond her years; her intelligence work had taken her to places where she had seen a lot of life in a short time. That night I stayed with her. The next morning as I jauntily wended my way back to my moth-eaten digs in Albany Road, I dared to think I had finally found someone I could love.

Sarah and I agreed to have lunch early the next week, over which we could finalize plans tentatively made for the coming weekend. We had only an hour so I booked a table at St Irvin's Hotel close to the office. Bad, bad mistake. Half the Service was there. Sarah was unsettled by the exposure given our liaison. I felt agitated and my anxiety mounted. Lunch was a disaster, not helped by slow service, during which we sat in increasingly strained silence. Mid-afternoon back at the office my telephone rang. It was Sarah. 'I won't be able to make it this weekend,' she said. 'Something's come up.'

I was hardly a world expert on women but I knew the kiss of death when I heard it. 'OK, sorry to hear that,' I said. A pause, and the telephone went dead. I sat there stunned. In a blur, I stumbled to the men's toilets and locked myself in a cubicle. The tears flowed. I just couldn't reconcile the rejection. In all other things I was capable, robust and resilient; why was I so useless when it came to relationships? That night I self-medicated. Sucking mints to cover my whisky breath, I dragged myself into the office the next morning. Miserable and hungover I somehow got through the day, which ended with me in bed by 8 pm with a belly full of fish and chips.

Awaking the next morning, I decided I never again wanted to experience the distress of relationship breakdown, whatever its form. I resolved to throw myself into my work and in the process honour my pledge to my mother to the fullest. Comparable priority would be afforded no other thing or person. I knew that my orchestrated promotion – more meritoriously my not-so-good friends Rupert Heneshaw and Freddie Ladler were on the same list – was designed to shut me up. I also knew that my posting to Indonesia, far away from the Service's centre of gravity, was to keep me out of sight and hence out of mind. Unaware of the high-level political imperatives driving events, I was oblivious as to why all this had happened. But I had survived the farce in East Berlin, somehow. I was now going to make the best of my second chance.

A week later I commenced language training. The language unit was housed within the headquarters building, but on the third floor in a wing adjacent to the communications centre remote from the Service's operational branches. Only rarely did I visit INS. At the end of the allotted six months, I passed both my final spoken and written language tests with flying colours. Administrative arrangements finalized; the lease on my Albany Road flat terminated; and a lacklustre farewell in the office with my INS colleagues, involving stale cake and a glass of cheap wine, and I was done. In early March 1968 I boarded British Airways flight 388 for Jakarta via Hong Kong.

Chapter 7 – Nought

Sam Cunningham from the Jakarta station using an embassy airport pass met me on the airside of the immigration and customs barriers. I was replacing Sam and would inherit things like his service-provided car and accommodation. We were to have a three-day handover. Sam's cover was as a political second secretary; as his replacement I was to adopt the same. We entered the diplomatic passport holder immigration lane. I bowled up to the counter and in my best Indonesian said, 'Selamat malam. Bagaimana anda?'

To my joy, the immigration official responded, 'Aku baik terima kasih. Selamat datang di Indonesia.' It was not because the official, in response to my enquiry, had confirmed his good health, while throwing in a welcome to Indonesia for good measure – I was ecstatic because he had understood my question and I his answer.

Waiting for my bags to arrive, Sam was moved by my over eagerness to prick my balloon. 'Indonesian's a dead easy language,' he said in the manner the jaded reserve for the new and enthusiastic, 'it's all phonetic.' Sam's evident irritation also caused him not to bother much with a handover. But I was happy to make my own way. The apartment I acquired from Sam after he left was thankfully close to the embassy – travelling any distance in Jakarta's maddening traffic was not for the faint hearted.

The station chief was a smooth Londoner named Noel Billings. He was declared to the Indonesians for liaison purposes, which meant the Service had formally advised the Indonesian Government of his true status. As with declared Service officers the world over, the objective of Billings's liaison was information exchange and, as required, inter-Service cooperation. The remaining three station officers, me now included, were undeclared. We were the field men charged with engaging in clandestine work. As far as the Indonesians and many in the embassy were concerned, we were Foreign Office diplomats.

Billings called me in once Sam had gone. 'Joe,' he said, 'I want you to get out into the community. Where there's an opening of an envelope, you should be there.' This was a reference to the never-ending stream of invitations the embassy received to cultural events and diplomatic receptions.

I nodded agreement. 'Handsome Scott told me I would also probably do liaison with junior CIA staff at the American embassy.'

If Billings detected my appropriation of Hanson's joke he gave no indication. Indeed, he fairly bristled. 'I manage all CIA liaison,' he said tartly. 'Your job is to be out there watching and noting. In everything you do, you are to keep me informed. You are not to move a muscle in anyone's direction without approval. If you see someone of possible interest tell me or one of the others. Got it?'

Billings made no mention of the agents the station had on its books. But I knew from reading cables in London that Mike Milligan, one of my subordinate colleagues, had a stable of agents. In those communications agents were referred to only by work names. Reading between the lines, though, most appeared to be either Indonesian academics or mid-level government officials.

The other of my subordinate colleagues was an extraordinary character called McNaught Collins. 'Call me Nought,' he said, 'as in zero. Everyone else does.' Nought was about to embark on his fourth year at Jakarta station. He had come to Jakarta directly from a three-year posting to Phnom Penh, reflecting that he was not in great demand back in London. Nought was only fifty-six but to me looked as old as Methuselah. He was apparently a wine connoisseur – and plainly the wine had won. Purple of nose, he was like a glorified in-house research unit. He did no work out of the office I ever saw, principally because he knew the Service would put him out to pasture when he finished in Jakarta. For all that, he was one of the sagest people I have ever met. Nought's value to the station was that he knew who was who in the Indonesian bureaucracy. His knowledge seemed to come only from a close reading of the Indonesian newspapers. But he was like a walking encyclopedia. Ask Nought about this Indonesian official or that and he seemed to know him like a brother.

Nought and I shared an interest in cricket. The Australian cricket team was touring England in the summer of 1968. Nought and I bonded while sitting up half the night listening to scratchy BBC short wave broadcasts of the Test matches. We chuckled together at the rich bucolic tones of broadcaster John Arlott and his evocative language. A particular favourite was Arlott's *The Lone Wolf at Cover,* his term to describe a solitary outfielder left to patrol a large swathe of the playing field while the rest of his teammates all hovered in the infield. *Cover* in this instance being a designated position on the cricket field and not of course a reference to the spy's perennial preoccupation. Nought and I endlessly enjoyed the unintended *double entendre* all the same. But I was callow at the time and treated our jocular adoption of it only as a nod and a wink to our secret work, never once suspecting Nought might attach a more serious meaning to the appellation. I grew to revere Nought. He became the only close male friend I ever had.

Meanwhile I did exactly as Billings had directed, unrelentingly so. I attended diplomatic functions most weeknights and every cultural event possible. I also filled the vacant vice-presidency of a UK–Indonesia friendship group, participants in which were a couple of pedestrian officials from the Indonesian Ministry of Culture and a variable smattering of Indonesian and expatriate British people. Monthly gatherings were held in a ground floor room in the Ministry. These were generally desultory affairs, so much so I would have quit the group were it not for my Sarah Sutherland-inspired commitment to career. About nine months into my posting, an annual general meeting, or AGM, was held and office bearers elected. Unsurprisingly, I was returned unopposed as vice-president. The Ministry hosted an after-meeting reception to mark the AGM's occasion. The promise of free food and drink attracted a larger turn out than usual, including several people I hadn't seen before.

I grabbed a glass of wine and started to mingle. I wasn't a natural conversationalist but found if I closed my eyes and jumped in I generally held my own. At receptions and the like I always kept an eye out for talent. I was open-minded about whom but by weight of numbers the focus was usually on Indonesians. Tonight was no different. My attention turned to a well dressed Indonesian man of about forty and small in stature in conversation with three Western persons. 'Hello, I'm Joe Lambert, British Embassy,' I said as I muscled in on the group. This was not rudeness. Receptions worked like this. Two of the Westerners moved on, leaving me with the Indonesian and a tall flaxen-headed woman in her mid-twenties. I offered them business cards in accordance with standard diplomatic practice. The man's card described him as the Assistant Deputy Governor of the Provincial Bank of Java, the PBJ. His name was Hartono Sumardi. The tall woman was Hilda Stadler, in-house counsel of the Jakarta office of Prince Rupert Minerals Pty Ltd.

I launched into trawling mode, using Hilda as a conversation point but all the while focused on Hartono. 'Where is PRM headquartered?' I asked her.

Hilda had a blunt, businesslike manner that appealed to me. 'Montreal,' she said. 'It's a Canadian public company with interests in gold mining here.'

'Are you French-Canadian?' I asked.

'No,' she said. 'I'm Swiss, from Basle. Other than English and Indonesian, I also speak French – and German and Italian. I found opportunities at home quite limited after I graduated as a lawyer. An employment agency alerted me to the PRM job. Indonesia's a long way from Switzerland and the job is quite challenging. But the experience will be good for my career. I'm very ambitious.' I liked her candour too.

'PBJ is a government-owned bank,' Hartono chimed in. 'It specializes in rupiah-denominated loans. These are offered as an investment incentive because they provide a facility allowing companies to meet their in-country expenses without converting hard currency. I've had past dealings with the friendship group and convinced Hilda we should come along tonight.' Hilda smiled a tight smile suggesting she had mixed feelings about this. 'Hilda and I are currently negotiating the terms of a new loan facility,' Hartono said. 'I can tell you she is a very tough negotiator and her Indonesian is excellent.' He smiled at her like a proud father.

We talked generally about minerals exploration in Indonesia. As I sensed the conversation was running out of steam, I decided to make my preliminary play. During training it had been drummed into us that Service officers needed a social platform. Golf or tennis club memberships were popular choices. I may not have been able to hit a golf-ball to save myself but I was a halfway decent social tennis player. I had joined the tennis club at the Republic Hotel.

'Do either of you play tennis?' I asked.

'Yes, quite well,' Hilda said with a confidence made charming by the absence of hubris.

'Not very well, I'm afraid,' Hartono said, smiling.

'Well Pak Hartono,' I said, using the respectful Indonesian form of male address, 'that makes two of us. How about we three play this Friday night? I'm a member at the Republic. I'll book the court for 7 pm for an hour. It's lovely under the lights.' Hartono consulted a small diary before agreeing he could make it.

Ever since my arrival, whenever I had suggested a possible target, usually an Indonesian, Billings and Milligan had pretended to consider it before rejecting it. I had discussed this with Nought. 'The Indonesian political elite is ripping off the place blind,' he had said. 'Spoils of victory; it's an era of excess. No wonder then that a lot of Indonesians further down the food chain – in government; the military; academia; you name it – are open to inducement. Who can blame them? Billings has been content to have Milligan rely on these sources, even if in my opinion many of the agents recruited are of dubious quality, not to mention expensive to run. The base fact, Joe, is they don't want you muddying the cosy waters.'

'So what should I do?'

'What is needed,' Nought said, 'is a really big fish, preferably a Russian. Someone with direct access to Soviet thinking, thereby avoiding dependence on Indon sources. A source in the local KGB station is the ideal. That's why we're here, supposedly, looking for reliable insights into Soviet efforts to build standing with Suharto.'

'OK,' I asked, 'if Billings is not interested in the Sovs how do I get involved?'

'It's difficult. The Soviets keep their people on a tight leash, usually only allowing them to leave the embassy in pairs or groups. My advice is to keep working on your tradecraft wherever you can. That way if the chance arises to nab a Sov, you'll ready to grab it.'

With Nought's advice in mind, I made the decision I would pursue Hartono without telling Billings or Milligan about him. *Apart from developing my tradecraft*, I thought, *he might appeal so much they can't help but agree to a recruitment attempt.*

I had considered enlisting a fourth player for my tennis date with Hartono and Hilda, so that we might play doubles, but decided it would spread the conversation too thin. On the night I told the others it was too hot to be running around for the full hour and suggested we play round-robin singles.

Hilda's long legs took her speedily around the court. She mercilessly disposed of Hartono, so much so that when I stepped up I thought I should ensure I suffered the same fate. And when I played Hartono I deliberately let him win, just in case his ego was in anyway bruised. Hilda was interesting. Her jaw set in determination when she played and she wasn't above muttering *Fuck it* after missing a point she might easily have won.

Over a lime juice, Hartono and I joked about our lack of tennis prowess and feebleness in the face of Hilda's onslaught. Hilda laughed along with us, while looking at me in a curious sort of way. I think she realized I'd been holding back.

But Hartono was the centre of my interest. 'What's the book value of PBJ?' I asked him conversationally.

'One hundred and fifty trillion rupiah,' he replied. By my calculation that was roughly fifteen billion US dollars. 'Please don't ask me how much of that is black money,' he added, laughing generously. 'We have a *don't ask* policy when it comes to deposits.'

Excitement coursed through me, overtaking caution and I didn't address the obvious – why Hartono was telling me his bank was corrupt. 'No, no of course not,' I said. 'I wouldn't dream of it.' *Is he trying to impress Hilda?* I wondered. 'I bet though you've got some well known names as clients?'

Hartono chuckled. 'We certainly do,' he said looking earnestly at me, as if Hilda wasn't there.

He's trying to impress me, by God, I'm sure of it, I thought, recalling Nought's advice about Indonesian officials and the current climate of malleability. Now here was Hartono seemingly fitting the mould. 'Perhaps we should catch up for lunch next week?' I said. 'I have a background in commerce and would like to get to understand the Jakarta business scene a little better.'

Hartono cast what I took to be a nervous look at Hilda. 'I will have to check my diary,' he said.

'No problems,' I said, 'I'll give you a call later in the week.'

Hartono smiled an awkward smile and said it was time to go. We all stood to leave. My mind was racing. I decided there and then that as a first step I needed to neutralize Hilda. I rang her the following Monday and asked if she would like to have dinner the coming Wednesday night. She agreed she would.

I booked a restaurant in the upmarket suburb of Menteng. With Swiss efficiency Hilda arrived on the dot of 7 pm. I can say hand on heart that despite her many appealing attributes, I had no designs on Hilda; career dominated my every waking moment. We negotiated some small talk. I got to the nub of things as our main course arrived. 'I think I put Hartono on the spot a little last Friday when I suggested we catch up to talk a bit of shop. What did you think?'

Hilda thought for a moment and then, fork in hand, waved in a gesture of dismissal. 'I am very ambitious and think you are too. If Hartono helps with your career, I would not be concerned with him being nervous about being seen dining with a foreign diplomat. If it's such a big deal for him, meet him somewhere private.'

An enzyme or whatever it was shot to my brain and my professional resolve crumbled, seduced by Hilda's cool confidence and career orientation. I knew then there was no need to warn her off. She was all business and not about to indulge in idle gossip about me tagging Hartono. I relaxed and the evening went from being a chore to a pleasure. At its conclusion, Hilda and I walked out into the still, hot night. I thought that was it for now and prepared to say goodnight. But Hilda had more robust plans. 'It's so hard to find decent men in this town,' she said, as if discussing the weather. 'Most I've come across want a little chicken for a girlfriend. Would you like to come to my place?' With that, she flicked up her skirt for an instant to reveal a buttock encased in panties bearing a leopard skin pattern.

A graduate of the Bootle docks, I was hardly a prudish person. But I'd be less than honest if I didn't admit to being daunted by Hilda's assertiveness. 'Sure, why not?' I said with more calmness than I felt. Hilda lived close by. Once there, she made a plunger of coffee and sat beside me on the couch. I never did get to finish my coffee. Come to think of it, I don't think I even took a sip.

But even as my relationship with Hilda progressed, I still couldn't shake the sense of intimidation I felt outside the restaurant. Her confidence and smarts; extraordinary linguistic skills; and old money European classiness all united to fire my self-doubt. I did all the right things, but to no avail. Just over a month in my loner instincts took control. Only this time my need to be alone was noticeably more urgent than usual. Hilda reacted with dignity when abruptly I called things off, barely pressing me for an explanation. My familiar depressive reaction left me hurt and wounded for weeks.

In parallel with my short-lived romance with Hilda, I set my sights on Hartono. The envisaged lunch never materialized. But when I telephoned him at his office he did suggest we meet up at the Gallery of Culture. In this discreet setting I made my pitch. 'If you can provide me a picture on the banking habits of any Indonesian minister,' I said, 'I can arrange for a cash payment in return.'

Hartono barely blinked. 'I don't have much on political figures,' he said. 'But two or three Deplu officials may be of interest.' Deplu was the abbreviated Indonesian name for the Ministry of Foreign Affairs. 'I would prefer US dollars, cash,' he added, smiling genially.

I was fairly tingling with excitement. Not even Billings could ignore this opportunity. I told Hartono I'd get back to him shortly.

I raced back to the office – raced being a relative term in the Jakarta traffic. Both Billings and Milligan were out, fortunately. I sauntered around to Nought's office, chest puffed out as if the modern-day incarnation of Rudyard Kipling. 'Just got a nice little fish on the hook,' I said, leaning casually in the doorframe.

'Tell me more,' Nought replied without enthusiasm.

'Shouldn't we talk in the safe speech room?' I asked. Now I was a master spy I wanted to play the great game by the book.

Nought was short with me. 'Indons couldn't bug us if their arse was on fire. Now this coup of yours – President Suharto I assume?'

'Not quite,' I said, a little peeved at Nought's sarcasm. 'A banker with info on payments made to corrupt Deplu officials.'

'Tell me the details,' Nought demanded abruptly. I told him all about Hartono and how I'd come across him. 'Wait here,' Nought said, 'and don't say anything to anyone until I say so.' He returned after a time carrying a file. Opening it, he pointed to a poor quality photograph of someone alighting from a taxi. 'Is this your man?'

The image was grainy but Hartono's face was clear. The trouble was the file referred to a PBJ source called Hendra Sutrisno. 'What's going on?' I asked, my apprehension rising.

'Seems Hartono was chasing some extra cash on the side,' Nought said. 'It's not unheard of among agents; that's why I wanted to check. Milligan already has him on the books but as Pak Hendra. Mike tries to photograph those of his recruits unlikely to appear in the newspapers or suchlike. Hartono's clearly unaware of Mike's amateur photography because his key judgement is that you and Mike comparing notes will not undo him. Silly foreigners confused by two Indonesians of similar descriptions, both with the same initials and working for the PBJ; that sort of thing. Hartono is probably his real name – if as you say he uses that with Hilda who's a bank client. He's likely hooked Mike by offering to sell him the political information he told you he didn't have, adopting the Hendra name to protect his true identity. He would have known only too well the risks involved in snitching on the political class.'

I was still not convinced. 'But what if Milligan and I see him when together? I say Hartono and Mike says Hendra.'

Nought thought about this. 'I suspect Hartono's relying on a combination of our compartmentalization and Jakarta being a big city,' he said. 'Mike will be running him as a sensitive source, only meeting him alone and after dark, and somewhere obscure. Hartono would have demanded the same of you. And Hartono will engage with Westerners only when he knows it's safe to do so. Otherwise, out there in the kampong he's invisible to us. All this virtually eliminates the risk of you and Mike stumbling over him together.'

Nought was right. It was a strict Service edict that officers should never unnecessarily expose sensitive sources to other Service colleagues. Nought's assessment also caused me to recall Milligan was away in Bandung the Friday night we played tennis at the Republic. Hartono must have known this. That's why he had checked his diary at the friendship group event before agreeing to play. This exemplified Nought's point about Hartono engaging with Westerners only when he thought it safe, while otherwise remaining invisible in his local community. 'OK,' I said to Nought, 'but why did Hartono attend the friendship group AGM? How could he sure Milligan wouldn't have been there and seen that he was calling himself Hartono? Once Hartono decided he needed to bring Hilda along as a foil he had no option to be anyone else.'

'Hartono has previously rubbed shoulders with the friendship group', Nought said. 'He knew that no self-respecting British diplomat would ever bother with a motley lot like it. Your name and where you worked would have been on the paperwork circulated for the AGM elections. This told him you were Service and also there was no chance of Milligan being there. We were hardly likely to send two people to work such a lowbrow event. He evidently calculated this was his chance to try and make some extra cash.'

'Even so,' I said, not wanting to believe what was becoming increasingly apparent, 'Hartono's scam seems pretty brazen.'

'He does sound desperate, I'd agree' Nought said, laughing. 'Perhaps he has a gambling debt or maybe has purloined money from the bank he needs to pay back in a hurry, who knows?'

I shook my head. 'The sneaky bastard wanted to sell me the Deplu stuff because he could ask top dollar for it. If he sold it to Mike as Hendra, he knew he would get little more than what he's already getting for the political intelligence he's selling him. And if

we were to have Mike ask *Hendra* for the Deplu material he would
have had fifty good reasons ready why that was not possible.'

'That's almost certainly true,' Nought said. 'But listen, we're
in a position to stay stumm on this. Neither Billings nor Milligan
know how far advanced you got and Hartono's not about to tell them
when he doesn't hear from you again. You've actually done well,
believe it or not. The groundwork you did was first class. The
experience will knock off your rough edges. You'll be a wiser man
next time around.'

I took leave in Singapore after completing a year at the post. It gave
me a chance to step back. I reflected on the bust up with Hilda and
decided I'd survived only by dint of being frantically busy. But the
experience had shaken me all the same. It occurred to me then that
strong and intelligent women like Hilda were the grown up versions
of the more assertive female students who had rejected me at
university in Liverpool. On the back of the Hilda experience, I felt
oddly relieved never to have been involved with any of them.

Professionally, I took encouragement from Nought's advice. I
had acquitted myself well with Hartono. I would ignore Billings's
negativity and keep plugging away and be ready to take any
opportunity that arose. I returned to Jakarta my ambition to succeed
fully restored. Nought was readying for departure. He had a sister
in Bath and would probably retire close by, perhaps to Bristol.

We had a boozy night to say farewell. I was well in my cups when Nought gently mentioned I needed to get married. 'Don't worry about Billings, Joe. No one in London takes him seriously. But even so, the Service prefers its men married and preferably to good English stock. Heterosexual domestic stability equals good security they think. It's a hangover from the Cambridge disaster.' I understood Nought was referring to the Cambridge University homosexual spy ring, whose number included the infamous former SIS officer Kim Philby who had fled to Moscow in relatively recent times. Nought shook his head, 'It's bollocks, total bollocks. You'll never find anything remotely official about this but believe me being married starts to get critical from about director level on. Old divorced sots like me are a dying breed.' Nought paused, as if debating whether to continue. 'You have *The Lone Wolf at Cover* make-up, Joey,' he said finally. 'It's how you're made. Being unmarried will hurt your career, no doubt, ...'

The warning about career catapulted me deep into drunken contemplation. *So it's not a joke about our work,* I thought. *He's warning the Service could brand me as a loner and, going to school on the Cambridge experience, treat me as a potential security risk.*

My preoccupation was such that it blotted out Nought's second warning, seamlessly following his mention of career implications, '... but being *The Lone Wolf at Cover* can also have far-reaching personal consequences.' I heard the words and understood they had been said gravely. But they just didn't permeate. I was too gone on the booze by this stage and reduced to doing one thing at a time.

My incomprehension convinced Nought to move on. 'They're going to send a woman called Penelope Hensworth, Doctor Penelope Hensworth actually, as station chief when Billings finishes six months from now,' he said. 'The Service has finally twigged the Indonesians have been filling his head with nonsense and is now in damage control. Penelope's an Islamic studies academic. She has spent many years here teaching and is well regarded. Wonderful linguist. The Service will get a decent return on her interaction with the Indons. It's really a masterstroke. She's first rate. She'll want you to take the initiative and be active in looking for recruits.'

Nought topped up our glasses; Beaujolais I think it was. 'I'll see Penelope in the UK and put in a good word for you. She used to rate me back when we worked together and I was on. Why don't you ask headquarters for a year's extension? It'll agree. You'll then have eighteen months with Penelope to use as a career launching pad. But remember, find some tart and settle down. It's important.' The next morning Nought claimed he couldn't remember past opening our third bottle. I didn't believe him for a second. In a reputed quest for budget savings, he wasn't replaced when he left.

Chapter 8 – Boris

Penelope Hensworth arrived in early October 1969. She was as Nought said she would be. In a matter of days the office atmosphere changed from cautious and restrained to relaxed and confident. Free of Billings's influence, Milligan became warmer towards me. By Christmas he had started to call me *Joey* and was happily responding to *Spike*. I returned from leave at the end of January 1970 with renewed enthusiasm to tackle the year ahead.

By now I'd grown to like the rank and file Indonesians who I found polite, honest and considerate in their dealings with foreigners. But liking the people was one thing and watching endless hours of traditional dancing, puppet shows and the like was quite another. The truth is, I guess, I wasn't sophisticated enough to appreciate its charms. But the cultural grind was at my cover's core. I stuck at it.

In early April I was given the opportunity to take a trip to East Java with the Deputy Chief of Mission, to Surabaya Indonesia's second largest city. The deputy was a bona fide Foreign Office diplomat. Ostensibly, I was on hand to be the note-taker at his calls on local officials. But wearing my cultural hat I had also arranged to attend a performance of traditional dance by a troupe from Central Kalimantan. I was keen to take up the embassy's invitation. Kalimantan had borne the brunt of Konfrontasi. In addition to

Indonesia's provinces, it now also housed the Malaysian states of Sarawak and Sabah. Any below the radar agitation by either of the formerly warring parties would likely first surface on the island. The event was a chance to keep an eye out for possible contacts.

Guests were invited at the conclusion of the performance to attend a reception on a riverboat anchored at a nearby canal. On boarding, I noticed a good-looking, fair-haired man in his late thirties I estimated talking animatedly in Indonesian to the event organizers. Speeches were made and refreshments served. Some speakers recognized dignitaries present in opening remarks. The blond man charismatically waved a hand when Mr Vasily Rykov, the Soviet Embassy's Cultural Attaché, was acknowledged. He looked briefly at me when well down the list plain old Joe Lambert from the British Embassy rated a mention. Vasily had two sullen colleagues with him. They stood silent and blank-faced, seemingly out of their depth while everyone, Vasily included, ignored them. The contrast with Vasily's easy charm as he set about working the Indonesians piqued my interest. I was sure Vasily would be of appeal to us, cultural man or whatever he was.

After a time, Vasily and I were invited to join dignitaries for photographs. I quickly exchanged business cards with him: *Counsellor (cultural affairs), Soviet Embassy Jakarta,* Vasily's read. The leader of the Kalimantan delegation, a man called Wahyu, was an especially enthusiastic photographer. He had a Nikon camera, small for the times. Seeking to conscript more photographic subjects, he placed the camera on a shelf behind the jerry-rigged speaker's podium and ran off to the far reaches of the room. People were milling around talking and laughing animatedly. Penelope had encouraged us to back our instincts, as Nought had foreshadowed. I made the split-second decision to walk to the back of the podium, where a huge public address speaker blocked clear vision of me. In the one action, I whipped the camera off the shelf and stuck it down the front of my trousers. My loose-fitting batik shirt covered the abnormal bulge in my groin. Sweating from the humidity but otherwise steeled, I locked myself in the boat's disgusting toilet. There I wound the film forward to protect it from exposure and removed it from the camera.

A moment of internal conflict suddenly overtook me. On one hand, I badly wanted to return the camera to Pak Wahyu. Like most Indonesians he was a courteous man and had certainly done me no disservice. On the other, I knew if I left the camera to be found *sans* film Vasily would understand something was up. I looked in the fly-spotted mirror. To my surprise a hard-eyed, uncompromising face stared back at me. I knew then that profession trumped principle. Exiting the toilet I walked to the starboard side of the boat, where on making sure the coast was clear I dropped the camera into the murky water. I returned to the reception room to find Pak Wahyu frantically searching for his property. Before too long he understood the camera had been stolen. His philosophical response masked his upset and satisfied his instinctive need to save face.

Spike and I developed the film when I was back in the Jakarta office. There were several good shots of Vasily, who had hitherto been unsighted. We assumed he had only recently arrived in Jakarta. It didn't really matter. He was here now and out and about.

Penelope praised my initiative. There was no pushing me out of the way and taking the credit. We cabled London with Vasily's details and how he had come to our notice, photographs to follow by diplomatic bag. Before too long a reply authorized by Brittingham's supervisor, the FADG in charge of South Asia proper, arrived. Vasily was a full-blown KGB hood by name of Nikolai Ivanovich Klimentov, born 1930 in Murmansk. He had known previous service in Turkey and Pakistan. The station was given the go-ahead to check him out. Headquarters allocated him the unimaginative code name of Boris. I was thrilled to be commended for my work.

We began trawling for Boris at diplomatic receptions, looking for points of access to him. Penelope soon discovered Boris had taken charge of a white Peugeot with gaudy red trim in which he drove colleagues to and from events. Its diplomatic licence plate was *CD 37 167*, the numerals *37* informing those in the know that the car Boris drove belonged to a Soviet diplomat. Penelope told me to focus on the car and see where it led me.

The Soviet Embassy was located in South Jakarta. It occupied a huge compound fronting onto HR Rasuna Said, one of the many vast, congested and bewildering thoroughfares flowing through Jakarta's chaotic heart. As a form of internal control, all Soviet staff were accommodated on the embassy compound. My initial reconnoitring revealed that vehicles driven by Soviet diplomats usually left the compound via a rear exit fronting on to Jalan Denpasar, an unusually wide secondary road offering several vantage points to monitor comings and goings safe from roving Soviet eyes. Penelope and Spike both agreed that for a month or so, I should alternate my stake out of the Sovs with the receptions and other events I usually attended. Just as I was beginning to think I was wasting my time, one Thursday night when on Soviet stakeout a Peugeot with a back licence plate of *CD 37 167* drove past me. It was dark inside the passing vehicle but my night vision binoculars made it possible to confirm the only occupant was the driver, Boris.

The numerals *15* on the diplomatic plates of the tiny vehicle I drove identified me as a UK diplomat. We had fished out a set of custom-made local licence tags held by the office. I placed them over the car's diplomatic plates when on stakeout. The subterfuge would not survive close inspection but in Jakarta's rough and tumble traffic, especially after dark, detection was unlikely. I gunned the engine and set off in pursuit.

Soon after passing me, Boris swung right and drove down a side street allowing him to turn left onto Rasuna Said. I followed, both hands tightly gripping the steering wheel as if willing my vehicle to overcome its lack of power. Boris drove like a madman, weaving through the traffic with all the skill of a local. I had done driving courses during training and vividly recalled one instructor telling me that Stirling Moss had nothing to worry about from me. I was now beginning to understand what he meant. Before long, I was struggling to keep up to Boris. But equally I didn't want to get too close in case he spotted me. The combination of my car and me spared me this worry – I could not catch him even had I tried. If this solved one problem, it raised another in the distinct possibility I might lose him. Fortunately, after each scare I again spotted Boris up ahead. For once I was grateful for the inestimable number of cars, motorcyclists and various others locked in their perennial struggle for a slice of road space.

Boris continued along Rasuna Said, through an area called Setiabudi One. Shortly after, he took a left exit onto a road tracing a rough semi-circle. He followed it until he reached the entrance to the Mata Aini hospital precinct into which he turned. There he skilfully squeezed into a parking space usually reserved for motorcycles. Boris sat in his car briefly, looking in the rearview mirror. He then locked the car and walked into the main hospital building. I would have liked to follow but decided to stay with his car, having calculated I was bound to lose him if after first trying to find a scarce car park I sought to follow on foot. I pulled off to one side, ignoring the parade of cars and motorcycles blowing their horns as they eased around me. Mayhem was a fact of driving life in Jakarta and my obstinacy attracted no particular attention.

Boris reappeared after about fifteen minutes. Without ado, he exited the hospital precinct but departed in the opposite direction from which he had arrived. I saw him leave but could not follow immediately; at least three other cars had pushed in and blocked my exit. Finally, as my anxiety levels were threatening to rise to code red, I reached the floodlit roundabout near Kuningan Village in time to witness Boris complete a slow rotation.

Only then did I recognize that Boris was engaging in tradecraft. The stop at the hospital was designed to detect any tailing person silly enough to be lured into the hospital building. I thanked my lucky stars. Had I followed him, as was my unrealized preference, Boris would have been sitting there waiting as I entered and the game would have been over before it had begun.

Conversely, the manoeuvre at the roundabout was to allow Boris to happen upon any suspicious-looking trailing vehicle, especially one driven by a Westerner. A second and this time larger sigh of relief escaped my lips. I had been lucky on two scores: had I not been impeded leaving the hospital in all likelihood he would have spotted me at the roundabout; and if I had been delayed just one minute longer, I would have lost him altogether. Fortune had shone on me. Satisfied his back was clear, Boris turned right and wound his way along this route until the road narrowed and became Jalan Karet Gusuran III.

Boris pulled up at number seventeen, a standalone two-level villa of whitewashed besser block with a traditional Dutch shingled roof. The dwelling was in a tree-lined area and nestled inconspicuously between nondescript apartment buildings. Its fence was made of rods of iron about ten feet in length and crooked at the top. Sheets of black steel covered the lower three-quarters of the rods preventing visibility through the fence. Two fixed sections of fence were inter-connected by concrete pillars painted white. A large sliding gate of the same construction made up the fence's third section. Boris quickly slid the gate open, drove his car inside and closed the gate behind him.

I parked my car about fifty yards past the villa and with the aid of passable street lighting monitored its entrance in my passenger-side wing mirror. An immaculately kept taxi soon pulled up. Its single passenger was a person whom I could make out was female. She pressed the intercom button on the concrete pillar near the gate. The gate opened slightly, just enough for her to slip inside.

The driver's side of my car was hard against a wall, deliberately so to oblige people walking by to pass on the passenger side. Even so, those bothering to look could see I was a foreigner. My presence unsettled the locals. As time dragged by, some young males started deliberately bumping into the car. I could have tried to offer an explanation for being there but that would have invited a barrage of questions as to who, what and why. I feigned sleep and tried to ignore the mounting interest in me. I knew that inevitably a posse of locals would force me to move.

After nearly three hours, as the community's tolerance was about to exhaust, the same taxi returned. The woman emerged and quickly hopped in the back seat. I could not see her as the taxi passed slowly by although I could make out the driver. He was a positively ancient Indonesian who wore a white peci, the Muslim skullcap favoured on Java. I began to follow, grateful to be moving. The taxi driver was oblivious to his tail. He headed back towards the Soviet Embassy compound but went further along Rasuna Said before finally pulling into the JS Luwansa Hotel. I followed into the hotel compound and parked my car.

The woman got out and the taxi drove off. I could see she was an attractive Eurasian. She did not enter the hotel. Instead she lit a cigarette and smoked it while apparently enjoying the night air. She then walked back down to the footpath running parallel with Rasuna Said and after going no more than 100 yards crossed the freeway using the first pedestrian overpass she encountered. I followed on foot, keeping my distance. She was unlikely to detect me initially; it was dark and there were people everywhere. But I knew I couldn't follow her indefinitely. I was a foreigner in a sea of locals and eventually she would become aware of me. I worried unnecessarily. Once across the overpass, the woman walked to the entrance of the Malaysian Embassy immediately to her right. After pausing momentarily to fossick for identification in her handbag, she was granted access and disappeared from sight.

In conference the next morning we agreed it was odd that a lone Soviet intelligence officer should be meeting one-to-one in a safe house with an apparently Malaysian diplomat. Less than four years had elapsed since the Konfrontasi hostilities had ceased; old wounds were still raw. It was possible of course that Boris was running the other party. But a meeting lasting three hours was a mighty long debrief. We were also bemused Boris should drive to the safe house in a vehicle carrying diplomatic tags, particularly as there was no indication of a following colleague guarding his back. This served only to invite the revelation the house Boris used was a Soviet safe house. All this was cabled to London. It tasked us to see if Boris and the Eurasian met regularly.

We decided we needed to monitor the safe house. But clearly no Westerner could park in the street night after night. Penelope, though, had the solution to our problem. It transpires she had been working for the Service throughout her years of teaching at Indonesian universities. Part of her secret work had been to establish a system of sleepers, Indonesian academics around the country to be called on as required, including to mobilize local watcher assets and the like. The network had been disbanded with Konfrontasi's end. But Penelope knew the whereabouts of some of its former Jakarta-based members.

Soon we had at our disposal a four-strong team of university students. All were critical of Suharto, young and idealistic, and keen to infer from our vague briefing that combating corruption by the Indonesian oligarchy was behind the task we set them. Each knew the hazards of challenging the state. Discretion was their byword.

The team got around on 125cc motorcycles, like a great majority of Jakarta's other residents. We estimated that working in shifts they could monitor the safe house at night but only for about a week. Eventually, the locals would tag them as not from the area and assume they were criminals or other undesirables not to be welcomed in the neighbourhood.

The following Friday the team advised the night before Boris had arrived alone at the safe house driving his Peugeot. A Eurasian woman had visited him shortly after, staying a couple of hours. At this point, we knew we had to get ears inside the safe house. But the station had no resources for that. It was time to bring in our American counterparts.

Chapter 9 – Betty

London accepted our recommendation to involve the Americans. The SIS station in Washington DC would approach the CIA. None other than Freddie Ladler authored Washington station's reporting cable advising the CIA was interested. Its Jakarta office would be in touch with Penelope.

Chuck Lindergarten was a muscular, crew cut, pugnacious ball of aggression. He was also head of CIA station, Jakarta. Only Chuck would know, at 4 am when supine in his bed, if Mr Self-doubt, he of the feet of clay, ever visited. But once on his feet, Charles H Lindergarten Jr. made clear to all and sundry he regarded himself as indestructible. 'P,' he said, comfortably seated in our safe speech room, 'this'll be a piece of piss. We'll get a listening team in there in the blink of an eye and see what this mother-fucking Russkie's up to. We'll either bribe the pembantu, and tell her we'll cut her throat if she blabs, or we'll pick the fucking locks and be in there quicker than shit passing through a goose.'

'Sounds good, Chuck,' Penelope said with equanimity. Whether she took seriously Lindergarten's stated preparedness to threaten the maid with murder was not clear. 'We'll leave the detail up to you.' Seamlessly she added, 'Would you mind if Joe sat in on the op?' She smiled sweetly at Lindergarten. Chewing vigorously, he didn't seem to realize she was playing him. 'Joe's one of our bright young things. It'll do him the world of good to experience how a listening post works.' In truth, the request had nothing to do with my career development. Penelope was covering off on the possibility our erstwhile allies might decide to withhold something from us.

'Not a problem,' Chuck replied expansively.

Two Thursday nights later I found myself in the enclosed back of a darkened van. The van's exterior declared itself in Indonesian to belong to *Comfy Removals*. Inside it was like a spaceship, with equipment securely mounted on racks welded to the vehicle's internal side panels. Bright dials provided the only light source. There were two Americans and me. I was given a set of headphones and a stool to sit on. We were parked on a vacant block of land no more than 150 yards from the safe house. The signals from the microphones the CIA had installed could be picked up from there.

We heard Boris arrive. He hummed gently to himself and put on softly playing music. The equipment gave signal strength indications for each microphone enabling us to know which room Boris was in. All sound was taped. After a time the intercom bell chimed. 'Come in Ibu,' Boris said, employing the courteous Indonesian female salutation to greet his visitor. 'I've had a difficult day. I'm looking forward to some relaxation.' In my mind's eye I saw Boris's charming smile. The woman, however, did not speak. The only sound we heard was footsteps as they walked up the stairs. The microphone in the bedroom boomed at full signal strength. We then heard sounds of water running from a tap close enough to be coming from the en suite bathroom.

The Americans looked at each other with concern. Running water was the enemy of the microphone because it obscured the sound of voice, making what was said in proximity to the water source difficult to hear. More to the point, running a tap was often a sign the target was aware of the microphone and taking steps to frustrate it. After some anxious minutes the water stopped. We then heard Boris say in Indonesian, 'I think that's enough bubbles.' With relief we realized that Boris and the woman had just run themselves a bubble bath.

The two must have been in the bath for a good hour. Goodness knows what they were doing. There was the occasional unintelligible sound and frequently the sound of water lapping. After what seemed an eternity the bedroom microphone picked up the sound of water gurgling as it ran down the drainpipe. The voices of Boris and the woman became clearer and we heard a bed complaining under their weight. Sounds of passion ensued. His voice thick with desire, Boris commanded the woman in Russian, 'Suck this, baby.' Whether or not she spoke Russian, the microphones made clear she complied.

On and on they went. The woman occasionally cried out, in Chinese according to one of my American colleagues. Finally, with one last bellow from Boris there was silence. After a long time the sound of a shower running could be heard, followed by inconsequential small talk as the couple leisurely re-clothed. They made their way downstairs. It'd been a nearly two-hour stay in the bedroom. Over the next hour they appeared to drink a cup of coffee together. *All very civilized*, I thought. The evening culminated with the flicking sound of money being counted and the woman confirming, in Indonesian, 'It's all there.' We heard her pick up the telephone. 'Pak Tasrip,' she said, 'I'm ready now. Can you come and get me please?'

Penelope Hensworth's integrity shone through. She argued persuasively with London I should be allowed to make the pitch to Boris. The Americans were Johnnies-come-lately; their claims to first dibs on him should be resisted. This worried me. 'Penelope,' I said, seated in her office, 'I hope you're not going too far out on a limb here. Frankly, I'm petrified I'll let you down.'

'Joe,' she said, 'Nought told me about you and how with opportunity you would grow into a very good intelligence officer. I agree with him. It's now your time.'

It went all the way to the DG. He finally sided with Penelope but with a rider in his instructing cable: *Contingency hand holding plans cleared at DDG level are first to be in place. Advice of such to London by close of business 8 May.*

Turkey celebrated Ataturk commemoration day on 19 May. Having served in Turkey, Boris was a good chance to be at the Turkish Embassy reception marking the occasion. And so it was. I sidled up to him and said, 'Nikolai Ivanovich, do you remember me?'

The use of his real name startled Boris, but only briefly. 'What do you want?' he asked in Indonesian.

With more calmness than I felt, I said, 'Friends of mine tell me you've been a naughty boy, little Chinese girl and so on. Your KGB masters in Moscow would put you against the wall if they knew.'

'You are mistaken,' he said, and turned to walk off.

'Find an excuse to meet me in an hour at the Borobudur Hotel, room 404,' I said. 'Otherwise you're in big trouble, I promise you.'

Chuck and Penelope were enjoying tea in room 404 when I arrived. Chuck had brought two pieces of muscle with him in case Boris got ideas. Both carried what appeared to be machine pistols with silencers attached. 'What do you think, Joe?' Penelope asked.

'Hard to say,' I replied. 'But he got the message alright.'

A curt rap on the door came forty-five minutes later. Muscle one ushered Boris inside and muscle two frisked him. Boris might have regarded himself as a modern-day Lothario but he didn't show much bottle. I wondered idly about boys' talk I'd heard to the effect that men who are good with women often don't have much heart. There again, Boris might have been pragmatically accepting the jig was up; or perhaps I was just self-consoling.

After some prompting, Boris told us in good English the Malaysian woman, Betty, had been an agent run by his predecessor. He had inherited her. The safe house had been used to debrief her while in service. 'But the recent arrival of a new Ambassador, a Malay nationalist,' Boris said, 'resulted in Betty losing her job as the Ambassador's secretary.' After a pause, seemingly reflecting on this, he added with apparently genuine indignation, 'For no other reason than she was one-third Chinese.'

'And then?' Chuck asked.

'She was sidelined into a position of social secretary, meaning her access to classified information was lost.'

'Yet you kept up the association?' Penelope said.

Boris was suddenly coy. 'She knew too much and should have been sanctioned.' We all knew he meant she should have been assassinated. 'But she was an attractive woman and understood the reality of the situation. I suggested we remain in touch, *informally*.'

'You old dog,' Chuck said, without humour. 'How did you manage this cosy little arrangement?'

Boris smiled briefly. 'It wasn't hard to pay her the same retainer by falsifying an entry in the agent cash log. There is no embassy oversight of this expenditure and few audits by the KGB in Moscow. Betty and I reached an understanding. She was to come to the safe house each Thursday night. If the curtain in the upstairs living area was open it was clear to come in. Betty uses an old Indonesian taxi driver. He treats her like his daughter and is totally loyal. She would meet him Thursday nights at the JS Luwansa Hotel and later he would drop her back there.'

'And what about the use of your diplomatic vehicle to travel to the safe house?' Penelope asked.

'The Peugeot is cover,' Boris said. 'It's deliberately distinctive to convey I am a cultural diplomat with nothing to hide. The KGB station has a pool of nondescript vehicles carrying Indonesian plates for secret work requiring clean transport. But a file number must be recorded on sign out. This means if something goes wrong the file will tell the station which job the officer was on. An abominable Georgian peasant administers the car pool. I don't like him and he doesn't like me. I know he regularly checks on me. He would have come to realize that each time I went out I was operating solo, without backup, which is very rare. This made me reluctant to make false entries. I thought it safer to use my diplomatic car.'

'OK,' Chuck said. 'But what does the embassy make of you disappearing by yourself Thursday nights if you don't have the intelligence task excuse? How do you explain that away?'

'Ordinarily,' Boris said, 'all in the embassy are forbidden to leave the embassy alone. But members of the KGB station have the authority to ignore the rule when they judge that operational needs warrant it. Naturally, this power is abused. The embassy hierarchy is wary of upsetting KGB people. Its compromise is to tolerate the abuse so long as the station officers concerned are restrained and discreet. Provided I go out alone only for a couple of hours once a week no one pays me any attention.'

'Even so,' Penelope said, 'you must have understood the risks associated with using your diplomatic vehicle?'

Boris shrugged. 'The diplomatic plates are no doubt an issue. But substituting local ones for them would protect only so far. The Peugeot is still distinctive. Anyone with an interest in it would know it is my car. That's why I take elaborate precautions against tails. I assume that despite this one of your people still managed to follow me to the safe house?' When Boris received no answer he said, lips tightly pursed and head slowly shaking, 'Trust me when I say whoever it was got lucky.'

Boris knew what was expected. We ran over plans for his weekly debriefing and how he was to pass us documents. He hardly argued. He knew for sure that the combination of tipping us the safe house's location and pilfering of funds was enough for the KGB to shoot him, even before it debated the merits of his liaison with Betty. I ran Boris until the end of my posting about a year later. The Americans were not at all happy having to rely on our product, but they were pragmatic and used *the most heavy lifting* argument to gain first in access to other sources jointly recruited.

Boris was eventually posted to Ecuador, for no apparent reason other than to give him a break from the Islamic world. With that we, the Brits, sold him to the Yanks. The Americans pushed Boris hard. It finally got too much for him, or maybe he simply got sick of it all. Boris was found sitting in his living room with fragments of his skull and brain splattered on the wall like someone had dropped a watermelon. A KGB service issue pistol lay by his side.

Chapter 10 – London

Despite the Service's emphasis on the NTK principle and the Chinese walls this built, word soon spread about that Joe Lambert was a bit of a star. It came as no surprise in late 1970 when my name appeared on a promotions circular. This time I felt I had earned it. My only disappointment was again seeing the names of Heneshaw and Ladler on the list. Not long before I left Jakarta in April 1971 Penelope had told me I shouldn't be shy about seeking promotion to the next level, which was to director. 'Don't wait, Joe,' she urged. 'When I was in London a couple of months ago, senior people were complimentary about you. If you wait before applying that sentiment could have dissipated.' I took heed of her advice. Penelope's husband was apparently a wheel in the City. She was done with the spying caper for good once she left Jakarta and would be returning to London and back to academia. The currency of her support for me within the Service would quickly whittle away.

I had been assigned a position in Indonesia section, back in INS where I had started. Bev Brittingham was still in place. But Hanson Scott had moved on, having left the Service and moved to Peking where he was now a stringer for the *International Daily*. In his place was a woman called Sue Freckleton. She had come in laterally from MI5, the domestic security service and, unproductively, the

Service's intelligence rival. It was clear why Five had given her glowing references; she was simply no good.

The idea of returning me to INS was that with Boris in play, the section was the best place for me. In hindsight, it wasn't a great management decision. I became proprietorial about Boris and was never happy at the way the station was running him. I chaffed at this and more realistically some of Sue's decisions. The truth is I became overbearing and full of perceived importance. The inevitable reality check came towards the end of 1971 when the directors' promotion list came out without my name on it. I'd followed Penelope's advice and applied, but without success. I only had myself to blame. An old adage rang in my ears: *You're soon in trouble once you start believing your own bullshit.*

I soldiered on through the first half of 1972, deliberately adopting a more collegiate approach to my work and colleagues. Bev Brittingham was badly overdue for a change of scenery. Personnel finally levered her out. A man called Patrick Hernandez took over as branch head. Patrick was a cold fish who took no prisoners. He offered no praise, not a scintilla, only blunt and stinging criticism as and when he thought it required. But at least he was consistent and treated everyone equally. Poor old Sue didn't last long under him. Quicker than you could blink, she was sent head spinning to one of the analytical units. Patrick called me in. 'I want you to act as director for the time being. When the directors' promotions are out later on we'll be getting someone off that list.' I found his message confusing. On the one hand, he had voiced confidence in me by selecting me to act as director. But on the other, he seemed to be suggesting I wouldn't necessarily be promoted. I rationalized with Boris on his way out in Jakarta, Ecuador bound, the powers that be had decided I needed the challenge of a director's job in a new area.

So much for positive thinking. The list came out at the start of October. I was mortified, gutted, to find I had missed out again. The insult to injury, at least so I thought, was that my nemeses Heneshaw and Ladler were now both through to director level. But the real insult came a couple of weeks later when Patrick called me into his office. Who should be standing there but Rupert Heneshaw. Patrick briefly conducted formalities. 'Joe, meet Rupert Heneshaw just back from three years or so in Bonn. He'll be taking up the INS director's job starting the week commencing 23 October. Have a handover brief to me by last thing Thursday and I'll look at it on Friday so Rup is ready to go on the Monday following.'

Fucking Rup, I seethed inwardly, mimicking Patrick's gratingly familiar reference to Heneshaw. I stood there unable to look at Heneshaw, knowing full well the beginnings of a superior smirk would be forming around the corners of his mouth.

Hernandez failed to notice, or possibly didn't care, that Heneshaw and I had not shaken hands. He looked up at me. 'Anything else?' he asked, a furrow forming on his brow. I couldn't trust myself to speak and shook my head before turning heel and leaving the office.

That night I let bad habits intrude until rather late at the Cambridge Arms, the local watering hole close to my rented flat in West Brompton. The next day, in the haze of a force five hangover, I prepared the brief requested. It wasn't my best work. But I managed to tart it up. It was in reasonable shape when I gave it to Hernandez on the Thursday afternoon. For all that, I was decidedly unhappy with my lot. Not much changed as the weeks passed. If anything my situation deteriorated owing to Heneshaw's willingness to tell anyone who would listen about the challenges he faced in fixing the mess Lambert had created while acting as director.

The year of 1973 arrived. Sitting alone one cold January night in the saloon bar of the Cambridge Arms, I tried to fathom why I had been overlooked for promotion. I reasoned that professionally there wasn't much daylight between Heneshaw, Ladler and me. My part in Boris's recruitment had been a significant achievement, but they had both completed assignments in high profile posts. What then was the factor in their favour? I could tell from my current interactions with colleagues I was no longer thought of as a yokel; Jakarta had been a defining posting for me. Whatever Heneshaw and Ladler thought about me, class prejudice was unlikely to be the difference. My mind turned to Nought's advice about getting married, about which I had done absolutely nothing since returning to London.

The Service is an organization imbued in secrecy. As a result, any gossip about people working there is shared avidly, freed as it is from the strictures of national security. It didn't take long to find out Heneshaw had married a Chelsea belle, part of the horsey set it seemed, while on mid-term leave from Bonn and that Freddie Ladler had married *a big toothed Texan* he had met during his Washington posting. The evidence may have been circumstantial but something told me Nought had been right all along. He always was.

Chapter 11 – Kathleen

There was an office social forum of which I had become aware called the Diners Club. Joining involved simply penning a short note containing a list of interests and placing it on a notice board in the staff recreation room. Interested persons contacted other interested persons to arrange dinner parties, dining out experiences and the like. The entire office had visibility of the notice board and I feared ridicule. But after staking out the board for a time I saw that quite a lot of people used it. Shortly after my birthday in March 1973, I took the plunge and put up a notice: *Joe Lambert; age 33; interests: cricket, reading and international affairs; extension 235.* I had included my age hoping this might encourage contact with people of a similar age group.

A fellow called Robert Charters rang. 'I'm calling about the Diners Club,' he said. He was obviously quite young. I wondered if my age strategy had gone awry. Robert was very nervous. 'My girlfriend, Phoebe, has a second cousin a few years older than her who has just moved to London. Her name is Kathleen Pennington. The cousin, that is. Sorry, I'm rambling here.'

'Take your time,' I said. My instincts were responding positively to the cues I was picking up. I liked Robert.

'Kathleen wants to have dinner. Rather than lopsided numbers, I wondered if you would be interested in joining us. I must be clear that neither Phoebe nor Kathleen is Service, if that's of concern.'

'No concern at all,' I said, 'and dinner would be great. I assume you'll make the booking? I live in West Brompton.'

'Pheebs and I live in Highgate,' Robert responded.

Five demerit points for the Pheebs bit, I thought. 'Goodness,' I said, 'when I first came here I lived at Kentish Town and thought that was a long way out.' He laughed and I restored his demerits.

'It's not too bad. And yes, I'll make the booking. But look don't worry. Kathleen lives in Mayfair so we'll eat in the city. What date suits you?'

My weekend diary was hardly overflowing but to save face I did the let me check routine all the same. 'How about Saturday 7 April?'

'That would work,' Robert said. He told me he would book for 7 pm and let me know where.

I presented washed and sober on the appointed night at the Ancient Islands steakhouse near Marble Arch. Robert and Phoebe arrived smack on time. They were the epitome of a nice young couple –

clean lines; stylishly dressed without hint of ostentation; and impeccably mannered. Robert worked in one of the administrative areas on the second floor. His work didn't allow him access to my area or mine to his. It was the first time I had met him.

At 7.10 pm Kathleen arrived. I assessed her surreptitiously. Her fair hair was long with a flicked fringe designed to give her an elegant lady about town look. But that initial impression was defeated somewhat, both by the fact the expensive couture she wore somehow didn't seem to fit her properly and her propensity for child-like mannerisms. I wondered when Kathleen told me she worked as a kindergarten teacher if this might have contributed to her social awkwardness.

Still the evening was pleasant enough. God knows what Kathleen thought about me but she was politely friendly throughout. We wound up about 9.30 pm. Robert and Phoebe had to rush for a train. I offered to walk Kathleen home. I nearly fell over when on the way she told me her flat in Adams Row was owned by a family trust. That was serious money. The half-hour stroll to Mayfair was otherwise unremarkable. Our evening culminated with a chaste handshake and vague mention of a staying in touch.

Proceeding past Hyde Park Corner and onto Kensington Road, I reflected the evening was like a nil-all football draw. You couldn't complain about the result but nor was there anything to get excited about. Why then did I write to Kathleen a week later suggesting an outing, just the two of us? The truth is the woman did not intimidate me. That might be put rather less kindly when juxtaposing Kathleen with Hilda, the Swiss from Jakarta. Be that as it may, I badly wanted to escape being pigeonholed as a bachelor loner and the threat to career this entailed. I never gave so much as a millisecond's thought to whether the pursuit of Kathleen might also help avoid the other pitfall in being *The Lone Wolf at Cover*, the personal consequences to which Nought had fleetingly referred.

Kathleen accepted my invitation to a Saturday matinee session of *The Mousetrap*. We had tea afterwards. She told me about herself, including she was turning thirty later in the year. Kathleen was evidently still missing her hometown of Maidstone in Kent, which at dinner with Robert and Phoebe she had wistfully termed the *Garden of England*. Her father, an accountant by trade, was the manager of the Shawcross butter factory in Maidstone. I didn't know then that he owned half the bloody company and was as rich as Croesus.

In the early 1970s prevailing social attitudes were such that, however ludicrously, unmarried women of thirty or more were generally thought of as doomed to spinsterhood. It didn't take much to detect Kathleen regarded her looming birthday with great apprehension. She told me she was a single child and until recently had lived at home all her life. Originally, she had hoped to be a schoolteacher, but 'when that didn't come to pass' ended up in kindergarten teaching. After a decade working in Maidstone a shift to London was necessary to gain wider experience. The round trip of sixty miles or so, Kathleen said, had deterred her from commuting from the family home. The night ended with a polite embrace and me pecking her on the cheek as we said our goodbyes.

And that's how it started. It would be wildly over-generous to say we fell in love because it suggests an intense relationship, gratifying sex and deep emotional attachment. Rather, the romantic dimension of our relationship was confined to us petting and occasionally, provided the light was off because she didn't want me to see her naked, Kathleen allowing me to fondle her breasts. The one time I asked for hand relief she primly replied, 'I don't do that. And as for the other, don't even think about it.' I assumed *the other* was oral sex. Nor did we ever stay together overnight sleeping in separate bedrooms. And whenever in Maidstone, I was accommodated as far away from Kathleen as the physical design of her parents' massive house allowed.

When courting Kathleen I found my loner instincts never surfaced, without which the relationship could not have progressed as it did. The reason was soon apparent enough. Although I was not uncaring about Kathleen, I had not invested much in the way of emotional capital in her and felt no anxiety for emotional security. This convinced me that only in cases of substantial emotional outlay did my need to escape trigger. My experience with Hilda in Jakarta suggested instances involving strong and intelligent women only exacerbated the problem. The illogicality baffled me and occasionally kept me awake at night. Around this time, usually in the wee hours of the morning, I sought to put meat on the bones of the tentative conclusion reached many years earlier at university, that somehow my mother's death was linked to my loner instincts.

For reasons unknown, perhaps an impulse to be rid of my long-held burden of guilt, I first pondered an act of God. This led me to decide my mother's suffering was an ethereal plan to force me from her; my leaving her at the critical juncture was not of my own doing but rather God's intention that my mother's distress should push me from her, effectively in an act of rejection. But bitter self-recrimination soon overtook my theory of spiritual rejection. Was I really blaming a deity in whom I had not the faintest belief for my reprehensible behaviour? I became gripped by guilt that I should treat my dying mother's misery as a pawn in some cockamamie, pseudo-religious attempt to explain away my abysmal conduct and later relationship woes. The extraordinary thing was the persistence of the shame I felt at this flirtation. Even years later any reminder of it would still invite a wave of self-condemnation.

Chastened by my temerity, I hastened to contemplate other explanations. My thoughts turned to psychological angles. I concluded that the trauma of my mother's death had sparked a drive to be safely alone from women of meaning to me. This translated in the romantic context into a fear of female rejection, a condition aggravated to morbidity by the Sarah Sutherland experience. The thesis I came to accept was that when anxious to cement a relationship my emotional outlay was prone to exceeding a certain threshold, beyond which I was vulnerable to the pain of female rejection. On detecting this my sub-conscious pre-emptively sparked the need to escape to protect me from the threat of rejection. The subsequent distress and depression arising from the involuntary triggering of this defence mechanism was the result of losing what I badly wanted in the first place. Such was my circular introspection. I found it infinitely more tolerable than the religious other.

Meanwhile I continued on with Kathleen. Her parents, Benjamin and Elizabeth, were substantially religious. Both Anglicans. They were noticeably unimpressed when I told them I was an agnostic – I spared them I was actually an atheist. My mother's tortuous death, reinforced latterly by my unhappy contemplation of spiritual rejection, had seen to that. But after a time Benjamin began to offer me a very weak whisky before dinner. I knew then I had finally been accepted into the fold.

Kathleen and I announced our engagement in September 1973. I proclaimed the happy news widely and loudly in the office. The word spread like wildfire.

Chapter 12 – Legacy

Around this time Penelope Hensworth re-entered my life, via a telephone call put through from the outside switch. Penelope was now living back in London. She was typically to the point. 'Joe,' she said, 'you should know Nought Collins is nearing his end. He would like to see you. He told me so.' Penelope gave me a Bristol address, telling me Nought refused to have the telephone at his home. 'If I were you,' she counselled, 'I would get over to the West Country soonish. He doesn't have long left.'

Nought, being Nought, had not bothered to stay in touch as he'd promised upon leaving Jakarta. But I remained endlessly fond of him and was shocked by Penelope's awful news. Penelope had called on a Tuesday. I calculated a letter posted that afternoon would reach Nought by the Thursday morning. I quickly wrote him a short note, explaining I would call at his home the coming Friday morning ex the London train. I then ran out to post the letter. On return to the office I completed an application for Friday leave.

I arrived at Nought's home in Bristol at about 11 am. It was a small, single-fronted, red-brick town home. The tiny front yard was mostly paved over; what greenery there was had clearly not received much attention in recent times. I rapped the doorknocker and heard the echo of its sound reverberate throughout the house. Silence. I began to panic and wondered if Nought had received my letter. Finally, the sound of stockinged feet moving very slowly could be heard.

I hardly recognized Nought. He still had the bulbous nose but was a wizened relic of what he once looked like. 'Joey Lambert,' he wheezed. 'What a sight for sore eyes. Come in, come in.' The house was not untidy in a major way. Nought explained he had two nieces who lived in Bath. Week about they came in and tidied up for him. 'They want to make sure they're in the will,' he said, smiling to show me he wasn't serious. 'Love to offer you a decent drink, Joe, but my innards have rotted. My sister has banned grog from the house as a condition of her daughters helping me out. They know I'd drink anything that was here. What the fuck have I got to lose?'

I made tea and we talked of the old days. After a time, I asked Nought if he remembered telling me the night of our knees-up when he was leaving Jakarta that I should get married.

'I do,' he said. 'And still valid advice too. Times are changing but the Service is a conservative outfit; it'll be the last to conform.'

'Well, I've just become engaged.'

Nought's reaction was not what I expected. Rather, he just looked at me, shrewdly assessing what I had said. Finally, he spoke. 'I loved my wife but I was young, ambitious and intelligent.

Brilliant some said. Too many other temptations. Never home and ended up fucking up the one thing that matters in life: real and lasting love. Lost my marriage, got on the slops and eventually found my way to the scrapheap.' Nought heaved for breath. 'Do you love this bit of crumpet you've got your hooks into?' he asked.

There was no point lying to him; he was too canny for that. 'If I was honest,' I said, 'there have been other occasions when I've felt a more powerful attraction. This is a different relationship. It's steadier, more a matter of companionship and mutual support than an emotional rollercoaster oscillating every which way.'

Nought made no direct response. Instead he said, 'Remember I also told you at the knees-up you had the makings of *The Lone Wolf at Cover*?' He smiled sadly at the memory.

'I surely do.'

'Did you ever stop to think what I really meant?'

'I thought initially it was just a joke, a reference to our secret work. But after that night I believed you were warning me of the danger to my career in the Service thinking of me as a loner because that's why it thinks Philby and Co. spied for the Sovs.'

'That's true, certainly. And it's still relevant to you. Although some day the Service will understand its thinking about the Cambridge lot is cockeyed and stop automatically putting anyone with loner tendencies in the same boat.'

Nought's eyebrows then knitted in a frown. 'But I was also trying to warn you about something a lot more serious. You weren't listening by then so I didn't push it. I wanted you to know that spying comes to destroy us if we allow it. It's the dark side of our dark business. You need to be aware, Joey, that total obsession with the black arts for too long will always lead to isolation and moral incompetence. One day we wake up and we're social outcasts; devious bastards unable to separate right from wrong, condemned forever to creeping alone across life's outer fringes.'

From over the rim of his water glass Nought checked he still had my attention. '*The Lone Wolf at Cover*, the solitary cricketer,' he said, 'is the perfect metaphor for it. Like us, he is cast out from the world and left alone to pad across a vast expanse. Only in our case we're removed not from the epicentre of a cricket match but from mainstream life, and what we're left to pad across is not bloody savannah it's the endless, frozen landscape of spying. Understand, Joe, all that stands between people like us who succumb to spying and *The Lone Wolf at Cover* is real love, the *real deal*. Nothing else can stop what is otherwise inevitable. I should know. I tried every alternative, the whole fucking lot.'

I didn't respond, a little disconcerted by Nought's rawness. Instead I reflected on him speaking as if still part of the Service, recalling he'd once told me of its capacity to claim people for life.

Nought stared at me with rheumy eyes and took another sip of water. He knew his appeal to my sense of self-preservation still hadn't overcome my fixation on career. He also knew just how badly I wanted him to encourage me to proceed with the marriage. Grimacing, much like a caring father reluctantly conceding to his son, he said, 'I guess for now you should try to make those who count think differently about you.' After a pause he added, 'But do so knowing this brewing marriage you've come here crowing about is going to end at some point. I can tell you that with certainty because there's no glue there. You might last ten days, you might last a decade. But it won't last forever. Ride it as far as you can I suggest. The longer you stay married, the more progress you'll make at convincing the fifth floor you're something you're not.' He laughed an anaemic laugh. 'That's Uncle Nought's last pearl of wisdom,' he said. 'I'm fucked, over and out.'

I left Nought heavy of heart. His final words rang in my ears. 'Don't fret for me, Joey. I'm in the acceptance phase now. I know what's coming and all I want is for the pain and feebleness to stop. One final thing: I don't want you coming to my funeral. I mean it. I really want you to remember me as I was. But I do want you to have this.' He produced from behind his back a small rectangular item that looked like a pencil case. It was no more than a foot long and an inch wide and high. 'Been passed down in the Collins family from father to son since the time of my great-grandfather. But as I fucked up, the line stops with me. If you have a son, Joe, be sure to give him this.' The box's outer leather skin was aged smooth with time and embossed with the seal of the Austro-Hungarian Empire. It was exquisite. The lump in my throat threatened to choke me as I realized the significance, and finality, of the gift. Nought could see this. He winked. 'Go well son.' Then he shut the door.

On the return journey I couldn't hold back the tears. My fellow commuters looked at me guardedly over the top of their newspapers. Back in London, I stopped at the off-licence on the way home. Sitting in the quiet of my flat I bid Nought goodbye. Nought died eight days later. His sister telephoned to tell me the news.

I slept poorly that night I returned from Bristol. Kathleen and I were to have Saturday lunch at her flat. I arrived hungover and subdued, telling Kathleen seeing Nought so ill and dire had upset me and caused me a disturbed night. I left out the bit about drinking three-quarters of a bottle of whisky. After lunch we decided to watch a re-run of *The Bridge on the River Kwai* on television. Cuddling on the couch I felt a primal urge to mate. Frankly I was scared, of what exactly I wasn't sure. When Kathleen warded off my attempts to put my hand down her underwear, I persisted. She became irritated. 'Joe, all this will come in good time. The church has taught me I must be a virgin when I marry and that's what I intend to be. Please try to control yourself.' With that, she got up and sat in an armchair.

'I think I'll try and doze if that's alright,' I said. 'I'm so tired.'

'Good idea,' she responded coolly.

Things remained strained for the remainder of the afternoon. There was no offer of dinner to consider. But as I was leaving, Kathleen suddenly said with forced brightness, 'Let's forget our tiff today. I'm sure you'll be a new man after a decent night's sleep.' We kissed goodbye with the promise to take a long afternoon stroll around Hyde Park the following day.

Chapter 13 – CIS

Kathleen and I were scheduled to marry on Saturday 8 June 1974. I mean that literally; we didn't select the date. Kathleen's parents wanted a big bash and figured the first opportunity of decent weather was in June. Kathleen never said anything to me suggesting she thought differently. Her parents paid all the bills and directed all traffic. They were not to be questioned. I was never consulted.

Professionally, 1973 had ended well for me. My name was on the directors' promotion list that came out in November. I was in no doubt my newfound respectability, courtesy of my well publicized upcoming nuptials, contributed mightily to me getting over the line. I took leave over Christmas while Kathleen was on holidays. Much of it was spent in Maidstone, where her parents' probing questions increasingly wore on me. I was glad to return to the office and my new position as director of Counter Intelligence Section.

CIS was one of two sections in CIB, Counter Intelligence Branch, and big brother to WPS, Warsaw Pact Section. With ten staff, CIS was a Service within the Service. Section members were mostly ex-military; two were former colonial policemen. All men. The role of CIS was to recruit selected Soviet personnel stationed in or visiting Britain. WPS did the same thing in respect of non-Soviet Warsaw

Pact countries, the Soviet Union's seven Eastern European communist allies.

CIS was permeated to its core by a cowboy culture. I first became aware of this early in my tenure when two section members and I were driving down Piccadilly in the middle of a working day in a beat-up-looking surveillance car. My colleague in the front passenger seat, a man called Bryan Cosgrove, reacted to a vehicle travelling in the opposite direction. 'That's fucking Kruchenykh, head of the Soviet consular office,' he screamed excitedly. 'Let's give the fucker a rev. Quick, before we lose him'

The other section member, the one driving, was junior to Cosgrove. 'We'll make him think we're some lads taking the mick because of his diplomatic plates,' he said, explaining Cosgrove's order for my benefit. With that, he pulled on the handbrake with such force that our vehicle turned 180 degrees. He then accelerated up Piccadilly in pursuit of Kruchenykh leaving traffic mayhem in our wake. I'd seen handbrake turns during training but never imagined they would be used unnecessarily in London traffic.

Once we'd pulled alongside the Soviet at traffic lights, Cosgrove who was closest to him proceeded to pull faces and make crude gestures. Kruchenykh resolutely ignored him while onlookers watched on in amazement. The lights turned green and he drove off. My colleagues watched him go, both grinning from ear to ear. I hoped my subordinates were showing off this once for my benefit. But it all seemed rather too well practised for my liking.

The night of the Piccadilly episode I reflected on the potentially serious political implications in what I had witnessed. That which unfolded was an intrusion against an apparently bona fide Soviet diplomat going about his business. The Sovs would lodge an official complaint with the Foreign Secretary in a trice if they ever thought their real diplomats were the subjects of Service harassment. And then there was the risk of the general public complaining about reckless driving antics. All that was needed was for someone to jot down a licence plate number. Either way, the Service chieftains would be in the political firing line.

The other problematic matter that shortly after came to my attention was the outright refusal of the CIS people to work cooperatively with MI5. Mind you, I don't think Five were altogether angels either. Of the Sovs targeted by CIS, those who were suspected of being intelligence officers but unable to be turned were supposed to be handed over to Five, which would investigate and where necessary make recommendation to the Home Secretary for that official to be expelled. But clearly this was not happening. The CIS approach, as explained to me, was to confront Soviet spies unable to be recruited and 'invite then to desist or risk getting a kick in the balls.' I was told with great relish about assaults in the toilets of seedy Soho clubs on intelligence operatives ignoring the warning, leaving them prostrate in foul urinals.

I accepted unquestioningly that uncooperative Soviet spies were being threatened with violence. But in doing their tough guy act, I think those claiming *actual* assaults overlooked the fact I had served in Moscow. On activation there I had been told of instances of Western intelligence officers returning home to find the kettle had just been boiled, indicating someone had very recently been inside their apartment. This type of psychological warfare was tolerated. But on both sides of the equation retribution was swift and brutal if the mark was overstepped. This gave rise, I had been briefed, to a gentlemen's agreement between the Americans and Soviets, which Britain and the other Warsaw Pact countries closely followed. Namely, the meting out of physical harm to intelligence officers and their families – narrowly confined to the spouses and children who usually accompanied married officers posted abroad – was off limits. But the agreement did not apply to deep cover agents or, depending on the circumstances, even people associated with intelligence officers. Here each side had open slather.

I concluded on the basis of the gentlemen's agreement that the claims of physical violence against Soviet operatives were concocted to intimidate me. Yet I was also aware that so long as established processes for dealing with disobliging Soviets were ignored, actual assaults were just one overstep away. In the event, this held calamitous implications for Service people in the field.

Mulling all this over, I had the inspired thought the flawed CIS culture was actually a gift, insomuch as it gave me an agenda to pursue in support of my career. I would propose to my masters the reform of the section, to make it less of a political and operational risk. Demonstrated management capability like this was essential to gaining promotion to branch head and beyond. Handled carefully, my initiative would sow this vitally important seed.

I decided the reforms I put up needed to place emphasis on good analysis and adherence to procedure. To be sure we had to retain some muscle – Positive Action capability as it was termed – for those occasions warranting it. But times had changed. Soviet spies were no longer big-eared ruffians in baggy suits who ate with their mouths open. The approach to what CIS did now needed to be more scientific. I worked up a hit list of staff I wanted to get rid of.

The head of CIB was a man by the name of Roger Saddington. Roger had a year to run until retirement but his mind was already on the golf course. He had seen a lot of war action and I respected him for that. But he no longer had any appetite for bureaucratic intrigue. This and his close affinity to the disciplined services background of the CIS people told me I would have to wait him out.

Chapter 14 – Phobias

The Service had a rule that officers could reveal their occupations to their life partners only once formally married, and subject to spouses first signing the Official Secrets Act. By 1974 the regulation was hopelessly outmoded in the face of growing numbers of unmarried couples living together. Yet change was slow in coming.

As my June wedding date loomed, I made the decision I should not wait until Kathleen and I married. I needed to tell her beforehand exactly what she was signing up for. One Saturday night in mid-May we were scheduled to go out for dinner. I arrived at Kathleen's flat about 6 pm. With about three weeks to go until the big day Kathleen by this time was in a state of high anxiety. She was in constant contact, and conflict, with her mother about the wedding arrangements. I was grateful to have been marginalized. Of the nearly 200 guest invitations sent I had invited not one person. I would have invited Nought. But he was dead. Robert Charters had agreed to be my best man.

'How are you? I greeted Kathleen. 'You seem a bit frazzled.'

'Well, wouldn't you be?' she replied with heat, a wild look in her eyes. 'I've been on the phone to my mother all afternoon and now there's some sort of problem with the flowers at the church.'

I could see she was close to tears. 'Sit down and catch your breath. I need to tell you something.'

'Yes,' she said distractedly.

I was now wondering if this was the right time and regretted not earlier deciding to ignore the Service's edict. But it was too late. If I didn't tell Kathleen now when would I? 'You know how I've told you I work for the Foreign Office?' Kathleen didn't answer. 'I actually work for the Secret Intelligence Service. Our role, broadly, is to ferret out information that can't be obtained by Foreign Office diplomats; information that other governments don't want the British Government to know.'

Kathleen looked at me like I was mad. 'Why are you bothering me with all this mumbo jumbo about information?' she asked. 'Surely I have enough things to worry about right now?'

I found Kathleen's manic look disconcerting. 'Well,' I said, 'when we're married you'll have to sign the Official Secrets Act, which is a legal undertaking not to discuss my work with anyone.'

Kathleen looked at me uncomprehendingly. Then she dissolved into tears and collapsed into my arms, her shoulders heaving violently as she wept like a wounded animal.

All of sudden I could think of nothing else other than Kat Phillips, the willowy Hungarian I had encountered in Soviet Political Branch after completing basic training, her world-weariness and its carnal effect on my protective instincts. Sexual desire soared within me. Kathleen and I kissed with hungry passion. She was wearing a pleated tartan skirt. I lifted it to her waist and lowered her gently to the carpeted floor. Kathleen's eyes were shut and her complexion flushed. Unprompted she raised her buttocks, allowing me to draw down the full white briefs she wore and discard them to one side. I was panting heavily and literally having trouble breathing. I pushed her skirt higher and saw a near rectangle of fine, dark pubic hair adorning her pubic mound. Immediately below, the convex of her labia majora, around which no pubic hair grew, projected like the smooth surface of a white peach. My lust was total. Urgency forestalled removing my trousers. I unzipped myself. Kathleen gasped as I plunged into her. Afterwards we lay there for a long time, both of us labouring for breath. Kathleen eventually pushed me off her with a grunt. Climbing to her feet, she smoothed down her skirt, scooped up her panties and disappeared into the bathroom.

Now sitting on the sofa, I regarded the large wet patch on the front of my trousers. I wondered about the absence of blood in the face of Kathleen's claims to being a virgin and the ease with which I had entered her. I simply didn't know enough about women to make up my mind one way or the other. Kathleen emerged from the bathroom. I smiled at her but she didn't smile back. 'You just couldn't wait, could you?' She spat the words at me.

I was taken aback. 'I thought it was more like WE couldn't wait.'

Kathleen ignored me. Instead she said, 'Look at your clothes; you're disgusting. I will get you a towel and want you to go into the bathroom and take off your trousers. Be sure to put the towel around you while you're in there. Don't think you're going to sit around here in your underwear like a common navvy. I'll put your trousers on the heater to try and dry them out.'

I felt seriously deflated. For the want of something better to say I asked, 'What are we going to do about dinner?'

'Obviously we're not able to go to the restaurant,' Kathleen replied scathingly. 'There's a new place opened over on Grosvenor Street selling takeaway. I'll go and get a pizza. If by the time we've eaten your trousers are not dry, you'll need to take a newspaper to cover your front when you walk home.'

I tried to make sense of it all while Kathleen was out. I had long known I wanted to marry Kathleen only because I feared the Service tagging me as a habitual bachelor. But we had an awful lot of incompatibility. I began to get cold feet and wondered if I could renege on the wedding at this late stage. Then I thought of the career costs involved. From the grave, Nought resolved my dilemma: *Ride the marriage as far as you can*, he had counselled. And that I concluded was what I must try to do.

We ate the pizza in near silence. Once finished, I asked Kathleen if she thought my trousers would be dry. They were but a big stain was visible. Kathleen thrust *The Times* at me when shortly after I readied to go, despite my protestation it was the dead of night outside. I was surprised when she kissed me lightly as I left – but should not have been. Walking home, after discarding the newspaper in the first refuse bin I encountered, it dawned on me she had made her own assessment. Kathleen was haunted by a morbid dread of spinsterhood and marrying me met her perceived needs. Consumed by her entrenched anxiety, as I was mine, she had decided the relationship had to carry through to marriage and beyond. Neither of us ever mentioned that night again. I never did resolve the question of Kathleen's virginity.

The night before my wedding I caught the late train to Maidstone after finishing work. I carried my groom's suit with me. Kathleen and her father met me at the station. Kathleen was in an upbeat mood. 'Darling,' she said, 'how wonderful to see you. Have you eaten?' We embraced. The lower halves of our bodies did not make contact, in deference to her father most certainly, but also as an act of chastity by Kathleen, who was determined to play the virgin bride. Over a cup of tea back at the house, I was informed the wedding plans had come together well.

Our wedding day dawned sunny but crisp. Kathleen's family customarily kept her from my sight. Robert Charters, Phoebe and I had breakfast together in the guest wing. Phoebe was to be a bridesmaid. She ate quickly and left Robert and me alone. Robert asked me how I was feeling. 'Nervous,' I said. He looked at me curiously. Robert was no dummy. I think he sensed the internal struggle I was having went beyond nerves. Alone, we talked a little bit of shop, mostly gossipy tidbits about who was going where. I produced Kathleen's wedding band and gave it to him.

The groom's vehicle deposited Robert and me at St Andrew's Anglican Church about ten minutes before Kathleen, accompanied by her father, was scheduled to arrive for the 2 pm ceremony. The church was in the Maidstone town centre, an oasis of beautiful old Norman design in the midst of a sea of ugly development.

Kathleen was traditionally late. My knees trembled as the service got underway. The church was small and packed to the gunnels. Invitations fell into two categories: those invited to the church and reception; and those to the reception alone. I couldn't help but think of the *B*-list diplomats in Moscow when I first became aware of this. I made a good fist of steadying myself. All the same, my memory of the service remains hazy. But all went to plan.

Words were said, rings placed on fingers and then we were done: man and wife.

Kathleen's parents had organized for a reception to be held at the nearby Town Square Hotel. Kathleen was overcome by excitement and squeezed my arm as we were driven away from the church. I was too busy trying to come to terms with what I'd just let myself in for to be too enthusiastic. But I managed a smile and said, 'Fantastic service, wasn't it?'

People were swarming everywhere when we arrived. The hotel reception room was overflowing to capacity. By now I was also starving, hardly having eaten all day. Kathleen and I were seated in the middle of the head table, with Kathleen's mother to my immediate left and her father at her right hand. Food was served, which I bolted down. Kathleen whispered I should eat more slowly; people were watching. I would have killed a man for a strong whisky by this point but all that was on offer alcoholically were sparse quantities of champagne. I didn't much care for the beverage but nonetheless rapidly sunk two glasses of it, earning me a sterner rebuke from my spouse.

The official part of the reception went on forever. Kathleen's parents both made speeches, with Benjamin's proceeding interminably. This was followed by other speeches, by this uncle or that and family friends of one guise or another, seemingly by the dozen. Just when I thought we were at the end another person would get the call. Finally, the speeches were done. But then Kathleen and I had to dance our bridal waltz, by ourselves in view of everyone. The last time I had danced was well over a decade ago and even then I was inside a bottle of gin. I worried I might fall over or worse trip up Kathleen. To applause befitting the winners of the all-England ballroom dancing championships, we tottered around. I think we were both relieved when other couples began to enter the square of parquetry demarcating the dance floor.

It was close to 10 pm before Kathleen's parents released us. Benjamin and Elizabeth were not stupid. They could see I was flagging. But I mattered little in their eyes. Not until Kathleen showed signs of running out of steam did they consent to our departure. While Kathleen was still running about the room inviting inspection of her wedding dress and generally being the centre of attention the show had to go on. I shrugged inwardly. Their little girl, I guess.

We were driven back to the family home to change. Kathleen was tired by now and had become surly towards me. Our chauffeur drove us up the M20 motorway towards London and onto Heathrow, where we had a room booked at the Terminal Five Hilton. Not much was said en-route. Kathleen perked up a little when we arrived, loudly announcing at reception for the benefit of anyone in earshot that we had a booking for 'Mr and Mrs Joseph Lambert.'

In the room and alone we sort of stared at each other. Kathleen declined my icebreaking attempt, an offer to make her a cup of herbal tea. She changed in the bathroom and emerged in pyjamas, jumping straight into bed and turning out her bedside lamp. I usually slept naked but fortunately had the wit to pack a pair of short pyjamas. I changed there in the bedroom putting on only the bottoms. The back of Kathleen's head was the only part of her visible as I hopped beneath the covers. 'Best we get some sleep,' I said. 'We've an early start for our flight to Madrid tomorrow.'

I was tired, exhausted actually, both from the physical demands of the day and the battle with my competing emotions. But I couldn't sleep initially. I summarized my position. Now we were married and to live together in Kathleen's flat, we no longer had the luxury of separate accommodation providing space for emotions to blow over each time we had a disagreement. Our relationship would soon be under strain. Yet if I were to go churlish on Kathleen we'd be done in no time. I had entered into the marriage only for the sake of my career. Having widely talked up the event within the Service, I would be the veritable Emperor without clothes if the union turned out to be stillborn. The blowback professionally and personally would be devastating. I had no option but to adapt.

No doubt both us had an end point when the marriage would no longer have a purpose to serve. But it was impossible to predict how long it would be before Kathleen judged she had proved she was not a spinster and I had no idea when being wedded would have satisfied my career needs. My focus could only be on keeping the marriage afloat while I needed it afloat. I concluded the marriage's survival prospects were best if I was restrained at all times. I resolved starting from the moment I awoke the next morning to avoid aggravating Kathleen, while also ignoring her moods and oddities. With that, I slept. Many years later, when the BBC television comedy *Keeping up Appearances* aired, I recalled devising this wedding night strategy. I marvelled at its similarity to the attitude taken by the fictional character Richard Bucket to the relentless pretentiousness of his equally fictitious wife, Hyacinth.

We had a quick breakfast at the hotel before proceeding to Terminal Five to catch our British Airways flight. Our honeymoon involved six nights in Madrid and a further four in Barcelona. Once on the plane, our respective spirits perked as the holiday feel took hold. We engaged in friendly banter while polishing up our limited Spanish. On arrival we completed formalities, changed some money and caught a taxi to our hotel in downtown Madrid. After lunch we hit the tourist trail. It was hot and we were both tired and sunburnt by the time we returned in the late afternoon. We ate an early dinner at a nearby restaurant. Back in our room, I rubbed Mercurochrome into Kathleen's sunburned back. I could feel her tenseness as we readied for bed. Unsure whether or not to play the amorous husband, I settled for a goodnight brush of my lips against hers.

The next day some of the thrill of being in exotic Spain was starting to ebb away as Kathleen, not entirely without reason, began to complain about the hordes of tourists clogging the streets. That night Kathleen had some sangria over dinner. This seemed to relax her; she even laughed exasperatedly at the rudeness of some of our fellow sightseers. In bed that night I touched her upper thigh over the material of her pyjama pants, kissing her on the lips as I did. Encouraged she did not pull back, I pulled down her pyjama pants only to find she was wearing briefs underneath. Not wanting to seem too anxious I started to kiss her again and tried to touch her breasts. 'Get on with it if you must, for goodness sake,' she hissed, her irritability doing nothing for my ardour.

The experience was nothing like that night in May, when something sexually remarkable had occurred. My drive was subdued and Kathleen unresponsive, our languidness feeding between us with compounding effect. Over the remaining eight days we had sex on three other occasions. Not much improved. By the end we were both relieved when the honeymoon was over. Being together all day, every day had broken new ground for us both.

Chapter 15 – Sheila

The timing of my wedding had been fortuitous in that it had occurred during my year of waiting. The way was now clear to make my career play once Roger Saddington had vacated as head of CIB. Three months after our honeymoon, I managed to get Kathleen to come into the Service, now located in Century House on Westminster Bridge Road in Lambeth. I met her at Waterloo Station and walked her around. There in the ground floor anteroom adjacent to the janitors' front counter she signed the Official Secrets Act.

In December 1974 Saddington hit the silk, as the old paratrooper liked to say. Kathleen accompanied me to his farewell at the Gascoyne club in Pall Mall. Saddington was too junior in the great scheme of things to warrant the DG's presence. But I thought it disappointing a DDG was not trotted out. CIB's supervising FADG, a man called Tom Inglis, was the senior attendee. He made the presentation. Formal remarks were tailored in deference to the universally unindoctrinated waiters.

On the tables guests were less discreet. I watched Kathleen's reaction to the many reminiscences. I don't think she understood, much less cared, what people were saying. She told me she wanted to go home as soon as dessert had been served. I put my foot down as gently as I could and told her we would wait until all the speeches were done and Saddington had received his crystal decanter. And then only after a respectable interval could we leave. She sat in wounded silence thereafter.

Early in 1975 Saddington's replacement arrived. Sheila Wilson was a lateral transferee from the Foreign Office. A lot of Service people, especially aspiring directors, were miffed an outsider could come in at the comparatively senior branch head level. I chose not to be one of them. If I didn't have a decent relationship with Sheila my grand plans would quickly run into the sands. Sheila was tallish and thin, about forty and with short hair. She paid no respect to superficiality, least of all in her personal appearance. I admired her mental strength not to run with the pack. More important, though, were her impressive professional qualities. She was always polite and collegiate, objective, and focused. And super bright. I liked that she was all business. I also liked that there was no hint of distracting sexual tension between us.

After Sheila had settled in, I sought a private audience and briefed her on my assessment of the section and its staff. I outlined the changes I thought necessary and why. Sheila listened intently, occasionally jotting down notes. 'The section,' I said, 'needs to develop a strong analytical capability. We need people who can deal with shades of grey and have the patience to undertake the long slog of definitive evaluation, people who do not live in a binary world where an immediate conclusion has to be reached and henceforth adhered to religiously. We do need to retain the capacity to drive cars fast and muscle up to the Sovs if necessary. But our Positive Action resources can only be deployed effectively if there's good analysis guiding their application and indeed governing the extent, if at all, to which they are deployed.'

'Go on,' Sheila encouraged. She was wary of being snowed and I didn't feel as though I had yet locked her away. But her commonsense was telling her what I was saying made sense. This captured her attention.

'As it stands,' I said, 'our ten section members have been in place for a long time. They all have ingrained habits and possess only the PA skill set. We need to get rid of six or seven of them and replace them with analysts and other intelligence officers prepared to tread softly, follow the rules and do the graft.'

I gave Sheila a list of names I thought we should move on. She took the paper but didn't read it. Instead she asked, 'And just how do you propose we do this?'

I paused. 'The tom toms are telling me Martin Mumford is poised to replace Inglis as our FADG when Tom goes in a few months from now. I know Mumford and think he'll listen to argument. We need to approach him at the earliest opportunity. He'll likely want to go to the DDG in the first instance and probably the DG. That's fine. But assuming there's ticks all around we can then go to Personnel about staffing matters and concurrently start talking to Five, the FO, the Home Office and others about getting some order into our affairs.'

Sheila considered this in silence. Then she nodded. 'OK, let's wait until Martin's in place. That will give us time to get nice and prepared.' I stood to leave. 'And Joe,' she said, 'if you tell anyone I've confirmed Martin's imminent promotion I will headbutt you. Is that perfectly clear?' The look on her face left me in no doubt she was serious.

Tom Inglis retired in late April 1975, whereupon Martin took up the FADG post. Sheila and I got in to see him a week or so later. We had made good use of our lead time, preparing a main paper detailing the reform proposal and refining a two-page executive summary drawn from it. Among other things, Sheila had insisted we include benchmarks – *metrics* she called them – by which the results of our reforms could be objectively measured. 'Martin may not want them,' she said, 'but they're becoming increasingly in vogue over at the FO. Given the space limitations in the executive summary, we'll mention them only in the main paper.'

Martin read the executive summary before inviting Sheila to speak to it. Sheila was generous in giving me credit. 'Joe has done most of the heavy lifting on this,' she said on beginning.

Mumford heard her out. Although he had listened intently as Sheila pitched my political and operational risk arguments, it was with disheartening dismissiveness he declared, 'It goes without saying that all Service officers have a duty to protect the organization's reputation and not do anything likely to put colleagues in the field in jeopardy.' Shortly after, he wound up the meeting. 'Leave the summary with me,' he said. 'I'm going to Washington next week for talks with the Agency. While there I will take a sounding on how the Americans are approaching counter-intel these days.' With firmness he added, 'You two just sit tight and do nothing. There's a lot to consider in this and I don't intend to go running upstairs until I've had the chance to fully weigh it all.'

Over the next couple of weeks I became increasingly impatient for Martin's adjudication on our proposal. I saw him briefly in the corridor after his return from Washington but he just smiled a hello as we passed each other. Martin would get back to us in his own time. I had just returned from buying lunch one day towards the end of May when Sheila came to my desk to say Martin had asked to see us at 3 pm. At 2.30 pm I had an extra strong cup of coffee in the hope it would sharpen me mentally.

Mumford was straight to the point. 'I checked out the Yanks as promised. They do put a lot of manpower into the type of analytical approach you advocate. At the same time, however, they still have significant PA capability. Two things come to mind here: one is they can afford to have the best of both worlds; and two they play across a larger PA field than we do.' I took the latter to be a reference to *wet affairs*, as the Americans called it, whereby certain enemies of the American state were eliminated as and when usually extreme circumstances demanded.

Martin proceeded to probe Sheila on the reform benefits, the costs involved and our proposed timeline for implementation, seemingly testing for weaknesses. Sheila addressed each issue with calm efficiency. And when Martin noted, 'The Americans are big on measuring reform effectiveness,' and asked what had been done in this regard, Sheila's diligence paid out its dividend in full.

'The main paper,' she said, 'contains metrics proposed for exactly that purpose. You'll see them on page fifteen.' Sheila proceeded to explain the logic behind each. 'The metrics will tell us whether or not the CIS reforms are appropriate as presented or if there's any remediation required. Either way, once they're bedded down they can then be applied seamlessly to Warsaw Pact Section.'

I thanked my lucky stars for Sheila, and her foresight.

I could tell Martin was also impressed; it convinced him once and for all we had been thorough. 'OK,' he said after a time. 'I'll put up this with comments added. Essentially, I'll be endorsing your proposal. I expect it will ultimately depend on what the boss thinks.'

The DG ticked off – lock, stock and barrel. I was ecstatic. Commuting home that warm June evening I was floating on air. Upon reaching the flat, I found Kathleen in a state of distress. 'Some bastard abused me today,' she exclaimed, when I asked her what was wrong. 'I was driving out to the Gloucester Hill nursery centre and forgot I had to take an exit off the A23 onto Gresham Road. I had to cut across in a hurry when I realized.'

I expressed sympathy for her dilemma. For six months now Kathleen had been getting around in a car her parents had bought her. It was safe to say she was not the ablest driver ever to grace London's streets.

'This … this *person*,' she said, 'was driving some type of lorry, speeding and not paying attention if you ask me. He had to put on his brakes in a hurry. What an obnoxious bully. He followed me all the way to the nursery and started yelling abuse at me, saying his load had shifted or something and it was all my fault and someone could have been killed; all that sort of nonsense.'

The more Kathleen rambled on, the more I had visions of a multicar pile up on the A23 motorway as she made her last second dash across lanes of traffic for the Gresham Road exit. But Kathleen was looking for tea and sympathy, not lectures on the need to drive with caution. I commiserated instead. 'As you say, this fellow was not paying attention and then wanted to blame you for his bad driving. Let's be thankful no one was hurt.'

Eventually, Kathleen settled down. Her mind moved to other things. Indicating with her head, she pointed out an ugly, prickly thing sitting in a pot on the mantelpiece above the fireplace. 'At least I was still able to buy what I wanted.'

'Is it a cactus?'

'Yes. It's Andean. They're very rare. I saw them advertised in the newspaper. Asking price was 100 pounds but I seduced the manager and got half off.' Kathleen giggled at the thought.

'So this rare cactus only set you back fifty quid?' I said in fake admiration.

'That's right,' she proudly replied.

I sighed inwardly. No doubt there was a greenhouse somewhere down the road pumping out rare Andean cacti for about five nicker a go. The silliness of it temporarily affronted my senses. But I easily let it go. Tonight, I was impervious to disenchantment.

Over the course of the year that had elapsed since returning from our honeymoon, routine increasingly had become my friend and sanctuary. I worked long and hard during the week, with early starts and late finishes. Sometimes I went in on Saturdays, or failing that did what work I could in the temporary office Kathleen and I had set up in the flat's second bedroom. Kathleen, though, had gone the other way, resigning from her kindergarten job at the end of 1974 for reasons I never fully ascertained. Thereafter, aided by the car she now drove, she had become an avid trawler of London's boutiques, underwritten again by her parents, this time in the form of a weekly allowance. Carry bags and other gaudy packaging bearing the name of Harrods and its ilk were ever-present in the flat on any given day.

Most Sundays involved a trip to Maidstone. On arrival, we would have morning tea with Kathleen's parents, followed by a light lunch. Afterwards Kathleen and I would visit one of her legion of relatives or family friends. I grew to hate the Devonshire teas invariably served. Kathleen loved nothing more than to sit with a cup of tea her hands positioned so as to give onlookers perfect vision of her rings of betrothal and speak endless nothings all afternoon. I was usually ignored, apart from pleasantries and Kathleen's occasional, 'Isn't that right darling?' I was happy with this; it gave me time to think about the week ahead.

Our love life, such as it was, directly linked to the Maidstone visits. My first inkling of this came one Sunday morning when Kathleen let her pyjama-clad buttocks touch my groin, apparently inviting my stimulation. I was at first unsure. But growing sexual need emboldened me and eventually I took her from behind. After which, Kathleen emerged pyjamas intact from under the covers and proceeded to the bathroom to shower.

It soon became apparent Kathleen's buttocks in my balls was a command to arousal. I assumed the fact we mated under the covers reflected Kathleen's wish that I not see her naked. The bizarre thing was the sexual encounter happened only on those Sunday mornings when we were to visit Maidstone. If we were not going to Maidstone, forget it. As our routine solidified, Kathleen even dispensed with the signalling and began to present bare buttocks to me, presumably to avoid wasting time on foreplay. Our copulation was always followed by an English breakfast Kathleen insisted on preparing, during which she would ask me questions befitting a dutiful wife, such as *How is work going?* Most other mornings she would ignore me while sitting on the couch engrossed in mind-numbing morning television.

With understanding came the realization that just like Hilda from Jakarta, Kathleen was the adult embodiment of young women I'd encountered at university in Liverpool. Only in Kathleen's case, I'd married not an assertive version but one fixated on a non-existent, romanticized image of marriage. The Sunday morning calls to sex; the cosy English breakfasts; and the Maidstone *Look, I'm married* afternoons, with Kathleen's rings and dumbstruck me exhibits *A* and *B* were all the acting out of a fantasy. Kathleen was a thirty-two-year old woman. Her abnormal behaviour was at first unsettling and then off-putting. Perhaps I should have tried to talk to her about it. But my pledge to give nothing and no one greater priority than my work remained my guiding star. So I tolerated Kathleen's fixation and in bed on the Sunday mornings in question made myself think lewd thoughts. In case you're wondering, the character played by Sarah Miles in the film *Ryan's Daughter* proved to be an excellent source of inspiration.

For all that, by the time of my CIS reform triumph in June 1975 the marriage had reached a form of equilibrium. Kathleen seemed to derive what she wanted from it by dint of the Maidstone Sundays and I never lost sight of why I had entered into the union. Kathleen existed in her bubble and me in mine. And when the bubbles overlapped we generally interacted evenly. This did not mean we didn't have our moments and to be sure Kathleen was not always at fault. But I stuck to my wedding night strategy and refused to court conflict. The upshot was that we soldiered on with reasonable stability, both of us with eyes raised towards our respective, if undefined, end points.

Chapter 16 – Katya

Head of Personnel, by now a different person to my original tormentor, summoned Sheila and me to his office. 'I see the DG's approved the restructuring of CIS,' he said, holding up a memo. The DG's trademark *C* was visible in the signature block. 'How do you want to proceed?'

I deferred to Sheila. 'The key thing is finding the right people to bring in,' she said. 'We envisage the rotation of six current staff may take as long as two years to implement, simply because the analysts we want to bring in may not be immediately available.'

'True enough,' Personnel responded. 'But I do have one chap we've been trying to place. He may work out for you.'

Sheila looked at me, inviting my input. 'We'd be happy to have a look at him,' I said, 'but on six months' probation if we do take him.'

Personnel smiled a knowing smile. 'His name is Harry Weideman. I'll get him to call into the branch at 2 pm this afternoon if that's alright.'

Sheila and I nodded in unison. 'The first of the existing staff we want to move on is a chap called Bryan Cosgrove,' I added.

'Fine with me,' Personnel said. 'After you've spoken to Weideman let me know if you want to take him. If so, I'll get Cosgrove up here and explain his redeployment options to him.'

Harry Weideman was a mathematician by training. He was twenty-five. With a name of obvious German extraction, I suspected Personnel's difficulty in placing him owed much to memories of the war among the cadre of older Service officers. That said, Harry was the very antitheses of a super confident, square-jawed Panzer tank commander. A slightly built young man with a wispy beard that resolutely defied proper growth, he was noticeably reluctant at interview to own up to an original name of Helmut; admit he spoke perfect German; or tell me that his parents, who had immigrated to the UK in 1953, originally hailed from Bavaria. But something told me Harry had promise; our insurance was we could be shot of him at any time in the ensuing six months. After checking with Sheila, I rang Personnel and told him Harry could start with us the following Monday.

In early August 1975 Personnel offered us the services of a young woman called Aneta Spa. Her surname was a shortened, anglicized version of her family name of Spasova, which her grandparents had carried with them when immigrating to Britain from Bulgaria. Aneta had a first in Russian studies and spoke Russian fluently. Sheila and I jumped at the offer. It was a double whammy, introducing not only an analytical skill set but also a female presence into a section too long populated by alpha males.

The section's new make-up began to gel. Soon it achieved a threshold of cohesiveness and was functioning well. Sheila and I spent the rest of 1975 liaising with MI5 and the Foreign and Home Offices. In November a multiagency consultative committee met for the first time. Information began to flow, slowly initially but then with greater confidence. Through the committee mechanism, we shared our records of known Soviet intelligence personnel with Five and they theirs with us. It amazed me that where the important business of identifying Soviet intelligence officials was concerned, both security services had operated independently of each other for so long. It was scandalous really.

Courtesy of the Home Office's involvement, we now also had earlier visibility of visa applications, photographs included. On three separate occasions we proposed in committee for Sovs known to us to be granted visas, where ordinarily a known intelligence background, not to mention making a false application, guaranteed visa refusal. We supported each proposal with a detailed assessment of the individual's worth and the likelihood of their turning. Ultimately, we pitched unsuccessfully in all three instances. Five took over. All had their visas cancelled at the direction of the Home

Secretary acting on recommendation. Disappointing, sure. But no one expected each and every initiative to come off. The important thing was the process was sound and well ordered. It would serve us well at some future stage.

Our internal reviews of the reforms were no doubt positive. Most of the metrics expertly identified by Sheila were being met. It was pleasing, and I could tell Mumford was pleased too. But I was far from satisfied. I badly wanted to hook a source of high and enduring quality. Time meandered by. Then one day when I least expected it, Katya entered my life.

It all started routinely, as these things invariably do. It was the late summer of 1976 and the Home Office had just provided us with details of visa applications by a Russian trade delegation planning to visit London. The delegation comprised six men and one woman, Emiliya Dmitrievna Kuznetsov, born Nizhny Novgorod on 22 September 1948. We ran each applicant through our processes and came up blank. *Nothing known*, we reported back to the committee. The delegation was planning an eight-day visit, arriving on the evening of Sunday 22 August and departing mid-morning on Monday 30 August.

CIS now boasted a staffing complement of four analysts and six PA staff. I assigned Harry and Aneta to the delegation. We three discussed the visit, perused the itinerary the Russians had provided and decided how we would run the rule over them. We agreed the visit's duration was a smidge longer than necessary for meetings beginning Monday and ending Friday morning. But we judged the itinerary was probably framed to allow the visitors some sightseeing on the last weekend. The delegation was to be accommodated at the Soviet Embassy in Kensington Palace Gardens, which was normal.

The visit began. Five had a permanent watching post in a flat on Bayswater Road from which it monitored the Soviet Embassy. Reflecting the contemporary spirit of inter-Service cooperation, it undertook to advise us of the delegation's departure each morning and of any missing member. Harry, Aneta and I working in tandem with our PA resources confirmed the delegation's arrival at its scheduled meeting and kept tabs to ensure none of the Russians ducked out during the appointment. The evenings were more demanding. The program included three mid-week night-time receptions. These ended around 8 pm, which meant that as with the other nights they were in town, delegation members were then free to carouse. Fortunately, the group was quite restrained by Russian standards. A couple of the men went to peep shows but most were tucked up in bed by 11 pm. At our mid-morning meeting on Friday 27 August we agreed all indications were the delegation was legit.

Emiliya was a serious young woman with a prosaic taste in clothes who wore her hair tied back in a fierce bun. Other than delegation duties, she kept to herself. Harry, however, had spent most of Friday reviewing PA watcher reports. By late in the day he had discovered that at various times, alone or with others, all six men in the delegation had consulted Emiliya on minor visit issues, such as car seating. Harry had come to me. 'Joe, these are chauvinistic Russian males. They normally wouldn't speak to a junior female colleague, let alone ask her opinion. Yet even on base trivialities, they're all treating Emiliya as if she's an authority to be respected.'

I scanned the passages Harry had underlined in the reports. 'I take your point, Harry,' I said. *Strike one for thorough analysis,* I thought. I was convinced enough to brief Mumford and Sheila.

Kathleen wanted to visit Maidstone over the weekend of 28–29 August. She didn't react well when on Friday night I told her work commitments would prevent me from going.

'For heaven's sake,' I said, 'we've been going there every Sunday for as long as I can remember. I'm sure your parents are not thinking I'm ignoring them.'

Kathleen scoffed. 'You think they don't notice you never want to make more than a day visit? Every time it's suggested we might stay longer, you're like some naughty school boy wanting to run back to London.'

'Look I'm sorry, but something has come up and I'm afraid that's the end of it.'

'Well fuck you,' Kathleen spat back. She rarely used bad language – perhaps she had overheard me when recently I had tried to adjust the television antenna in the flat's roof void. 'I'm going over tomorrow morning and staying the weekend and a few extra days as well.'

I made no answer.

'Enjoy work,' she said sarcastically, slamming the door as she left the room.

I was in the office bright and early on Saturday morning. The day passed without any sign of Emiliya leaving the embassy. I began to wonder if we'd outsmarted ourselves; if our analysis had made a mountain out of a molehill. Nonetheless, I was still in the office early on Sunday 29 August, even if my expectations were low. Then about twenty-five after nine my telephone rang. It was Aneta, who was duty analyst for the day. 'The cousins have just rung to advise that madam' – our informal identifying term for Emiliya – 'left home on foot a short time ago. She's on her own. Cousins are in touch at a respectable distance.'

'OK,' I said, my senses enlivened by the news of Emiliya's Sunday morning escapade. 'I'll get wheels and others in here. You get here ASAP.' I hung up and rang our standby PA man and Harry as well.

An hour later the four of us sat in my office. I rang Five on speaker. The voice at the other end was obviously that of a former policeman. 'Bayswater post without access to mobile resources 8 am to 10 am this morning due to one-off implementation of new shift roster. Fortuitously, five-person mobile unit with comms en-route to Israeli Embassy staging through post when target left home at 9.03 am. Decision taken to deploy this unit. Target initially walked east towards Notting Hill, briefly stopping at Lloyd's Bank to adjust a blue raincoat she wore. Asset behind withdrew assessing possible window reflection back check. Asset two in front maintained touch. Target then walked north, then west before entering Paddington underground at Bishops Bridge Road entrance. Asset three alerted and able to establish contact. Rode to Baker Street in same carriage as target. Target spent eighteen minutes at Baker Street doing back checks, giving asset four time to get in place. Four had visual all the way to Euston underground. Observed target exiting towards Euston aboveground. Asset five at Euston too late to attach but searched aboveground and chance sighted target boarding 10.14 am Leicester train departing platform seven. Asset five confirmed with platform ticket collector that target presented return ticket to Milton Keynes Central. Report ends.'

Five, I thought, *God bless their cotton socks*. Addressing my colleagues, I asked 'Why Milton Keynes?'

Harry jumped to his feet. 'Just going to the janitors' counter to grab their newspapers. I seem to recall I glanced at something in the paper this morning mentioning Milton Keynes.'

We found what we were looking for in the *Sunday Times* – a short paragraph in a side column on page eight informing readers a public forum on the future of UK nuclear power and technology was to take place today at the Great Linford Hotel in Milton Keynes. We didn't need to read past that. 'Right,' I said, 'let's go.' Turning to Aneta I said, 'Aneta, you're duty analyst and will have to stay in the office in case Five needs to contact you. Harry and I will go. While we're gone could you update Mumford and Sheila please?' It actually suited to have Harry with me. The place would be full of scientific eggheads and Harry fitted the stereotyped description. Our PA man rocketed us up the M1 at a great rate of knots.

Harry and I entered the Great Linford's conference centre and took seats towards the back of the room. It was a large venue comprising two meeting rooms made into one by the opening of heavy-duty plastic concertinaed doors. We scanned for Emiliya. Harry spotted her on the room's right flank, about three rows from the front. She took some spotting because her hair was no longer in a bun but instead cascaded down across her shoulders. She wore a tight-fitting woollen maroon top. Emiliya's chair was turned inwards at forty-five degrees affording her line of sight to the speaker's podium on the hall's raised stage. The position of her chair also allowed her to monitor the hall entrance with a subtle rather than dramatic turn of her head. 'I think we're on to something here,' I whispered to Harry. 'Emiliya's practising tradecraft if I'm any judge.' I was positive Emiliya would have scrutinized Harry and me when we walked in. But presumably aided by Harry's appearance, we must have passed muster. *If in doubt, cut and run* was the golden rule of fieldwork. Yet there Emiliya was, still sitting there.

The symposium, as the program grandly called it, featured eight speakers. Protestors in the audience chanting slogans and being generally disruptive frequently delayed proceedings. Security guards removed them. About half past four the convener drew proceedings to a close. Emiliya had done nothing all day, bar sit there. But at the end of the event she made a hasty beeline for a wire-headed boffin in his late forties I estimated, whom I knew from the program as Dr Geoffrey Tyler, a nuclear physicist from the Atomic Weapons Research Establishment.

AWRE was a top-secret agency housed within the Ministry of Defence charged with developing Britain's nuclear weapon capability. We could see now that Emiliya had abandoned the overly long and loose-fitting skirts she usually wore for a short, tight-fitting navy-blue number. I couldn't hear what she was saying to Tyler but she was clearly charming him out of the trees, smiling broadly while touching and curling her beautiful mane of black hair. 'Harry,' I said urgently, 'go and find a telephone and ask that Mumford, Sheila and Aneta meet us somewhere halfway between here and London. The truck lay-by at Luton seems as good a choice as any. And also find out what time the trains to London run. We're going to have to move like lightning on this.' Harry disappeared.

Five minutes later, as soon as Emiliya had finished talking to Tyler and began to leave the hall, I charged into the ruck of people taking refreshment and grabbed Tyler roughly by the arm. 'Sorry about this mate,' I whispered in his ear, 'but I have to speak to you right now.' Tyler stood there, startled by my approach.

A woman about twice the size of him descended. 'What do you think you're doing?' she asked haughtily. 'I'm Geoffrey's wife. Don't you come in here and start manhandling him.'

'Sorry,' I said, 'I'm with the house security detail and something's come up.'

'What?' she demanded.

'I'll tell you shortly but first let me speak to Dr Tyler.' I was very grateful she had not asked me for identification.

Tyler and I pulled to one side. I assessed he would know all about the Service. Working where he did he was assuredly a customer of ours. 'I'm SIS,' I said. 'That woman in the maroon top – what did she say to you?'

'Nothing much,' he said. 'She's French, delightful accent.' He fished in his pocket. 'Here,' he said, producing a business card, 'see for yourself. Her name is Marie Brunelin and she works for the French Government's Atomic Energy Commissariat. There's a global conference in Vienna in a fortnight. I'll be a keynote speaker and as it turns out she will be there as an observer. She has to get back to Paris tonight and couldn't talk long. But she wanted to be sure we caught up in Vienna. Her work relates to a lot of the stuff we at AWRE are doing on Chevaline.'

I looked at him blankly.

'You know, the new front end system for Polaris,' he explained patiently, as if talking to a child. 'The program, if not the detail, was announced about two years ago by then Prime Minister Wilson.'

'Dr Tyler,' I said, 'I have to leave you now. There's some very urgent business that needs my attention. Tell your wife I had received information suggesting the protestors here today were planning to target you as you left. Say it became obvious to you I was over-reacting once it was clear all I wanted to do was give you a general warning. Please do not say a word about this to anyone. The matter is very important to national security, I assure you.'

Tyler shrugged. I could only hope he was taking me seriously. I wasn't sure he was.

Mumford and the others were already waiting at the Luton lay-by when we arrived. I briefed them. 'Emiliya is clearly KGB; she was all tradecraft and tits today. It's obvious the Russians are planning to spring a honey trap on Tyler in Vienna. The KGB somehow got wind of the fact the Five monitoring post had no call on mobile assets for a two-hour window this one Sunday morning and found out this coincided with the symposium. The trade delegation visit was mounted to allow Emiliya make the initial approach to Tyler on the last day because all things being equal she wouldn't be followed on leaving the embassy. A few back checks along the way and no one would know about the Milton Keynes visit. But they were sadly out of luck today. Even so, the Russians have done their homework. Tyler's wife is a harridan. Terrifying. They're banking on him being prepared to do almost anything to avoid upsetting her.'

Mumford interrupted me, asserting his authority and taking charge. 'Sounds like a whole lot of planning and effort has gone into Tyler's targeting,' he said. 'My guess is when they show him the photographs they take in Vienna, they'll ask him to part only with minor information without telling him what they really expect. The

Russians will know that pilfering low-level stuff will only put him in a deeper hole and make it more difficult to resist their real demands once they're made.'

'What do we do now?' Sheila asked Mumford.

'Views anyone?' he said.

I didn't want to make myself unpopular with Mumford or in particular Sheila by imposing myself too much on the decision-making. Time, however, was critical. 'Look,' I said, 'it's really up to you senior people. But we've tumbled her and tonight, before she gets back to the embassy, is when she's most vulnerable. If she's ever going to come across, it'll be now. I think we need to act immediately. She's bound to be on the train arriving London at 7 pm; we should pitch at Emiliya then, when she gets off the train.'

Sheila and Mumford considered this. 'OK,' Mumford said, 'Who pitches?'

By now I was in too far. Before anyone else could speak I said, 'Aneta and me, with all others currently present, including PA personnel, to be in the background.'

'Why you two?' Sheila asked, but not with hostility.

'One,' I said, 'if Emiliya comes the *I don't understand* routine Aneta can speak to her in Russian. And two, I saw her in action today. I can make clear I saw everything and we know exactly what the Russkies are up to. And if she decides to shout sexual proposition, those in the background can deal with any authority or white knight who might come to her rescue.'

'Let's move,' Mumford said. 'Sheila, Joe and Aneta, you travel in the same car as me. We can discuss tactics on the way.' This time we rocketed down the M1, Euston station our destination.

Aneta and I got to platform seven just as the 7 pm train from Milton Keynes arrived. Emiliya was now wearing her blue raincoat and had retied her hair in a bun. We followed her until she reached the concourse. It was a Sunday night and not much foot traffic was around. I walked up behind her. 'Emiliya,' I called with enough volume to ensure she heard me. She turned. I could tell she was shocked but her eyes were defiant. 'There's something we need discuss. If I were you I wouldn't run off. Your life and the welfare of your family back in Russia are both in grave danger.'

Ignoring me, she continued walking, quickening her pace. Aneta ran ahead and impeded her path. Then to my surprise she slapped Emiliya hard across the face. 'Listen to what he says, bitch,' she said in Russian, she later told me, 'or else you'll spend the rest of your waking days as a whore in a military brothel.' With that,

147

Emiliya retreated to the concourse's darkened perimeter and waited for us to join her.

Driving down from Luton, Mumford said the biggest thing going for us was that Moscow Centre would not tolerate failure. It marked hard. Serious failure was effectively a death sentence. I thought of Jakarta and how the threat to reveal Boris's litany of errors to his masters led him to agree to work for us with barely an argument. Martin had also indicated that owing to Emiliya's relative youth, we should assume she had parents or other close family still alive. As he put it, 'What we don't need is someone telling us to get stuffed because they personally are stoic enough to take what's coming. We need to leverage off the family.'

'I watched you today, Emiliya,' I said, with what I hoped was icy menace, 'and can tell you that you've fucked up. We now know you're KGB and going after Tyler with a honey trap in Vienna in a couple of weeks.' Emiliya's face remained impassive. 'There's at least two ways to play this. We can make a ruckus about kicking you out and get the media involved. I don't need to tell you what your bosses in Moscow would think about this and how they'd react.' I looked stone-faced into Emiliya's eyes, 'If we do go public, you'll also need consider what happens to your family. You know as well as me they'll be sent to the gulag. Not much of an end for mater and pater is it?' I could see the defiance begin to be replaced by fear. I knew then this was our point of leverage.

We all thought a double-headed outcome was possible should Emiliya wish to avoid the publicity option. Mumford had outlined the parameters en-route to London. 'Tyler,' he said, 'will feed the Soviets chaff but only once they start making real information requests, when they judge he is fully hooked. Until then he will provide the marginal information they seek.' I admired the simple genius of it. The substantive information requests made by the Soviets, once confident Tyler was on board, would identify the key gaps in the Soviet nuclear program. These we would fill with disinformation. The result would be catastrophic. 'And separately,' Martin said, 'Emiliya would become a rare and much sought-after Service asset, one spying for us direct from the KGB's heartland.'

'What's the other option?' Emiliya asked softly, the slight tremble of her bottom lip as she spoke revealing that the magnitude of the threat to her family had now sunk in. She was all but turned.

'You go back to Moscow tomorrow and tell them all's on track. Then go to Vienna and execute the honey trap. After you have passed Tyler to his handler you will remain on our books giving us everything you can on anything you can. I hardly need remind you we'll be looking closely at the quality of the information you give us.' I didn't need to go on.

Puzzled, Emiliya asked, 'Besides recruiting me, you want the operation against Tyler to go ahead as well?'

'I'll spare you the details, Emiliya,' I said, 'but the short answer is yes.' Emiliya stared poisonously at me. She knew she would be branded as criminally irresponsible for allowing herself to be tracked to Milton Keynes and while there alerting us to the KGB's intricately planned honey trap. There was no escaping the unpalatable consequences for her and her family of this failure. With grim reluctance, Emiliya nodded her acquiescence.

I wanted to finish soon. Any further delay and Emiliya would be fielding questions from the embassy about what took her so long to get home. The delayed train excuse only ran so deep. 'The arrangements for channelling information to us will be worked out ahead of Vienna and conveyed to you there. Now piss off back to the embassy before anyone starts to wonder where you are.' I touched her on the arm as she started to leave. 'One last thing, what's your real name, date and place of birth?'

With something akin to military precision she replied, with pride I thought, 'I am Katya Lyubimova Vasilieva, born in the Hero City of Leningrad, 30 June 1948.' Aneta scribbled in her notebook as Katya spoke.

Chapter 17 – Vienna

Back in the office that night we shared a glass of whisky. We weren't terribly upbeat because there was still the problem of Geoffrey Tyler with which to deal. 'I will have to talk to the DDG first thing tomorrow morning,' Mumford said, 'and then likely the DG. Until they're consulted we can't be sure they'll agree to us doing anything involving Tyler.'

'How do you propose to broach it with them?' Sheila asked.

'I will argue the national interest dictates the honey trap should go ahead,' Mumford replied. 'Without it Katya will be known to have failed and likely be eliminated. With that, we would lose the rare opportunity to sabotage the Soviet nuclear program while at the same time be denied a prized source within the KGB.'

'I think you should also emphasize we don't need to know if Tyler takes up Katya's offer of a night in bed or if the Russians have to drug him,' Sheila said. 'That might soften the blow.'

'It could, I agree,' Mumford said.

'There's also the fact,' I said, 'I effectively told Tyler this so-called Marie Brunelin was a French spy. Upstairs might view this as an impediment to going ahead. But equally Tyler appeared to take what I said with a grain of salt. That makes me think, should it become a bone of contention, it could be argued he would likely be amenable to an explanation it is now clear Marie is not spying for the Frogs. Sorry for the stuff up, etcetera.' The others responded with a combination of slow nods and grunts of agreement.

Of course we all recognized that even should the disinformation sting get off the ground, it would not run forever. Sooner or later the Russians would wise up to it or tumble to the fact of Katya's spying for us. As a result, both inextricably linked operations would fall over together.

Mumford came down Monday afternoon. He looked exhausted. I think he had received quite an earful. He told Sheila and me that only with the greatest reluctance had the DG ticked off, and then only after speaking with the Minister's office. The DG had nominated Sheila to approach Tyler as soon as possible, not formally in his office but somewhere unobtrusive, to explain away my approach at Milton Keynes.

Two days later Sheila reported the night before, having followed him to the Tesco supermarket near his home in Brentford, she had been able to collar Tyler as he emerged from the store. Sheila cast herself as someone humbly apologetic. She explained it was all a terribly embarrassing cock up; hence her informal approach. The Service hoped Dr Tyler would accept its sincerest apologies. Marie Brunelin was not a French spy. In the days since the symposium she had been thoroughly checked out. We'd be most grateful if you didn't mention our mistake to Mme Brunelin, you know English-French relations and all that.

Tyler was apparently contemptuous. 'I thought so,' he had said. 'I think that character who set upon me at Milton Keynes was a sandwich short of a picnic.'

We moved to planning for Vienna. There was a lot to do and not much time. As a first step, we made discreet enquiries through the Ministry of Defence to determine Tyler would be staying at the five star Erdberger Wien Hotel, walking distance from the conference venue, the Burgtheater. We then sent Harry to Vienna, whereupon booking into the Erdberger and using his fluent German he was able to confirm the hotel was holding a booking for Mme Marie Brunelin.

It had been decided on high that SPB, specifically Moscow Affairs Section, would take over running Katya as soon as CIS had finalized her recruitment. We left it to MAS to develop a plan on how Katya would contact her handlers from Moscow station on her return from Vienna. Finally, we tasked our Vienna station chief Alexander Pickering to find us a discreet hotel where we could interview Katya. Sandy confirmed overnight a double room had been booked at the Hotel Gabriela on Rilkeplatz for Mr and Mrs Jeffries. That was to be Aneta and me.

The Gabriela was about five of Vienna's huge city blocks from the Erdberger; close enough for a prompt return to the Erdberger but far enough away to be reasonably sure of not running into people we'd rather not. The conference was to be held over three days. When it broke on the first night seemed the best time for Katya to come to the hotel. Eight o'clock was selected. Sheila was delegated to forewarn Katya of this.

We knew KGB people would be around the conference and all over the Erdberger. But we inferred from the Milton Keynes exercise, where she operated alone, that Katya enjoyed a high degree of operational authority. We were confident she had only to utter the words *operational requirements* for any would-be watchers to back off. On Katya's arrival at the Gabriela, Sheila would shepherd her to the room where Aneta and I waited. I was acutely aware Sheila was doing a lot of the legwork and me more the guts of the operation. But Mumford was calling the shots and Sheila seemed to accept the arrangements without question.

The day before the conference we flew to Vienna. Aneta and I travelled together, separately from Sheila. We surveyed our room after we had checked in. Its furniture included only a tiny two-seater couch and we knew we could hardly request a couch large enough for someone to sleep on. 'Looks like we'll both have to sleep in the bed,' Aneta said.

I detected she was a little unsettled at the prospect. I offered reassurance. 'Aneta,' I said, 'right now I'm so on edge that the thought of a tryst with you in charming *olde-worlde* Vienna is the last thing on my mind, I promise you.'

Aneta nodded and smiled. I was grateful for her determined professionalism. All the same, she was taking no chances. As we readied for bed, she emerged from the bathroom in a hotel robe under which she wore her pyjamas and I think her underwear. I wore boxer shorts and a tee shirt.

I was glad when morning came. I didn't sleep very well and nor did Aneta as best I could tell. After breakfast we sought the advice of front counter staff on tourist activities and set off ostensibly to do these, all the while looking for tails or people overly interested in us. The risk of Katya running a double game on us was at the forefront of our minds. We continued the trade work during the afternoon. By late afternoon we were satisfied we were clean.

Katya was nothing if not punctual. Sheila ushered her into the room on the dot of 8 pm. Sandy and Harry arrived ten minutes later after watching for following foot traffic from differing vantage points. At first nothing was said while Aneta frisked Katya, even taking her to the bathroom to disrobe as a precaution against her wearing a wire. When the preliminaries were done, I asked Katya to take a seat. 'When will the move on Tyler take place?' I said.

Katya smiled briefly. I couldn't help thinking how beautiful she was. 'He's a conservative man. But ultimately he's a man. I doubt it will be tonight but tomorrow night I suspect it will happen.'

'You mean you think he'll get involved with you by choice?' I asked, earning myself a withering look from Sheila that said, *We don't care how it happens, remember?* Without waiting for an answer to the question, I quickly moved on. 'Please tell us what you know about how Tyler is going to pass information to the Russians and how he will be provided with shopping lists.'

'In London, mostly through a dead drop,' Katya said. 'But when Tyler travels to the places where AWRE weapons production occurs, such as Burghfield and Cardiff, he will likely meet face to face with a handler, in a pub for example.'

'Tyler's work also takes him abroad frequently. What happens then?'

Katya shrugged. 'I suppose he will be required to carry material for passing over at the other end and will receive further instructions at the same time.'

'When will he be asked to begin supplying information?'

Katya understood my question. I found her intelligence seductive. *I really enjoy talking to her*, I thought, surprised to think this and distracted by the need to contain my galloping emotions.

'I don't know for sure, but my strong guess is he will be initially tasked to supply what the Americans call chicken feed.'

'I'm familiar with the term,' I said, doing my best steely Joe.

Katya stared intently at me, mocking amusement in her eyes. 'Maybe for six months or more,' she said. 'When Moscow Centre judges he is in too far to back out, our demands will escalate.'

I looked at Sheila. I could tell that like me, she was thinking Katya's insight into running Tyler was a pointer to the quality of the information from inside the KGB she would supply. I hoped Sheila wasn't reading my other thoughts.

I found it unnerving to watch Katya's resilience evaporate when I asked her about her family, transforming from defiance to fear in the blink of an eye even though she tried to hide it. We all agreed later she was not telling the truth when she said her parents were dead, and she was unmarried and an only child. The look of panic in her deep, dark eyes when I talked about the ramifications for her family of selling us out said it all. I wanted to put my arms around her.

Sheila then took over. 'Assuming everything goes to plan, you'll be back in Moscow on Thursday. On the following Saturday, you're to go to the Russian State Library at 2 pm. Provided you think you are clean, fifteen minutes after you arrive you are to remove a scarf you'll carry in your handbag, put it on and tie it loosely around your neck. If anytime thereafter you have suspicions, untie the scarf and we'll abort and have another go the following Saturday, same times plus one hour. Remember from the moment you put on the scarf untying it is the signal you will rely on if you detect trouble. Assuming you are satisfied all is in order, leave the library a couple of minutes after 3 pm and proceed to Biblioteka metro station and take the 3.10 pm train from platform Three south to Metro Kropotkinskaya. From there walk to the Pushkin Museum of Fine Arts and position yourself in the Numismatic Collection exhibition. Someone will contact you there.'

'I understand you,' Katya said sullenly, her distinctly Russian pout further arousing my distinctly conflicting protective instincts.

Interview done, we stuck a document under Katya's nose. She signed it in her native Cyrillic language. Aneta saw her out. Sheila rang a tame number in London where Mumford and his DDG had situated themselves. *A Service flat somewhere,* I thought.

'The insurance company has agreed to settle,' Sheila said. To a question I didn't hear, she responded, 'Yes, the entire claim.' Sheila rang off. 'Right,' she said, 'let's jot down key impressions for our lessons learned debrief.' Reaching for her handbag, she extracted a bottle of whisky before adding with a broad smile, 'After which we can have ourselves a well earned drink.'

I wasn't part of the delegation that met with Tyler in an obscure office in Service headquarters. That chore fell to Mumford and Sheila. Mumford apparently had opened by saying it had come to the Service's attention that the Russians had pulled a stunt in Vienna placing him, Tyler, and indeed British national security at risk. Tyler did not deny it and did not ask how the Service knew. He was never asked to provide a blow-by-blow description of how the honey trap unfolded. Presumably he thought we knew, which I think we may have thanks to my out of order question to Katya.

'He was very anxious to confess,' Sheila told me later. 'When I telephoned him at his office that morning he sounded panicked and had readily agreed to talk to us.' Tyler had brought with him the photographs the Russians had foisted on him in Vienna. I passed when an opportunity to have a look at them came up.

According to Mumford, Tyler was most relieved when told there would be no recrimination over him allowing the Russians to copy the documents he had with him in Vienna, including one carrying the low-grade classification of *Restricted* that really shouldn't have been out of the office. 'My off-hand mention that Mrs T need not know about matters was not lost on him,' Mumford recalled. 'He knew whereas government might forgive his transgression, the home front situation was far less certain.'

Tyler apparently stiffened up somewhat when advised that government forgiveness was conditional upon him passing initially genuine then doctored material to the Russians. An intelligent man, he was immediately suspicious of the Service's involvement. Martin had told him straight-faced the Service had no prior knowledge of the compromise and did not think Mme Brunelin had knowingly assisted the Russians. 'Sometimes this sort of lie is necessary, Joe,' Mumford was to explain. 'The chance to feed disinformation to the Russians stands to put back their nuclear program for years, long after they discover Tyler's material is a con.' I understand Tyler cheered up a little when Mumford hinted a word in the ear of the Queen's Birthday Honours Secretariat might be appropriate.

Chapter 18 – Bellona

The branch head promotions for 1976 did not materialize owing to uncertainty about how many positions were available in the face of deep budget cuts by the Callaghan Government. When the list came out in the first week of February 1977, my name was on it. So was Freddie Ladler's. But not Rupert Heneshaw's. I indulged in some schadenfreude on that score.

That afternoon I literally bumped into Heneshaw as he left the men's toilets as I was entering. It was as if he could read my mind because as soon as he saw me he abandoned any attempt to avoid me and drove his shoulder into my chest. I charged back at him. We stumbled back into the toilet block coming to a stop only when Heneshaw became pinned against a bank of hand basins. A stalemate quickly ensued: we were both about the same size and weight. Gripping the lapels of the other's suit coat, and with no one party able to gain the ascendancy, we became locked in a dance of death. Finally, the toilet flushed in one of the cubicles. We looked at each other, knowing neither of us could afford to be caught engaging in fisticuffs in the office. We released our holds simultaneously and went our respective ways.

Sheila had been away. She returned the day after my run-in with Heneshaw and came to my office, a broad smile on her face.

'Well done, Joe. I was convinced the CIS reforms you drove and your lead role in Katya's recruitment made you a shoo-in for promotion.' I thanked her. I really did owe Sheila. There were several branch heads around the place who would have cheerfully elbowed me out of the way to take the glory for themselves. 'I've also received some good news on the career front,' Sheila said.

'Really?'

'Yes, word reached me last night that I have been successful in a Foreign Office promotion round. I'm to head the Defence Coordination Unit.'

'Fantastic, Sheila. Just great news. Sincerely sorry to see you go all the same; really sorry, actually.' The position Sheila was taking up was the Foreign Office equivalent of FADG.

'I'm happy to be going back to the FO, Joe. It values level and consistent performance, whereas this outfit requires notable, if not spectacular achievements. I'm not sure I want to spend the rest of my working life trying to destroy the lives of other human beings just to get a promotion.' I stood and we embraced awkwardly.

Sheila left the Service shortly after. I occasionally saw her when over at the Foreign Office. But even when we did get to speak we never reminisced. Soon we just waved to each other without stopping. Our work was our only point of commonality; it was natural we grew apart. Personnel asked me if I would stay on another year running the branch in Sheila's stead, to bed in a new CIS director and oversee the reform of Warsaw Pact Section. You never said *No* to Personnel if you knew what was good for you.

In early 1978 I was summoned to a meeting in the ADDG's office. Rodney Charlesworth was the incumbent. He was expected to have visibility of everything ranging from blocked toilets and non-functioning lifts to the viability of the Service's security vetting and its resource requirements. I pressed the lift for the fifth floor a few minutes before the meeting's scheduled start. When it opened, I stepped in to find Freddie Ladler and a man in his mid-thirties I'd seen around but whose name I did not know also heading to the fifth floor. Ladler had been best man at Heneshaw's wedding back in 1970. From the day we three had joined the Service together, he and Heneshaw had been joined at the hip. Ladler's body language radiated hostility, prompting me to recall my contretemps with Heneshaw in the men's toilets a year ago. He stared at me coldly. Neither of us spoke. Stepping out of the lift, the third party extended his hand to Ladler and me in turn. 'Brian McGowan, pleased to meet you,' he said. 'I guess we're all off to see the ADDG, eh?'

Charlesworth got straight to the point. 'This blasted government,' he said, his inborn instinct to protect his career against possible political blowback preventing him from using a stronger adjective, 'is making life difficult. Cuts here, cuts there. Unless we can do more with less, our capacity to service our current obligations, let alone expand them, will be severely tested. That's where you lot come in.' McGowan smiled a relaxed smile. Ladler and I did our best impersonations of Easter Island statues. 'You three,' Charlesworth said, 'have been chosen to do a root and branch review of the Service. No holds barred. You'll have access to all areas, top to bottom. Your terms of reference are simple: cut costs while generating greater operational efficiency.' He paused to let his instruction sink in. 'You'll have until the end of the year to complete your report. Don't waste our time with crap. We want good, practicable and well reasoned recommendations.'

Nodding at Ladler and me, Charlesworth told us, 'We've chosen two operations people because you'll need to look at every country in the world where we have an operational presence and examine how processes can be made more efficient.' Looking now at McGowan he added, 'Brian's job is to conduct a comprehensive cost estimate for each individual recommendation. Whatever you arrive at, overall there has to be demonstrable increases in operational efficiency married to a reduction in costs.'

Charlesworth went on to advise we'd be accommodated in offices on the fifth floor. We'd be starting on the Monday of the next week. A scribe would be provided to assist in drafting our report. 'Any questions?' he asked, with just enough aggression to make clear he didn't want any. As we began to leave, Charlesworth said, 'I perhaps shouldn't say this, but you three may be interested to know you have been handpicked by the DG. I don't think I need spell out what a feather that is in your respective caps.' He then looked down at his papers, already onto the next item in his in-tray.

We rode the lift down together. None of us spoke. I was first out at the fourth floor. McGowan bade me a cheery, 'See you on Monday.'

'Will do, Brian,' I responded. 'Cheers.' I could see McGowan's look of puzzlement as the lift door closed; the tension between Ladler and me was all too obvious.

Back in the privacy of my office, I punched the air. Being handpicked for anything by the DG was a big deal. I could not have dared to hope for a better legacy from the CIS reforms; my selection to do the review clearly signalled those upstairs thought I was management material. All things being equal, next stop was FADG. My élan faded a little with the realization I would have nearly a year of working cheek by jowl with Ladler. But like Scarlett O'Hara, I decided to worry about that tomorrow. Sitting at my desk, I tried to get back to work. I started reading a document but was soon only staring at it while thinking happy thoughts.

A knock at the door caused me to lift my head. It was Trent Davis-Dennison, T double D as we called him, the now director of CIS. Trent was a soppy public schoolboy who in truth had been promoted too quickly. I guessed he would toughen up with time; he had better, otherwise the Sovs would eat him for breakfast. But I liked him. He was intelligent, polite and no spoiled brat. 'Joe,' he said, 'I've a bit of news that may be of interest.'

'Yes?'

He hesitated. 'Well a mate of mine in Soviet Political Branch mentioned a certain Service source, work name of Bellona, is no longer with us. He said you had a bit of history with Bellona.'

I could see Trent was now wondering if he would get his friend into trouble for telling me this. 'Double, don't worry old son,' I said. 'I'm not about to run off and tell anyone you've passed on a bit of harmless gossip.'

He smiled, relieved. 'Yes, apparently a bit of rough treatment in Lubyanka before being put up against the wall.'

Bellona was the codename given to Katya.

I thanked Trent, while trying to remain impassive. He left. I shut the door and immediately began to shake uncontrollably. Katya had survived about sixteen months. The last of that time did not bear thinking about. I knew only too well what rough treatment in Lubyanka entailed. I thought about her recruitment. Through her defiance and then submissiveness, Katya had made clear she would have had the fortitude to reject our approach but for the consequences for her family of her operational failure. 'She spied for us in order to give her loved ones as much time in the sun as possible,' I said softly to myself, shaking my head in sad wonderment. 'She would have known one day the balloon would go up.' The deeper I lapsed into rumination, the tighter I drew the shroud of anguish surrounding me. I held my head in my hands as guilt momentarily overwhelmed me. 'No wonder once we had pressed her into service she was giving us the crown jewels,' I said out loud. Mirthlessly, I smiled. She and Nought would have understood each other.

That night I decided to walk home to clear my mind of upset. I reflected on the loneliness of my marriage of convenience and why I entered into it. Usually I was able to push such thoughts aside and singularly focus on my career. But tonight I could not. Sexual and emotional attraction to Katya fuelled by memories of her beauty and strength of character intruded and refused to budge. I tried to tell myself this infatuation was making me sentimental; my silly male protective instincts were distorting my thinking. I determined to snap out of it. But every time I tried I couldn't get Sheila's parting words out of my head. I had destroyed this remarkable young woman, and in horrible certainty her family as well, all in the name of my career.

As Kathleen and I drove back from Maidstone on the following Sunday evening, I decided there was a silver lining in Ladler being on the root and branch review team. Since the news about Katya I had been consumed by self-disgust and disgust for my profession. For the first time since the Konrad debacle in East Berlin, I was seriously questioning whether I wanted to stay with the Service. But the last people on earth to whom I wanted to reveal any weakening of spirit was Ladler and, by association, his boxing kangaroo sidekick Heneshaw.

The review soon bogged down. As soon as I suggested something, Ladler dismissed it as rubbish. I returned fire. About a month in, we had made precisely zero progress. Our scribe, Brenda, sat in her small office polishing her nails.

One day Brian asked Ladler and me to come into the conference room in our suite of offices. He shut the door with a crash that would have been heard in the DG's office at the far end of the corridor. 'Right,' he said, hands aggressively on his hips. 'I'm sick to death of you two liabilities. You're both like fucking children. If we don't get our finger out, this exercise will turn into a disaster for us all. I'm fucked if I'm going to sit here waiting for you two to grow up.' I noticed then for the first time that although Brian had a natural inclination to affability, he also had substantial steel in his backbone. It came as no surprise to me a decade later when he succeeded Charlesworth's successor as ADDG.

But for now, neither Ladler nor I spoke. We both knew what Brian said was true but each of us refused to be the first to concede. Brian came to our rescue. 'What you're going to do is effectively divide the world into two. Each of you will work independently from the other on one of the halves. Fortunately, Brenda's got good writing skills. As you make notes she'll write it up so the report's not obviously separately written. Clear?' Ladler and I both nodded. 'Good,' he said. 'Let's get to it. There's a lot of time needing to be made up.'

Ladler and I did as instructed. We both worked hard. Often we would be in the office together late at night or on weekends, just the two of us. We didn't speak but nor did either of us go out of the way to antagonize the other. I took on Eastern Europe, having served there. Ladler took the other high profile field, relations with the United States intelligence establishment. It was during this time I came across the files recording the political circumstances of my recruitment into the Service and later activation as *Leonard*. It was also when I saw Petr Klaus's report vindicating me from responsibility for the Konrad disaster, which in the political climate of the day explained why the Service fell over itself to make good and send me to Jakarta.

On discovering these files, I put them to one side and began reading only late in the evening when all the others had gone home. I had rung Kathleen to tell her I would be late, very late. It was only when dawn began to peek over London's rooftops that I locked the files in my safe and went home.

Once back at the flat, I had some coffee and a long shower. Kathleen was up by the time I emerged from the shower. She asked me what I had been doing all night. The question was really a stalking horse for enquiring whether I had been with another woman. But she appeared to sense I was telling the truth when I simply answered, 'Working.' After breakfast I lay on the bed for thirty minutes resting my eyes. Then I dressed and headed back into the office. Riding the bus, I realized that my career drive had now rekindled, marking my recovery from the news of Katya's demise. But as I entered the office, from out of nowhere, a powerful sense of emptiness briefly engulfed me. After years of paying it absolutely no regard, I recalled like yesterday Nought's warning about the personal cost in being *The Lone Wolf at Cover* and how the only thing standing between it and me was real love.

The report turned out a triumph. Brenda had written it brilliantly. Those reading would have thought a team of happy campers compiled it. Ladler had mostly reached the same conclusions as me about where operational efficiencies lay, and Brian's ability to make a silk purse from a sow's ear where money was concerned bordered on genius. The DG put on an afternoon tea when the report, after surviving Charlesworth's critical perusal, was presented to him. I knew then we were in good odour.

Brian proposed we go and have a pint that night. I managed to get him to one side. 'This is a bit difficult,' I said. 'There's a lot of bad blood between Ladler and me. I would be more than happy to buy you a drink, God knows I owe you that, but socializing with Ladler is unfortunately a bridge too far.'

Brian laughed raucously. 'Just half an hour ago, Ladler said much the same thing to me.' Shaking his head in mirth he said, 'Tell you what, you and I should have a drink tonight. Freddie's got some bash at the US Embassy, apparently. I'll catch up with him tomorrow night.' Brian was still chuckling when later we caught up at the Three Stags pub near the Service.

Chapter 19 – Done

The branch head promotions list came out as the end of 1978 approached. Heneshaw had been promoted, meaning he had now caught up to me. I had little doubt Ladler had clued him up on the direction in which the Service was heading. Heneshaw would have been well placed at interview to impress the panel with his insights into the type of outcomes the Service was seeking. Not long after, Personnel called to tell me he wanted to send me to New Delhi as station chief. India was where East and West frequently intersected making head of station New Delhi a prestigious Service assignment. I was given a week to think about it.

I also learned on the Service gossip treadmill Ladler had been offered Lisbon. In April 1974 there had been a coup in Portugal by a group of left-leaning army officers. In the aftermath of this so-called Carnation Revolution, the Sovs suddenly had a situation on the southern fringe of Western Europe they could exploit. US President Gerald Ford had publicly warned of Soviet penetration in Portugal. The number of diplomats at the Soviet Embassy in Lisbon grew exponentially. An urgent need arose to develop reliable sources, particularly within the resurgent Portuguese Communist Party. Virtually overnight, the Lisbon posting had gone from a backwater to a position of prime strategic importance.

The following weekend I casually mentioned to Kathleen the Service wanted to post me to New Delhi. I expected her to refuse point-blank and wondered if our marriage's end might now be in reach. To my surprise, Kathleen began to wax eloquently about the wonders of the sub-continent. And her enthusiasm refused to wilt. She told anyone who would listen that we were 'Off to Ind-yaar,' as she liked to say. I knew she had read Jim Farrell's *The Hill Station* and wondered if the book's sympathetic treatment of India and the exotic images it conjured had influenced her thinking.

Whatever my reservations, come March 1979 we landed together at New Delhi's Palam Airport to take up our three-year assignment. India was a British Commonwealth country. I would be working out of High Commission and not an Embassy, although the difference was in name only.

I was fretting as to how well Kathleen would manage the posting. The first few weeks at a new post could be quite dislocating after the excitement of getting there had rubbed off. Most High Commission UK staff resided on a purpose-built compound also housing the High Commission office block – the Chancery, as it was known in diplomatic parlance – and High Commissioner's *Official Residence*. But owing to the nature of my work, we were located off compound. There were pros and cons to this. The upside was welcome avoidance of the endlessly unhappy compound politics, the main downside being the house's erratic water and electricity supply.

Kathleen managed to keep herself busy for the first month. We had three house staff: a dhobi who did our laundry; a bearer who cleaned the house and would have cooked if we had wanted it; and a mali, a gardener, who looked after the yard. We also had a night watchman, our chowkidar, who gave new meaning to the concept of a static sentry. Kathleen found all this a novelty and, as if in some sort of time warp, was soon penning letters back home describing the challenges of managing the staff. She also appeared to enjoy the dinners numerous colleagues put on to welcome us to the post. Our settling in went a lot smoother than I had anticipated.

As head of station I was declared to the Indian overseas intelligence agency, the Research and Analysis Wing, or RAW as it was better known. I had four staff, all of whom were undeclared and held diplomatic cover as First or Second Secretaries. Although liaison with the Indians was my meat and drink, I also had supervisory responsibility for covert operations. My masters in London were keenly interested in Indian arms purchases, principally from the Russians. They also held a brief for the wider Warsaw Pact sphere, particularly the supply to India of Czech small arms and plastic explosive. India was thus a hotbed of espionage, especially in and around New Delhi, one potentially offering Britain and its allies priceless intelligence on the status of Eastern Bloc weapons development. Of course, this information was treated with great secrecy in the Indian system and had to be ferreted out. Our task was to penetrate India's labyrinthine defence procurement bureaucracy. This was quintessentially the definition of easier said than done.

One of my early undertakings was to go over the station's assets. Of our existing sources, no one person was especially productive. Similar to that encountered on arrival in Jakarta, all of the fifteen agents we were running were academics or middling government officials. My aim was for the station to perform at least to the same standard as under my predecessor. But this was the bare minimum. I really wanted to do much, much better.

Kathleen's first stomach bug came just on nine weeks into the posting. The British doctor attached to the High Commission prescribed antidiarrheal medicine, plenty of filtered water, and rest. Kathleen was instantly cured of posting life. Following our arrival, she had engaged with other spouses for morning teas and exercise classes. But she now became increasingly withdrawn. Making telephone calls to the UK was a nightmare. Each time she tried it took forever to get through. And when she did the line appeared to be shared with six other parties, each babbling incoherently to English ears. Goodness knows what Kathleen's family in faraway Maidstone made of it all. It certainly didn't impress Kathleen.

After three months Kathleen declared she was taking a trip home. She was gone for more than a month before returning. A matter of weeks later she again returned to the UK, this time for a longer period. Her third return to India lasted a couple of months. It was now obvious the end of our marriage was in sight. We might well have struggled on much longer had we remained in England. But the pressures of living in a culture alien to us had hastened our shaky union to the precipice. My honest impression was of Kathleen experiencing a form of neophobia, her wariness of the unknown temporarily overriding her existing discontent. But the die was cast. Close to the first anniversary of our arrival in Delhi, Kathleen announced she was taking yet another trip home. There were no histrionics but this time her departure was somehow different. Watching her resolve as she boarded the airport bus taking her to the waiting British Airlines flight, I had a strong sense of finality.

And so it was. For a time afterwards Kathleen never contacted me. I wrote her a letter but it went unanswered. After about six months, she wrote to tell me she would not be returning and ask for me to arrange for her furniture in store in London to be released to an address in Maidstone. Kathleen had clearly moved back home. I complied. We never spoke again and just over a year later when the divorce papers turned up, I signed away any claim I might have to Kathleen's assets on the understanding she would do the same for mine. As Nought had suggested, the marriage had been ridden as far as it would go.

Chapter 20 – Chowdhury

For all the artificiality of our relationship, Kathleen's departure left me feeling empty and alone for a time. I didn't miss Kathleen *per se* and knew her return permanently to the UK was best for her, and me. All the same, I felt my isolation acutely. I refocused on my work with greater intensity. I knew the staff thought I drove them too hard but didn't care. 'Get out there and look,' I instructed them, reliving my diligence in doing the groundwork when in Indonesia. 'I want each and every conceivable opportunity run to ground.'

This saturation approach was eventually to pay dividends. At a reception one evening in May 1980, one of marginal importance that most times no station officer would attend, a man called Golam Chowdhury, a Bangladeshi, bowled up to Jessica Cole, the youngest and least experienced of my staff. 'I do not earn enough to put my eldest child into the British school here in Delhi when he comes of age next year,' Chowdhury had told Jess. 'Khaled is my first boy. He is the most important.' We suspected Chowdhury was a Bangladeshi intelligence officer because he then told Jessica, 'I have access to information of considerable interest to your government.' We judged it likely this throwing out of bait also indicated he knew Jessica was Service. Jess did well, probing him on his connections to the Indian bureaucracy, which on face value seemed vast, and then parking him with the promise to get back to him.

It didn't take much to find out that Chowdhury was a declared member of Bangladesh's overseas spy agency, the National Security Intelligence. NSI was poorly resourced and, in light of Bangladesh's dire financial situation, paid very low salaries. We cabled London proposing an offer to Chowdhury of a scholarship to the British school for his son under the auspices of the Thames Development Company. TDC was a private company contracted to deliver the UK Government's health and education aid programs in India. Its reign was short-lived but from 1979 to 1984, when the privatization experiment was abandoned, TDC was the line authority for such matters. Its office was housed within the High Commission.

London queried us on funding. We argued the Service should reimburse TDC its costs in London. The TDC office at post would administer the scholarship. But it was sensible that none of its large contingent of Indian staff became aware an internal transfer of funds had funded the bursary. I did not tell headquarters how Shirley Astbury, the post's TDC office head who was briefed on my status, had reacted indignantly when I first raised the possibility of a scholarship with her, telling me 'TDC is not an intelligence plaything.' Fortunately, our London people also came to see the prudence in them squaring away all other arrangements with TDC's head office. We were given approval to explore the opportunity.

The day of the recruitment attempt arrived. These were always nerve-wracking affairs. Chowdhury's was no different. I wanted

Jessica to do the recruitment pitch, knowing only too well how important it was to get early successes under one's belt. Chowdhury seemed keen; all in all, it shaped as an ideal undertaking on which to cut her teeth. Chowdhury had told Jess he wanted to meet her late in the afternoon in the coffee shop of the Taj Mahal Hotel, a run-down establishment near the Red Fort in Old Delhi. Jess left. Philip Brownlie, another of my staff was to follow separately, riding shotgun for her. Time ticked by. I was waiting in the office when a visibly upset Jessica walked in, accompanied by Philip. Clearly all had not gone according to plan.

'I had to park some distance from the hotel,' Jess said once she'd calmed down. 'The car park is only small and it was full. As I was walking back to the hotel, some young fellow jumped off his scooter taxi and groped me. His mouth was bright red with betel nut. Then some of the others joined in.' The effort of making the explanation caused Jessica to tip over. She dissolved into tears.

'I was a good way back watching Jess's back,' Philip said. 'By the time I got to where the commotion was taking place, there must have been 500 people gathered watching.'

'What happened next?' I asked.

'The hotel security eventually came down and ushered us into the hotel,' Jess sniffled in reply. 'They asked if I wanted the police called. I told them I didn't.'

'Are you hurt?' I said. 'I mean do you want to see the High Commission doctor?'

'No, I'm just teed off, that's all.'

'Thanks to some bad luck with parking, Jess,' I said, 'you've just experienced first-hand one of the big challenges of working in this city. Everywhere a Westerner goes there are a thousand pairs of eyes watching. It's particularly difficult for you because most uneducated Indian street lads, and that's the majority of them, think young Western woman are promiscuous. It's a stereotyped image courtesy of our film, television and advertising industries. The problem's doubly bad when they're tanked out on betel nut.'

Jess nodded. 'Don't I know it,' she said bitterly. Turning to Philip, she asked, 'Did you get to speak to Chowdhury?'

'No,' he said. 'I looked in the coffee shop but didn't see him. Presumably he'd taken off.'

'Let's not worry about Chowdhury right now,' I said. 'Jess you get some rest and we will re-set tomorrow.' Jess lived on the compound. 'Philip, would you walk Jess home please and then come back here?'

Waiting for Philip to return, I counselled myself to hold my nerve. Fortunately, I had at the time an incomplete appreciation of Chowdhury's value. *Don't be panicked into removing Jess from the op or taking control yourself,* I thought. When Philip returned I told him what we were going to do. 'Jess has just fallen off the spy's equivalent of a bike,' I said. 'We've got to get her back on and soon. Tomorrow night I want you to find Chowdhury and bring him to my house. I don't care what time. Just find him and bring him there, and Jess can then pitch at him. It's not as discreet as I'd like but let's see if we can prevent the op falling apart and Jess with it.'

I spoke to Jess first thing the next morning and told her of my plans. She was grateful for the second bite of the apple. Her mouth set in determination.

Philip arrived at my home that night around 10 pm with Chowdhury in tow. I hadn't bothered to stand down the chowkidar; the mere thought of coming to work seemed to put him into a deep sleep.

'He took some finding,' Philip told me after Jess and Chowdhury had gone into my study. 'Eventually, I tracked him down at the

Empire Club enjoying a few whiskies with some of his RAW buddies.'

The mention of the RAW people alarmed me. 'Did any of the RAW guys become suspicious?' I asked as calmly as I could.

'Hard to say,' Philip said. 'They did look me up and down, though. The only thing I could think of was to tell them I needed Chowdhury to shift his car.'

I didn't say anything, but the chances of the RAW contingent being convinced by the shift the car excuse seemed remote. I didn't blame Philip. What was he to do? He was working on the run. The risk now loomed large that RAW was on to us.

Jessica and Chowdhury emerged from my study after an hour. 'We have an understanding,' Jess said, evidently pleased with the outcome. The deal Jess had clinched was for a one-year TDC scholarship to the British School commencing in January 1981 and, starting immediately, 250 US dollars a month for *expenses*, to be paid from the station's US dollar float.

I shook Chowdhury's hand. 'Good to have you on the team,' I said, pleased for Jess more than anything. But thoughts of damage control had become my priority. 'I understand you were socializing with some RAW contacts when we dragged you away. Do you think there are any grounds for concern?'

Chowdhury read me like a book. 'Mr Lambert,' he said, 'are you familiar with the saying that my enemy's enemy is my friend?'

'I am indeed.'

'Well suffice to say that RAW was actively involved in the emergence of the independent People's Republic of Bangladesh from the former territory of East Pakistan. RAW unquestioningly regards its Bangladesh counterparts as allies. The agreement we have reached will not attract RAW's scrutiny, of that I am very confident.' He smiled roguishly, his head wobbling in the distinctive South Asian manner.

I actually tried to agonize. *By any measure*, I thought, *I have cause to be worried half to death.* But Chowdhury's assertion, especially the self-assurance conveyed by his vigorous head-wobble, defeated my pessimism. I felt supremely reassured.

Chowdhury was to last about eighteen months. He had an amazing array of senior contacts in the Indian bureaucracy, a veritable menagerie of sources from whom he extracted a stream of high-quality information. True to his word, the Indians appeared to pay him no attention whatsoever, not even the odd cursory look. He roamed around New Delhi at will, which made him an easy source to run. Soon we had a standing arrangement that each week he would come to my home late at night to pass over documents and provide other useful information. He was going so well that within three months we had bumped up his monthly cash payment to 500 dollars.

This happy situation dramatically reinforced the depth of residual enmity between India and Pakistan. RAW was neither silly nor lazy, anything but. It all boiled down to the simple fact that while Chowdhury was a perceived ally in the struggle against the despised Pakistan, he was free to do as he pleased.

After a total of nearly six years in Delhi, Chowdhury's tenure expired and he was recalled home at the end of 1981. His replacement was from the Bangladeshi elite, a thunderously wealthy young man who was easy to dislike. We tried but got little traction with him; he could have bought and sold the entire High Commission. With Chowdhury in place, however, we had made much hay while the sun was shining. I derived enormous satisfaction from the station's 1980 and 1981 performance assessments of *Performing Exceptionally*.

Chapter 21 – Agnes

$\mathbf{A}$ new High Commissioner arrived around the time of my forty-second birthday in March 1982. Sir Aubrey Stevens was on his last assignment, a fact of which he made no secret. An old soldier, he was also a vastly experienced diplomat and above all a decent human being. But as old age encroached, it was becoming apparent he was trading on his reputation. Already he relied enormously on his deputy, a woman called Belinda Crawford-Brown, who capably ran the mission and did all the work. Nonetheless, Sir Aubrey and Lady Hanna liked to entertain. Around two months after his arrival, I found myself an invited guest at a dinner party at *The Residence*.

Sir Aubrey and Lady Hanna's guest list was eccentric, mixing ambassadors and also-rans like me. But *The Residence* dining table in seating sixteen, a smallish number by diplomatic standards, was still large enough to sort the sheep from the goats. The sheep at the top end of the table, along with the High Commissioner and Lady Hanna, were the Ambassadors of Ireland, Belgium, and Greece all with accompanying spouses, and some wheel from the Exchequer in London with a suspiciously young-looking female aide.

Shirley Astbury, the TDC office head, also had a jersey. A preposterous character replete with a monocle and cravat partnered her. He claimed at one point he was an exiled Polish Count. He and his consort sat opposite each other in the table's middle reaches, as if the person in charge of the seating plan, like me, wasn't sure if the Count was for real. I tuned out on the occasions when he addressed those assembled as if holding court, while all the while madam looked on in unrestrained admiration.

Sitting with me at the goats' end of the table, remote from ambassadorial company, were Belinda and her husband and an English woman with long auburn hair, who looked to be in her mid-thirties. Her name was Agnes. I was on my best behaviour and drank sparingly.

I found Agnes an engaging personality. When she smiled her green eyes sparkled and her high cheekbones enhanced the warmth she exuded. Her business card declared her to be Agnes Huntington, Indian Operations Manager of an organization called HOPE, the acronym standing for Humanity, Opportunity, Purpose and Evolution. HOPE was a London-based non-government aid outfit that, according to Agnes, did good works in the developing world. From what she said, her particular operation ran on the smell of an oily rag. Its focus was mainly on refugee groups in India. Agnes said her largest growing client group was displaced Afghans, who were especially disadvantaged because the Indian Government refused them refugee status. This caused my ears to prick up.

The Soviet-Afghan war commenced in December 1979, about nine months after my arrival in New Delhi. By 1982 there was still a dearth of knowledge in both London and Washington about the situation on the ground in Afghanistan, particularly away from the urban centres. All SIS stations within reasonable proximity of Afghanistan were tasked to gather any information available. Beginning as a trickle and then in greater numbers, Afghans fleeing the carnage had begun to arrive in India. Most were from rural areas. The high probability was that among them were potentially valuable sources of intelligence on the Soviet war effort in the provinces. To date, we had been unable to get alongside any of the Indian officials involved in monitoring this influx and were obliged to rely on information given us by RAW. It surprised me London seemed reasonably happy with this product, which I considered inadequate. Whatever, headquarters did not press us into greater effort, saving that for our beleaguered colleagues in Pakistan.

But with Chowdhury now out of the picture, I badly wanted a new source, someone like Chowdhury who was sufficiently productive as to convince head office New Delhi station was continuing to perform above and beyond expectations. I asked Agnes if it would be possible to inspect the centre HOPE had established on New Delhi's outer limits.

She smiled warmly. 'You are most welcome,' she said.

I do confess my heart gave a little skip in response. But I quickly refocused on work priorities. 'I'll be in touch in the next few days,' I told her.

I decided to write to Agnes and arranged for a High Commission driver who knew the HOPE centre's location to deliver my note. His instructions were to wait for a response. He returned later in the day and gave me back my note now annotated with Agnes's blunt reply: *OK for visit Thursday 27 May 2 pm.* It was signed, in confident cursive script, *Agnes C Huntington, IOM, HOPE UK.* I found Agnes's handwriting inexplicably attractive.

The drive to the HOPE centre took us on a narrow, poorly maintained road. Once we had passed the airport I was lost. The driver informed me, when I asked if we were going in the right direction, if we overshot our destination we would eventually end up in Jaipur a further 160 miles to the south-west. After what seemed an eternity, when we were about twenty miles from Delhi, we reached a collection of ramshackle buildings surrounded by a rickety wire fence. 'Welcome to the HOPE centre,' Agnes said, bounding out of the hut that served as her office. She carried a huge smile on her face. Her hair was tied in a bun and as might be expected she wore no make-up. She was clad in trousers and a shirt and shod in heavy boots. The swell of her breasts against her shirt did not escape my attention. But I'd come with determination to act the hardcore professional and that's what I intended to do.

Agnes gave me a conducted tour of the facility. Along the way, I rehearsed my lines on why I was interested to visit. I came at it from a consular perspective saying the High Commission was hearing from the Indian police that persons suspected of being Afghans were targeting the homes of Western representatives in New Delhi. The sizeable British private sector community was among those most at risk. Agnes pouted doubtfully when told this. 'I really don't think any of these poor beggars would have the means to get to New Delhi let alone rob anyone there,' she said.

I played my hoped for trump card. 'What if I gave you some names and descriptions? Could you keep an eye out for these people?' The information I had was provided by RAW. The names and background meant nothing to us; indeed, I wasn't fully convinced such persons actually existed.

Agnes became indignant. 'First thing, Sport,' she said, her derision amplified by emphasis on the word *Sport*, 'I'm here primarily to worry about the welfare of these people. And secondly what sort of description are you going to give me? Aged before their time, traumatized half to death, wearing rags around their heads, not to mention loose-fitting trousers? That should narrow it down to the last five million possibilities.'

I was strangely unmoved by this sarcasm, when usually I would need to suppress my irritation. 'Hearing you loud and clear,

Cobber,' I said, my counter use of antipodean mimicry tumbling out of me in a wave I recognized as pure affection. Whether Agnes detected this I couldn't be sure, but her eyes sparkled and a smile began to form around her lips. I smiled back, effortlessly matching her warmth. 'Tell you what, if in your busy life you come across someone who was a government official back home or a university professor or anyone who just speaks a bit of English, could you let me know?'

'OK, deal,' she said. 'Sorry, this job can be so bloody thankless. At times I feel I have quite enough on my plate without anything more.' She laughed generously, shaking her head with exaggerated bemusement. Then, after taking my arm briefly in order to direct me, she escorted me back to her site office. Over a cup of tea and digestive biscuit, we swapped our experiences of living in India. Finally, it was time to go. We shook hands. The cool firmness of Agnes's handshake was like an electric shock but with difficulty I remained po-faced.

A feeling of elation washed over me as my driver started to wend his way back to New Delhi. The following day I sent Agnes a note asking if she wanted to see a film during the next week, at the US Embassy cinema to which the High Commission's UK staff had access. *The Sting* was showing.

Agnes's response simply said, *Sounds good. See you there at 7 pm Tuesday.* It generated far more excitement in me than the words could ever have possibly warranted.

On the day of the movie I was on tenterhooks. *Christ Joe*, I thought, *you're carrying on like a lovesick puppy. Get a grip. She's probably got a husband and three kids back in London and is only being polite.* I was conscious too that since my visit to the HOPE centre any thoughts about finding a replacement source for Chowdhury had been pushed to the back of my mind. I was preoccupied only with Agnes, especially with not making a fool of myself and scaring her off.

I arrived at the entrance to the US Embassy compound far too early. From his secured guardhouse, the marine on duty watched me as I paced up and down the street. I decided to explain to him I was waiting for a friend. *A boy from Middle America*, I thought, as he looked at me unsmilingly through the bulletproof perspex window. This only added to my nervousness. Then I saw Agnes walking up the street. We shook hands and greeted each other warmly. Suddenly we were laughing and talking, as if we had just taken up from where we left off at the centre.

People often tell me *The Sting* is a great movie. I'll have to take their word for it because even though I sat through it, I have no recollection of it. Rather, all I can remember was the pleasure it gave me to sit in the cool and quiet of the theatre with my shoulder intermittently touching Agnes's. Above all, I recall the scent she wore. Like everything about her, I decided, it was perfect. Not too strong or sweet but uniquely feminine and stimulating to the senses.

The movie finished. I walked Agnes back to her car, a locally made model known as an *Ambassador*, which was a knock-off of the old British Morris Oxford design. The car had seen better days. I was pleased that when an old Indian man arrived, Agnes introduced him as *Gulam, my driver*. The old man and I shook hands. He reverently opened the door for Agnes, who sat in the back seat. Images of Malaysian Betty and her taxi driver flooded back.

'How about we go somewhere for dinner next week?' I suggested leaning through the open window, trying to act casual.

'I'd really like that,' Agnes said, causing my heart rate to quicken. 'Before then, though, I'm having people over for drinks at my house this Friday night. Why don't you come along? Many of my friends and associates haven't met a real live diplomat before.' She threw back her head in laughter. Before I could answer Agnes said, 'Bring a bottle of booze if you like. Number five Nehru Place, off Mathura Marg. Any time. Thanks for a lovely night, Joe. Early start for me tomorrow so best get some sleep.' I watched the car drive off slowly, resisting a powerful urge to run after it. Only when it was out of sight did I return to my vehicle. There has never been a snippet of information I have guarded more carefully than Agnes's address. As soon as I reached my car I rifled through the glove compartment for a pen and wrote it down lest I forget a single detail.

I had long abhorred attempting to get somewhere only to end up lost. It frustrated me and often made me cantankerous. I wanted to avoid any possibility of this on the Friday night at Agnes's. Accordingly, I was up before dawn the following Thursday and drove out to find her house. I had asked the High Commission's drivers for instructions for getting onto Mathura Marg but did not want to reveal my ultimate destination. The sun had fully risen by the time I located Nehru Place. Logic told me that finding number five would be straightforward now I knew how to get to the street. It was time to get out of there before someone saw me. But I was fixated on finding out exactly where Agnes lived. I wanted to imagine her curled up in bed. In a fit of consternation, it dawned on me she might not be curled up in bed alone. Only after a struggle did I manage to push the concern to one side.

I decided to risk a single slow pass down Nehru Place. If I didn't find number five in one go I would bail out. There was now too great a chance Agnes might spot me to consider multiple passes. Halfway down the street I had the panicky thought she might be an early morning walker. After an interval, I spotted the numeral 5 crudely painted on the gate of the pedestrian entrance to a house otherwise protected by a high stonewall. Mission accomplished, I sped off as quickly as I thought reasonable. There was no doubt in my mind an unseen night watchman from one of the surrounding houses, squatting silently in the shadows, would have observed me. I just had to hope that news of my preliminary exploration did not get back to Agnes.

I arrived at Agnes's house on the Friday night with carefully studied lateness, to be greeted by her offering congratulations on my ability to find the place.

I felt great relief. The gods had smiled on me; my Thursday morning reconnaissance had escaped her notice. 'Not easy in the dark,' I said, 'but I've got reasonable radar.' The radar fib being harmless enough but an egregious falsehood all the same.

Agnes accepted my bottles of red and white wine. 'Come in,' she said. There was a mix of European and Indian guests. We went through endless introductions. I usually tried to remember names as a matter of trade practice but didn't bother to apply myself. I chatted away, waiting for a chance to speak to Agnes. While struggling to be a good civil servant and defend the UK's trial privatization of aid delivery to a serious young Indian sociology student, I felt a tap on my shoulder. It was Agnes. She handed me a glass of wine. 'Let's go out to the back garden and drink this where it's cooler,' she said, smiling broadly. 'You can tell me all your darkest secrets.'

We sat on a bench under a small Banyan tree. Agnes told me she had been in the development game for a long time. At one point she had her own business. But her partner had fleeced her. 'I mixed the personal and business,' she said, 'and paid the price for it. Graeme was my partner in both spheres. It wasn't a good arrangement. I became a registered bankrupt but was discharged five years ago. I work for HOPE for wages. My contract expires in October 1985. I haven't given any thought to what I'll do then.'

We sat in relaxed silence for a time. 'Are you still angry at your partner?' I asked.

'No,' she responded. 'I was disappointed for a time, yes, but never angry. I have a relentlessly forward-looking philosophy. It's best to forgive and be rid of all that negative energy. Anger's such a counterproductive emotion.'

Forgiveness; no negative energy; anger's such a counterproductive emotion. For some reason each of these sentiments struck a chord with me. It was not until many years later that I understood why.

Agnes smiled at me. 'What about you, Joe?'

I explained I had been a diplomat since 1965. 'I was married once but not now.'

Agnes looked at me and spoke softly. 'Not all that long ago, was it? I couldn't help noticing the faint indent on your finger where your wedding ring once was.'

My marriage to Kathleen had expired about three months shy of six years. I would have liked it to remain on track until I had made a realistic attempt at FADG. For this reason, I had continued to wear my wedding ring well past the time we had formally divorced. But I eventually came to realize the only person I was fooling was myself. The word would have been out in the corridors of London headquarters much earlier, from around the time Kathleen left for good, if for no other reason than the fact my allowances had to be adjusted down once I became an unaccompanied officer. News like that spread rapidly across all walks of Service life. Six months ago one Sunday night I had taken off the ring and put it in a drawer. It had stayed there since. I smiled back at Agnes. 'You're in the wrong job you know.' She chuckled. 'Yeah, not all that long ago,' I said, 'but it was on the skids for a long time beforehand.'

Agnes and I subsequently went out together two more times; once for coffee and cake, the other for dinner to celebrate her thirty-eighth birthday. Mid-meal on the occasion of her birthday celebration, Agnes suddenly became serious. 'What do you think about the work I do, Joe?' she asked. 'Do you think it's worthwhile or just a waste of time, money and effort?'

My mind harked back to an ill-tempered discussion the preceding Monday with Shirley Astbury, when she had chided me about Chowdhury's scholarship. I foolishly allowed myself to become upset, mainly because I thought Shirley was dredging up past irritants in the hope of inventing problems. The discussion quickly degenerated. My telling Shirley to stop looking for excuses why her programs were not meeting benchmarks and focus on resolving her differences with the Indian Government upset her enough. My parting retort, 'That if TDC dispensed with all the staff perks coming off the top of the aid budget, there'd be money galore to go around,' left our relationship in tatters.

Of course, Agnes's work brought her into frequent contact with Shirley; indeed, some of what Agnes did relied on TDC grants. 'I fear Shirley's been in your ear,' I said, 'and suspect I've been verballed.'

Agnes didn't deny my assumption. 'I'd be interested to hear your version of events,' she said evenly.

I looked into Agnes's intelligent eyes, sensing this was a make or break moment. *Straight down the line*, I thought, *no fudging, no embellishment.* 'Shirley's upset because I told her that until she sorts out things like policy settings and anti-corruption measures with the Indian Government, her programs can't deliver what they're meant to deliver and just waste taxpayers' money. TDC wants to be first in line for other contracts should the UK further privatize its aid delivery. Shirley knows that substandard outcomes in India will harm TDC's prospects and reflect badly on her. That's why she wants to blame others for the fact she's struggling to get her program settings right. I never raised HOPE with Shirley. But for the record, I think it's a very different organization. HOPE can operate effectively despite government, whereas the TDC model needs a functioning partnership with government to work properly. HOPE's designed to plug holes too small for outfits like TDC and operate in areas not of priority to stretched government. Simple as that.'

Agnes considered this. She was smart enough to know I was telling her the unvarnished truth. I sensed her trust in me mount. 'On balance,' she said, returning my candour, 'I agree with you. Shirley's a good person and wants to do right by those she's trying to help. But I have noticed, to be brutally honest, she's reluctant to deliver hard messages to the host government when it's warranted.' Agnes laughed. 'That's what I'm best at.'

I smiled at Agnes all the while thinking, *Bloody Shirley; it will be a while before she gets a Christmas card from me.* Agnes picked up the wine bottle, recharged my glass and sat it down. She stared directly at me for a good ten seconds before breaking into an amused smile. I knew then I'd passed some sort of character test. Euphoria, a cascading waterfall of happiness, swept over me. 'Good,' I said, 'now we've got that out of the way, let's sort out Arthur Scargill.'

Scargill was a controversial UK trade unionist, a polarizing figure who readily divided public opinion. Agnes roared with laughter causing some other restaurant patrons to look up. 'Sorry,' she whispered, 'but you are such a funny man.'

We parted on the best of terms, kissing tenderly when I dropped her off. I drove home feeling like an excited schoolboy. Sleep that night was impossible. The next day I suggested to Agnes we have dinner the coming Saturday night at the Star of India restaurant. I did so on the recommendation of an FO colleague who claimed that, rupee for rupee, it was the best dining experience in Delhi. I was anxious the evening should be a resounding success. My relationship with Agnes was heading somewhere and I was hell-bent on its speedy consolidation.

On the Friday afternoon preceding our planned outing, however, I received a note from Agnes saying she was laid low by a stomach bug. She thought it unlikely she could do Saturday dinner. I dropped everything and drove to Agnes's house. 'Madam is sleeping, Sir,' her housemaid said, with sufficient firmness to make clear my seeing Agnes was not about to be countenanced. I left a note saying I would come over at 6 pm the following night.

I then drove to my house and roused the bearer who was sleeping in a wicker chair on the front porch. 'Madan,' I said, 'I want you to cook the spatchcock that's in the freezer and make me a cucumber and yoghurt salad, and naan bread. Wrap it in foil please and put it in the refrigerator. I will be needing it tomorrow night.'

Agnes was sitting up in bed looking wan when I arrived. She had just showered as her damply falling hair revealed. In an act of spontaneity coming to me as naturally as drawing breath, I kissed her lightly on the forehead and whispered, 'Poor baby.'

Agnes showed no surprise. Like me, she knew our relationship now extended beyond a simple friendship. 'I think I'm just about over it,' she said, shaking her head. 'For a while there I thought I was going to die. Seriously.'

I showed Agnes the food I had with me. 'I thought we could have a picnic. Let me get you a plate and bib and prop you up. Eat as much or as little as you want.'

Agnes brightened. 'That's wonderful of you, Joe. The food looks beautiful. I've hardly eaten for days but with just the sight of it I can feel my appetite returning.'

There was only the one bedside light. As dark came its glow reflected softly on us. The surrounding gloom had the effect of isolating us in our own cocoon remote from the outside world. It was still and quiet. After we ate, I removed the soiled utensils and sat next to Agnes stroking her hair. She took my hand and kissed it.

With that, I kissed her fully on the lips. She wrapped her arms around my neck and drew me to her. My hand found the inside of her nightdress and caressed her firm breast and jutting nipple. 'Joey,' Agnes whispered. I took away the bedclothes. 'Be gentle darling,' she said, 'I'm still not a hundred per cent.' The smell of Agnes's intoxicating perfume pervaded my senses. We coupled slowly but with growing intensity. Then we slept. I woke the next morning still in her arms. I felt like the happiest man in all of India.

Chapter 22 – Unmasked

My being declared to RAW made it inevitable my identity as an SIS officer would become widely known among the New Delhi intelligence community. The Service understood this. The important matter of liaison with the Indian intelligence services for one thing required the head of station to be declared. Moreover, the incumbent was often an officer earmarked for promotion to FADG – leading to a management role and little subsequent on the ground clandestine work. If not promoted, the incumbent thereafter was restricted to declared postings. I'd gone to New Delhi hoping for the former; Noel Billings in Jakarta was an example of the latter. Early into my posting, in May 1979 to be specific, the KGB station in New Delhi, once alerted to me by its RAW contacts, had reported my status to Moscow Centre as a matter of standard procedure.

And just how do I know this? The answer is because it came from information supplied by a senior KGB source. What's more, the material the source provided went far beyond a tidbit about the KGB station reporting on who and what I was. What reached me, late in 1991, was in fact a comprehensive, blow-by-blow description of the KGB's involvement in the events starting from May 1979 that were to impact on me over the next eleven years. It's a critical part of how my story unfolded from here on in. For now, I'll call the KGB source *our source*.

The KGB's Second Chief Directorate was responsible for counter intelligence. *Our source* was to explain that it kept files on known foreign intelligence officers. These were cross-referenced by a sophisticated card system to files kept on all Western diplomats. The huge number of people undergoing investigation made the vetting process very slow, especially the standard procedure to which I was initially subjected. But it was efficient, even if it took a full eighteen months, until the end of 1980, before the investigating sub-directorate had established that undeclared and under diplomatic cover, I had served abroad in Moscow and Jakarta.

This led to further enquiries, more cross-referencing to ascertain if any notable events possibly involving me had occurred in either location during my tenure. A further year elapsed, for which I understand there were later some internal recriminations. Finally, however, the sub-directorate completed its investigation. The KGB had concluded that Boris's suicide in Ecuador was linked to his likely recruitment by Western intelligence while stationed in Jakarta. When the sub-directorate identified my posting in Jakarta had overlapped with Boris's by at least a year, it raised a flag – but nothing more. Boris had remained in Jakarta for over a year after I left and the KGB, suspecting the Americans, had no inkling I'd been involved in his recruitment. Moscow was a nil return.

The identity, however, of those responsible for Katya's recruitment remained a big-ticket item for the KGB. After completing its protracted investigation the sub-directorate passed my details to the CPG, a small specialist investigation unit responsible for examining intelligence personnel, British especially, for signs of a possible link to Katya. The KGB station's RAW contacts had provided it with a colour photograph of me, which by now was in the hands of the CPG. Katya did not know my real name. But during interrogation, *our source* said, she had provided a detailed description of me as the prime architect of her recruitment, from which a Photo-FIT had been constructed. As I'd grown older, and my wavy fair hair darkened, my physical features had become all the more unremarkable. My clear blue eyes and pale complexion remained, though, and Katya did tell the KGB I was left-handed.

The CPG soon noticed the resemblance between the Photo-FIT and the RAW photograph when it did the standard comparison. It immediately tasked the KGB station in New Delhi to confirm I was left-handed, just under six feet in height and that I spoke with a slightly bastarized London accent. I later learned the KGB station was able to provide confirmation of my personal characteristics via a source in the High Commission, work name of Basil, most likely a locally employed Indian reporting directly to the Soviets.

On receipt of the station's response, the CPG examined my history. An educated guess was made I was in London on a home posting during the summer of 1976 at the time of Katya's recruitment. More substantially, my cover as a junior second secretary in Jakarta up until May 1971, when contrasted with taking up the senior role of station chief in New Delhi in March 1979, indicated I had made significant career advancement over this eight-year period. The CPG identified that Katya's recruitment was the type of achievement necessary to power progression like this.

On weighing all before it, the CPG eventually concluded I was Katya's recruiter. With that, I was elevated within the Second Directorate to the status of a *Person of Significant Interest*. The elevation automatically triggered a request to the KGB station in New Delhi for a detailed background investigation.

By late 1982, *our source* told us, the Second Directorate had a report before it indicating I had divorced subsequent to arriving in New Delhi and was now involved with an English woman heading a private UK aid organization. The report recorded for the benefit of the KGB psychologists that coincident with entering into this relationship, my general demeanour had become noticeably more buoyant. An assessment of my potential for recruitment was rated at low to negligible. My assessors concluded I was a moderate drinker, leaning towards teetotalism – how that dovetailed with monitoring conducted during my Moscow days I never found out.

As March of 1983 approached, Agnes and I began to discuss my return to the UK. I had been granted a year's extension by head office. But having now completed nearly four years in Delhi I was subject to the Service's then informal rule that by this time officers risked becoming sympathetic to host country perspectives – *captured by the natives* as it was universally known. One morning while still in bed, I told Agnes I wanted to spend the rest of my life with her. She responded by kissing me, before telling me with much solemnity she loved me too. I had quite substantial savings by this time and was earning a salary whereby servicing a mortgage was feasible. On the spur of the moment I said, 'I'm going to buy us a house.'

'Where?' she giggled.

'Somewhere in London,' I replied, gesturing vaguely. 'And more to the point it's going to be OUR house, not my house.'

Agnes suddenly became serious. 'Joe, are you sure? I want to be with you forever. But you know I have to see out my contract with HOPE. They were very good to me when I was nearly down for the count and I feel I owe them.'

I knew Agnes was effectively asking me if I was sure our relationship could survive eighteen months of commuting. I was unfazed by her caution. Agnes was unquestionably a strong and intelligent woman and usually my loner instincts would be on a hair-trigger. The litmus test was whether they would kick in and I would again be overwhelmed by my cursed need to escape. But nearly a year into our relationship, there was no sign of this. On the contrary, I lived for Agnes and hated being apart from her. I was an open book – nothing of my emotional being had been withheld from her. My one secret, or so I thought, was my work. Agnes and I were to holiday for a week in the UK when my posting finished. Once there, I planned to tell her I was Service.

I surmised that whereas with Kathleen my *Lone Wolf at Cover* persona failed to trigger because my emotional outlay fell under a lower threshold, with Agnes there was no trigger because my emotional outlay had exceeded an upper threshold. With this, my loner instincts, the visible symptom of my sub-conscious protection mechanism, were suppressed. Nought had spoken of real love, *the real deal.* I now knew what he meant. It was not a sensation or reflex generating emotional outpouring; rather it was the serenity, the inerasable calm and sense of emotional security, which distinguished it. It was an exhilarating and liberating feeling.

Chapter 23 – Shukhov

Around the time Agnes and I departed for the UK, on the fourth floor of KGB headquarters on Lubyanka Square in central Moscow General Sergei Shukhov called the KGB Operational Steering Committee to order. *Our source* was in attendance. As described by *our source*, Shukhov was a giant man, stretching some six foot, four inches into the air. He worked hard at his physical condition and unlike many of his contemporaries did not overwork the vodka bottle. At fifty-three, he was fit and hard, physically and mentally, and ambitious and ruthless with it. For all that, Shukhov was a heavy smoker. He claimed it helped him think.

Topic four on the agenda referred to SIS officer Lambert, Joseph. On reaching it Shukhov said, 'You will have all read the Second Directorate's recommendation,' while simultaneously enveloping his colleagues in the foul-smelling smoke of his Latvian-made cigarette. *Our source* dwelt on Shukhov's smoking habit. Rumour had it that as an act of rebellion the Latvians substituted linoleum for a portion of the tobacco going into the manufacture of the cigarettes they were obliged to export to Russia. This apparently had two advantages: it reduced manufacturing costs; and expanded the incidence of smoking-related illness among the Russian populace. If Shukhov had heard the rumour he appeared unconcerned by it. *Our source* told us he smoked forty of the filthy things each and every day.

Shukhov had given his colleagues half a minute to refresh their memories before continuing. 'The overall assessment is Lambert would be difficult to recruit at this time. But he has caused untold cost to our nuclear weapons research program and orchestrated substantial leakage of vital intelligence on KGB global operations. We cannot and will not let this go unremarked. This takes us to the psychiatric report at annex B.' *Our source* told of Shukhov waiting impatiently while the other committee members caught up. 'You will see our chief psychologist, Dr Gradsky, assesses Lambert is unusually emotionally dependent on a woman he is now involved with following the breakdown of his marriage.' Rifling through his papers, Shukhov said, 'Yes, here it is. Agnes Claire Huntington, born Hungerford UK on 10 June 1944, an employee of an English non-government aid organization.'

Shukhov stubbed out his cigarette and folded his hands letting them rest on the table in front of him. He spoke earnestly, *our source* said. 'The proposal before us is to eradicate Huntington, creating an emotional vacuum in Lambert's life to be exploited. That is, into the vacuum we will insert a woman whom we assess will provide Lambert the same emotional fulfilment as Huntington does currently. Our operative will ultimately be tasked to recruit him. The aim gentlemen and lady,' Shukhov had said, twinkling as *our source* put it at the only female in the room, 'is to recruit Lambert while posted to an important head of station role, where he will enjoy access to high-grade American, NATO or other alliance material.' Shukhov invited questions. No one spoke.

'Good,' Shukhov said, turning to the First Directorate representative. 'You are to task your Spetsnaz sub-directorate to plan and execute an operation to eliminate Huntington. This involves no breach of unwritten protocol. She falls outside the gentlemen's agreement we have with the West applying to intelligence officers and their families.' *Our source* thought Shukhov had deliberately paused to underline the point. 'The elimination must take the form of an accident and arouse no suspicion,' Shukhov continued. 'If Lambert so much as thought the Soviet state was behind it he would assuredly refuse to work for us.'

Dismissing the First Directorate with a curt nod, Shukhov more graciously addressed the head of the Third Directorate, the person who was actually destined to become *our source*. 'Dr Gradsky predicts that after Huntington's death, Lambert will sink back into his work. This was his response to his divorce and at his age it is unlikely his behavioural pattern will change. The operation I intend involves your Directorate assisting Lambert to the fullest extent possible win promotion to the next level in the SIS. Only at that senior level will he be eligible for the appointments we want him in before recruiting him, the likes of head of station Washington, Brussels or Bonn.'

Shukhov looked around the table. Again there were no questions.

Agnes and I flew from New Delhi to London on the last day of March 1983. The following morning we made our way to a rented cottage in the Cotswolds town of Bourton-on-the-Water where that night we belatedly celebrated my forty-third birthday.

On the second evening as we sipped red wine, both of us feeling pleasantly exhausted after our walk to Cleeve Hill and back, I told Agnes I was with the Service. She smiled at me. 'Joe, I've suspected that for some time.' I looked at her, stunned. Agnes laughed, shaking her head. 'Poor darling,' she said, 'you must know there are no secrets among the Brit colony in Delhi. Several people all but told me you were a spy. When Shirley Astbury complained to me you had once hijacked her aid program for immoral purpose she effectively confirmed those rumours.'

I shook my head, abashed by the realization that while I was out and about in New Delhi taking my cover so seriously, all and sundry were aware I was acting out a charade. Agnes placed her hand on my neck and drew my lips to hers. 'Honestly, it doesn't bother me one bit what you do for a living. I love you. That's all that matters.' Agnes was silent for a moment. 'But we need to hang in there until I'm finished with the HOPE assignment. Then we can get on with our lives together.'

'We can handle that Aggie,' I said, using the sweet nothing I often cooed in Agnes's ear in our most private and intimate moments. 'We will coordinate our leave and spend it back here in this house I'm going to buy, or occasionally go somewhere on holiday. I can tell you nothing is going to come between us now.'

We said our goodbyes a couple of days later. Agnes went to Hungerford to spend some time with her parents and I returned to London to a furnished flat in Battersea I had leased for six months. We spoke by telephone each night. We agreed I shouldn't go to Heathrow to see her off; the parting would be too painful for us both. Then Agnes was gone and back in India.

We wrote to each other every day. The archivist who managed receipt and dispatch of the High Commission's diplomatic mailbag, and with whom I was passing friendly, had agreed to act as our go-between, placing Agnes's letters to me in the diplomatic bag to London and passing on my letters to Agnes when the bag arrived in Delhi. The exchange of letters was a second-best option but better than nothing. Each letter I received from Agnes I devoured hungrily. I slept with them while they were fresh so that I might keep the smell of her perfume in my nostrils as long as possible.

Agnes was next entitled to leave in late October. We had agreed she would return to the UK for its duration. I began counting the days.

In the interim, I returned to work. This time as head of SEB, Southern Europe Branch, supervising sections respectively looking after Greece, Turkey and Cyprus; and Italy, Yugoslavia and Albania. As fate would have it, Rupert Heneshaw was my fellow branch head. He had oversight for Central Europe and Iberia Branch comprising a section looking after the Iberian Peninsula countries and another covering Belgium, Switzerland, and Austria. But Heneshaw and I didn't see each other much and there was little overlap in our work.

We did have a weekly meeting every Monday morning with our jointly shared supervising FADG, an insipid character by the name of Reggie Sullivan. Reggie had come into the Service at a lower level some years earlier from the RAF. He was widely regarded as the worst performing of the Service's eight FADGs. It remained something of a mystery as to how he had managed to get himself promoted to such a senior level.

Usually I would have chaffed at working for Reggie; he was not the right person to be supervising me if it was promotion I was after. Unlike Heneshaw who had two or three powerful benefactors, not least his former boss in Bonn who was now a DDG, I had no such support. Indeed, the fifth floor had recently told me of its *disappointment* that after two highly productive years Delhi station's output should have tailed off over the remaining two years of my assignment – when of course my principal interest was Agnes. But I didn't care in the slightest. I was full of joy and nothing could worry me. I now knew where my priorities lay.

I began to scan *The Times* classifieds for houses to buy. I was dismayed by the price of anything decent. Nothing up to my limit looked remotely suitable. One sales agent suggested I look further out than central London and its near environs. A week or so later he alerted me to a listing in Brent Cross that met my needs. The house in question had a small rear garden and was situated on the left flank of a six-house terrace row set back from the main thoroughfare of Clitterhouse Road. Directly opposite stood the large expanse of the Clitterhouse Playing Fields.

Boyhood memories of playing cricket in North Park in Bootle flooded back. I was sold. This is where Agnes and I would set up home. I saw my bank manager during the following week and signed a contract to buy. I moved in on Saturday 17 September 1983, whereupon I took endless photographs and wrote Agnes a long, heartfelt and no doubt utopian letter. The following Friday, once the photographs had been developed, I lodged the letter with the diplomatic mail people and began waiting with keen anticipation for Agnes's reply. How sweet was life.

Chapter 24 – Aggie

I was in a deep sleep. Something had awoken me. I realized it was the telephone on my bedside table. We had an exfiltration going on in Albania at the time and my first thought was something had gone wrong there. The crackling line, on which other conversations in Hindi were clearly audible, soon made me realize the call was from India. I looked at my watch. In London it was 2.30 am on Monday 3 October. That made it 10 pm the previous day in Delhi. Agnes never called. It was too difficult and expensive. But I assumed she was making an exception, calling at this odd time in a rush of excitement having just received the house photographs. I was instantly awake and anxious to talk. 'Hello, hello,' I yelled into the mouthpiece.

'Joe, Joe can you hear me?' came the reply from an English woman, but not one who was Agnes. 'Joe, its Heather Willmington from the High Commission in Delhi. It's taken an eternity to get through.' Heather was the go-between for the letters Agnes and I wrote to each other.

A cold chill washed over me. I tried to remember Service techniques for remaining calm. 'What's going on?' I yelled.

Suddenly it dawned on me that Heather was crying. I could hear her sobbing and gulps of breath as she sought to regain control. 'Joe, there's been a terrible accident. Agnes has been killed. A runaway lorry hit the HOPE bus on the Delhi ring road.'

I tried to speak but couldn't. I honestly thought I was dreaming. Instead I sat on the edge of the bed holding the telephone handset hearing scratchy speech coming from it but not comprehending anything. How long I sat there holding the phone I don't recall. My next conscious memory was looking at my watch and finding it was now 4 am. Without warning I was violently ill, vomiting the contents of my stomach over my knees and onto the bedroom floor. Then I cried, my wailing coming in heaving waves that strained my rib cage. I fell to the floor and lay there in my own vomit praying to the God I didn't believe in that this was all a terrible mistake.

I spent the remainder of Monday in an incoherent state, stumbling around the house in unceasing distress. I ate and drank nothing. The Service was always alert to unexplained absences from the office. It packaged this as a staff welfare concern but it would not be too cynical to say its real motivation was a morbid fear of an SIS operative suddenly popping up in Moscow: twenty years on, the ghost of Kim Philby was alive and well. I have a vague recollection of the telephone ringing throughout Monday but I just ignored it.

Viscerally, from deep in the pit of my stomach, I knew that the news of Agnes's death was not a mistake.

It was dark by the time a team of janitors assisted by a Service locksmith entered my house to find me dishevelled and soiled and lying in the foetal position on the kitchen floor. An ambulance was called and I was shuttled off to a remote ward in the Croydon Heights private hospital, a facility regularly used by the Service. After forty-eight hours of sedation, a Service welfare officer accompanied by an in-house shrink came to see me on the Thursday morning. By this time I was coherent enough to tell them what had happened. They left to be replaced after a time by Richard Samson, a hard-nosed character who didn't like me much. He had recently replaced the now retired Rodney Charlesworth as ADDG.

'You've had a severe shock, Joe,' Samson said. 'We want you to stay here until you're fully recovered and then we can talk about getting you back to work. We've placed you on sick leave effective as of Monday last. You don't need to worry about anything.'

I suspected Samson was saying only what he was expected to say and in fact regarded my falling apart as one big inconvenience he didn't need. But I didn't care one way or the other. 'I need to go to India, to Delhi,' I said, 'to find out exactly what happened. I want to bring Aggie back home.' I instantly regretted using my privately affectionate name for Agnes and the fact that saying it nearly caused me to dissolve into tears. I tried to steady myself.

Samson looked at me without expression. 'Agnes's family was notified of the accident through Foreign Office consular channels,' he said. 'They agreed Agnes should be cremated in India. The cremation took place two days ago. Her parents travelled there to attend the ceremony. Agnes's ashes are to return to the UK with them; they might even be back by this time.' I understood the need for cremation to take place as soon as possible. There was not much available in New Delhi in terms of morgues. Even in the cooler winter months bodies went off very quickly.

'Even so,' I said doggedly, 'I need to go there and see for myself what happened.'

I detected the slightest hint of irritation in Samson. 'You know the Service rules, Joe. We can't agree to you returning there and running around New Delhi asking this and that person questions and so on.' He paused. 'We have to be particularly firm on this point given your … ugh … emotional state. Sorry.' His jaw set in resolve.

I exploded. 'Well you know what, the Service can stick their rules where the sun don't shine. You and the rest of them can all get fucked. I'm going to go to India and that's that. I will fucking well resign if I have to.'

Samson was no longer in sympathy mode; he was now the take no prisoners, merciless bureaucrat he needed to be to make ADDG. 'You have signed legal obligations binding on you for life regardless of whether you're still in the Service's employ or not. This gives us the authority, as circumstances require, to have the personnel registry withhold release of your private passport, or even for us physically to restrain you from travelling. If you know what's good for you, you won't force us down that path.' He stood to leave. 'New Delhi station has obtained a copy of the official police report into the accident. Against my better judgement, I am prepared to give it to you to read, should you choose to. Once you have read it you are to return it to the Service. A condition of furnishing you with the report is you sign an undertaking not to make a copy of it.' Without another word he left the room.

The next afternoon I was sitting out of bed trying to soak up the last of the weak sunshine coming through the window when a Service courier arrived with the police report. He thrust the undertaking not to copy under my nose. I signed it with ill grace. Only then did he hand over the report. 'It needs to be returned within three days,' he said, handing me a card with a single telephone number on it. 'Ring when you're ready for the pick up.'

I hopped back into bed, propped myself up with pillows and began reading. The report was written in convoluted English. Tea drinking, cricket and bureaucracy were said to be England's main legacies to India; in the last of these the document's language did not disappoint. The gist it conveyed was that around 1 pm on 2 October 1983 a HOPE minivan travelling along Shantipath had merged onto the dual carriageway ring road. I could picture the road junction. Shantipath ran through the middle of the New Delhi diplomatic precinct. I had merged off it onto the ring road many times, recalling the act was one demanding a close watch for speeding, poorly maintained heavy vehicles inexpertly driven. Anil Kunderan, a HOPE employee, was driving the minivan. Its passengers were Agnes and two other local HOPE employees, Singh and Subramanya.

The minivan was reported by an eyewitness, and confirmed by another, to have merged *seemingly unsighted* into the path of oncoming traffic. Conditions were clear – which meant the usual level of pollution haze. A lorry driven by one Subhashchandra Ramchand collided with the van. The lorry was carrying a load of Upla, the Hindi word for the dry animal dung cakes used for cooking by India's lower castes. Owing to the weight of his load, the driver's attempts at braking had little effect causing the minivan to be pushed 150 yards up the road. Ramchand sustained only minor injuries whereas all four in the minivan were killed more or less instantly on impact. Dental records had positively identified each of the victims.

The report appeared comprehensive and I was aware of no raised eyebrows where the Foreign Office, or for that matter the Service, was concerned. I lay back in the hospital bed. Reading the report had exhausted me. I could only hope Agnes had been killed outright and had not experienced fear or pain. Dinner was served. I had no appetite and pushed it away. Something other than the obvious was bothering me. I finally realized my concern was that Agnes would not allow an incompetent or dangerous driver behind the wheel of a HOPE vehicle. Before permitting this she would drive the vehicle herself. It followed that Kunderan, the HOPE employee driving the minivan, was a safe and reliable driver. Yet the police report was to the effect he had driven into the stream of oncoming traffic without taking adequate care. There it was, the piece of the puzzle not making sense.

Of course, what I didn't know then was that the lorry driver, Ramchand, received 1,500 United States dollars for his part in the accident, the two eyewitnesses 500 dollars each, while the assistant sub-inspector who compiled the police report obtained 1,000 dollars by not asking too many questions, including why the drag marks caused by the minivan as it was pushed up the freeway by Ramchand's truck began in the merge lane. Nor could I have known that within six months Ramchand would die in mysterious circumstances while allegedly drinking toxic home-brewed alcohol and the two eyewitnesses would have disappeared from sight.

Lying there in the quiet of the hospital ward, I thought long and hard about what to do next. I decided to write to Agnes's personal driver, Gulam. I knew neither the Foreign Office nor Service would have spoken to him. Apart from the fact he was not involved in the accident, this was how the world of international relations worked. The death of Agnes and her colleagues was a policing matter. Jurisdiction to interview anyone in relation to it resided with the Indian police. The Indian Government would complain bitterly if uninvited a British civil servant sought to usurp this authority. Richard Samson's anxiety about me returning to Delhi behaving erratically and embarrassing the Service was driven by this concern. That I would be acting in a private capacity made no difference.

Suddenly I had energy and purpose. I asked the night nurse to find me some writing paper and envelopes. My letter to Gulam was written in the knowledge he would not understand English and the expectation that the person reading it to him would have only basic comprehension. Thus, I phrased it in child-like sentences and hoped this would cause no offence. On both the envelope containing the letter and at the head of the letter itself I wrote, *Please arrange for an interpreter to read this letter to Gulam.* The essence of my letter was to ask Gulam what had happened in his opinion.

I then considered how best to get the letter to Gulam. I had no address for him, did not know his surname and in any event placing reliance on the chronically inefficient Indian mail service was out of the question. I would have to rely on HOPE passing the letter to him. My instincts told me that as a result of my outburst, there was a good chance Samson would have arranged for the interception of any letter I sent to the High Commission. I elected, therefore, to write to HOPE's head office in London. The phone book gathering dust at the bottom of my bedside cabinet provided a mailing address in Ladygate Lane in Ruislip.

I began to draft. My letter to HOPE explained my relationship to Agnes and told of my admission to hospital on receiving the news of her death. I explained that Agnes was like a daughter to Gulam. I wanted to commiserate with him privately. Hence the letter to Gulam was sealed and marked private and confidential. I told HOPE I knew Agnes would want me to do this. This was a calculated tug of the heartstrings aimed at ensuring HOPE's best effort to deliver the letter. I requested HOPE forward any response from Gulam to my Brent Cross address.

I was now on a roll and after I had finished the letters to Gulam and HOPE, I decided to write to Agnes's parents. There was not much I could say beyond offering condolences and noting my own intense sense of loss. But I did want to see Agnes's ashes and hear about her memorial service. I asked if I could visit them in Hungerford in the coming weeks. Finally, as midnight came and went, I wrote to Heather Willmington the High Commission archivist to thank her, sincerely, for contacting me and, for the benefit of anyone reading my mail, to say I had seen the police report and regrettably nothing more could be done.

I placed the letters to Agnes's parents and Heather Willmington on the side table. I would ask the hospital chaplain to post these later in the morning. Word would reach the Service I was writing letters and no doubt it would like to know to whom. The letters to Gulam and HOPE I secreted away; no one need know about these. Maybe I was paranoid but better to be sure than sorry.

My letter writing signalled I was on the mend. The medical people kept me in over the weekend but allowed me to go home on the Monday, a week after I had been admitted. I was to have a further two weeks' home rest before returning to work. A Service-provided taxi took me home. As soon as it was out of sight, I had dashed to the corner post box and posted my letter to HOPE containing my letter to Gulam. My house, once a symbol of hope and happiness, now felt like a mausoleum. Without Agnes, buying it suddenly seemed pointless. I had the irrational thought that things would be so much better if only I could sell the house. But I also knew I could not rush headlong into a fire sale. For one immediately practical purpose, I wanted to see if there was any response from Gulam.

I visited Agnes's parents in Hungerford during my two weeks of convalescence. They had responded promptly to my letter welcoming my proposed visit. Staring gloomily out of the train window, I estimated Agnes's parents would be both in their late sixties. When I met them they looked twenty years older. They were beyond consolation. Agnes's death, it seemed, would hasten their own. They welcomed me as family, telling me the last time they had seen Agnes she was the happiest she had ever been.

The harmony, however, later frayed at the edges when abruptly I declined their offer to attend a chapel together to pray for Agnes. I instantly regretted bristling. The proposal had caught me off guard and evoked past thoughts about ecclesiastical links between my mother's death and my hitherto dysfunctional relations with women. This stirred feelings of self-disgust, which mixed toxically with my torment over Agnes. 'How can there be a God,' I had demanded, angrily, 'when you think about what has happened to Agnes?' The atmosphere became awkward. I hoped they understood just how upset I was.

After two hours I judged it was time to leave. I think they were pleased to be left to their grief. On parting, Mrs Huntington gave me a vial of Agnes's ashes from the antique ceramic vase positioned next to a photograph of Agnes on the chiffonier in their sitting room. She also gave me a wallet-size photograph of Agnes, taken when Agnes last visited her parents prior to her fateful return to India. I hugged Mrs Huntington and shook her husband's hand. I felt better for this and the tension it dissipated. I was glad to have visited. It was a duty done.

A deep melancholia settled over me as I walked to the station, induced by my lingering study of Agnes's radiant face in the photograph I'd just been given. I made the return trip in miserable solitude. My spirits revived marginally upon reaching my home when I found waiting for me a letter from the HOPE CEO, one Rebecca Normington. Rebecca's letter expressed sympathy for my loss. She also provided a welcome assurance that a HOPE staffer imminently scheduled to visit India would carry my letter to Gulam with her and arrange for an interpreter to read it to him.

I had been back at work for over six weeks. Christmas 1983 was fast approaching. On return home one night I found an envelope bearing HOPE's insignia pushed through the front door post box. It contained a short note saying, *For your information, Rebecca* and a smaller, unstamped letter addressed to *Mr Jospet Lambart*. The writing on the smaller envelope was wavering and barely formed, seemingly written by someone very old or young – or unaccustomed to writing in English. I tore open the envelope. The letter's opening sentence read, *I am Ranjane. I write for Gulam S V Gaekwad.*

Gulam's letter was formulated in the bygone style of colonial India. I found its excessive deference irritating but understood the tone taken was consistent with that of a lower caste Indian man writing to an English overlord in those different times, when India and Indians generally were less assertive. This gave me reason to think the contents of the letter accurately reflected what Gulam had told his interpreter. Gulam was of that generation. Anything too confidently phrased would have caused me to wonder if a later generation scribe had inserted his or her own interpretation.

When I finally got to the letter's substance, what I read caused me to stagger backwards, nearly falling. On my knees with sweat pouring down my face I re-read the text. *Rusavasi they kill her. Cousin lari man tell my friend. Rusavasi pay Lari man and 2 his drink wallah. Pay Pulis to.* Rusavasi was the Hindi word for Russians; lari the word for lorry; and the *drink wallah* reference explained that both witnesses were the lorry driver's drinking companions. *Pulis* meant police, but Gulam did not expand on his allegation of police corruption. Nor did he offer any theories as to why the Russians had killed Agnes. But deep in my bowels I knew his information was correct, deriving as it did from the Indian street where nothing bar nothing escaped the myriad of onlookers.

My aching knees caused me to stand. I knew instantly the murder of Agnes and her colleagues related to my work. There was no other explanation. My mind turned first to Boris and then Katya. With chilling realization growing to horror, it slowly dawned on me that Katya's recruitment was the critical issue. Katya would have identified me to her interrogators as the SIS officer most responsible for it. In Boris's case, he wasn't alive to say anything when his suicide inevitably raised questions of recruitment.

The disinformation we fed the Russians through Geoffrey Tyler and Katya's treasure trove of intelligence had seriously hurt the Soviets. This was one huge body blow to the KGB's pride. That's why the Service had put Tyler in cotton wool, arranging for him to take up a headmastership at a remote research school in Warwickshire shortly after he had been made an OBE in the 1978 Queen's Birthday Honours List. Even so, some form of retaliation against the Service was still expected. But revenge against an individual intelligence officer with no attendant intelligence benefit was virtually unheard of. To do so was to be uselessly vindictive and further no intelligence interest. Even were the officer cowed, the parent organization continued on institutionally unimpaired.

At another time this might have told me something. But buried by grief I gave no credence to the possibility that Agnes's death was anything other than a straight-out tit for tat revenge killing. It was a belief to which I clung tenaciously for ages, years in fact.

Now in the moment, abject desolation began to mount. Just as my career ambition had caused Katya's death, so too had it now caused Agnes's. 'God help me,' I whispered. 'My pointless, bloody useless career. Forgive me Aggie, please forgive me.'

Chapter 25 – Ronnie

I sat at my kitchen table all night, thinking. Despite the freezing cold I did not turn on the heat, not even a light. Still in my suit and wearing my overcoat, I moved only when the bedside alarm went off at 6.30 am, its sound resonating around the house on the chill morning air. The lack of sleep seemed to have no effect. I felt awake and alert. My nocturnal contemplation had told me I now owed a solemn duty to Agnes. The Russians may well have acted with unconscionable vindictiveness – to the extent that they thought it necessary to use the smokescreen of the accident to try and disguise this. Even so, my self-absorption with career had provoked their conduct. My unequivocal obligation was to find out who in the Russian system gave the order to kill Agnes and then kill that person. After that, it was no longer important if I lived or died.

For several hours throughout the long night, I had considered how best to find out who gave the order. I finally decided it was through a defector. For every Russian who defected to the British or other Western allies, ten others defected to the United States. I needed to ingratiate myself with the Americans. This involved two aspects. One was becoming known to and trusted by them. The other was to be able to request defector information from the CIA additional to the defector debriefs the Agency routinely shared with the Service. Washington station chief met both criteria. But this was a much-coveted assignment. Further complicating matters was that obtaining the appointment necessitated my promotion to FADG.

The Service's long-standing practice was to appoint the Washington station head from the pool of head office FADGs. But I had determined the next rotation shaped to be different. Of the eight FADGs currently in headquarters, two had already done the posting; one I knew was earmarked for Bonn; and Brussels would have to be filled soon. Rumour also had it that Martin Mumford was about to be promoted to DDG. Two others, I calculated, would want to stay in London to maintain profile in the race for promotion to the same level. And then there was Reggie Sullivan who was going nowhere. I decided a promoted branch head would likely secure the appointment when it was announced. That would be about eleven months from now, in November 1984, ahead of the scheduled February 1985 take-up.

I was confident that if I put my best foot forward at every opportunity, I could see off most of my peers aspiring to advance to FADG in the next while. But I also knew that to realistically seek elevation to FADG, I would first have to repair my standing with the Service. There was for one thing the psychiatric angle. I resolved to argue that my breakdown came as the result of personal trauma, not the consequence of work pressures, and note I had bounced back in a week. A second issue was trickier. I had railed against the ADDG Richard Samson to the point where I was sure he would have instituted precautions to prevent me ducking off to India and causing all sorts of chaos. This insubordination would be a certain impediment to promotion. It had to be addressed, somehow.

As for the actual appointment, I eventually concluded Freddie Ladler was the major stumbling block. The more I thought about it, the more certain I had become that up on the fifth floor Ladler was already earmarked as the Service's next US point man. He would have cultivated a host of CIA contacts during his posting to Washington. Many of these would now be rising through the ranks. He also had numerous close friends in the CIA's London station, aided by the fact he was married to an American. And I knew Ladler would soon threaten FADG. In September 1982, after returning from Lisbon earlier in the year, he had been placed as head of Southern Africa Branch. It was no secret this two-year attachment to SAB was designed to broaden his experience ahead of a slated return to US work. I needed Ladler out of the picture. Only then could I compete more evenly with other contenders.

I shaved, ironed a shirt and put on my best suit. After which I walked to the station with resolve and purpose, exhaling billows of steaming breath as I went. Coincident with angling for promotion and a posting to Washington, I would work towards discrediting Ladler – just how I did any of these things I did not know yet.

I took no leave over Christmas and New Year. The office was virtually deserted for that week and into the first week of 1984. There was little work to do; it was as if all the spies in Southern Europe had gone to ground. I used the time at my disposal to take stock of what I knew about Ladler. Worryingly, it was very little. I decided I should try and find out more about his personal details. But bowling up to personnel section and requesting a look at his file was clearly out of the question, and I wasn't about to start inquiring around the Service into things like his politics and financial affairs.

I did recall, however, that many Service officers had entries in the Foreign Office Staff Appointments Handbook, widely known by its nickname of the Breeder's Guide, or the Breeder's for short. The Breeder's was not classified but nor was it freely available, much less publicly accessible. Copies were usually distributed to senior Foreign Office staff, to give them ready access to staff background they could consult as required. The idea for Service officers was an entry in the Breeder's added an extra layer of cover for when they were posted abroad under the guise of political officers. To be sure there were copies of the Breeder's located within the Service. But the personal assistants to the various FADGs and DDGs held these. In keeping with Service mores, copies were kept under lock and key and had to be signed out. My operation against Ladler, however, had one non-negotiable rule: *no footprints*.

I rang Ronnie Waterson at the Foreign Office on spec. Ronnie had been a political officer in New Delhi for some of my time there. We were not close friends but had got on quite well professionally. I was pleasantly surprised when he answered his telephone. Ronnie explained he and his wife were planning to ski in Switzerland in February and he wanted to preserve his leave. I could tell he wasn't sure whether or not to mention Agnes. I saved him from his dilemma. 'You will have heard about my recent my loss,' I said.

He agreed he had.

'I hardly need tell you,' I said with a deliberately maudlin air that wasn't hard to contrive, 'it really gutted me; knocked the stuffing clean out of me.'

'Well, you wouldn't be human if it didn't,' he commiserated.

'True enough,' I said. 'But I'm slowly on the mend, which brings me to the purpose of this call.'

'Go on,' Ronnie said. I could hear the apprehensiveness in his voice.

'It's a bit embarrassing actually Ronnie, but man-to-man I have to tell you that I'm feeling extraordinarily lonely right now and in need of female company. There's someone at the FO I am considering approaching with a view to forming a friendship. Let me hasten to add I'm not chasing a quick roll in the hay here. That's the last thing on my mind. It's just that right now...' I let my voice tail off. It all sounded a bit lame to my ears.

But Ronnie was sympathetic. 'How can I help?' he asked.

'Do you mind if I duck over to your office this afternoon and have a quick peek at the Breeder's? It's like getting into Fort Knox to get hold of a copy here.'

Ronnie laughed, relieved. 'Of course,' he said. 'I was conjuring all sorts of things for a moment.'

I laughed back, companionably I hoped. 'Thanks ever so much Ronnie. I'll see you about 3 pm.'

Ronnie ushered me into his office at the appointed time. We chatted idly for a few minutes. Fortunately, he appeared not to have realized that on the telephone I had deliberately built up the impression I was going to ask him for something major only to make a relatively simple request, resulting in his eager agreement to my lower level proposition. But now Ronnie was in a bind. When I suggested I'd best have a look at the Breeder's and be on my way, he fidgeted uncomfortably with his tie. 'Look Joe,' he said eventually, nervously wringing his hands, 'I'm not sure I can informally give out private Foreign Office employee information. The practice is to share this stuff on a strict official needs basis.'

I did my best to look crestfallen but said nothing.

'Tell you what,' Ronnie said, 'if you tell me who you're interested in, I might be able to help.'

I pretended to brighten. 'How about I tell you who it is but you let me read the entry myself? Truth is I'm not entirely sure what I'm looking for. I'm a bit muddled as you can imagine.'

Ronnie looked doubtful. I raised my eyebrows and smiled a sad smile. 'OK,' he said, shaking his head. 'Who's the lucky girl?'

'Sheila Wilson,' I replied.

Ronnie looked at me incredulously. After a considered pause, he said gently, 'Joe, you know she bats for the other side I take it?'

'It's the company I'm after,' I said. 'We did some good work together once.'

Without another word, Ronnie handed me the book. To my great relief, he then stood and said, 'I'm just going to the gents. I'll be back in a tick.' Trying in my mind to stay one step ahead of our conversation, I had been unable to decide how I would look under *L* when Ronnie, were he watching, would have been expecting me to go to *W* at the rear of the book.

Ladler's entry was brief and not completely up to date: Frederick Godfrey Ladler, born 28 September 1940 in Walton-on-Thames; educated at Cambridge University where he read for the Law Tripos; married Mary-Beth Quinlivan on 8 July 1969; one son, Barrington James born 1972, one daughter, Julianna Felicity born 1976. The rest was a chronological recitation of bogus placements in FO work units, interspersed by entries indicating postings as Second, later First Secretary (political) Washington from June 1967–August 1971 and Minister (political) and Deputy Head of Mission Lisbon, April 1979–July 1982. I scribbled down each and every detail. I had just flicked to the *Ws* when Ronnie returned. I handed him back the book. 'Perhaps you're right,' I said. He smiled grimly.

Returning to the office, I summarized what I had had. Ladler had been born in the Surry stockbroker belt, intimating a conservative-leaning family background; was better educated than me; and his American wife, with whom he had two children, was of Irish extraction. I reflected on the monumental effort expended to obtain not much. *Almost certainly not worth it*, I thought, *but who knows*?

Chapter 26 – Rhodesia

That night at home I sat disinterestedly watching television. I had become a virtual teetotaller during my time with Agnes. With her death and my plunge into permanent sadness, I hadn't reverted to the habit of heavy drinking. I used to drink my whisky on the rocks, preferably in cut crystal glasses, allowing me to knock back shot after shot, as was my want when depressed. Nowadays, I settled for a double whisky in a long glass, added ice and diluted it with a mixer. I liked the feel of a glass in my hand. Whatever that said, nursing a single whisky and ginger ale got me through the long, lonely nights and left me clear-headed and fit for work the next day.

The 10 pm news came on. It carried a report on a conflict in Zimbabwe between rival tribal groups. The country was the former British colony of Southern Rhodesia or informally, Rhodesia. The story cut to the Leader of the Zimbabwe Opposition, a white Zimbabwean called Ian Smith. I knew of Smith, long a thorn in the side of the British Government, having seen his name in the National Collection Requirements issued monthly by the Cabinet Office Intelligence Coordinator.

In some context or other, the news program made mention of Smith's arch conservatism. I sat bolt upright. There as the analysts liked to call it was the triangulation I was seeking. Smith the far right conservative; Ladler from a likely conservative background in Britain; and by dint of his stewardship of SAB calling the shots for the Service on intelligence gathering in Zimbabwe. I tipped the remainder of my drink down the kitchen sink and climbed into bed. *Tomorrow*, I thought, *I'm going to start to make some progress.*

I was in the office by 6.30 am. The janitors gave me a bemused look as I charged in. But they were discreet men who never asked questions. My branch operated a card index system for each country of responsibility. Explained simply, if an issue concerning a country coming under the branch's purview arose with a country outside of our remit, say Brazil for example, a dated entry for the relevant country would be made under *B*. These entries usually directed the enquirer to a file where details of the matter could be found.

For each of the branch's supervised countries, I looked under *Z* for Zimbabwe. Nothing. I then did the same for *R* for Rhodesia. The Yugoslavia index directed me to a file containing reporting from Belgrade station dating back to 1967 about Yugoslavia supplying Rhodesia with manufacturing equipment in breach of sanctions imposed by the government of Harold Wilson. The sanctions, which carried United Nations endorsement, had been applied after a November 1965 Unilateral Declaration of Independence, a UDI, by the then Ian Smith-led Rhodesian Government.

The file told me that Smith's whites-only administration had held powers to govern Rhodesia's internal affairs, while the colony remained under British suzerainty. But Smith wanted out and out independence, hence the UDI. For all that, no country formally recognized Rhodesian independence, principally because Smith's regime had effectively repudiated the principle of majority rule by enacting electoral laws making it impossible for most of Rhodesia's majority black populace to qualify to vote.

Yugoslavia's involvement in the UDI matter meant that related reports sent by stations other than Belgrade were also on file. To my great interest I saw a report from Lisbon station advising Rhodesia had established an office in Lisbon subsequent to the UDI, despite Portugal's official policy of non-recognition. Later-dated documents gave up that the office, effectively an embassy in all bar name, had remained in place until the Carnation Revolution of 1974. Portugal's own involvement in sanction-busting was also noted in several Lisbon reports. These included repeat instances during the period between the UDI and the Carnation Revolution of Portugal shipping oil to Rhodesia via its African colony of Mozambique.

I sat back and admired my handy work. Less than a decade had elapsed since Portugal was up to its armpits in assisting Rhodesia frustrate the British sanctions. The extent of governmental assistance signalled substantial public support within Portugal for Smith's Rhodesia. It could be safely assumed that remnants of this pro-Smith rump would have been alive and well during Ladler's tenure as Lisbon station head.

I decided to find out more about Ian Smith. To that end, I visited the British Library the following weekend. Smith, it transpires, flew for the RAF in the war. His extraordinary gallantry caused me to wonder if any sane person could be that brave. Politically, however, Smith was less impressive. His critics, and there were many, mainly derided him as a far right racist who regarded the white man as superior to the black. It occurred to me that just as there were surely pockets of support for Smith in Portugal, the combination of his war record and politics would mean the same applied in Britain. As if in confirmation, I later discovered that on the night of the signing of an agreement in London in 1979 paving the way for Zimbabwe's independence and the election of its first black government, Smith boycotted the event, dining instead with former RAF colleagues.

The resilience of the support for Smith in the UK and Portugal, I reasoned, would depend a lot on how Zimbabwe had fared since independence. Not well was the conclusion I soon reached. The credibility of the country's leadership was in tatters, much to the disappointment of those who had anticipated the growth of representative democracy. Not only had prime minister Robert Mugabe signed an agreement with distinctly undemocratic North Korea to train and equip the Zimbabwe army in an effort to put down the current tribal unrest, he had also made recent public references to a preference for a one-party state. Added to which, Zimbabwe's economy was in free fall. These were all factors bound to have Smith's supporters saying, 'We told you so.'

This prompted a final piece of research at the British Library involving the *Who's Who in UK Business*. Under *Ladler*, I found five entries. But only one, Godfrey Randall Ladler, Principal Partner of Phoenix Investments PLC, was chair of the Elmbridge Borough Conservative Committee. The entry also noted a marriage to Coral Howlston-Browne in 1936 and three unnamed children, two sons and a daughter. Walton-on-Thames, where the Breeder's told me Freddie Ladler was born, was located within Elmbridge Borough. 'That's the old man, I bet,' I whispered to myself. This apparent unearthing of Ladler's father, and his company, and the proof of Freddie's conservative background it appeared to offer now made going to the trouble of consulting the Breeder's seem worthwhile.

The 1984 working year began in earnest the next week. On the Monday morning, 9 January, after Heneshaw and I had our usual start-of-week meeting with Reggie Sullivan, I returned to my office and consulted the branch's copy of the UK companies' index. The entry for Phoenix Investments was brief: *A privately owned company with a paid up share capital of two million pounds; specializes in offshore investments for both retail and institutional investors.* I rang the number I found in the telephone book. The switchboard operator answered. 'Good morning,' I said in my best upcountry brogue. 'It's Clarrie from UK Parcels. I have a package here that's addressed to a Mr Frederick Ladler. But the address is care of his father Godfrey at your company ... yeah here it is, Phoenix Investments, 44 Tachbrook Street, Pimlico. I don't want to send a driver out on a wild goose chase if I can help it. If we dropped the parcel around would it be going to the right person?'

The operator was a young woman of pleasant disposition and disarming guilelessness. She laughed lightly. 'Yes, I can confirm Freddie is Mr Godfrey Ladler's son. Drop it off and we'll make sure it gets to Godfrey.'

'Thanks darling,' I said, and I meant it.

The next day, 10 January, I told my staff I had a lunch meeting. Proceeding to Waterloo Station, I entered the men's toilets on the concourse level. In a booth I changed out of my suit into jeans, a dirty shirt, sports shoes and an old parka. I stuffed my office attire into the brief case I was carrying and put it in a locker. Moving as quickly as I could without running, I boarded a Jubilee train alighting at Green Park where I did a quick back check. Satisfied the coast was clear, I hopped a Victoria line train to Pimlico tube station.

A short distance up Tachbrook Street, I found the Phoenix Investments office. The young woman at reception, who also operated a desktop telephone switchboard, sounded like the one I had spoken to the day before. Affecting a cockney accent, I told her I was interested in an offshore investment because of the potential tax breaks it offered.

After a short wait, a thickset man in his late forties with crinkly hair came out and ushered me into a side office. He introduced himself as Dennis Davison. I responded in my adopted cockney, 'Brian Spinks, nice to meet you me old china plate.'

Davison ignored my abuse of the English language. 'What can I do for you?'

'Well, I anticipate coming into a sizeable sum of money in the near future,' I said.

Davison raised his head sceptically. 'How so?' he enquired deadpan.

I adopted a smug expression. 'Daddy's about to head to the afterlife,' adding for Davison's benefit in a mock southern United States accent, 'and ain't nobody left but lil ol me.' I smiled conspiratorially at Davison's expressionless face. 'Father,' I said, using the noun facetiously, 'has a house in Walworth, South London. They tell me it's likely to fetch about 300,000 quid.'

'Where exactly is it?' Davison asked.

I was ready for that. '198 Rodney Road,' I said. 'An old area but now making a comeback I'm reliably informed.'

Davison took notes and then asked for identification. In 1984 driver's licences with embedded photographs were still a couple of years off. The absence of photographs made the illicit use of the paper licences of the day a less complicated undertaking. I produced a licence in the name of Brian Spinks, with a Putney address. Davison jotted down its details. 'The address is an old one,' I said. 'Haven't got around to changing it just yet.'

After confirming on Monday 9 January that Frederick Ladler was Godfrey's son, and now set on visiting Phoenix Investments, I had become concerned I should have phoney identification with me. A bogus Service driver's licence was the ideal choice. But these had to be signed in and out, which would infringe my *no footprints* rule. There was also the trifling matter that use of clandestine Service property for personal reasons was a criminal offence.

Owing to these complications, I may well have chanced it without identification had Heneshaw not volunteered in our earlier Monday meeting with Reggie he had authorized one of his juniors to draw a licence for a training exercise later in the week. I cornered the junior in the corridor after lunch and told him in hushed tones I needed the licence by day's end for a one-day NTK purpose. He was very green, and daunted, but nodded resolutely when I said he was not to mention this to anyone. He slinked by at the end of the day to give me the document. I promised to return it to him the next afternoon under similar NTK circumstances. 'Good field training for you,' I assured him with a wink.

What I didn't count on, after giving him back the licence late on 10 January, was the silly bugger would go to the domestic documents registry where he asked a clerk named Teresa English to note the issue card to reflect I was in possession of the licence from 9–10 January. I was only to learn of this many years later.

For now, however, on taking back the licence from Davison, I pretended to be suddenly indignant. 'Listen, what's this got to do with me? All I want to know is where I can put 300 grand without this fucking government taxing the eyes out of it.'

Davison had seen it all before and wasn't fazed. 'We get a lot of tyre kickers come in. It's important we know that you're serious.'

'I'm bloody serious, mate, trust me.'

Davison's body language told me he was far from convinced, but my producing a licence now had him interested enough to be doing a mental calculation of his commission if I did turn out to be genuine. 'Fine,' he said. 'Where do you live right now?'

'Got a bird,' I said. 'We shack up out the back of her olds' house.'

'Address?'

'67 Clifton Gardens, Maida Vale,' I told him. It was currently a building site.

'Telephone number?'

'Mate, we're in the fucking granny flat. Who has a phone in there?'

Davison shook his head slightly. 'Did you have any particular investment preference?'

I told Davison I'd be happy with anything paying reasonable interest. 'What I want,' I said, 'is to avoid paying UK tax.'

Davison said this was easier said than done. 'Apart from the United States, Canada and Singapore,' he said, 'the UK doesn't have a lot of Double Taxation Agreements.'

'What the bloody hell are Double Taxation Agreements?'

'Treaties with other countries that recognize if you've paid tax overseas you don't need to pay it here.'

'Right,' I said, stringing out the word so as to convey I hadn't understood at all. I then made my play. 'A mate of mine told me about investment opportunities in a place somewhere in Africa. In mining he said. It started with Z but I can't remember it. Apparently it's all in the news.'

'Your adviser probably means Zambia,' Davison responded. 'There are some companies involved in copper mining there but I wouldn't recommend them. The political risk is through the roof.'

'No, no, wasn't Zambia,' I said, pretending to rack my brains. 'Like I say it's on the telly. I seen something on it myself just the other day.'

'You don't possibly mean Zimbabwe, do you?' Davison asked.

Uncurling my left index finger and pointing it towards Davison's chest, I exclaimed, 'That's it mate, that's it.'

Davison put down his pen and closed his notebook. He had given up on me. 'Sorry Mr Spinks but Phoenix does not recommend investment in Zimbabwe. Politics,' he said, turning the palms of his hands upwards. 'There hasn't really been a decent investment environment there since the 1960s. And now the political risk is off the scale, much worse than Zambia. We took the decision quite a long time ago to give Zimbabwe a wide berth and to date nothing's convinced us to change our mind.'

I pretended to be flummoxed. 'Well what the fuck is Wally talking about?'

Davison stood. Our interview was over. 'That,' he said, 'you'd have to ask Wally.'

Originally, I had hoped to start vague smoke and fire rumours that Freddie Ladler, a conservative-leaning Service officer, was using his position to pass information to Smith's supporters in the UK and Portugal in support of Smith's return as prime minister. The gutter press thrived on this sort of stuff, especially when spies were involved. There was no great difficulty in anonymously feeding the tabloids allegations and flimsy evidence. They were tooled up for it and for circulation's sake prepared to splash around headlined innuendo, even if on any objective assessment the claims could be easily debunked. And the mud, once thrown, always stuck. But while researching I came to realize there was one big problem with this approach – that Mugabe was so obviously on the nose. The very real risk existed, I decided, of people thinking that Zimbabweans would be better off with Smith in charge. The upshot I feared was random approval across the Service for Ladler's apparent daring.

A link between Phoenix Investments and Zimbabwe thus became indispensable. This was how I would convey via the tabloids that altruism was the last thing on Ladler's mind. People loved to think the worst. They would still perceive of Ladler using his inside knowledge on Mugabe to aid Zimbabwe's reversion to an Ian Smith government. But the mere hint of an economic benefit would also persuade them his currying of favour with conservative white Rhodesia was aimed at enriching his father's company. Human nature being what it is, it was unnecessary to spell out how or when this supposedly would be achieved. I had allowed myself to believe the critical link would exist. It was a body blow to find it didn't. But there was no time to contemplate my situation. I rushed back to Waterloo Station, changed into my suit and returned to headquarters.

Reggie Sullivan swept into my office even before I had time to hang my suit jacket. He was fraying at the seams. 'I've been looking everywhere for you, Joe. That was a bloody long lunch.'

'Yes,' I replied, 'the cork got stuck in the port bottle.'

Reggie really was a feckless sort of character who was easily distracted. 'I remember that happening at a mess dinner in Aberdeen one night, actually,' he said, demonstrating yet again his infamous propensity for verbiage. I inwardly rolled my eyes. Fortunately, Reggie was feeling harassed and quickly returned to topic. 'The

DG's just announced Martin Mumford's been bumped up to DDG. He'll be in charge of the US and West Europe and our supervising DDG. I have to have a full brief on our current state of play to him by close of business tomorrow night. Can you get a Southern Europe Branch brief to me please, deadline noon tomorrow? Rupert's already half-finished his branch's brief.'

Good old Rupert, I thought, resentment rising in me at Reggie's implication that, unlike me, Heneshaw was not letting him down.

I called in my two directors and requested section briefs no later than 10 am tomorrow morning. Their positive response caused me to reflect that branch head was probably the happiest level in the Service. The directors were usually ambitious and hardworking, insulating the branch head from staff complaints about workload and the like, whereas the FADGs stood between the branch heads and the ever-demanding fifth floor. I sighed deeply. If only Agnes was with me life would be so perfect. That I might not be content to sit at branch head for the rest of my career was not something I considered. Tears welled in my eyes. I felt a sense of loss bordering on physical pain. 'Those cunts,' I cursed bitterly, unsure whether I was referring to the likes of Ladler and Heneshaw, those responsible for Agnes's killing, or both. 'I'll show them. Somehow I'll get around today's disappointment and get back on track.'

Resolve restored, it occurred to me Mumford's promotion was an opportunity to begin repairing my standing with the Service, damaged by my insubordination to Richard Samson. That night, long after even my directors had gone home, I sat in my office drafting and redrafting a letter to Mumford. Only when satisfied with the content did I turn my attention to the handwriting in which I would present it. The script needed to be ragged but not illegible; the writing needed to convey I had dashed out the letter in about ten minutes rather than taking all night, as had been the case.

My letter did not overly flatter Mumford. He was too grounded to be seduced by sycophancy. I simply congratulated him on his promotion, noting it came as no surprise to me. With careful calibration lest I sounded too familiar, I noted our shared professional values. I mentioned Agnes and the devastation of her death but assured Mumford I was up and going on all cylinders. I said I thought I needed another overseas assignment, one taking me away from London and distancing me from bad memories. An English-speaking country like the US was of primary interest. The ideal was to get promoted and go there as station chief. I concluded the letter by again congratulating him on a promotion well deserved, signing it informally as *Joe*. I managed to squeeze the whole thing onto one A4 page. The truth is I would have mowed his lawns for a year if it had helped my case. But Martin was his own man. I had to hope my light touch kiss of his arse did the trick.

Chapter 27 – TransRho

Unbeknown to me at the time, Dennis Davison of Phoenix Investments fame was also something of a secret agent. It all stemmed from a clandestine arrangement he had with a lawyer called Harold Blanckenberg. Not that Dennis thought of himself as a spy. What he did was simply a variation of the *commission received for product sold* model that underpinned his income stream.

A UK permanent resident, Blanckenberg had been born in Pretoria, South Africa's national capital and also capital of Transvaal Province. He had a long-standing retainer with the so-called Vereeniging group, named after the provincial city in Southern Transvaal of that name. The group comprised sixteen members, all of whom were born in Vereeniging and had lived there most of their working lives. By 1984 fourteen members were in their mid-to-late seventies and two were over eighty. Between them they owned sixty-eight per cent of the issued script in a company called TransRho. TransRho's name reflected the Transvaal origins of its major investors and that the company's main asset was a diamond mine in Rhodesia.

Until 1965 and Ian Smith's UDI, TransRho had been a very successful operation. It was listed on the stock exchanges in London, Johannesburg, and Salisbury, as Rhodesia's capital was then known. But the sanctions imposed on Rhodesia after the UDI destroyed TransRho. By 1968 its shares were worthless, trading at one-halfpenny in London down from a 1964 high of twelve pounds, four and six. The regulatory authorities suspended trading in the stock. But creditors were paid from Vereeniging group members' private funds and the company was never wound up.

After the UDI, group members had mutually pledged not to sell their holdings. Instead at different times they lobbied the Smith regime; the British, South African and Portuguese Governments; and even the United Nations. It was all to no avail. The Eastern Bloc, led by Russia, was with Portugal and South Africa at the forefront of sanction-busting. Russia and South Africa, however, were major diamond producers and neither had any interest in encouraging more production. Britain and the UN were passively sympathetic, leaving only Portugal as a possible outlet for the sale of TransRho diamonds. A couple of shipments went out via Mozambique. But when the combined force of the Western and Eastern superpowers pressured Portugal to desist, the government in Lisbon quickly complied. Smith needed the Ports on side for higher priorities, such as ensuring Rhodesia's oil supplies, and was not about to take on Lisbon over a single commercial entity. Admirably true to their word, the Vereeniging group all went down the financial gurgler together.

Upon Zimbabwe's independence and the lifting of sanctions, Robert Mugabe had made encouraging noises about stimulating mineral exports. Old and embittered and wanting their money back before they died, group members had reactivated Blanckenberg's retainer with instructions to keep an eye out for any interest in the UK for investing in the Zimbabwe minerals sector. The group was singularly fixated on putting right the perceived wrongs of two decades earlier. To this extent they wore rose-coloured glasses, failing to heed contemporary messages coming out of the Mugabe Government to the effect that compensation-free government acquisition of resource deposits was under consideration.

It was from *our source* that much later I learned about Blanckenberg, his secret relationship with Dennis Davison and all about the Vereeniging group. The account *our source* provided explained how it was a seemingly trivial item, the driver's licence I had used during my visit to Phoenix Investments, came to spark a series of events destined to become the very essence of my story.

The agreement Harold Blanckenberg had with Dennis Davison was that for every expression of interest in the Zimbabwe mining sector of which Dennis became aware, Blanckenberg would pay him ten pounds for the basic details. Dennis had contacted Blanckenberg after the *Brian Spinks* visit to Phoenix Investments. He provided Blanckenberg with the address of the house supposedly worth 300,000 pounds and the nominated Spinks home address, neither of which, as Blanckenberg found, existed in the form I had represented. Dennis also gave Blanckenberg the number of the licence that as

Spinks I had used for identification. Blanckenberg had a low-level source in the Driver and Vehicle Licensing Agency. His DVLA contact was later to inform him the licence holder details could be obtained only by written application to the DVLA director.

In early February 1984 Blanckenberg telexed all this in a report to the Vereeniging group. The report drew the erroneous conclusion, based on the dummy addresses and evident subterfuge, that the Spinks charade was an attempt at intelligence gathering on behalf of unidentified persons predicting improvement in the Zimbabwe investment climate. It also contained the details of the bogus driver's licence, with Blanckenberg simply noting it had not proved possible to verify Brian Spinks as the registered licence holder.

By prior arrangement, Blanckenberg's telex went to the de Bruyn real estate office in the Johannesburg suburb of Saxonwold, owned by the son of one of the Vereeniging group. Its transmission took place at a time when the Soviet Union was without diplomatic representation in South Africa, having severed relations in Cold War strategic opposition to South Africa's policy of apartheid. It was also an era when the Soviets, in search of widespread political support on the African continent, were financing black South African movements, principally the African National Congress.

A black South African man called Jacob worked as a driver for de Bruyn real estate. Jacob had been told to drive the Blanckenberg report to Vereeniging. He did so, but not before detouring to Soweto where his ANC controller had photocopied it. The Soviets were particularly interested in Western country efforts to access Southern African minerals. When told by the ANC of the Vereeniging group's wish to reactivate exports to the West, the Soviets had urged a source be found to inform on the group. Jacob had been recruited because the ANC knew the de Bruyn real estate office was the Vereeniging group's window to the world.

ANC operatives subsequently smuggled the copy of Blanckenberg's report to the KGB station in the Soviet Embassy in Maputo, Mozambique. The station sent it to Moscow. A Moscow Centre analyst, intrigued by Blanckenberg's inability to confirm the licence holder details, astutely decided further investigation was warranted. After consulting *our source*, she tasked the KGB's London station to get to the bottom of the matter.

KGB London station had on its books a Sergeant Garry Bullock of the London Metropolitan Police. A competent policeman, apparently, with a wife and two young sons, Bullock nonetheless had a weakness for horse racing. The station had become aware of this in 1982 through a starting price bookmaker who often extended Bullock credit. In short order it had snared Bullock using a Czech intelligence officer called Tusar, who told Bullock he was a Czech immigrant willing to pay for information on a business rival. Once entrapped Bullock had nowhere to go. This was long before enlightened times when gambling addiction came to be treated for the illness it was. Bullock knew he would lose his job and be publicly humiliated if his employer became aware of his problems.

Our source was initially unaware of Bullock. This is because the KGB station's demands on him, via the Czech Tusar, were usually low-key; mainly details of motor vehicle ownership, silent telephone numbers, and the home addresses of certain persons. Bullock was sick, not stupid. The KGB station understood he would soon realize that Tusar could not have interests sufficiently broad to warrant all the requests he made. But it calculated it was easy money – in the pre-computer age accessing police records left no electronic trail. The judgement was sound. Bullock did not quibble when Tusar later told him he was working the Czech émigré community selling his services as a procurer of useful information.

Our source became aware of Bullock when Tusar reported that after giving Bullock the Brian Spinks name and licence number, Bullock had tried to tell him the information sought was beyond his, Bullock's, level of access. This deepened the mystery first raised by Blanckenberg prompting *our source* to order the heavies be put on Bullock. The following day Tusar revisited Bullock bringing with him a man from the KGB London station, a splayfooted thug from Siberia whose job specifically was to intimidate. Forty-eight hours later Bullock told Tusar, 'The driver's licence used by *Brian Spinks* is a bogus issue held by the SIS and on 10 January it was in the possession of an SIS officer named Joe Lambert.'

Bullock also told Tusar he had just resigned from the Metropolitan Police, after confessing his double life to his wife the night before. *Our source* discussed this with General Shukhov, the man who had ordered Agnes's execution. The normal response would be to shop Bullock to the British authorities, as a warning to any other would-be waverer among London station's stable of compromised civil servants. Eventually, however, Shukhov directed Bullock be let go. His ultimately swaying judgement was that with the emergence of my name, it was best to avoid arousing the interest of the British security services. Bullock's was a case of a happy ending. In the world of spying it was a rare event.

Bullock's version of events came to light many years after his exchange with Tusar, when a senior Service officer interviewed him, the same officer who later debriefed *our source*. Bullock said the Siberian thug had threatened him with ruin if he didn't comply with the information request. Bullock was in no doubt the threat was real; as a policeman, he said, he knew a hard man when he saw one.

Bullock said he had initially discovered the licence file was protected, meaning either MI5 or the Service was the licence custodian. This is why he told Tusar he had no access. Now under duress, he had checked with an MI5 contact who gave a negative response. With that, Bullock rang Teresa English in the Service's domestic documents registry. The two were professionally acquainted. When Bullock told Teresa the licence had come up in a traffic context on 10 January, she had confirmed it belonged to the Service. She was allowed to tell Bullock this. But then Bullock had said, 'On the QT Tess, could you tell me who signed it out last, just in case there is a next time?'

Teresa should have clammed up. But on studying the licence issue card before her, she had recognized her initialled entry. 'Yes, yes that's right, Joe Lambert had it that day,' Teresa had said.

'I instantly regretted my mistake,' Teresa later explained to the Service. ' "Garry," I had said, "That is strictly *entre nous*. I really shouldn't have told you that; I was just thinking out loud." '

'Safe as houses, Tess,' Bullock had responded.

Within six weeks of telling Tusar he had resigned, Bullock and his family had relocated to Edinburgh, home to his wife's maternal grandparents. Bullock overcame his addiction and went on to be a successful executive with a local security company. It was in Edinburgh that the senior Service officer interviewed Bullock, after a Service other had earlier tracked him down.

Chapter 28 – Ladler

In late April 1984 General Shukhov received a follow-up report from the KGB station in London. It expanded on the station's earlier advice that I – Joe Lambert, a known SIS officer – had made enquiries to a private company about investment in Zimbabwe using an alias supported by a bogus Service driver's licence. Shukhov shared the update report with *our source*. It conveyed that the principal partner of the company in question was one Godfrey Ladler, now confirmed as the father of Frederick Ladler an SIS officer who had come to the KGB's notice when head of SIS station Lisbon. The report noted my motive for approaching the company remained unclear. But given one possible explanation identified by London station, it did include details on a certain Jeremy Waller and the minutes of a political meeting held in London in May 1979. Shukhov also told *our source* that his search request to the KGB registry, instigated on receipt of London station's update, had now produced a newspaper article on a man called Silva.

Shukhov observed it was obvious something was afoot. He and *our source* both agreed that one SIS officer would not usually undertake clandestine activities against an immediate relative of another. If there was an official reason for the approach, British law generally required it to be declared. They soon decided it could mean only one thing – that I had engaged in rogue conduct.

Shukhov instructed *our source* to find out why I had approached Phoenix Investments. 'We don't need be too subtle about this,' he had said. 'Find out where Lambert lives and let's get an asset to approach him face to face. If our London people are correct about what he is up to – and they could well be – and provided we can live with whatever is Lambert's end objective, this shapes as a golden opportunity to assist him gain promotion.'

Our source described how Shukhov's intensity had visibly mounted; soon his eyes were burning with energy. 'This is the key moment,' Shukhov told *our source*, 'the chance to set Operation Citadel in motion. I can feel it in my moody Russian soul. Use only your best assets. And don't fuck this up, no matter what.' Operation Citadel was the code name the Russians had given to the plan to exploit my emotional vulnerability and eventually recruit me.

Our source was in fact a man – aged thirty-six and a tall, straight-backed soldier. He had started military life as a cadet before becoming a stone-faced ceremonial guard goose-stepping up and down in front of Lenin's tomb in Red Square steadfastly ignoring the ever-present throng of tourists. From there he had been talent spotted by the KGB and accelerated up the ranks. On receiving Shukhov's instruction, *our source* had thrown Shukhov a crisp salute and snapped his heels. But the gnarled Russian Bear had apparently just waved him away and reached for another of his vile cigarettes.

It was a Sunday afternoon in early May 1984; the first hints of summer were in the air. My front door bell rang. I opened it to find a small woman of about sixty on my doorstep. She carried a large handbag about half the size of her diminutive torso. 'Yes,' I said with aggression, thinking she was some variety of religious nutter.

'I am Valerie O'Hare,' the woman answered in a thick Irish accent. 'I would welcome the opportunity to speak to you about a matter of considerable importance. You may call me Mrs O'Hare.'

Taken aback, I stood to one side allowing Mrs O'Hare to skip nimbly by me. We stood in my sitting room strewn with the Sunday papers and empty coffee cups. If she noticed the mess she gave no indication. 'It has come to my attention,' she began immediately, 'that posing as some laddie from the boon docks, in January this year you called on a London-based investment company, the principal partner of which is Mr Godfrey Ladler father of an SIS colleague of yours, Frederick Ladler. Please tell me why you did that.'

I don't know what stunned me more – the knowledge she had or the audacity with which she presented it. 'Who the fuck are you?' I asked angrily.

As a precaution against my anger getting the better of me, Mrs O'Hare retorted, 'Don't get any ideas of throwing me into the street sonny boy. My driver would just love to be summoned here in doors to belt the living tripe out of you.' I looked out the window but could see no car. 'He's a young tough and he's no more than five minutes away,' she cautioned.

Still standing but now more measured, Mrs O'Hare said, 'I represent a group of people who have suffered untold harm at the hands of the British Government. We have a global network of like-minded friends. One of our allies heard about your antics, your supposed interest in investing in Zimbabwe, and let us know. But they had no details other than your alias. After a little detective work about which I won't bore you, we found it was you who made the approach and subsequently came across the Frederick Ladler link. We know the identity of many SIS officers. A simple check of our records confirmed Ladler is a colleague of yours.'

Mrs O'Hare was now comfortable enough to sit down. 'It's as plain as day Mr Lambert you are up to some sort of shenanigans and this is not part of your official work. A decision was made to assist you achieve your objective provided the outcome involves a black eye for the British Government.'

'No doubt this act of kindness was decided on by the Provos in a safe house up the Shankill Road,' I said sarcastically.

'Something like that,' she responded, seemingly confirming she was working for the Irish nationalists, but then adding with caustic derision and a twisted face to match, 'to be sure, to be sure.'

My head was spinning. Sitting in my living room was a woman who appeared to be telling me the IRA was here to help, while simultaneously seeming to resent me assuming she was IRA. And in any event, why would the IRA want to help me? If not IRA, who was she? Mrs O'Hare could see I was struggling to make sense of it all. 'Let me make you a cup of tea,' she said. As she did, I made the decision to tell her I thought Freddie Ladler was mixed up in a pro-white Rhodesian group and wanted to make enquiries before going to the Service chiefs. But Mrs O'Hare was no pushover. 'Joe, Joe,' she said, as if my great aunt, 'what was going to Phoenix Investments supposed to tell you about that? Stop playing games and let us help you. Otherwise this whole damnable thing will blow up in your face.'

Many things flashed through my mind. But most of all I thought of Boris in Jakarta all those years ago and my private condemnation of him for not showing more spirit. But now I understood why he had rolled over as easily as he did, despite the awful feeling I was about to dig myself into a hole I would never get out of. Like Boris, I was boxed in. The siren call of capitulation was overpowering, in my case in the face of this obviously informed woman who would not and could not be deflected.

I spoke so softly I could hardly hear myself. 'I wanted to discredit Frederick Ladler for personal reasons – I wanted him out of the running for a particular position I am after. Ladler has responsibility for intelligence gathering on Zimbabwe. My first instinct was to paint him as politically motivated, wanting to help overthrow the Mugabe Government. But Mugabe's making such a hash of things, I didn't want anyone in the Service actually giving Ladler credit for going out on a limb to assist Mugabe's political opponents. I decided I could be sure of discrediting him only if he was seen to be using his position for personal gain. That's where his father's company came in.'

'I see,' Mrs O'Hare said. 'Tell me, what position is involved?'

'Head of SIS station, Washington,' I heard myself say.

'And the reason?' Mrs O'Hare asked. 'Why are you so keen to do Ladler in the neck, Joseph?'

Mrs O'Hare's question and her use of the longer version of my name ignited a spark of irritation within me. It was as if she was a priest taking my confession. The perceived religious connotation upset me – for much the same reason that Agnes's parents had upset me when suggesting we go and pray for Agnes; my lasting self-censure for once briefly thinking my relationship travails were religiously bound to my mother's death.

Resentment stoked my failing resolve. Anything to do with avenging Agnes, I decided, would remain in my confidence. 'Ladler,' I said, 'is a privileged prat who thinks people of my background don't deserve to be in the Service. He is desperate to become Washington station head. I wanted to take the position instead of him.' Mrs O'Hare's eyes focused on me as she listened intently. 'I intended to show Ladler was prepared to assist white Rhodesians, or Zimbabweans if you prefer, regain power because of the economic benefits to his family. My plan was to feed a sniff of this to the tabloid press and let it do the rest. That would have put the bastard back in his box and opened up the Washington job to me at his expense. But after visiting Phoenix Investments I found it had no ties to Zimbabwe on which to base the suggestion.'

Mrs O'Hare did not press the point. Instead she removed an envelope from her oversized handbag and held it in the air. 'We do have some clever people. The essence of your plan to publicly link Frederick Ladler to conservative white Rhodesia was a popular theory among our thinkers, even if the reason why was not clear. That is why I brought this with me.' Opening the envelope, she produced a newspaper clipping dated 17 June 1979. The caption below the photograph dominating the article was written in Portuguese. Someone had attached an English language translation: *Pictured at a recent private party marking the opening of the Jardin Verde shopping centre on Avenue Duarte Pacheco in downtown Lisbon are the developer, Mr Francisco Pinto Silva and Mr*

Frederick Ladler, Minister at the British Embassy. I studied the picture of a smiling Freddie Ladler warmly shaking hands with a swarthy individual, a half-smoked cigarette insolently hanging out of the man's mouth.

'Silva was an active participant in Portugal's busting of Rhodesia sanctions,' Mrs O'Hare said. 'He started as a rent-seeker but grew to hate the black Rhodesians because they stood between him and his business objectives. Silva was imprisoned in Lisbon for two years from 1971 to 1973 on fraud charges and while incarcerated recruited followers to his cause.' In spite of my stress and confusion, I laughed to myself. Here was Freddie Ladler freshly arrived in Lisbon and out and about trying to work out who was who in the zoo. Somehow this Silva character had got his hooks into Freddie before he had time to realize he shouldn't be seen associating with this racist crook, especially in public.

I started to speak but Mrs O'Hare held up her hand. 'Your inclination to discredit Frederick through his family was sound enough. But you were looking at the wrong side of the family. Frederick's mother, Coral, has a half-brother going by the name of Jeremy Waller. Waller is the name of her mother's second husband. Hence the connection with the Ladlers via Coral's maiden name of Howlston-Brown is not obvious. Waller is a vocal supporter of Ian Smith and all Smith stands for. There is considerable publicly available evidence that Waller and his cronies support subjugation of the blacks and the restoration of white rule in Rhodesia.'

'Well a bit bloody late to be telling me this now,' I said resentfully.

'Despite Jeremy's extremism,' Mrs O'Hare continued, ignoring me, 'he hasn't been completely disowned by Godfrey Ladler and family. Coral forbids it. She apparently holds to Christian principles and thinks blood is thicker than water. Jeremy, therefore, still gets invites to birthday parties and other assorted soirees. From what we understand, Godfrey, Frederick and the other children tolerate the arrangement under sufferance. This will change when the whole world comes to know about Jeremy's familial ties to the Ladler clan, including that he is Frederick's dearly beloved uncle.' She chortled briefly at the thought.

'The fact you found no evidence to support your economic benefit story,' Mrs O'Hare said, 'matters not. The political aspect will work just fine. The photograph with Silva is important grist to the mill where the family link between Waller and Frederick is concerned. People will note Frederick's conservative background and choose not to believe in coincidence. The separate Silva and Waller associations each will reinforce the other's perception that he is indelibly linked to people who couldn't give a tinker's cuss about the welfare of black Zimbabweans. Now that you've confirmed our suspicions, we'll make sure the whole world knows about Frederick, his racist uncle and the criminal black-hater Silva. I can assure you once the tabloids are finished no one will be thinking Frederick is a sainted soul wanting to do right by Zimbabwe.'

Mrs O'Hare paused and looked at me with narrowed eyes. 'I now want you to listen closely to what I have to say next.'

'OK,' I said, perversely intrigued by what was to come.

'The story about Ladler will break in the press on Wednesday next week. Two days later, that is the following Friday, you will get a telephone call at work at 3.30 pm. The call will be routed through from the Foreign Office. The caller will be a man called Cuthberson. He will tell you he has a document to give you. You will arrange to meet him that evening. When you do, Cuthberson will explain how it is he has the document. Take careful note of what he says; you will need to tell your superiors all about this.'

'Is this really necessary?' I said irritably. 'Why can't you just get the bloody thing from him and give it to me. And anyway what's so important about it?'

'If you allow me I will explain,' Mrs O'Hare said reprovingly. 'A second press leak would be too blunt, too choreographed and suggestive of orchestration. Thinking minds would focus on this and not the document's content. Your giving it to your Service gives it gravitas. This subtlety will cause your people to take the document at face value and treat it seriously. For that reason, how you come to take possession of it will be the subject of intense scrutiny. Obtaining the document by the means described will survive that examination. It is essential you receive it from Cuthberson.'

'If you say so,' I replied superciliously.

'I do say so,' Mrs O'Hare said firmly. 'The document Cuthberson will give you is the minutes from a meeting of a now defunct group known as WRR – standing for White Rule for Rhodesia – held in Bexly, South London in May 1979 a month after Rhodesia's last pre-independence election. The minutes show WRR passed a resolution calling for Ian Smith's reinstatement as Rhodesian Prime Minister, Smith having been replaced after the April election by a stooge, a black cleric called Bishop Muzorewa. WRR's politics are not important and make no sense anyway; everyone knew Smith was still calling the shots. The important thing is the list of attendees. One you will find will be Jeremy Waller. Oh ... and it may aid your quest to be posted to Washington to point out to your superiors another attendee was a Mr Reggie Sullivan, one of your colleagues also I believe.'

Mrs O'Hare checked her watch and declared it was time she left. I sat there bewildered after she had gone. So many questions flowed through my head. I had a stiff drink and thought hard. I didn't know much about the IRA but doubted it had the intelligence network to pull in all the information this mad Irish woman had thrown at me. And to boot, the woman seemed very unhappy to be labelled IRA. Surely it was some sort of trap? I convinced myself it was a Service operation aimed at getting me to confess, something I had done meekly notwithstanding my reticence about avenging Agnes. I was sure I was dead meat, a carcass swinging in the breeze.

I waited for the knock on the door and Special Branch's command to lie on the floor and not move. But nothing happened. I drank some more. Midnight. Nothing moved. *Maybe they're coming for me at 4am,* I thought, *that's when a person's resistance is reputedly at its lowest ebb.* Sleep was impossible, even with half a bottle of whisky on board. Two am became three and then four. Nothing. I fell asleep on the couch. At 6 am I stirred. I made a cup of coffee. Convinced I would be arrested on arrival at the office, I shaved and showered. 'Time to face the music, Joe old son,' I said to myself as I headed out.

The janitors gave me a cheery welcome. En-route to my office, people I passed in the corridor wished me good morning. One of my directors poked his head in to ask how was my weekend. I looked and felt like shit. 'A bout of food poisoning,' I told him. 'Bloody takeaway curry.' He commiserated. Reggie Sullivan appeared at my door and the sight of him startled me. I retained just enough composure to sell him the food poisoning line, triggering a Reggie diatribe about Asian immigrants. It was a long day. I went home smack on the official finishing time of 5 pm.

'Get some rest,' someone shouted as I left.

On the train home I tried to fathom if the Irish woman could possibly be genuine. But an old truism dominated my thoughts: *If it's too good to be true it probably is*. And even were she for real, would the IRA settle for temporarily embarrassing the British Government or would it want something more, something from me?

Mrs O'Hare had stopped at a phone box a respectable distance from my house after leaving that Sunday afternoon. From there she rang a number in Ilford where her KGB controller waited. A summary of her report was flashed to *our source* in Moscow. It indicated that Raven, to use Mrs O'Hare's work name, had advised the successful completion of the first phase. The report also conveyed that my stated objective in visiting Phoenix Investments was to discredit Frederick Ladler because he thought me socially unworthy of being an SIS officer. To that end, Raven reported, I wanted to deny Ladler the head of SIS station, Washington position and rub salt in the wound by taking it myself. The report concluded by citing Raven's expressed expectation I would be OK by Friday, when the second phase was to occur.

Our source said Raven was a contractor. He explained the logic behind using her was to give the approach to me a readily identifiable anti-British organizational context. This gave it credibility. 'Without the IRA pretext,' *our source* said, 'Lambert's mind might have wandered. Shukhov and I had agreed this would risk Operation Citadel's compromise, either by him not taking the bait or worse suspecting that Raven was working for the KGB.'

When told Mrs O'Hare had nearly given the game away by displaying her distaste for pretending to be IRA, *our source* dryly noted she had obviously spared her controller this when reporting. Mrs O'Hare was a mercenary, he said, pure and simple. She had never held a sectarian brief for either side of the Irish troubles. But her father had been very pro-Unionist. After he was murdered by the IRA, she came to hate it albeit for personal rather than political reasons. 'It took a lot of persuading,' *our source* admitted, 'but eventually she did reluctantly agree to adopt the IRA cover. In hindsight it was probably a mistake to use her. But people with her skills were not to be found on every street corner.'

Chapter 29 – Scandal

I spent most of Monday evening lying on the couch pondering my situation. One half of my brain was telling me to confess to the Service before my circumstances became even more precarious; the other was arguing I owed Agnes and urging me to carry on. Overarching all of this was the pending IRA intervention. If Mrs O'Hare were on the level the hares would truly run on Wednesday when the tabloids went for Ladler. If she were not, I wasn't sure.

Was it an IRA blackmail play? *Unlikely*, I thought. I was no use as an SIS mole. The Service's Irish Affairs Branch was a discrete unit, comprising mostly military types adept at weapons use and paramilitary tasking. I was as remote from the Irish sub-Service as the clerk who clipped my ticket at Waterloo Station. I wondered what else it could be. Earlier thoughts resurfaced of Mrs O'Hare being a player in a Service op against me. Was the Wednesday deadline set to give me a chance to come in of my own volition?

I slept Monday night with one eye open waiting for a knock on my door, which never came. Badly sleep deprived, but at least without a throbbing hangover, I staggered into the office on Tuesday morning. Everything and everyone seemed normal. But there again the Service was full of good poker players. I had two cups of strong black coffee and actually made inroads into my backlogged in-tray.

By lunchtime, however, I could no longer occupy my mind and was in a state of heightened anxiety. Time was running out. If I was going to own up to the Service, I needed to do so before the end of the working day. I studied the photograph of Agnes I carried in my wallet, the one her mother gave me. Past memories overpowered me. Agnes was the only woman I had ever loved, the only woman for whom my affection continued to outweigh my debilitating loner instincts. She was the *real deal*, exactly as Nought had identified. I couldn't let her murder slide by, not when it had been my fault. At 6 pm I went home. From tomorrow there could be no turning back.

Again no sleep. Again no knock on my door. I rose at 4.30 am and turned on the radio to listen to the 5 am BBC news. No reports of any scandals. I accepted then Mrs O'Hare was the Service's stalking horse. Fretting I would be denied what I needed to do and resigned to what was to come, I paid scant attention to the 6 am bulletin. Thus when the words *scandal* and *government* emanating from the radio permeated my fug, I wasn't sure what I was hearing. I rushed out of the house. The newsagent's shop was still in darkness. I waited impatiently for the 6.30 am opening time advertised on the door in gold lettering. The newsagent arrived seven minutes late, yawning and unenthused. I watched him through the shop window as he began slowly unwrapping bundles of newspapers he brought in from the shop's rear entrance. He looked up and smiled a weary smile when I opened the main entrance door, ringing the customer alert bell. 'Won't be a moment, sir,' he said.

I fixed on the unopened bundles of papers in the manner that a hungry lion sizes up an intended kill. Only with the greatest of willpower did I restrain myself from attacking them. I pretended to peruse the magazines, while internally screaming at the newsagent to hurry up. Finally, the papers were on the shelves. I scanned them at speed. The *UK News* and *The Examiner* went hardest, both carrying the story in screaming, red-bannered front-page headlines.

I bought both papers and rushed back up the road into a doorway where I could read them without being too obvious. *Our Spies secretly working for Smith* was one front-page headline; *Racist link to UK intelligence* led the other. Both papers prominently featured the words *alleged* and *unnamed sources*. None too subtly each portrayed Ladler as a white supremacist holding to WRR objectives, emphasizing his family ties to Waller and reproducing part of a rancorous letter that, in a WRR capacity, Waller had written to *The Times* in early 1979. Seamlessly, much mischief was made of Ladler's photograph with Silva and Silva's sanction-busting activities. Readers were then apprised that Ladler was *understood* to be an SIS officer with oversight for gathering intelligence on Zimbabwe, nakedly invited the deduction he was using his position in aid of racist white Rhodesia. It was skilfully done, even if the tabloids had a lot of experience when it came to character assassination. Paying lip service to balance, both publications noted the Foreign Secretary had been unavailable for comment. I returned home and readied for the office. 'Remember,' I sternly instructed myself, 'act surprised by the news. Like everyone else will be, not least Freddie Ladler.'

The lights were on up on the fifth floor when I arrived. Virtually everyone I saw seemed to be carrying a tabloid newspaper. I saw Martin Mumford about to hop in the lift, heading for the fifth floor. He looked grim and tired, no doubt having been awoken in the early morning. But he was calm and measured at the same time; made of the right stuff our Martin. He held open the lift door as I was about to walk by. 'Been meaning to thank you for your letter at the start of the year, Joe. Much appreciated. It's times like this you wonder whether getting promoted is worth it.' But he smiled and winked while saying it. I knew then for sure I was in the clear, for now. *God knows where this rollercoaster will end,* I thought, shuddering at the possibilities.

Foreign Secretary Howe refused to comment. His press secretary told enquiring media to do so would only dignify the fatuous nonsense that had been printed. In the end, as the press continued to bay, the Government Press Office issued a low-key statement. The announcement's untroubled tone belied the welter of frantic activity behind the scenes during the course of the day. The statement formally refuted the allegations as unfounded speculation and indicated the Foreign Secretary's full confidence in Ladler. Nor did it concede that Freddie worked for the SIS, referring to him only as a senior and valued member of Her Majesty's diplomatic corps.

The DG had then quietly moved Ladler to the Service's training branch. 'Just temporarily, for a couple of weeks,' I believe the DG told Ladler. Then everyone settled back and waited for the matter to blow over.

The relief I felt on realizing the Service was not behind Mrs O'Hare's visit was short-lived. I now had the IRA, or whomever it was, to manage around. My ambition was to cope with whatever demands were made of me long enough to find Agnes's murderer and take retribution. Provided this was achieved, nothing else mattered.

In the absence of any other explanation for its hatchet job on Ladler and what was about to follow, I tentatively concluded the IRA had opted for a fox in the henhouse type of strategy. The Government and Service had dismissed the newspaper allegations against Ladler for the patent nonsense they were. Without more, the matter would quickly fade from memory. But evidence forty-eight hours later of another senior Service officer, Reggie Sullivan, with ties to a ratty white supremacist group linked to Rhodesia would have the fifth floor beginning to second guess itself. The focus would be on a possible pro-white Rhodesia cell within the Service. I guessed the IRA's objective was to send the Service on a wild goose chase, hoping it would waste time and money trying to run the matter to ground and fall into tension with Whitehall in the process. Beyond burdening the Service with this relatively minor inconvenience, any outcome from the strategy likely to seriously damage the British Government escaped me. I metaphorically shrugged; presumably the IRA knew what it was doing.

I also took as incidental to the perceived IRA strategy the benefits befalling me: the praise coming my way from the Service for uncovering the minutes and Reggie Sullivan's connection to the WRR zealots; and the reviving in Service minds of the question marks that, courtesy of the press allegations, had briefly hovered over Ladler. After all, the IRA had no substantive interest in my wish to deny Ladler the Washington posting by taking it myself. Yet on the facts as I understood them, I benefitted more than the IRA. I was puzzled but reasoned I did not have the full story.

In any event, I was not about to look a gift horse in the mouth. Should everything be allowed to quieten, Ladler would return from his temporary exile and re-assume pole position in the race for appointment as head of Washington station. The second intervention potentially offered a slight loosening of his grip on the Washington job. And unearthing the minutes might also hopefully mean my task of gaining promotion just got that little bit easier. My attention turned to the telephone call I was to receive on Friday.

Chapter 30 – Cuthberson

At 3.35 pm on Friday, my telephone rang. It was the Foreign Office switchboard. 'Mr Lambert,' the operator said, 'I have a Mr Cuthberson on the line for you.'

A click was followed by silence and then a weedy voice spoke. 'My name is Garrick Cuthberson,' he said. 'I was given your name by Anthony Delminico.' The name *Delminico* was familiar but I couldn't place it. Cuthberson jogged my memory. 'I understand you and Anthony worked together in an embassy in the Far East.' Then I recalled – Flight Sergeant Delminico had been attached to the office of the Air Attaché during the last year of my posting to Jakarta. Occasionally he was present when the station consulted the Attaché on matters of mutual interest. Delminico was much older than me but we were both junior-ranked and a bond of sorts developed between us. He knew my real status.

'Yes, yes that's true,' I said. 'How can I help you?'

Cuthberson was either a very good actor or genuinely nervous. 'I have a document I need give you. Anthony is now retired and lives in Brighton. I went to him initially and he advised me to hand it over to the Foreign Office. He gave me your name. That's why I'm ringing,' he added unnecessarily.

On the off chance the switchboard operator was listening, I strung Cuthberson on. 'Can you tell me what this is all about please?'

'I'd really rather not talk on the blower,' he replied.

I pretended to consider this. 'OK,' I said with an air of reluctance. 'I'll meet you at 6 pm in front of the WH Smith bookstore on the Strand. Please be punctual.'

'Yes Sir,' Cuthberson replied.

Cuthberson was waiting for me when I arrived. He wasn't hard to spot, and not only because he was the only person standing awkwardly in front of WH Smith with an expectant look on his face. He was also a rarity that in person he looked exactly like he sounded on the telephone – tall and gangly with a prominent Adam's apple. He gave me a manila folder from his backpack. I opened it to find the minutes of the WRR meeting as Mrs O'Hare had promised.

'Two questions,' I said. 'How did you get hold of this and why are you giving it to me?'

Cuthberson cleared his throat. He had practised for the queries. 'In 1979 I was in the RAF and posted to RAF Northolt. I clerked for the adjutant to Wing Commander James Battersy, the Squad Commander. Battersy's dead now by the way.'

Go on,' I said.

'Well one day Battersy comes in with a ream of handwritten notes and asks me to type them up – nice like. That's them,' he said pointing to the manila folder. I nodded to him to continue. 'Well, I ain't real bright but I knew what I was typing was the record of some sort of political meeting. I typed them on one of them new typewriters with a memory. After Battersy had gone, I printed out a copy. I've left the RAF now but have kept the papers for some reason.'

'OK,' I said, 'that's how, what about why?'

Cuthberson took some time to collect his thoughts. 'A week ago, last Friday night, I got a phone call from Jenny Delminico, Anthony's sister. Totally unexpected. I've never met her; never knew he had a sister, actually. Spoke like a Geordie. Said she was ringing on Anthony's behalf to ask if I still had a copy of the minutes I typed up in May '79. I said yeah, I have as a matter of fact. I asked her why she wanted to know. She said she couldn't answer that; she was just enquiring on behalf of Anthony.' I opened my mouth to speak but Cuthberson beat me to it. 'I had told Anthony about the minutes not long after I typed them and showed him the copy I had made. He didn't say much but I do recall him rolling his eyes and saying something like, "That fucking Battersy. The lazy sod." I wouldn't say Anthony was angry with me. He just warned me not to let on to Battersy about making a copy saying, "He'll kick your arse until your nose bleeds if you're not careful." Anthony never raised it with me again.'

Warming to his narrative, Cuthberson pressed on. 'Anyways like I say I kept the copy. Dunno why; just being bolshie towards Battersy probably. Put it away in my service trunk. For years now haven't even given them papers a second's thought. It was only when Jenny rang that I remembered I had 'em. She says ring Anthony on this number on Wednesday afternoon and he'll explain why he now has an interest in the minutes. Then at lunchtime Wednesday I was up the High Road and seen the *Examiner*. I shit myself. I thought fucking hell, the stuff in the newspaper is on the same gunk the minutes are on about and here I have Jenny ringing me about them. I ring Anthony, quickish-like. I like him. He was the senior NCO – you know, non-commissioned officer – in my squad when we were both working for Battersy.'

'I'm listening,' I said.

'Anthony's ill – heart or something like that. He told me he couldn't get involved but insisted I give the minutes to someone before I got into trouble. Ordered me, really. He didn't say why I'd get into trouble but I knew never to question Anthony. He gave me your name and the Foreign Office telephone number.'

'Tell me,' I said, 'why did you ring this afternoon and not Wednesday afternoon, yesterday or this morning for that matter?'

Cuthberson looked at me, puzzled. 'Well it were you who asked to be called at half three today, weren't it?'

'But we've never spoken before today.'

'Yeah, that's true. But Jenny rang again, ten minutes after I'd spoken to Anthony, this time to tell me when you wanted me to call.' With that, Cuthberson started walking away. His intuition was sending him warning signals. He was scared and wanted out.

'How do I contact you?' I called. He made a shrugging motion as he walked but didn't turn or answer. I watched him disappear into the night.

I walked along the Strand to my old stamping ground of the Strand Castle Hotel. Sitting in the saloon bar, I nursed a whisky, ice and soda as I tried to distil Cuthberson's explanation. The facts were this: the IRA, for want of a better name, had learned from Anthony Delminico that Cuthberson possibly had a copy of the incriminating minutes; someone pretending to be Anthony's sister confirmed he did; that same someone also arranged for Cuthberson to call Anthony so as to be given my name; and shortly after, the same woman instructed Cuthberson when to call me to ensure that, as the IRA intended, the Service became aware of the minutes forty-eight hours after the initial Ladler allegations. Delminico's pretend sister with the supposed Geordie accent was part of the O'Hare group of this I was sure, almost certainly Mrs O'Hare herself.

But there were at least four other questions requiring answers. One easily guessed at was how did the IRA know about the minutes? Like every other amateur hour, ragtag group the WRR would have been a security shambles. There could be no doubt that many persons, IRA agents included, would have had access to its documents. Indeed, it would not have surprised me if secreted away in the Police Special Branch files gathering dust was the very document I was about to spring on my Service superiors.

But what made the minutes so important? I decided the IRA must have found smoke on Ladler at some point past, seemingly prompting it to think about using what it had against him. And on discovering the WRR minutes containing the names of Jeremy Waller and Reggie Sullivan, I supposed it judged this particular set of minutes to be the ideal complement. With that, the IRA's fox in the henhouse strategy to distract the Service had presumably been born. The decision on timing, to have the minutes surface forty-eight hours after the publication of the original dross on Ladler, was probably the final plank in their planning.

But why rely on me giving the minutes to the Service? What happened if I dug in my toes and refused to cooperate? I recalled Mrs O'Hare saying that prior to her visit to my home her *thinkers* had made an educated guess my strategy was publicly to link Freddie Ladler to racist white Rhodesia. I decided the IRA's analysts had calculated, subject to confirming this intention, I would go along with delivering the minutes to the Service. It seemed high-risk to me. But the IRA apparently believed my handing over of the minutes was necessary to generate the gravitas supposedly required for the Service to take them seriously.

Unanswered though was the question of the link between the IRA and Anthony Delminico. How did they find him? Did he act voluntarily or were the frighteners put on him? And crucially why did he direct Cuthberson to me? The simple solution would be to contact Delminico and ask him. I now wished I had asked Cuthberson for Delminico's telephone number.

Chapter 31 – Delminico

I returned to the office and rummaged around until I found the Brighton telephone book. There were two *A Delminicos* listed. I rang the first number. A man answered. 'Siapa nama Anda?' I said.

Silence. Then a haughty voice said, 'I have no idea what you are talking about, whatever it is you want.'

'Sorry,' I apologized, 'it seems I have the wrong number.'

I rang the second number. A male voice said, 'Hello.' I could feel the tension coming down the phone line. I knew then it was Delminico. Nonetheless, I also asked this man his name using the same Indonesian phrase. He laughed softly and replied, 'Nama saya Anthony. Thought I might be hearing from you.'

'So, what's the story?' I asked. 'Best you spit it out because my employer is going to want answers when I show them this document I received earlier tonight from you know who.'

Delminico said he understood. I heard the shuffling of papers.

'Battersy,' Delminico said, knowing that Cuthberson would have told me about him, 'was a madman. Very right wing politically. Racist. Hated the black Africans in particular. He was always trying to get RAF colleagues to go to events on the pretext they were gatherings of old flyers, when they were actually political meetings in support of that white politician fellow out in Southern Africa who flew for the RAF in the war. I only got sucked in once. Battersy was an officer and I was an NCO; he more or less ordered me to go even though he shouldn't have. Unfortunately, I didn't have the backbone or the means to leave immediately I twigged what was going on. Battersy had driven me there for that reason. So I just got pissed on the free beer.'

'That's fine,' I said, 'but it doesn't explain why you set that long streak of misery on me.'

'About a fortnight ago I had a visit from a fellow named Kelvin Fullerton. Showed me his South African passport. Kelvin said he was trying to find a cousin of his named Geoffrey Fullerton, whose mother was about to expire at some great age. Her dying wish was to see her son again. Geoffrey had been wild and headstrong and had lost touch with other family members several years ago after moving to England. The only person Kelvin knew of who might have been able to help trace him was James Battersy. Geoffrey was apparently an associate of Battersy's. But Battersy was dead. Someone had suggested that Battersy's former RAF colleagues might be able to help. I had served under Battersy in number 32 Squadron and Kelvin found me from RAF records.'

'So Kelvin's found you. What then?'

Delminico cleared his throat. 'Kelvin confided in me that Battersy had politically influenced Geoffrey. The two had been active in a London-based organization supporting white rule in Rhodesia. It was all very embarrassing, but if I was able to point him to any RAF person who had been an associate of Battersy's, particularly anyone who might have also been with the same organization, that could open up fresh leads. I wasn't nimble enough in my brain. I should have said I knew nothing about the group or anyone linked to it. But Kelvin seemed a nice chap and I did recall silly Garrick once showing me a copy of minutes he'd typed up of a political meeting Battersy chaired. I gave Kelvin Garrick's name, wished him good luck and thought that was the end of it.'

Delminico paused to sip something, water presumably. I also heard the turning of a page. I wondered if I was jumping at shadows by thinking he was very well organized – speaking notes seemingly prepared and glasses of water by his side. The water tumbler was set down on a wooden table and Delminico continued. 'But on Monday this week Kelvin reappeared. He said he had an odd request but there was 1,000 quid in it for me. My RAF pension has been considerably eroded by inflation; I was interested, but cautious. I said, "Tell me what you want and I'll decide." '

'And what did Kelvin ask and what did you decide?' I said, trying to hurry Delminico along.

'Kelvin said something about the newspapers going ballistic on Wednesday with a story on Rhodesia. Told me to expect a call from Garrick regarding the minutes of a meeting on Rhodesia Garrick had in his possession. I knew that Kelvin meant the minutes Garrick had typed for Battersy. Kelvin said, "Tell Garrick to give the minutes to the Foreign Office before he gets into trouble. Your RAF records show you once worked in the British embassy in Jakarta. You will know a suitable Foreign Office person you can direct him to." When I asked the obvious questions, all Kelvin would say was he was assisting the police on a confidential matter relating to the minutes.'

'And?'

'I told him to fuck off,' Delminico said. 'The whole thing was far too strange for my liking, more like your line of work. But he just gave me the FO telephone number as if I had said *yes*. All I had to do was tell Garrick to ring the FO and give him a name and the number. Then I could say I had health issues and I'd be cut out of the loop. When I told him *no go* again, he was not so friendly anymore; got nasty in fact. Said if I didn't comply I'd be putting my family at risk. I live alone since my wife died. All I have is my kids; they're my life. I'm not as strong as I used to be and couldn't risk putting them or their families in harm's way. So reluctantly I agreed. You must understand I was scared stiff, for the kids and grandkids not myself. I felt I had no option. Thinking back to my time in Jakarta, your name came to mind in the circumstances.'

Delminico seemed to be crying. I wasn't sure. His extra-loud sniffling sounded fake to me. 'So you took the grand and did what he asked.' It was a statement not a question.

'Yeah,' Delminico whispered.

'OK,' I said, 'let's leave it there. Someone from the office will be down to see you in due course. You may need to make a formal statement to the plods, I really don't know at this point.'

'Night Joe,' he said, and hung up.

The immediate effect of Delminico's version of events was to draw my mind to a droll joke currently doing the rounds. The set-up question was: *What's the difference between the IRA and Dublin Gas?* The punch line answer was: *The IRA gives a three-minute warning.* I was not drawn to the joke's dark humour, far from it. I was drawn to its subtext – that the IRA relied on publicity to achieve its political objectives. In other words, the IRA did not deal in non-attributable outcomes, much less the subtlety of which Mrs O'Hare had spoken. On the contrary, being openly known as a threat to public safety was its stock in trade. But the IRA had not bothered to claim responsibility for the earlier Ladler material. And now, in channelling the minutes through me, it was forsaking the opportunity to build, with or without attribution, on this initial embarrassment of the UK Government. The Service would deal with the minutes privately as it did every other internal problem, irrespective of how much gravitas my handing them over engendered. Yet Delminico had just detailed the hoops the IRA had jumped through – the planning, the expense, the risks. Where was the corresponding benefit? The Service inconvenience angle no longer cut it.

I realized then that Delminico's confession had told me two things. It had confirmed once and for all that Mrs O'Hare was not IRA. And it had also revealed there was something else, something obscure and undoubtedly sinister behind the O'Hare group's determination that I furnish the Service with the minutes. But why the group should want this I had now not the remotest idea. There were no fairies at the bottom of the garden. The thought that the exercise was intended for my benefit simply didn't enter my head.

The mystery of it all caused me to reflect on my conversation with Delminico. There is a rule good spies follow when building cover, or legends as the romantics like to call it: stick as close to the truth as possible and deviate only when necessary. Delminico appeared to have adopted the same approach. I suspected he was intimidated by this Battersy maniac, as reflected in his warning to Cuthberson, and had attended more WRR meetings than he liked to admit. Whoever the O'Hare group was, they had likely found Delminico's name regularly appearing in the WRR records and come to know he had served with me in Jakarta. With that, Delminico self-selected as the lynchpin in the group's mission to have me personally deliver the minutes to the Service. Delminico had admitted to accepting a 1,000 pound bribe, under duress allegedly, to direct the minutes to the Foreign Office. It was not hard to imagine him agreeing for the same consideration to voluntarily direct the minutes to me.

But Delminco's cover story meant he could not plausibly hold a copy of the minutes. He had to find a credible conduit to me. That being so, it was no significant leap of faith to conclude Delminico had proposed Cuthberson as the credible conduit, subject to the O'Hare group confirming Garrick still had his copy of the minutes. Delminico had tacitly admitted this; telling me he had alerted Kelvin to Cuthberson and how Kelvin on his return visit had effectively confirmed Cuthberson's possession of the document. Garrick was the ideal choice. His ingrained RAF training guaranteed he would obediently follow any instruction from Delminico, his former senior NCO; and his explanation for having the minutes was watertight.

Equally, though, I knew that unless I'd badly misjudged Delminico his story would collapse under expert questioning. I was sure Kelvin from South Africa – whom I later learned was Irish and, as suspected, part of the O'Hare group – was the alias used by the man who had approached Delminico with the offer of the bribe. But

I doubted very much *Kelvin* had pedalled a long lost cousin story. That was a secondary concern. More worrying was Delminico's line he had chosen me at random to be the recipient of the minutes. Once the fiction was revealed, the Service would want to know why Delminico had been instructed to direct Cuthberson to come to me. It was no consolation that I might get away with it by playing dumb when the investigators set on me. Being specially chosen to receive the minutes would preclude my promotion and snuff out any hope I had of gaining the Washington station head appointment.

My nerves were jangling when after completing one more urgent task I rang Martin Mumford at his home.

'Martin there's something I think you need know about tonight. Unfortunately, it's not possible to go to Reggie.'

Mumford was typically unflustered. 'Should I come to the office?' he asked.

'I'm in a position to come to you,' I replied. 'Probably best we do it that way.'

'Sure thing,' he said. 'See you shortly.' I liked the way he was prepared to rely on my judgement.

Chapter 32 – Reggie

Martin lived in Wimbledon, in Somerset Road close to the famous tennis stadium. It was a lovely area but how he and his family put up with the crowds each year during those two weeks in July was anyone's guess. Tonight, however, that was the last thing on my mind as my taxi wound its way to his home. Martin perused the minutes at speed. I didn't need to point out Reggie's name; his raised eyebrows told me he had seen it. 'Right,' Martin said, 'from the very top. Tell me how you came to be given this document.' I ran through the conversations with Cuthberson and Delminico in detail. I made no mention of the suspicions I had about Delminico, or of him apparently having prepared notes. It was nearly 11 pm by the time Martin had stopped asking questions. 'I think we should pay Reggie a visit, right now,' he said. 'Then depending on how things turn out I might need to brief the Old Man.' I could see Martin was wary of more press allegations appearing overnight and wanted to be sure the DG was up to speed. I had anticipated this and made preparations before calling Mumford.

Reggie Sullivan lived in a modest home in Fulham. Cheap houses were the means by which civil servants and other members of the middle classes managed to live in such posh suburbs without over capitalizing. I had never been to Reggie's house. But Martin clearly had because he drove there through a bewildering number of side streets. On the way he told me he would prefer I wasn't there, me being Reggie's subordinate. But it was getting late and he couldn't interview Reggie without a witness. It took a little time to rouse Reggie. Eventually, a light went on upstairs. Martin smiled at me as the sound of footsteps walking down stairs could be heard on the still night air. 'I hope Reggie hasn't been sucking too hard on the gin bottle,' he said drily.

Reggie was in pyjamas with a dressing gown tied loosely around him. His scowl evaporated when his sleepy eyes finally told his brain it was Martin Mumford standing before him. He ushered us into the sitting room, glancing at me with barely concealed irritation. Mumford spoke the instant we were all seated. He thrust the minutes at Reggie. 'Reggie, what can you tell me about this meeting you apparently attended?'

Reggie looked at the document now in his hand trying to understand what it was. He retrieved a pair of reading glasses from a side table and stroked his chin as he read. 'Yes, yes, I do recall this event. What a bunch of inconsequential no-hopers.' He placed the minutes on the coffee table in front of him and looked Mumford squarely in the eye. 'You'll have seen a fellow called James Battersy chaired the meeting. I served in the RAF with Jimmy for a number of years. He and I became friends of sorts having come through the system basically at the same time. We stayed in touch after I left the RAF and joined the Service. Jimmy was hyperactive;

it was no surprise to me when he died of a heart attack a couple of years back. He convinced me to go to this particular meeting,' Reggie said, nodding at the minutes. 'He said it would be a gathering of a few RAF mates and threw some familiar names about. When we got there, not one of the promised names was to be seen. I was right peeved and sat up the back taking no part in proceedings. I had no idea they were going to write me down as an attendee.'

I could tell Reggie was telling the truth. He pursed his lips to continue but Martin broke in. 'You were a Service officer at this point, Reggie, and this was a meeting of people actively working against government policy, however unimpressive they might have been. You knew the rules. You should have reported the incident.'

Reggie leant forward, his reclining leather lounge chair squealing in protest. He scratched the back of his head and looked hard at Mumford. 'So I should have, Martin,' he said ruefully, 'so I should have. But honestly, they were such a bunch of ...' He settled for shaking his head after struggling unsuccessfully to find a suitably pejorative adjective.

'I do accept it may have seemed trivial at the time,' Mumford said. 'But we have to presume the *UK News* and its fellow travellers will know you are Service. You know as well as me that with a little effort and friends in the right places, officers at FADG and above can usually be identified. Right now there's a risk of these rags leading their Saturday morning editions with salacious headlines similar to what we saw earlier in the week about Freddie Ladler. If this eventuates, the matter has the unfortunate consequence of building on Wednesday's effort to the point where it gives the whole beat-up some credibility.'

Reggie was crestfallen. 'I do understand, Martin,' he said, wringing his hands in anguish.

Mumford went on. 'Taken in isolation, Reggie, I would normally treat an indiscretion of this limited magnitude as something that could stay between you and me. But in the current circumstances, I do have to brief the DG tonight because of possible media fallout tomorrow. The DG's not going to be very pleased with you, or with me waking him up this time of night. Sorry, but that's what has to be done.' Reggie looked at the clock on the mantelpiece. It was now past midnight. He shuddered, bemused that after so long something so minor as this should rebound on him.

With that, we all sat in momentary contemplation. Then the still of the night was broken by the switching on of a light in the hallway behind a pair of closed frosted-glass sliding doors. Seconds later, the doors began to open. The design of the doors was such that the person opening them had to slide both doors apart using shallowly recessed handgrips. The effect was that for an instant, the person opening was obliged to stand in full view of any sitting room occupant with both arms fully extended.

Alerted by the switching on of the light, we were all looking up when the doors fully opened. Standing there, arms outstretched, was a small woman. With the light shining behind her, the nightgown she wore was rendered transparent. Through the diaphanous garment, I could clearly make out her firm breasts and the dark nipples appointing them, and below a wild bush of jet-black pubic hair. The stirring in my loins reminded me how long it had been since I was with a woman. Reggie was mortified. He jumped to his feet. 'For God's sake, Imelda,' he said, before shepherding the woman back into the hallway and closing the sliding doors behind him. A tense and hurried conversation could be heard. Then came the sound of the woman crying and Reggie in softer tones imploring her, 'Go back to bed, Immie, I'll be there shortly.'

Reggie re-entered the room. Bad had just become worse. If one subscribed to the trilogy of bad luck theory, a meteorite was about to hit Reggie's house. 'The maid,' he said simply, a hangdog look on his face. 'From the Philippines. Glenda's at her sister's.' Martin and I glanced at each other. We didn't speak but a clear communication passed between us. The message conveyed was that neither of us passed moral judgement on Reggie for shagging the maid while Mother was away. My tolerance, however, derived from knowing emptiness and loneliness within a marriage and appreciating in those circumstances the allure of the maid's firm young body. For Martin though, ever the pro, his concern was only for the Service. Morals and the Service were not comfortable bedfellows; indeed, morality was regularly discounted in Service councils. What had caught Martin's attention was that Reggie was having sex with a foreign national. It could be safely assumed he had not lodged a contact report declaring the liaison. Reggie, therefore, had placed himself in a position of vulnerability. His potential exposure to exploitation rendered the Service liable to risk.

Reggie stood there. I sat mute. We were both waiting for Martin to speak. Martin used the silence sublimely. For fully ten seconds he said nothing, signalling to Reggie his extreme displeasure. Then quietly he said, 'It's time for us to go, Reggie. We will talk later. But first I need to use your telephone if I might.'

'Certainly, Martin,' Reggie said, as if an obliging valet in a high-class hotel. Right arm outstretched, he squired Martin to the instrument sitting on a small mahogany table in the hallway.

Martin rang a number and waited patiently for it to be answered. A gruff voice could be heard to say, 'Hello.'

'Colin,' Martin began, it was strange to hear the DG, Sir Colin Jameson, being called by his Christian name, 'something has come up I'm afraid. I need to speak to you before the morning. Possible media and ministerial interest.' I didn't hear the muffled response. Martin replaced the receiver and to me said, 'Right, let's get going.' Without a backward glance at the hapless Reggie we left the house.

Martin addressed me while he drove, 'You'll need to wait in the car while I brief the chief.' I nodded. Whether he saw that in the dark didn't matter. It was an order.

'Martin,' I said, 'I anticipated that some defensive media points might be necessary. In the taxi to your place, I roughed out a few words for your consideration and possible use on an *As Needed* basis.' I had in fact written the points in the office after speaking to Delminico, but before calling Martin, knowing for certain by then they would not be necessary but nonetheless giving great care to their content. I was genuinely terrified by what was happening around me. But equally I was driven to take every opportunity to enhance my reputation with the Service bigwigs in order to counteract my show of indiscipline to the ADDG Richard Samson at the time of Agnes's death. The DG was my primary target but if I happened to impress Martin on the way through then well and good. It was all about building personal capital with them; positive memories they would store away for future retrieval as and when my name arose in one decisional context or other.

But if Martin was impressed he didn't show it. 'Let me have a look at them when we get to Kew Gardens,' was all he said.

We pulled up outside a large apartment block on Bushwood Road. The front of the block had views of the Thames and the back of Kew Gardens. I assumed the DG would be up the top somewhere and have a lovely vista, provided he ever had time to take it in. Mumford was gone only about twenty minutes. He'd clearly had a very direct conversation with the DG. He started the car. 'Where exactly in Brent Cross are you, Joe?' he asked. 'Time to get you home.' I made noises about getting there under my own steam. 'It's past one in the morning,' Martin said. 'If I left you to your own devices we'd never see you again.' He laughed at the suggestion. 'I need to brief you anyway. The DG liked your talking points. He thought they were very good for something drafted in the back of a taxi.' I disguised my pleasure at hearing this. I had been sure Martin would tell the DG the points were my own initiative but not so sure about them winning the DG's approval. 'The DG,' Martin continued, 'was about to brief the Minister's Chief of Staff as I left. I am to get Bill Rimmington and Special Branch people down to Brighton first thing this morning to quiz this Delminico fellow.'

My warm feeling evaporated. Rimmington was in charge of Service Internal Affairs. A former copper, his excessive politeness, steely gaze and extreme doggedness gave him something of a menacing air. Delminico wouldn't last ten minutes with him; Rimmington would then come looking for me. Martin was speaking again. 'Naturally, I told the DG about Reggie's undeclared attendance at the WRR meeting, and his liaison with the maid.' He paused to collect his thoughts or perhaps for emphasis, I wasn't sure. 'This is probably unnecessary for me to say, but to avoid any doubt I want you to understand whatever Reggie has been up to and what happens to him is none of your business. Got it? Not one peep from you, thank you.'

'Understood completely, Martin,' I replied. We drove on in silence. On reaching my house, Martin wished me goodnight. He said he would be in touch later on in the day.

I lay on my bed unable to sleep, wound up like a clockwork spring. 'Is it time to give up on all this, Aggie?' I said to the unused pillow next to me. 'I'm not sure I can cope with the strain.' I knew she would say *yes*, but only because she cared for me. I stroked the pillow. A surge of affection steeled me. *No,* I thought, *I've made my decision. That's it. That's final. I will never again question this course I've set myself on.* With the profound sense of this resolve setting in stone, my head immediately cleared and I slept.

Reminiscent of that awful night when I received the news Agnes had been killed, I was woken by the jangling telephone on my bedside table. It was Mumford. 'Joe, Delminico's dead. Suicide the Brighton police are saying. Single pistol shot under the chin.'

'Christ almighty,' I exclaimed with genuine surprise.
'Did he give you any hint he might do this?'

'No,' I said with honesty. 'I did tell him the cops were likely to interview him. He wasn't thrilled but seemed to accept it was going to happen. Christ … where would he have got the gun?'

'That and many other questions remain to be answered,' Martin replied. 'Come into the office in two hours' time; we'll have a council of war and see what it throws up.'

I now had a private car a two-door, light-blue Ford Anglia. I had bought it nearly six months ago because it was cheap and sufficient for my modest needs. Being Saturday, parking was available at the Service. I felt faintly ridiculous as the Anglia putted along towards Lambeth, unable to match it with the more powerful machines racing by. I reflected on the latest turn of events as I drove. I couldn't bring myself to believe Delminico had killed himself; assuredly it was the O'Hare group covering tracks. But as to what tracks I had no firm ideas. For now, though, I had to push these puzzling thoughts from my mind and focus on the attention that would be paid to me when I reached the office.

Mumford chaired our meeting. Other than me, Bill Rimmington and an off-sider were also present, as well as a taciturn woman from the Executive Support Unit, who would later brief the DG. A younger woman took notes. Rimmington opened the batting. 'Special Branch,' he said, 'had contacted the Sussex constabulary at

304

7 am, just on three hours ago. They had been instructed to pick up Delminico and hold him *voluntarily* at Brighton Crowhurst Police Station until Special Branch and I arrived to question him. When the police could not rouse Delminico, they forced entry. They found his body in the study. No sign of break and enter. The corpse is currently awaiting post mortem. Initial reports indicate he died of a single gunshot wound administered under the chin, the bullet exiting the top of his skull via the roof of his mouth. A Smith and Wesson pistol has been recovered and is undergoing forensic testing. Investigations are underway as to how Delminico came to be in possession of the gun. He was not the registered owner of it or any other weapon. Updates as available.'

Mumford asked if for the benefit of those present I would go through the events of last night, Friday 11 May 1984, up until the time I had called him. I was well rehearsed and smoothly delivered my spiel. I concluded by noting a connection between the two events of the past week was evident from the fact that a woman posing as Delminico's sister had contacted Garrick Cuthberson in the days before the story on Freddie Ladler broke. Clearly someone was orchestrating a campaign against the Service. Delminico had been key to unlocking the puzzle. With his death, the one lead we had as to who was pulling the strings was gone. My point in making these blindingly obvious observations was to prompt those assembled to think the story about Freddie Ladler ran deeper than first assumed. I could tell they all agreed something was up; they could hardly have thought differently.

My biggest headache was Rimmington. His copper's nose was fairly twitching. He was watching me; I could feel it, and his instincts were telling him my involvement wasn't as innocent as I was making out. Mumford asked for thoughts, as was his habit. 'Special Branch expects to pick up Garrick Cuthberson in the next couple of hours,' Rimmington said. This did not faze me; the O'Hare group's strategy relied on Cuthberson confirming my story.

I snuck another look at Rimmington. I reasoned my main point of vulnerability was whether anyone, such as a neighbour Rimmington might interview, had seen Mrs O'Hare come to my house. I could provide no ready-made alibi for such a visitor. But I had come to realize the choice of a little woman of advancing years was a canny one in that Mrs O'Hare presented benignly and was not someone readily recalled to mind. She was also a professional. On arrival, she had dwelt no more than five seconds on my doorstep before pushing past me into the house and away from the gaze of any casual observer. Nor did her driver drop her at my front door. Instead she walked to my home from a distance away, much as if she were a local returning from church. And her precisely timed departure told me the driver was not static at her pick-up point but passed by the location at a pre-arranged time.

Mumford wound up the meeting with a summary. He avoided any firm conclusions. He would wait, he said, for more details from the police before proceeding further.

I reflected on Rimmington's edginess as I drove home. I especially thought about just how difficult it would have been explaining to him the sizeable time gap between the finish of my call to Delminico and calling Mumford, when I wrote the *As Needed* talking points I had told Martin were drafted in the taxi. It had been a calculated risk to try and impress the DG with a carefully crafted set of media points represented as something formulated quickly and off the cuff. I knew of course the precise times I had called Delminico and Mumford would be confirmed. I had intended simply to say I had made notes after speaking to Delminico, before calling Martin. It was now clear I had underestimated the danger in this. Once on the scent, Rimmington would not have been fooled by flimsy excuses.

The combination, however, of Delminico's death and British bureaucracy had shielded me from Rimmington. Plans were afoot for a new Service building, prompting the money people to extend the life of the current office's 1960s-vintage telephone switch. Accordingly, the time of calls in and out the Service was not recorded, unless made through the operator. It had been safe to tell the meeting that my call to Delminico concluded later than it did.

I also thought about Rimmington inexorably squeezing the admission out of Delminico he had been instructed to tell Cuthberson to come to me. The most I thought was the O'Hare group would have regarded my avoiding tricky questions on the subject as a bonus on top of its reason for killing Delminico. It never occurred to me I was the intended beneficiary of Delminico's murder; that as with the delivery of the WRR minutes I had to be seen as snow-white by the Service. Not until *our source* told us did I learn that my protection from the instruction issue alone had been judged reason enough to kill Delminico.

Monday morning in the office was tense. I saw Reggie slink by when he first came in. He was bowed, literally, and carried the air of a beaten man. Reggie spent all day on the fifth floor, returning to the area only late in the afternoon. He spoke to no one before leaving, carrying a large cardboard box full of books and personal items.

Shortly after, Martin Mumford called Heneshaw and me to his office. 'Reggie,' he said without ceremony, 'has accepted a placement at Fort Monckton, effective as of tomorrow morning. This obviously leaves vacant the position of FADG Southern and Central Europe and Iberia Division. Personnel expects an FADG round will be finalized towards the end of the year, in about six months' time. A promotee from the round will permanently fill the SID position. Pending that, each of you will act as FADG SID for three months. Right, who wants to go first?'

I looked at Mumford and Heneshaw. I was not thinking about going first or second. I was thinking how being asked to act in a senior division head position was evidence that any image problems I may have had on the fifth floor as a result of my hospital bed disobedience towards Richard Samson had now subsided. Delivering the WRR minutes to the Service and writing the media talking points for the DG had erased past sins. I suspected these two matters had also helpfully backed up the assurance I was again firing on all cylinders contained in my letter to Mumford congratulating him on his promotion.

I was on a roll. From here on I would be judged only on how well I did the job. Time to strike while the iron was hot. 'I'll go first, Martin, if that's alright with Rup.' The realization the Samson incident was behind me had made me chirpy; the *Rup* bit was an intended turn of the knife.

Heneshaw smiled as if he had just bitten a rotten apple. 'Fine with me,' he said through gritted teeth.

Mumford knew we hated each other and I could see he saw the funny side of the exchange. He dismissed us like the silly schoolboys we were.

Chapter 33 – Weinberger

On the first day of my acting stint Martin poked his head through the door of my office in the late afternoon. 'Thought I'd let you know that using the pistol's serial number the police traced the weapon used to kill Delminico to the Langford Armoured Van Company out at West Drayton near Heathrow.' I noticed Martin didn't say the weapon with which Delminico committed suicide. 'The company reported the weapon missing from its armoury in 1982. But a police investigation failed to find it. Then in 1983, after a Langford technical support officer called Gerard Hopgate had been killed in a car accident, an empty ammo clip belonging to the weapon was found in his locker. The police searched Hopgate's home and made other enquiries but drew a blank. They've now re-activated the investigation. But I'd be very surprised if it sheds much light on the circumstances of Delminico's death.'

'Perhaps Hopgate sold the gun to Delminico, simple as that,' I said.

'It's possible,' Martin said, unconvinced. 'My gut feel is we're not going to make much headway on this one way or the other.'

What neither Martin or I knew until *our source* came over was that Hopgate had sold the pistol and ten rounds of ammunition for

2,000 quid to a bloke he literally met in a pub. The buyer, posing as a criminal planning a blag, claimed he was of Croatian background. He indicated he would pay good money for a weapon and ammunition and asked Hopgate, who liked to pretend he ran the Langford armoury, if he could oblige him. Hopgate was clearly in an incautious rush to take the money on offer because he accepted the Croat's assurance he would file off the pistol's serial number. Once the weapon was in his possession, the Yugoslav operative posing as the would-be criminal gave it to his KGB controller. The pistol was placed in the KGB London station's secure vault, waiting for a rainy day when it might be used.

Good preparation breeds good luck. The gun replete with serial number became the ideal tool for a man called Jack Kelly to use when the station needed to engineer Delminico's suicide at short notice. Kelly was a former soldier, who after completing a term of imprisonment at the Maze Prison in Northern Ireland, had been dishonourably discharged from the Irish Guards. With any number of people after his head, he had ended up on the island of Bequia in the tiny Caribbean country of St Vincent and the Grenadines, where according to *our source* he came to the attention of Cuban talent spotters. 'Using Venezuela as his transit point to the world,' *our source* said, 'and forged travel documents supplied by our people in Caracas, our Caribbean operative solved quite a few pressing problems for us. Usually for a fee of 10,000 US a hit.'

Hopgate's demise was not a tidy-up exercise, as might reasonably be suspected. He could never have led police to the Yugoslav, who left the UK shortly after buying the pistol. Hopgate simply went to sleep while driving in the Herefordshire countryside and died instantly when his car hit a Post Office telegraph pole.

As Mumford predicted, the investigation into Delminico's death ran into the sands. Rimmington stored the details away in his mind and soon set about attending to other pressing matters. The police had been in touch to advise that someone claiming to be SIS was passing off dud cheques. 'Hope it's not the DG,' he had joked to some in the Service as he set out to call on Scotland Yard.

The final stanza of Delminico's death was played out some months later in the Court of Her Majesty's Coroner for Brighton and Hove, where an open finding was recorded. For the Service, therefore, the mystery of the Freddie Ladler and Reggie Sullivan matters remained exactly that.

In June 1984 the DG made his annual official visit to the United States. Martin Mumford, as the DDG responsible for relations with the Americans, accompanied him. Most of the visit was spent out along Route 123 in Virginia at the CIA's Langley headquarters, where the DG and Martin spent two full days locked in discussions with the CIA Director, William Casey, and other senior CIA staff.

Their program also included calls on the Secretaries of State and Defense, George Schultz and Casper Weinberger respectively.

Defense Secretary Weinberger's maternal grandparents had been born in Britain. It was well known he took more notice of general developments in the UK than many of his contemporaries. The conversation in Weinberger's Pentagon office began by covering familiar ground, principally the usual US complaint about carrying too much of the financial burden for the Western intelligence effort against the Soviets.

But Weinberger then switched tack, addressing the DG. 'I briefed President Reagan last week,' he said, 'on the business in the London tabloids last month concerning that guy of yours, Ladler. I'm reliably informed Ladler is a good chance to come here next year to head up the SIS station in your embassy. The President and I agreed in principle it might be best if someone else took up the appointment. Perhaps Ladler can have a go next time. I do believe the President is going to talk to Schultz and Casey about this.'

The DG told Martin afterwards his first instinct was politely to tell Weinberger to bugger off and leave the Service administration to him. But for a moment he had wondered if the Americans had wised up to the second Rhodesian matter involving Reggie Sullivan. Then something had told him that Weinberger's intervention was political. Even so, the DG had admitted to Martin, any relief he felt that the

Service's dirty laundry had not been aired soon turned to caution. Long experience had taught him discretion was the better part of valour when in the political galaxy alongside political heavyweights. This need for prudence, Martin later told me, was undoubtedly the reason why the DG replied to Weinberger as he did. 'Certainly Secretary, we will take into account your and the President's views when deciding who should come over next.' Martin also told me that Weinberger had smiled, having decoded the DG's response.

On the plane home, the DG explained to Mumford why he had bowed to Weinberger's sugar-coated dictate. 'Unless I'm badly mistaken,' he had said, 'with a Presidential election coming up this November the Republican Party is concerned about Reagan being seen to countenance the appointment of a senior British intelligence officer with alleged ties to white supremacists to conduct liaison with the CIA. The Democrats will run hard on this, including regurgitating the allegations against Ladler in the domestic media. The risk the Republicans identify is that Ladler's appointment could antagonize those voters who fail to consider the fallaciousness of the allegations against him. And as we both know, Martin, in the largely inward-looking US that might be a sizeable slice of the electorate.'

Later on in the flight, Martin said, after the dinner service, the DG had retuned to Weinberger matter, having apparently given it more thought over his Beef Wellington. 'Not only is it prudent to avoid political ructions,' the DG had said, 'it would also be unhelpful to the Service if the Ladler allegations resurfaced. At some point tomorrow, I will call in the ADDG and that fellow Brian McGowan who has just been made Personnel and instruct them not to consider Ladler for the head of Washington station appointment next year.' Ladler was a certainty for promotion to FADG, the DG had confided to Martin, but the Service could find something else for him to do. 'And to be doubly sure of calming any American nerves,' the DG had added, 'Ladler can stay on his training project for a while longer than originally planned.'

Mumford's opening up to me on the DG's conversation with Weinberger and what flowed from it was not idle gossip. Martin, you see, was the senior Service officer who debriefed *our source*. What Martin revealed about the DG's exchanges with Weinberger was in fact a small part of the comprehensive briefing he provided me on the saga that was to become my story.

Martin delivered this comprehensive briefing in December 1991, some seven-odd years after the Washington visit, after his debrief of *our source* and other enquiries had been completed. Henceforth, I shall call it Martin's *Final Briefing*.

Chapter 34 – Heneshaw

I had felt comfortable from the outset in my acting FADG SID role, dealing competently with the day-to-day issues that arose. An early task had been to get across the detail of every current activity in the division on which the fifth floor could conceivably demand answers; it was simply not interested in hearing *I don't know.* I was pretty well across the activities of my branch but needed quickly to get up to speed on the happenings in Heneshaw's area. I had called him in. He had been cold but nonetheless responded apparently truthfully, if economically, to all my questions. Nor did he object when I had asked for a detailed brief on his branch's activities to be on my desk within forty-eight hours.

But by July, with half my acting period already elapsed, I was growing increasing anxious to make an impact, to set a discernable benchmark from which I would stake my claim for advancement to FADG. In mid-July my wish appeared to be granted. It was in the form of a *Secret* cable from our Berne station recommending a recruitment attempt. The proposed target was a Soviet, not Russian but an ethnic Kazakh. His name was Yerik Massimov, First Secretary (scientific) at the Soviet Embassy in Berne. The station reported that Massimov often made work trips alone within Switzerland. But it cautioned this might not be significant owing to his fringe role in the embassy. Rather, in the station's estimation,

Massimov's appeal was his apparent influence, lowly position notwithstanding. His regular mingling with senior embassy people and a single glimpse of he and the Ambassador deep in conversation suggested a possible political connection in the station's estimation.

I was keen to pursue the opportunity. A halfway decent scalp like Massimov snared on my FADG watch would be sure to give impetus to my promotion prospects. But I didn't want to display my eagerness when first discussing the proposal with Heneshaw, who was the branch head responsible for Berne station. I pretended instead to be undecided. Privately, though, I agreed with Heneshaw's assessment that while Massimov's work didn't seem to be particularly important, his access to the embassy's senior people made him someone who could later assist us in landing a bigger fish.

The station's report made clear that Massimov was most susceptible to recruitment when his work took him to the Institute of Plant Sciences in Zurich. There in the absence of any restraining influence, he appeared to throw all caution to the wind. The upshot was he concentrated more on Zurich's clubs and brothels than on how to grow cabbages, and in the process splashed money around with reckless abandon. His behaviour bore all the traits of someone vulnerable to bribery, a honey trap, or a combination of both.

As part of the charade to disguise my enthusiasm, I still voiced caution early the next week when Heneshaw, now *very* keen, pressed for a proposal to go up to Mumford recommending a recruitment attempt. But then, with the air of someone initially neutral who on weighing the facts had tipped to one side of an argument, I agreed. I had Heneshaw draft a submission recommending a bribery pass with a cash threshold of 2,500 US dollars per month. Subject to Martin's endorsement, I would instruct the station to pitch at Massimov on those terms when next he was off the leash in Zurich.

I sold the submission vigorously to Mumford, in marked contrast to my downbeat performance with Heneshaw. Martin didn't say much but I detected he was pleased with the proposal's brevity, in that I did not burden him with detail, and its fiscal conservatism. Always cautious, he slept on it before making a final decision. But after we had spoken the next morning, when I again pushed for an affirmative response, Martin had signed off. 'Go for it,' he said, throwing the papers into my in-tray, a wide smile on his face.

The Monday after it had been tasked, Berne station citing a Swiss Air contact advised Massimov was to travel to Zurich the next week. I opened my diary to Wednesday 1 August 1984 and made a note to that effect.

The day arrived and I looked forward with anticipation to the station's cable confirming that Ringo, the Service's work name for Massimov, was in the bag. That never came. Instead there was a phone call on the secure line from the station chief, Justin Campbell-

McLoud. Heneshaw and I activated the phone's speaker at our end. JCM, as we called him, sounded rattled. 'We got to Ringo in the coffee shop of the Howard Hotel in Regensdorf, Irene Rogerson and myself. It was very strange. He kept saying, in excellent English by the way, "Who the fuck are you two? I told you no more contact until the university job was sorted out." Rather than categorically identify ourselves, we just put to him we could do two and a half K a month if he'd help us out with some info on the embassy. That sent him bananas. "What do you mean 2,500 dollars a month?" he said, adding something like you know full well I want half a million plus the other arrangements. He then clammed up, apparently realizing by now we weren't whoever he thought we were. We were at a loss by this stage and decided it was a no sale, at least today.'

Heneshaw looked at me waiting for me to respond. 'Put all the above in a report and get it to us,' I instructed JCM. 'We'll have to see where this goes.' Looking enquiringly at Heneshaw, who shrugged his shoulders, I added, 'Neither Rupert or I have any inkling of what's got into him.' We left it there.

I went and briefed Martin, telling him that on receipt of JCM's report I planned by return cable to direct the station to make discreet enquiries. We both knew this would include JCM quietly speaking to the CIA station in Berne. 'Keep me informed,' Martin had said.

JCM never got the chance to sound out the CIA station – the Americans beat us to the punch. Unbeknown to *most* of us at the time, the CIA had a concentrated and urgent interest in Massimov, who was far more important than he appeared. The Americans were on the cusp of recruiting him. But immediately following Berne station's approach, Massimov told them the incident had badly scared him and now all bets were off. After obtaining video footage from the hotel that very night, the CIA went apoplectic. It started in Washington the next morning where the SIS station chief was called into Langley to have a new arsehole torn for him, as some Agency types were fond of saying. The poor devil knew nothing and could only promise to report the American concerns back to headquarters.

Shortly after our receipt of Washington station's report, Tommy DeLuca, CIA station head in London and bureaucratic knee-capper extraordinaire, came in to perform a similar anatomical adjustment on Mumford. Martin had asked me to be present. I was nervous knowing I largely carried the can for the fracas. Tommy, who was built like a Greco-Roman wrestler, could be very intimidating. But it was a privilege to watch Martin in action. He first allowed DeLuca to blow off all his Italianate steam before saying calmly, 'Please don't come in here carrying on like a complete prat, Tommy. We don't have ESP. How could we have been expected to know you were chasing after the same body?'

'I wish I could give you chapter and verse on him,' DeLuca responded, noticeably struggling to maintain his outrage in the face of Martin's swami-like composure. 'Then you Limeys might understand the scale of the trainwreck you've caused.'

Martin countered politely. 'We now unequivocally accept the individual in question was of major importance to the Agency, Tommy. But to repeat, we had no visibility of this at the time.' DeLuca glowered but didn't answer. Martin continued, but this time with deliberate hostility. 'If you, and I mean the royal you, the CIA, had the common decency to ask us to steer clear of him, we would have considered the request. Now get the fuck out of here before I have the janitors throw you in the street.'

DeLuca stood to leave. 'You should know Schultz is going to call Howe. There'll be hell to pay. Have a nice day.'

'Close the door, Joe,' Mumford ordered. I did, dreading what was to come. 'This is not great, unfortunately,' Martin said, 'and you'll have to take responsibility for this. It was your op after all. Our political masters will curdle under US pressure; in fairness they really have no alternative. We'll need to make a *mea culpa* and admit we should have run Ringo's recruitment past the Yanks.'

But Martin,' I protested, 'that means gaining American approval for every single thing we do.'

'No, it doesn't,' he said, with enough force to make me regret saying what I just had. 'It comes down to intuition and judgement about when to consult and when not. The bald fact is the ability to make the right call eight out of ten times sorts out who gets to FADG and who doesn't.'

I felt for the first time ever some resentment towards Martin. 'Why didn't you tell me to consult then?' I asked with heat.

Mumford chose to ignore my testiness. 'Your submission depicted Ringo as small beer, of no real intrinsic value in himself but someone who might open doors to others. It also excluded the detail Berne station provided, such as his freedom to travel alone, hobnobbing with embassy heavies and the fact he threw money at every call girl in Switzerland. I have no issue with any of that. Where low-level recruitments are concerned, as this ostensibly was, I rely on the FADG's judgement as a matter of course, including on whether to consult the Americans. But now knowing the detail, I can say Massimov's conduct comes across as extreme and really should have been a signal to you to proceed cautiously, including consulting the Americans. I can't be doing the FADG's thinking or reading cables from supervised stations on behalf of the FADG. I have my own problems requiring my undivided attention.'

I nodded, suitably chastised. Mumford declared it was time he got on. He walked around his desk and opened his office door. Arm outstretched he ushered me through the doorway, offering as I passed, 'Sometimes it can be counterproductive to try too hard, Joe.' I heard his message loud and clear. I had just learned a valuable lesson – the hard way. Stewing over this as I returned to my office, I happened upon Heneshaw in corridor conversation with Ladler, temporarily upstairs from his exile in training. Both were laughing at something. But what caught my attention was how pleased Heneshaw looked. I found it hard to fathom in the circumstances.

The DG called in Mumford and me to tell us what he planned to put in his letter to William Casey. 'Mr Howe has elected not to apologize to Mr Schultz, preferring instead that we convey our regrets at senior officials' level,' the DG said. 'And I have been given the dubious pleasure.' Directing a withering look at me, he added, 'I am very disappointed at this turn of events.'

'I take full responsibility Director General,' I said. 'The operation ran entirely under my guidance and it was an error of judgement not to consult the Americans.'

'Fine, thank you. That will be all,' the DG responded, closing the book on the matter. Martin and I both turned to leave. The DG held up his hand as if preparing to wave us goodbye. 'Martin, could you stay please? There's another matter I want to discuss.' As I opened the door, the DG called out to me, 'The sun always comes up Lambert, remember that.' I wasn't entirely sure what he meant. I guessed, though, he was saying now that you've gone down let's see how you get up. It made me think of the old Confucian parable, something along the lines of: *Our greatest glory is not in never failing but in rising each time we fail.*

Suitably inspired, I spent the last of my acting period trying to do as good a job as possible. Then it was back to my old office, while Heneshaw took charge of the division. I supported him much as he had me – with an economy of assistance.

The winter had set in as we waited for the outcome of the FADG round. There were three positions up for grabs. Twelve candidates had made it to the interview stage. I had my interview one morning in early October and spent the afternoon lamenting what I omitted to say. Heneshaw had his interview shortly after. The sparkling new suit and red tie he wore gave him an air of authority causing me to fret as I saw him walk by. He returned an hour later looking even more confident to my jaundiced eyes. I also heard on the grapevine Ladler been interviewed. This was further grounds for disappointment. Ladler had only recently returned to Southern Africa Branch. My hopes had been raised for a brief time that his extended stay in training meant the hatchet job done on him had actually sidelined him from the promotion round.

Friday 16 November 1984 and the telephone on my desk rang. It was Brian McGowan. He avoided any small talk. 'Joe, a circular

announcing the FADG promotions will issue on Monday. Your name is not on it. Since becoming Personnel I've tried to lessen the disappointment for people missing out on promotion by letting them know in advance. It's not much but I hope it's something.' I started to speak but Brian talked over me. 'I can tell you the matter back in August told against you. But I can also tell you the chief and others have been pleased with the way you picked up yourself. For a handful of candidates not being promoted, you included, I am authorized to advise that by mutual agreement, Reggie Sullivan is leaving the Service early in the new Financial Year, 12 April to be precise. The circular, therefore, will indicate a reserve list is to run for six months, to May 1985. Keep that in mind.'

I brightened a little. 'Are you saying I'll go up shortly after 12 April next, Brian?'

'No, I am most definitely not giving you that guarantee. All I'm saying is you are one of a small number of unsuccessful candidates who will be considered for promotion in this current round once Reggie leaves.' Brian rang off.

A dark cloud descended on me as I thought it through. Even were I promoted next April, the new head of Washington station would already have been in place for two months. My gloom was deepened by the thought that Agnes's last eighteen months with HOPE in India would now be over. If it weren't for the horrible events of October 1983 she would be back in my arms at Brent Cross, safe and sound. Wearily I packed my papers, put them in my safe and spun off the combination lock. *I haven't had a decent drink for two years*, I thought. *Perhaps tonight I should.*

I wasn't even able to attempt to get out of bed until noon the next morning. After so long without a hangover, I had forgotten what it was like. I hated feeling brittle and lethargic. It was a salutary reminder I was no longer the strong young man of my twenties and thirties. I knew then this was the end of my heavy drinking days.

Although fully recovered by Monday morning, I was seriously demotivated. Fortunately, things were quiet. It was early afternoon when the promotions circular came out. The internal courier brought me a copy. It took some willpower to look at it. The successful candidates would be listed alphabetically so I began from the bottom of the list on the circular's second page. A woman called Alison Meagher had been bumped up to fill the SID vacancy. I'd heard only good things about her. Taking a big breath, I flicked to the first page. 'Fucking hell,' the words involuntarily escaping my lips: Rupert Heneshaw to head of station, Washington; and Frederick Ladler to head a new division, the Falklands Intelligence Unit.

The reason for Rupert Heneshaw's smugness in the corridor that I had noticed when returning to my office after receiving Martin Mumford's dressing down was not revealed to me for many years.

When it was, Martin was again my source. Only this time, the information came to light not as part of his *Final Briefing*. It came as an addendum of sorts to it, in 1996 nearly five years after the day in December 1991 when Martin and I had sat closeted for eight hours in the study of his Wimbledon home.

At the time of the Massimov operation, a loud and aggressive former marine called Maurie Sanity was attached to the CIA London station. Sanity eventually retired from the CIA in 1992. While in service he had gained a reputation for wanting to make his intelligence colleagues think he knew everything that was going on. Those he worked with used to joke that Sanity was a walking misnomer. In 1996, twelve years after JCM's pitch at Massimov, Sanity was diagnosed with inoperable brain cancer; he knew he wouldn't see out the year. Since Massimov, Sanity had carried a guilty conscience. Now with the end in sight, he wanted to unburden himself of this. He contacted the CIA.

The gist of Sanity's deathbed confession was that in July 1984, when drunk, he had told the SIS officer Rupert Heneshaw about Massimov and how the Americans had come to know the Kazakh was a prime mover in the Soviet biological weapons program. He did so prompted by Heneshaw's mention to him of the Service's interest in apparently the same person. Sanity said he warned Heneshaw the Brits should back off telling him that, with American encouragement, Massimov pretended to be a drunken womanizer.

This kept the unwashed off his back – Swiss counter-intel; even his own people. All the while the Americans were secretly negotiating a deal with him. 'We've sunk a fortune into him,' Sanity said he had told Heneshaw, 'but now, after nearly two years, we're close to making him an offer.'

The CIA contacted the Service to seek an explanation. Up on the fifth floor it was recalled that I was in charge of the division at the time of Massimov. Mention of my name still caused the odd political palpitation. The Service overlords were wary of giving the Lambert matter new life in Whitehall. A safe pair of hands was required. Names were mooted. Finally, it was decided to recall Martin Mumford, retired a year by now, to interview Heneshaw.

Mumford contacted me after interviewing Heneshaw and explained the political circumstances of his recall. He said my comment on his draft record of interview was crucial to properly rounding out his report. I returned to England especially for the occasion.

'It started at a dinner party I attended at Freddie Ladler's house the Friday night of the week Berne station had proposed we pitch at Massimov,' Heneshaw had told Mumford. 'Several from the CIA London station were there, Maurie Sanity included. We all got drunk and packed our wives off home with a view to getting down to some serious drinking in Ladler's poolroom. No sooner had we started than one of the Americans left. I said to Sanity something to the effect that Barney boy must be slowing down in his old age.

'It was then Sanity had whispered to me, "He's flying to Berne tomorrow – our Berne boys have got some scientific wallah, a Sov, on the line and they want a bit of help."

'I remarked that our people over there had recently cast the rule over a scientific fellow from the Soviet Embassy and wondered if it was the same person.

'Sanity asked whether he was a Kazakh.

'I played dumb and said I wasn't sure. Sanity then became alarmed and warned me the Brits should back off.'

'And what followed?' Martin asked.

'Nothing initially,' Heneshaw said. 'Sanity knew he had blabbed and soon went home feeling remorseful. I was too pissed to do anything. In fact, I never got home until 5 am. Three hours later my wife Genevieve and I were woken by my son Timothy making breakfast. He was unwell then, with Attention Deficit Disorder, and never stopped to think. But he's fine now.'

'Just the facts, please,' the record showed Martin had said.

'I began to consider what I would do with the gold that silly Sanity had dropped in my lap,' Heneshaw had continued. 'Normally I would not have hesitated to arrest the collision course Berne station was on with the Americans. But I also knew significant blame would fall to Lambert if the station got in the way of the American efforts to recruit Massimov. This caused me to wonder.

'The one big advantage I identified was that Sanity would swallow glass before telling anyone he had spilled the beans. I contemplated the possibility of not alerting the Service. Sure the Americans would bitch and moan if the station interfered with its plans, but that would wash over once they had Massimov on board. And if the British cross cutting actually resulted in the Americans not recruiting Massimov, denying them strategic advantage in the biological theatre, I figured the Yanks were resourceful enough to find someone else capable of delivering the same outcome.

'I decided to take the chance to give Lambert a kick in the nuts while it existed rather than try to read the Cold War tea leaves. You have to understand I was very tired, rationalizing somewhat and in truth still half-tanked when I made this decision.'

'Yet that's where you left it,' Mumford had said. 'Even after you'd caught up on your sleep and was thinking more clearly.'

'Lambert had been excessively cautious in agreeing to put up the Massimov op to you,' Heneshaw had responded. 'If that was any guide, another opportunity to professionally harm him might not arise. Lambert and I had a dust up in the men's toilets way back in 1977. He had just been promoted to branch ahead of me and I could tell he was revelling in my disappointment. Ever since I had wanted to get even; I wasn't about to take that from a bumpkin like him.'

The record showed no spoken reaction from Mumford. Just Heneshaw telling him, 'That was the clincher. That's why I stuck to the course of action I had decided on.'

And the implications for Heneshaw in admitting he did not alert the Service to the American interest in Massimov, preferring instead to inflict damage on me? None really. Heneshaw had proved just how shrewd he was. He had summed up it was now a different time and much water had flowed under the bridge. Once she knew the facts, Alison Meagher who had succeeded Sir Colin Jameson as DG in 1993 – nine years after her elevation to FADG SID – opted for the political safety of doing nothing. A slap on the wrist for Rupert, a telephoned apology to her American counterpart, and then a line drawn under the matter. There was no time to dwell in the past.

Chapter 35 – Citadel

I'm told the snow fell voluminously in Western Russia in January 1985. I'm also told General Shukhov took advantage of this to enjoy a week's cross-country skiing at Zavidovo before returning to work in mid-January. He started the year by reviewing Operation Citadel and decided that after its initial spurt it was now flagging and needed fresh impetus. He said all of this to Colonel Dmitri Aleshkovsky, head of the Third Directorate and the man who in 1990 became *our source*. But first he had to wait because Aleshkovsky was on leave for another week. Aleshkovsky's deputy, Major Zamir Umarov, some years later told a third party – which then told the Service – how Shukhov had been mightily displeased when told this. He had rudely declined Umarov's offer to see him in Aleshkovsky's stead.

When he did get to open up to the third party, Umarov explained that he had never won Shukhov's confidence. He was an Uzbek Muslim and Shukhov was not about to trust anyone who wasn't from good Russian stock. Umarov had specifically recalled Shukhov's rudeness in January 1985. 'I was insulted,' he had said. 'Only a year earlier I had completed four arduous years as station head in Jeddah. I had done an exceptional job under intense scrutiny from the Saudi security services. Yet on return to Moscow that arsehole of a General, Shukhov, had blocked my promotion.'

Martin Mumford's *Final Briefing* fully detailed Aleshkovsky's meeting with Shukhov first thing the following Monday. 'This was a watershed moment for two reasons,' Mumford was to tell me. 'It was Aleshkovsky's first hint that Shukhov's bond to Operation Citadel extended beyond a close professional interest. It also led to the events directly following, the significance of which Aleshkovsky said he never could have guessed at in his wildest dreams.'

Aleshkovsky had soon dispensed with the small talk on detecting Shukhov's irritation at being kept waiting for a briefing. 'The Irish contractors and the Caribbean operative have successfully completed their tasks,' Aleshkovsky said without further delay. Shukhov knew well this was a reference to the O'Hare group and Jack Kelly. 'The press coverage on Ladler was ideal and, unhindered by anything the Brighton go-between might have said, Lambert passed the WRR minutes to his Service. The success of this phase of Operation Citadel is reflected in the Sullivan fellow's shift to Fort Monckton.

'Lambert's promotion status, however, remains unclear,' Aleshkovsky continued, 'and unfortunately we can do no more than watch and wait.' Sensing Shukhov's displeasure, Aleshkovsky had hastened to explain. 'SIS division heads using their real names have long interfaced with UK academia. But SIS academic contacts are telling the journalists and others we use that since last May's bad press on Rhodesia no new SIS division heads have been sighted. I think this is the SIS applying the lesson of the WRR minutes, of how

Sullivan's status being known to many academics exposed the SIS to the risk of more press beat-up.' Aleshkovsky was right. Eight months earlier the now risk adverse DG had ordered that newly promoted FADGs should avoid contact with certain UK institutions.

A raised hand stopped Aleshkovsky as he went to go on. 'Even if you are correct, Colonel, your report is still not on progress, it's only back-fill and excuses,' Shukhov had said, his eyes flint hard.

Shukhov had then taken a deep breath, seemingly trying to push aside his growing anger. 'I can see that your knowledge of Operation Citadel needs to be expanded,' he said. 'You should be aware just how fortuitous it is that Lambert's objective in going to Phoenix Investments related to a wish to be posted to Washington as head of station. For your information, Colonel, Operation Citadel never intended anything but Lambert's promotion and his posting to Washington as SIS station chief. I know back in March 1983 when first announcing Citadel I told the Steering Committee that head of station Bonn and Brussels were other possibilities. But that was a security measure, a precaution in case we had a talker in our midst.'

Shukhov lit a cigarette and motioned Aleshkovsky to continue. Aleshkovsky noticed Shukhov was now smoking *Camels* instead of the odious Latvian things. But he gave it little thought; in light of the General's update, his focus was on delivering a forward-looking briefing. 'Sir,' he said, 'the incumbent SIS head in Washington has not yet been replaced. If Lambert takes up the posting his promotion will have been achieved and we can be confident the objective of recruiting him while alongside the Americans remains in reach.'

Shukhov did not respond, his unspeaking stare telling Aleshkovsky he wanted more. By his own admission, Aleshkovsky filled the vacuum unwisely. 'Our strategy has by no means failed if Lambert does not become Washington station head,' he said. 'If promoted, he will still be very senior in the SIS and his recruitment offers other meaningful intelligence opportunities. It is a matter of degree. It just means our strategy has succeeded to a lesser extent.'

Aleshkovsky then told of the uneasy silence that ensued. Shukhov broke it by heaving violently from his chair, its screeching on the office floor as it slid backwards startling Aleshkovsky. 'Listen to me you fucking *krestyanskiy*,' Shukhov growled, his heated use of the Old Russian word for *peasant* underlining his menacing ferocity. 'All I want to hear is how you intend to achieve Operation Citadel's objectives. Don't give me this bullshit about degrees. Unless you want to see yourself posted to forward operations in Afghanistan, you are to ensure Lambert's promotion, if that is still necessary, AND his posting to Washington. Get that through your thick head. Once he is in Washington your Directorate will also fast track his ingratiation with the Americans. The objective is for Lambert to spy for us from within their privileged inner sanctum. When it suits us best, we will shop him to his own side. As a result of his betrayal while in the Americans' confidence, the US–UK special relationship on intelligence cooperation, the engine room of the Western intelligence effort against the Soviet Union, will be crippled for decades. Citadel has no room for degrees. Now get to it and get me results, soon. Dismissed.'

Aleshkovsky saluted and pirouetted. He had left the office, he later said, with more spring in his step than he actually felt.

On Aleshkovsky's return to the Third Directorate, his deputy Umarov had enquired of him, 'How was the boss Dmitri Aleksandrovich?'

The two men were friendly despite their different backgrounds. Aleshkovsky trusted Umarov. He was occasionally indiscreet with Zamir when needing an outlet for his frustration. 'It's all close hold, Zam,' Aleshkovsky said. 'But between us I can tell you we're leaving a trail of bodies like Hansel and Gretel trying to pull in some Brit. We even topped his girlfriend in a fake car crash for God's sake. The *gruppenführer* is like a mad dog with a bone.'

The Nazi ridicule caused both men to snigger and the tension to ease. Aleshkovsky returned to his office. He needed to think. It was when reflecting on Shukhov's white-hot anger that Aleshkovsky first began to wonder if the General actually had skin in the game.

Chapter 36 – Libya

From Aleshkovsky's perspective, the situation deteriorated in February 1985 when Rupert Heneshaw took up as head of station, Washington. Aleshkovsky told Martin Mumford that on reporting this to Shukhov, the General had been grim but otherwise surprisingly restrained. He did, however, pointedly order Aleshkovsky to determine my promotion status *without delay*. Unable to rely on his usual sources to identify recent SIS division head promotees, owing to the restrictions imposed by the DG in May 1984, Aleshkovsky chose innovation. He tasked all KGB Residents, as station heads were also called, to report the name and seniority of all known or suspected SIS officers active at any time in their jurisdictions. 'I had calculated,' Aleshkovsky told Mumford, 'this blanket approach would soon reveal Lambert's promotion status.'

Aleshkovsky began to receive responses. One was a report in March 1985 from the KGB Resident in Cairo. 'He informed me,' Aleshkovsky said, 'that a senior SIS officer, Frederick Ladler, had recently called on the General Intelligence Directorate.' The GID was the Service's Egyptian counterpart. And KGB station, Cairo had an asset within the Directorate who sat in on Ladler's call.

Aleshkovsky said the Cairo Resident's report indicated Ladler had been candid with the GID, telling it he had only recently been promoted to division head and allocated the Falklands Intelligence Unit job. Ladler had explained the FIU had been formed because Argentina's economic recovery since the UK–Argentina Falklands War in 1982 had revived British concerns it could make another attempt on the Falkland Islands – the windswept British overseas territories off Argentina's East coast over which the initial seventy-four-day conflict was fought. Ladler had also volunteered he expected to be in the Falklands job for the next few years.

There's quite a bit of background to Ladler's call on the GID. Most of it comes from documents Martin Mumford unearthed, papers he allowed me to read at the time of his *Final Briefing*.

The first of these is the record of a conversation between the DG and Ladler early in 1985, shortly after Ladler had taken up the FIU position. The DG had reminded Ladler that most of the UK's Falklands casualties resulted from Argentina launching Exocet missile attacks on British warships. Ladler's main task as FIU head was to stymie any Argentine effort to rejuvenate its warfare capacity, in particular to obtain more Exocets from the French manufacturer, directly or through third parties.

The record shows that Ladler's supervising DDG Digby Carhiddy was also present, he of the David Niven moustache and silver cigarette case. Carhiddy was from the automotive industry. He had entered the Service at a time when the idea of Service operatives secreted in the business world had undergone a growth spurt. From there, he had skilfully ducked, weaved and manipulated his way up the Service's pecking order, ascending to DDG in 1982.

Ladler had enquired about the restoration of the UK's diplomatic relations with Argentina. As might be expected, these had been broken with the on-set of the Falklands war. The record shows the DG had forewarned him, 'This is a way off. You should expect to be in the FIU job for four to five years.'

'Always have a grip packed. The travel demands will be significant,' is Carhiddy's recorded contribution.

Freddie didn't know at the time – indeed, I'm not sure he ever knew – of the DG's earlier undertaking to Secretary Weinberger to exclude him from the US theatre until the posting rotation after Heneshaw, at least four years distant.

More Service records, this time Freddie Ladler's reporting cables, show that he was coolly received when visiting the French overseas intelligence agency, the DGSE. Ladler's report surmised this was a hangover from a secret communication during the height of the Falklands conflict sent by Margaret Thatcher to President Mitterrand demanding the French Government take positive steps to deny Argentina more Exocets, particularly through sales to third parties.

The French had complied. *But clearly*, Ladler had written, *the DGSE is still feeling wounded by the upbraiding.*

Another Ladler cable reveals he did not fare much better when he called on Italy's SIS equivalent, the SISMI. The Italians, apparently, remained upset that their significantly favourable trading relations with Argentina had been disrupted as a result of European Community economic sanctions imposed on Argentina at the outbreak of the Falklands conflict. Now with the export of ships and other lucrative items again on foot, Italy wanted to avoid any repeat disruption. The SISMI, Ladler advised, was unreceptive to the suggestion that Italy might curtail exports to Argentina and its allies of items capable of aiding the deployment of Exocet missiles.

Freddie Ladler's recorded experiences in France and Italy are germane to the fact that shortly after the Falklands war began on 2 April 1982, Libya's dictator Muammar Gaddafi offered to provide Argentina with Exocet missiles and other *matériel*. Gaddafi appears to have done so because, disingenuously, he chose to interpret Britain's military response to Argentina's invasion of the Falklands as an act of imperial aggression. For all that, Gaddafi proved to be a straw man in that the promised Exocets never materialized. But Libyan mortars and ammunition did find their way to Argentina.

Ladler had set out his intended approach to Libya in a strategy paper he distributed to the DG, Carhiddy and FIU staff. Libya was a second-ranked priority – top billing went to those countries of South America most likely to help Argentina. Absent a British toehold in Tripoli – for reasons unrelated to the Falklands, the UK's diplomatic relations with Libya had been broken in 1984 – Ladler proposed to monitor Libya on the cheap, with the assistance of Western allies with commercial or colonial ties to Libya. France and Italy were the prime candidates. But the attitude of the DGSE and SISMI convinced him to revise his thinking. With that, he turned to Egypt.

To say UK–Egyptian relations had a fractious history is an understatement. The most prominent disagreement was the Suez crisis of late 1956, resulting in the severing of UK–Egypt diplomatic relations from 1957–1959. Some say the howls of international condemnation that followed Britain's decision, with France, to invade Egypt seeking to wrest control of the recently nationalized Suez Canal marked Britain's decline as a great power. The forced resignation of UK Prime Minister Anthony Eden certainly made clear in hindsight that less pre-emptive measures to protect the UK's strategically important oil supplies might have been preferable.

No so well known is relations were again severed from 1965–1967. This time because of Egypt's membership of the pan-African Organisation of African Unity and its annoyance that British prime minister Harold Wilson should have ignored its calls militarily to remove Ian Smith after Rhodesia's 1965 UDI. Instead the Organisation interpreted Wilson's opting for economic sanctions as tacit repudiation of the principle of majority rule and an affront to Rhodesia's black populace. Along with most of its members, Egypt broke off diplomatic relations with Britain in protest.

Despite these historical tensions, Ladler's strategy paper identifies he chose Egypt for two reasons. In 1977 Egypt and Libya had clashed over Israel policy, provoking a four-day war. By 1985 diplomatic relations had still not been restored. The simple geographic fact that Egypt sat on Libya's eastern flank was Ladler's second reason. The land border between the two countries was highly porous. Each had agents aplenty in the other's territory.

Ladler had written an advance memo to those of his staff who in March 1985 accompanied him on the GID call. He had warned they would encounter residual anti-British sentiment. *For that reason*, Ladler wrote, *we should not be too cute when speaking with GID. We need to be as open as possible.*

Colonel Aleshkovsky admitted to Mumford the information on Ladler was virtually the only return of substance his grand plan had elicited. 'By late April 1985,' he had said, 'I was deeply frustrated by the lack of progress on something so basic as Lambert's promotion status. So, inspired by Shukhov's example of simply asking Lambert why he called on Phoenix Investments, I decided to do the same thing.'

Chapter 37 – Clarity

That's how it was, one cold and rainy Saturday morning in early
May 1985, that a dapper man of about forty sporting a beautiful
cashmere overcoat approached me in the car park of Sainsbury's
Brent Park supermarket as I loaded groceries into my car. 'Mr
Lambert,' he said in pucker English, 'Valerie O'Hare sends her best
wishes. She would like to know if you managed to get promoted as
a result of the little help we were able to provide last year?'

The man's mention of promotion initially caused me to recall
the telephone call from Brian McGowan in the last week of March,
when Brian told me I was to be promoted upon Reggie Sullivan's
retirement. Brian, though, had been apologetic. 'The promotion will
not take effect until 1 October 1985,' he had said. 'Reggie has been
agitating for his RAF service to be included in his lump sum long
service leave pay out. And now Legal's changed its tune and sided
with him. We hadn't budgeted for an extra single payment.
Reggie's agreed to take what's owed to him in wages. He will go on
leave until he formally retires on 30 September. The FADG round
must conclude when the reserve period expires in May. Announcing
your promotion now means you are still formally promoted in the
round, only the promotion won't take effect until October.'

'Well?' the man said, jolting me back to the present.

I tried to think of a suitably cutting response. But distracted by my thoughts all I could manage was to say huffily, 'I'm being promoted at the start of October, actually.' Then my anger took over. 'Who the fuck are you people?' I yelled, forcefully grabbing the man's overcoat with both hands and shaking him hard. Other shoppers paused to watch.

The man ignored my question and with strong arms removed my hands. 'Thank you for confirming your promotion as of October,' he said evenly. Then looking down at the lapels of his expensive overcoat, which I had lifted and twisted out of shape, he added in a flash of anger, 'You should not be so ungrateful. Your promotion was our only intention all along.' The man immediately calmed himself. Straightening his coat, he said quietly, 'Please don't make a scene. I should think the last thing either of us needs is a policeman asking questions.' After staring at me briefly, he turned and walked away.

I was too bewildered to run after him. The words *Your promotion was our only intention all along* rang in my ears. My astonishment came not from the man reinforcing the conclusion I had reached the night after speaking with Anthony Delminico, that the O'Hare group's strategy was something more complex than a plan to inconvenience the Service. No, it was that seemingly goaded by my shaking of him, he had just solved the piece of the puzzle I could not fathom. He had just told me that the O'Hare exercise –

Freddie Ladler; Reggie Sullivan; Cuthberson and Delminico – was all aimed at helping me. That was the strategy. With clarity came instant, clawing apprehensiveness: if there is one surely immutable rule of the Universe it has to be there is no such thing as a free lunch.

Aleshkovsky was to tell Mumford that the combination of Shukhov's apparent personal interest in Operation Citadel and latterly my not achieving the Washington posting had made him very cautious. 'Even so,' Aleshkovsky had said, 'I still wasn't entirely convinced Shukhov's threat to send me to Afghanistan was serious. But I'd seen it happen with other KGB sub-Director Generals. I had my family to consider and was determined not to push my luck. The instant my operative provided the advised date of Lambert's promotion I had rushed to Shukhov's office.'

'Sir,' Aleshkovsky had said, 'You will recall that in February a man called Rupert Heneshaw took up the head of SIS station, Washington position. Heneshaw has a wife and three young children and lives in Falls Church, Virginia. I regret it has taken so long to gather the additional information we have been seeking. But we now know Lambert takes up a promotion to the Washington station head level this October and that his rival Ladler, although already eligible for the Washington appointment, appears likely to be tied up on other matters for a number of years.'

Aleshkovsky told of Shukhov having a coughing fit when starting to respond. 'He was literally barking,' Aleshkovsky said. 'It was a good minute before he had settled down.'

When Shukhov was able to speak he noted that the delay in my promotion taking effect was actually advantageous. 'We need to convince this Heneshaw to go home,' Shukhov had told Aleshkovsky, 'particularly with Ladler now out of the picture. No physical harm must befall him, his wife or children. But if, for example, the brats are unable to adjust to life in Washington, Heneshaw may be compelled to put family before career. Get me a plan so I can explore this angle. If Heneshaw goes home maybe Lambert can still yet take up the Washington position.'

Aleshkovsky said after leaving Shukhov his mind was racing. 'I was preoccupied with the need to come up with a plan for convincing Heneshaw to go home; at the same time I thinking about the General's coughing. It had sounded almost consumptive, like he had tuberculosis. It reminded me of my paternal grandfather, then my guardian, who died from cigarette-induced emphysema when I was ten, just two years after my father was killed in operations during the 1956 Hungarian uprising. The cough explained why Shukhov had switched to smoking *Camels*, even though I knew, and I suspect he did too, that by now the damage would be done. It was the first sign I'd seen that his health was seriously on the wane.'

Chapter 38 – Timothy

Of all those Aleshkovsky gave up, Martin Mumford was to tell me, it was William and Barbara Whetstone where he evinced the most regret. The Whetstones were Russians and so-called illegals – having entered the United States from Mexico over a decade earlier posing as US citizens returning from vacation in Cancun. The family name they took belonged to a two-year-old boy, who in 1955 accidentally drowned in a dam on the family potato farm outside Sonna, Idaho. Like Aleshkovsky, both Whetstones were from Soviet military families and had lost mothers as toddlers, then fathers under a decade later to combat incidents. Aleshkovsky had gravitated to a Red Army cadet residential college at age eleven, when his remaining guardian, his grandmother, died. The Whetstones, conversely, had been orphaned, falling easy prey to the KGB illegals training program, where in their late teens they were paired. Aleshkovsky identified closely with them. This drove his empathy.

Living in Falls Church, Rupert Heneshaw commuted daily from Northern Virginia to the District of Columbia where the British Embassy was located. Service people posted to Washington were briefed to expect driving difficulties in winter when it came to the black ice on the bridges over the Potomac River linking Virginia to the District. But apart from areas like Georgetown in the District's Northwest quadrant, where rents were out of control, no family could safely reside in DC owing to the prevalence of drug dealing and violent crime. It made sense for the Heneshaws to live in Virginia, or in Maryland the District's other adjoining state. Virtually all bar Washington's most senior diplomats did.

Other than Timothy, who was now fourteen, Rupert and Genevieve Heneshaw had two girls, aged ten and eight respectively. The girls were enrolled in a local junior school and Timmy the also local Omar N Bradley High School. Knowing the Heneshaws had settled in Falls Church, Aleshkovsky had tasked the Whetstones to keep an eye out for any information on the family, either from their work or membership of the Falls Church Baptist Church.

Barbara Whetstone worked as an administrative assistant at the Omar N Bradley High School, a position specially selected because of the information it offered on US Government officials and foreign diplomats resident in Northern Virginia. As the end of the summer school term neared, Barbara sighted a letter sent to the Heneshaws by the Assistant Principal, Miss Bates. The letter requested a private meeting between Bates, and Rupert and Genevieve. Barbara knew why. Timmy had not settled despite every opportunity to adjust to his new school and classmates. His reputation for disruptive and unruly behaviour, and the effect of this on other students, was well known by teaching and administrative staff alike.

Miss Bates's record of interview indicates she had warned the Heneshaws that, in the school's opinion, Timmy might have Attention Deficit Disorder. Apparently Rupert had scoffed, accusing her of overanalysing adolescent hijinks. Bates had countered to the effect that while ADD was only a recently discovered condition, the research on it was proving very conclusive.

Genevieve had asked Bates about next steps. Bates suggested that over the summer break, Timothy have a couple of sessions with a school counsellor, with a view to him starting off the autumn term on a good footing.

According to the record, Rupert had objected *stridently*. 'I know my son and his qualities better than people who have spent just five minutes with him,' he had said. 'I don't think Timmy needs your amateur psychologists, thank you.'

Bates had clearly decided to go straight to her bottom line. 'Mr Heneshaw,' she had replied, 'I'm afraid that unless Timothy undertakes the preliminary counselling, the school may not be able to accept his enrolment for next term.'

Genevieve appears to have rescued the sinking ship. She is on record as asking Bates to excuse her husband's rudeness, offering work pressures as an explanation. Genevieve undertook to ensure that Timmy attended the counselling sessions.

Barbara Whetstone provided her conduit to the KGB Washington station, a Hungarian trade official, with a copy of Bates's notes at a crash meeting at a safe house the night of the interview. The report reaching Moscow Centre also contained Barbara's assessment that if Timothy ran into trouble with the police, and the trouble was sufficiently serious, the State Department would likely get involved. In cases involving children State usually consulted the relevant school. In Timothy's case, Barbara had said, the school would be sure to recommend the boy return to England owing to his behavioural problems.

Aleshkovsky was to debrief that Shukhov had summoned him on receipt of Barbara's report. 'Shukhov asked me what I thought,' he told Mumford. 'I said I agreed with Barbara. But I also sounded a note of caution, saying something to the effect that we don't want the mother taking the children home and Heneshaw staying on. The trouble the boy gets into would need to be significant, something normally involving a custodial sentence.'

Shukhov had nodded in agreement before adding, 'There's the matter of timing. We don't want Heneshaw on a plane before Lambert's promotion takes effect. But we also don't want to wait too long after Lambert is promoted in case he is siphoned off somewhere and becomes unavailable for the posting.'

Aleshkovsky had recounted how Shukhov was fighting for breath, taking in only short, shallow bursts of air. 'To spare him the discomfort of a back and forth conversation,' Aleshkovsky said, 'I suggested the Third Directorate mount an operation to get the boy into hot water with the police around the last week of August, while on summer term break. In proposing this timing, I mentioned something about the Americans being sympathetic towards the family. "It's not as if the father will have broken the law," I said. "They won't be asking him to be gone within forty-eight hours, unlike some other diplomats." ' Aleshkovsky said Shukhov had laughed uproariously at this, causing him to cough and splutter and his face turn purple. As to the trouble to be visited on Timothy, Aleshkovsky had suggested they ask the Whetstones.

'Within three days,' Aleshkovsky told Mumford, 'not Barbara but her husband William – code name Alpha – had responded. His cover work was as a paralegal in the office of the Virginia State Juvenile Court. He suggested pinning a marijuana trafficking offence on Timothy. Alpha said the Virginia legislature had recently amended the State's criminal code to place the onus on any person possessing over 100 grams of marijuana to prove they were not trafficking the substance. Trafficking was a far more serious offence than possession and usually led to a custodial sentence.'

Aleshkovsky related to Mumford how Shukhov had focused on the proving of personal use aspect. 'Shukhov was intrigued by

Alpha's opinion,' Aleshkovsky said, 'that because proving personal use was near impossible, the law now effectively deemed anyone with over 100 grams of marijuana to be trafficking. We finally agreed we should proceed on this premise. Although this meant we no longer had the need to find people to say they bought the drug from the Heneshaw boy, we still had to plant the stuff on him and then bring him to the attention of the police. I said this to Shukhov.'

But Shukhov had just shrugged according to Aleshkovsky. 'These matters can be overcome,' was all he said.

Despite Shukhov's evident wish to press ahead, Aleshkovsky said he still had reservations about costs. He chose his words carefully. By now the Kremlin had forbidden mention of the deterioration in the Soviet economy. 'I put to Shukhov that the operation would require a large team and for security reasons, team members would need to fly to Washington from various Western European capitals posing as tourists. I took care to make clear the team's insertion would be very expensive.'

Aleshkovsky told Mumford of his surprise at Shukhov's response. 'He was almost fatherly,' Aleshkovsky said, 'addressing me using the familiar form. This show of mellowness reinforced the impression I had gained that Shukhov's illness was quite serious.'

'*Tovarishch*,' Shukhov had said, 'the operation against the Heneshaws is an unavoidable stepping-stone to Lambert's recruitment while ensconced with the Americans. Lambert has caused us untold damage. I concede that in the current economic climate retribution alone may not justify the cost. But the price of a few airfares and hotel rooms is nothing compared to him becoming our agent while within the American inner circle. The destruction of the US–UK intelligence relationship is the minimum compensation we can accept for the harm he has done us. I do not want the lesser option of recruiting Lambert only as a source in the SIS. I want him recruited while he is in Washington cuddling with the Americans.' Aleshkovsky said Shukhov was now struggling to get his words out. 'The KGB is well resourced even if other agencies are not,' he had croaked. 'The Third Directorate has the budget to do what is necessary. Just get me results, Dmitri Aleksandrovich.'

I was later told the extraction of Aleshkovsky and his family to the West – his wife and four young children – took place in March 1990. The Russians at the time were paying close attention to vehicular traffic crossing from Russia into Finland. A decision was taken for Aleshkovsky to invent an excuse to commandeer a military plane to fly him and his family to Vladivostok in Russia's Far East. He pulled it off somehow, apparently under the guise of educating his children about the vastness of the Motherland. The Aleshkovskys' exit thereafter entailed a bribe to a ship's master and, I understand, some delicate high-level negotiations with the Japanese as regards the vessel making an unscheduled berthing at Akita on the island of Honshu, ostensibly for boiler repairs.

The nature of the extraction was such that the Aleshkovsky family had to travel very light. This limited greatly the material Aleshkovsky could bring over with him. But I did get to see the translated versions of the handful of papers he took from his office safe. For some reason, Aleshkovsky had decided to retain all documents relating to the Timothy Heneshaw operation. Among these were the planning proposal prepared by the team undertaking the operation and its subsequent implementation report.

The documentation revealed that a six-strong Soviet team – three pairs of men and women travelling separately – arrived in Washington on Wednesday 21 August 1985. Advance reconnaissance by the KGB Washington station had revealed Timmy's main holiday routine to be a karate class each Saturday morning at the Tysons Corner shopping mall in Northern Virginia, a short drive from his family home. Afterwards, he and two classmates had hamburgers, fries and cokes at *Mo's Burgers*. Using a contrived excuse to enter the karate centre locker room, the KGB station had first inspected and then photographed Timmy's white *Adidas* kit bag. It had determined all that Timmy carried in the bag was his karate uniform, gym shoes and a towel.

The team calculated that 200 grams of marijuana, packaged into twenty sachets of ten grams each, could be added to the bag without a noticeable change in weight, provided it was substituted for the towel once dampened by Timmy showering after his karate class. Sachets would be placed in each gym shoe. To give the impression of attempting to secrete the marijuana, the soles of the gym shoes would be hollowed out and the shoe insoles replaced over the sachets inserted in the cavities. Then a total of 148 dollars in used small denomination notes would be placed inside the gym shoes on top of the insoles. The money would alert any enquiring police officer to the need to inspect the shoes.

Plans were formulated for separating Timmy from his bag and temporarily substituting an identical replica bag of the same weight for the original. Near the end of the boys' lunch at *Mo's* was the time chosen for the separation. Having completed their karate class and now eaten, their young minds would be receptive to other stimulus.

The KGB station reconnaissance had also revealed that when hanging out in the mall after Saturday lunch, Timmy and his friends always visited a clothing store called *Young Man*. For hip boys living in and around the national capital, *Young Man* was the place to be seen. There was no evidence the boys ever bought anything. But the team calculated the store tolerated their visits in the hope it was a prelude to their parents buying them the items they liked.

The *Young Man* shop had a large sign at its entrance declaring: *Shop Lifters will be Prosecuted – No Exceptions.* Electronic scanners were installed at the store's exit to detect clothing items still bearing an electronic security tag, which was normally detached on payment. On Friday 23 August team members had gone into *Young Man*, where they placed an electromagnetic hood around the tag on an expensive shirt. They then left the store with the shirt without triggering the alarm.

Once in possession of Timmy's original bag, the shirt would be placed in the bag. When the boys entered the store the next day, team members carrying the original bag would follow. They would remove the hood re-arming the shirt nestled deep in Timmy's original bag, now also containing the concealed marijuana and money in his gym shoes. At the first opportunity the original bag would be re-substituted for the replica Timmy had unwittingly carried to the store from the restaurant. On Timmy's exit carrying the original bag, the now unshielded shirt would trigger the shoplifter alarm; the police would be called and the shirt, money and marijuana discovered. The operational bonus identified in the planning paper was that Timmy would have a shoplifting offence hanging over him in addition to the drug trafficking matter.

The operation proper was implemented on Saturday 24 August 1985. It was a complex and risky undertaking. The team's one big advantage, according to the KGB child psychologist's assessment attached to the planning proposal, was the boys' immaturity, impulsiveness and adolescent curiosity, all of which would run unfettered without parental supervision.

The team's implementation report conveyed that the operation was flawlessly executed. Timmy and his friends had occupied a booth in *Mo's* close to the restaurant's entrance. They ate quickly, noisily and messily. A team pair – posing as French tourists – triggered the distraction as soon as the boys had sat back, appetites sated. The resulting commotion sparked by the female team member as the male member suddenly slumped over near the entrance to *Mo's* attracted the boys. They had run excitedly from the restaurant, as operational planning had envisaged. A second team pair slid into the booth vacated by the boys, where their training bags still remained. If asked to move by restaurant staff, this couple was to act as Spanish tourists without good English. They were to secure the booth long enough for the male from the third couple to arrive.

When he did, dressed in the mall cleaning contractor's uniform and carrying the replica bag in a large black heavy-duty garbage bag, the exchange reportedly took less than thirty seconds. With this, the couple securing the booth departed the restaurant and the team member now holding Timmy's original bag spirited it to a van in the car park where technicians got to work to hollow out his gym shoes.

That done, the man now wearing ordinary clothes exited the van with a large *Macey's* carry bag hidden in which was Timmy's compromised original bag. His female colleague told him at their rendezvous point that on resuming his seat in the restaurant booth, Timmy had not given his kit bag a second glance. The pair had watched the boys leave the restaurant and then shadowed them as they meandered through the shopping centre. Finally, the boys had entered the *Young Man* store.

The re-substitution apparently also went smoothly. The male team member later reported it took him less than two minutes to arm the shirt in Timmy's original bag and slide it into the position where Timmy had carelessly dumped the replica, before setting off to roam around the store.

Withdrawal was equally uneventful. The man simply scooped the replica bag into the *Macey's* bag and concealed it with a covering shawl. He then approached his female colleague, now engaged in distracting a sales clerk. 'We've just arrived from Stockholm,' he said to the clerk. 'I'm feeling very tired all of a sudden. I must drag my wife away and get back to the hotel. My apologies.'

The faux Swedish tourists reported hearing the distant sound of an activated store alarm as they departed the shopping centre.

358

Chapter 39 – Washington

It was the first week of October 1985. I was FADG North Asia Division and had been for a whole three days. But I was far from content. I was troubled because even though gaining promotion had been one of my key objectives, the companion objective of the Washington posting now seemed unachievable. After Heneshaw, Ladler would likely be posted there. In the new era where station chiefs regularly did four-year stints or more, the wait could be as long as a decade. By then, even if I won the posting, it would probably be too late.

The telephone rang. It did constantly. *I really don't feel like another problem just now,* I thought.

Martin Mumford's voice caused me to sit up in my chair. 'Still interested in Washington station chief?' he asked. 'I seem to recall you mentioning this in the letter you kindly wrote me after I was promoted early last year.'

I was flabbergasted and could scarcely believe what I was hearing. 'M-m-most certainly, I would be Martin,' I stammered. 'Thank you for asking.' A million questions raced through my mind. 'But how come it's suddenly available?'

Martin didn't answer the question; he simply said, 'Let me speak to McGowan, he's acting ADDG at the moment. Either he or I will get back to you.'

As for Rupert Heneshaw, the consequences of Timmy's troubles were made known to me two months later, on a wet afternoon in London in the first week of December 1985. The Deputy Chief of Mission in Washington, a senior Foreign Office diplomat, was on home consultations and had called on the Service. As Washington head of station-designate I sat in on the meeting.

It transpires that on the first working day of September 1985, after the Virginia police had filed a report with the State Department, Heneshaw and the deputy had attended a meeting called by State's Chief of Protocol. 'Hillary Hamelworth,' the deputy had said, 'is a no-nonsense type of woman. With 142 countries represented in Washington, there are always sensitive issues requiring her attention.' According to the deputy, Hillary was especially businesslike this particular morning. 'The essence of what she said was that whereas the shoplifting matter might conceivably be treated as a misdemeanour, the drug trafficking allegation against Timothy was of grave concern.'

The deputy volunteered that Heneshaw had tried to respond but Hamelworth's body language had shut him down. 'She wasn't finished yet,' he said, smiling ruefully. 'The extra she wanted to impart was to the effect that the protocol office had spoken to Timothy's school, which had advised that Timothy had already received counselling for unruly and sometimes unsavoury behaviour. "The United Kingdom may be the United States' closest ally," Hamelworth had said, "but we cannot tolerate conduct like Timothy's, notwithstanding he is a minor. Do I make myself clear?"

'Heneshaw just exploded,' the deputy said. 'I could hardly believe his transformation from urbane and unflappable spy to this rabid, angry figure. Heneshaw essentially said that Timothy had denied everything, but he was very aggressive in the way he spoke.

'Hamelworth was completely undaunted,' the deputy said. 'She's one tough cookie. She just looked at Heneshaw and said, "Mr Heneshaw, the United States Government has no issue with you personally. And I am not here to give you gratuitous advice on how to raise your son. But Timothy cannot stay in this country. I am instructed, therefore, to tell you that by 30 November this year Timothy should leave the United States. In the interim, no charges will be laid against him. I might add for the sake of completeness that we have no plans to make you *persona non-grata*; indeed, we have no legal basis on which to do so. But should you not comply with our request as regards Timothy, a submission will go to Secretary Schultz recommending he contact his UK counterpart, Mr Howe, to raise our concerns. I expect that call, were it to eventuate, would result in your recall by your own government."

'Rupert again let his emotions boil over, alas,' the deputy said. 'He was fairly spitting his words and used some extremely coarse language. I decided it was time to intervene. I thanked Hillary for making the position clear. I then added for Heneshaw's benefit, principally because I thought his conduct unbecoming for a British diplomat albeit one from the Secret Service, that I would brief the Ambassador on our meeting – which I duly did.'

Of course, I had not a clue about the Russian operation against Timothy Heneshaw when on a freezing winter's day on 19 December 1985, I arrived in Washington to take up the role of SIS station chief. It was nineteen years to the day since my inauspicious debut for the Service in East Berlin. The notional length of my assignment was four years.

My first three months in Washington took place in the usual blur of preoccupations bedevilling new *arrivées*. The introductory side was unrelenting, particularly over the first couple of weeks when Christmas and New Year fell. Around this time, I christened myself the *plumber with leaky taps* insomuch that while I was adept at the social interaction with colleagues and counterparts my job demanded, I was happiest when alone with my memories. For the unversed, the equivalence is of a plumber out and about fixing everyone else's leaky taps but putting up with leaky taps at home. I took an apartment in McLean, Virginia and braved the daily commute to the District.

It was clear from the attitude of the CIA people I first encountered that Heneshaw's legacy lived on. They were polite to a fault and did what had to be done, but no more. I sensed an air of caution, of borderline distrust. In my own interests I even tried to argue Heneshaw's case, making the obvious point that he had done nothing wrong; it was his son who had gone off the rails. The Agency guys, though, felt they had been burned. The Heneshaws were not the people they had been led to believe. It was a barrier I didn't need and one that had to be overcome if I was to fulfil my secret quest to identify Agnes's killer.

My station was large, some twenty-one people in all. The station deputy, an officer at branch head level, looked after the day-to-day running of affairs. In a structure reminiscent of head office, two director-level staff answered to the branch head. This freed me to concentrate on the bigger picture, with no issue larger than my liaison with the CIA. My other staff trawled the big Washington diplomatic community and related professions. Eastern Bloc diplomats, journalists, and academics were never far from our thoughts. Mindful of the nothingness of many of the agents we had on the books in Jakarta and New Delhi, I was discerning when approving recruitment proposals to London. *No empty vessels* became my mantra.

The Americans were relaxed about us conducting operations on their turf, provided we avoided American citizens, as we were relaxed about them doing the same in the UK, reciprocal citizenry terms pertaining. This ostensibly happy state of affairs was underpinned by an agreement that any resulting product was always to be shared, even if sources were not usually revealed. The Service suspected the Americans often withheld product and were not averse to targeting British citizens when it suited them. But as a sign of Britain's demise as a global power and its strategic reliance on the United States, we honoured the agreement to the letter for fear of incurring big brother's wrath.

The branch head I inherited as my deputy was a man called Prosser. He had formerly been Heneshaw's number two. We gelled quite effectively. It was during the remaining six months of his assignment he opened up about Heneshaw's reaction to the State Department's direction his son should leave the United States. Prosser said he had never seen Rupert so angry. The dressing down he had received from the Ambassador for his behaviour during the meeting with the Chief of Protocol had not helped his mood. Prosser said Rupert had complained bitterly that he had been denied natural justice. 'The fucking State Department,' he had told Prosser, 'had simply closed its mind on questions of guilt or innocence once the school had told it Timmy had been in trouble. I've half a mind to stay in Washington just to be a rock in State's shoe – but for the fact I would miss too much of Timmy's development by seeing him only every few months.' According to Prosser, Heneshaw had even said,

'Any of the other kids and I'd be able to tough it out.' Prosser said he wasn't sure if Rupert was serious or just angry.

It was not until much later that I learned of the elaborate Soviet plan behind Rupert Heneshaw cutting short his Washington posting. Despite the passage of time, I still felt a tinge of regret for Heneshaw's son who then had just been a boy, and a troubled one at that. But much later still, with the advent of Maurie Sanity's deathbed confession to the CIA and the revelation of Heneshaw's intention to harm me professionally by not alerting the Service to the American interest in the Kazakh scientist Massimov, I became more sanguine. Years and years had passed. All I thought was, *What goes around comes around.*

1986 rolled by. I worked ferociously hard at ensuring the station ran at maximum efficiency and in cultivating my CIA contacts. The Agency was a broad church. Many CIA people I encountered were robust and roughhewn individuals, all clones of Chuck Lindergarten from yesteryear in Jakarta it seemed to me. I chose always to be hail-fellow-well-met in their presence and was grateful that my working class origins equipped me to pull off this act. But the bookish ones were usually the more senior and hardest to get close to. They scared me. Most of them were incredibly intelligent individuals. I worried each time we talked about this defector or that they would see through me and perceive my real intent.

Aleshkovsky told Mumford it was a Friday evening in late September 1986. 'I recall winter was fast approaching,' he said. 'All over Moscow people were cleaning boilers and fixing heating pipes in preparation for it. I had earlier requested a meeting with Shukhov and got into see him towards the end of the day. Instead of sitting at his desk, Shukhov suggested I sit on the sofa in his office.'

'Can I offer you a glass of vodka, Dmitri Aleksandrovich?'

'Despite our often-testy relationship,' Aleshkovsky said, 'I had warmed to Shukhov as it became clear his health was failing. I accepted his offer. Shukhov had slumped wearily in his armchair after preparing our drinks. The mere exertion of it was causing him to gasp for breath.'

'Emphysema,' Shukhov had said, once his lungs had absorbed enough oxygen for him to speak. 'It will cause me to cease working at some point and eventually kill me. Salut.'

'We then downed our vodkas in a single gulp,' Aleshkovsky said. 'Shukhov refilled our glasses. He became reflective, talking positively about Mikhail Gorbachev's elevation in February 1986 to General Secretary of the Communist Party of the Soviet Union. Among other things, he commended Gorbachev's anti-alcohol campaign, instituted to address chronic alcoholism among Russian men. Even so, Shukhov had a glint in his eye. He was sure, he said, that us imbibing a little tonight would not cause too much trouble.

'We drained our second glass, also in a single gulp, and began talking generally. I was surprised by Shukhov's apparent interest in my family and my children's progress at school. It was not until we were onto our third glass of vodka that he turned to business.'

'Tell me about Citadel,' Shukhov had said.

Aleshkovsky said by now he was feeling affected by the vodka. Rather than risk forgetting something he had referred to his pocket book notes. 'I reported,' he said, 'that now ten months into his assignment, Lambert appears well settled in Washington. I explained about the monitoring we did of Route 123 so as to gauge such things as the length of his meetings at Langley. I said we were also watching the homes of senior CIA people at nights and weekends, looking to sight Lambert's car, so far without success.

'Even so, I told Shukhov, there were signs of an incremental warming in Lambert's relations with the CIA. We based this on a recent sighting of Lambert at dinner in a Georgetown restaurant with Charles Kudermann, the CIA Deputy Director, and other senior CIA people. I finished with my assessment that while Lambert appeared on his way to winning the Americans' confidence, it would be slow going unless we instituted measures to foster closer ties.'

Aleshkovsky said Shukhov had considered this at length. 'Let me take you into my confidence, Dmitri,' he had said, the glint in his eye now gone even if his tone was still fatherly, 'something I rarely do with anyone in this madhouse. You should know I am personally invested in Citadel. Katya Lyubimova Vasilieva, remember her?'

Aleshkovsky told Mumford that Shukhov's admission of personal investment in Operation Citadel came as no surprise – he had suspected it for over a year now. But the mention of Katya as the subject of this personal investment was a new development. 'I was certain the vodka had not loosened Shukhov's lips,' Aleshkovsky said. 'He was choosing his words deliberately and carefully. "I do, General," I had replied with deliberate blandness. "I recall she was uncovered as a British agent in December 1977." '

All of a sudden, Aleshkovsky said, there was tension in the air, as if Shukhov was about to reveal something very secret about Katya. But an instinct seemed to have stopped him at the last moment. 'The General owed his career, and in every likelihood his life, to trusting no one and always holding his cards close to his chest,' Aleshkovsky said. 'I have no doubt he intended a moment of substantial openness but ingrained caution prevented it.'

'I was close to Katya's father,' Shukhov eventually had said. 'It killed him when we executed her. When we discovered Lambert was behind her role in compromising the entrapment of the British scientist in Vienna and her recruitment as an ongoing agent, I devised Citadel and the plan to destroy the US–UK intelligence relationship. It's an ambitious outcome I'm seeking. That's why I've been so fastidious and demanding of you.'

'Speaking intensely had caused Shukhov to labour for breath,' Aleshkovsky said. 'I waited for him to recover.'

'With the assistance of an oxygen mask,' Shukhov said on regaining his composure, 'I may be able to work a couple of more years during which time I would like to see Citadel reach its conclusion. After that, I'll go to the Dacha to die. The tumblers are falling into place, Dmitri, and I have no time to waste. Right now, this very instant, I want you to feed Lambert some red meat. Make the Americans love and revere him. Then early in 1987, after the CIA has had a chance to fully weigh Lambert's value, we will introduce a woman I have handpicked. I propose to call her Sunlight. I will tell you all about her shortly into the New Year.'

'Shukhov was now physically exhausted,' Aleshkovsky said. 'He did offer me a fourth vodka but only to be polite. I left feeling light-headed and clear at the same time. I now realized that Shukhov was engaged in a personal crusade linked to Katya – even if at the last minute he had decided to withhold the real how and why of this.

'Nonetheless, what he had said did explain why he was throwing a fortune at Citadel and moving with such precision. It also explained why he was prepared to kill Lambert's girlfriend and her co-workers, however uneasy I still felt about that. And I could now better understand why he had ordered the tidy-up killings of the Indian lorry driver and attesting witnesses involved in the woman's death, and separately that of the ex-RAF fellow in Brighton we used to channel the WRR minutes to Lambert.'

Chapter 40 – Ritchie

Ritchie Ross – what can I say? The deck was stacked against him from the word go. Charles Kudermann, the CIA Deputy Director, told me much about him one Sunday afternoon as we sat in the study of Kudermann's upmarket Georgetown apartment sipping Pappy Van Wrinkle's Family Reserve bourbon whisky. Aleshkovsky was later to complete the Ritchie story, his perspective from the Russian side plugging those gaps Kudermann could not fill.

Ritchie had an unusual background for a sailor, a submariner in fact. He had been brought up as a landlubber on a dairy farm outside the small South Dakota town of Millbank. Indeed, he never saw the sea until he was nearly nineteen. His father was a frequent binge drinker who although a decent, hard working man when sober underwent personality change when drunk. His dropping dead at age forty may have come as a relief to the family, but the dairy farm soon fell into dysfunction. The Co-op foreclosed on the lease about the same time as Ritchie's mother took up with a man from town who Ritchie said hated him from the day he laid eyes on him.

In 1961 aged eighteen Ritchie left for Chicago with vague notions of following in the footsteps of Jake Manders, one of Millbank's favourite sons who had played football for the Chicago Bears before the Second World War. But Ritchie was no Jake

Manders. When footballing opportunities did not arise, he found himself unable to find work. Scared and hungry, living off food stamps and sleeping rough, Ritchie was saved from utter destitution only by the good offices of the Chicago City Mission. It was while dossed in the charity he learned that some before him had escaped their circumstances by joining the armed services. It seems Ritchie knew the location of the Naval recruitment office on Chicago's north side. In any event, that's where he lodged his application to join the Navy. The mission boss provided character reference and management told Ritchie he had a bed for so long as it took for the Navy to make a decision.

The timing of Ritchie's bid to join the Navy was fortuitous in that a month later, a life-changing incident occurred that could have derailed the whole process. 'Ritchie was still very coy about it years after,' Kudermann told me. 'We had to prise it out of him.' Kudermann related how Ritchie was sexually molested by one of the mission's male volunteers. It was an era when checks on volunteers' backgrounds were cursory at best. The incident apparently entailed Ritchie waking one morning to find the volunteer performing oral sex on him. Ritchie was eventually to tell the CIA he allowed the process to reach its biological conclusion because of the irresistible pleasure he experienced. Only when the man sought to kiss him did Ritchie react.

Mission management later told the CIA it accepted some culpability for Ritchie's molestation. But he had half-killed the man and conduct so violent could not be tolerated under any circumstances. Ritchie had been asked to leave immediately. The mission's compromise was not to make a police report or withdraw its referee support for Ritchie's application to join the Navy.

Thrown out of the mission, Ritchie had wandered Chicago's streets for half a day before finally going to the Naval recruitment office. His timing was impeccable; the office had just received word that his application had been accepted. Ritchie was given a train ticket to the US Navy Great Lakes Training Centre and a cash advance of twenty-six dollars and fifty-four cents to cover expenses. He was to report for duty in one week.

Ritchie used most of his cash advance to rent a room at a fleapit hotel not far from Chicago's Union station. Lying on his bed he was faced with that unholy pairing of time to kill and no money to do it with. Ritchie told the CIA he had become bored and depressed. Only with the greatest reluctance did he then confess that before too long he had begun to think about the man's skilled arousal of him. Blushing like a choirboy, Kudermann said, Ritchie told the CIA that not once, not twice but three times he had brought himself to orgasm, experiencing after each climax a deep sense of self-disgust.

Ritchie appears never to have had another homosexual encounter. But vivid memories of his one remained. Ritchie lamented he had only to think of the man to be instantly filled with demanding lust. This led to him gaining a reputation as a needy and frequent user of prostitutes, earning him several unflattering nicknames. The only alternative – to get blind drunk – was not always feasible, or preferable. Little did Ritchie's detractors know that after each sexual release nauseating self-loathing consumed him. The internal conflict, the CIA shrinks were to conclude, left Ritchie pathologically anti-social and clinically paranoid.

In 1958 three years before Ritchie joined the Navy, the US nuclear-powered submarine *Nautilus* had circumnavigated the North Pole icecap without surfacing. The vessel remained continuously submerged for over four days. *Nautilus* had been able to complete the extraordinary feat because of its sophisticated internal navigation system, a type of gyrocompass that was unaffected by the pull of the Pole's magnetic field. Alarmed at this advance in American warfare capability, the Soviet High Command had tasked the KGB to give priority to recruiting sources within the US Navy submarine corps.

Despite the prestige and many practical positives attaching to the *Nautilus* feat, for the Navy an unwelcome and enduring development was a drop-off in internal volunteers for submarine service. Sailors all well understood the *Nautilus* had come perilously close to being trapped under the ice cap while in the

Bering Sea, whereupon its complement would have faced a slow and unimaginably terrible death. It was also appreciated that following on from the success of the *Nautilus*, other risky undersea ventures were likely as the US sought to press home its strategic advantage over the Soviets. It was one thing to find a relative handful of derring-do astronauts to take the plunge into space, but quite another to find the many numbers of suitably adventurous types to crew submarines testing new frontiers beneath the unforgiving sea. The shortage of submariners was still a headache for the Navy by the time Ritchie signed up for his initial four-year term.

From graduating basic training as a Seaman Recruit, Ritchie was posted to the US Naval base in Norfolk, Virginia. It was at Norfolk that he became aware the Navy was anxious to attract internal recruits to its submarine service. Although he had grown up in the wide-open spaces of South Dakota, the quiet isolation of the undersea appealed to Ritchie. He signed up. The Navy psychiatrists of the day, under pressure to pass potential recruits fit for submarine duty, erred on the side of generosity in concluding Ritchie had a harmlessly benign personality. In 1963 Ritchie was posted to the New London submarine base in Groton, Connecticut. Aleshkovsky later said that to the best of his knowledge, it was in Groton where Soviet talent spotters became aware of Ritchie's sexual proclivities and mulling loneliness. But he was a very junior sailor and only of limited value. He was filed away for another day.

The CIA consensus was that Ritchie made a reasonable fist of being a submariner. He spent many years at sea and inched up the non-commissioned ranks. But he was renowned as a loner and the solace he found at sea seemed only to entrench his anti-social tendencies. By the late 1970s Ritchie's career had plateaued at Petty Officer Third Class. Recruits into the submarine corps were now plentiful and the selection processes more effective.

In 1980 in a sure sign his career was spiralling down, Ritchie was transferred to a shore job at the new King's Bay submarine base near St Mary's, Georgia. He hated sitting behind a desk and the administrative work he did. The turn of the knife as far as Ritchie was concerned was this reduced him to a lowly clerk, the ultimate insult for a formerly seafaring submariner. The job did involve Ritchie handling highly classified material relating to propulsion systems on the US Atlantic fleet's nuclear-powered submarines. Even so, Kudermann told me, this did nothing for his damaged self-esteem. Forever a piston engine man, Ritchie had not the faintest understanding how the systems worked. At age thirty-seven, Ritchie came to realize he was all but washed up.

While on leave in Atlanta one evening in the summer of 1980, two women sat next to Ritchie in a bar. Ritchie told the CIA that neither of them looked like hookers, yet unprompted one began to talk to him. Ritchie said he often drank a lot in regular female company. It helped overcome the inadequacy he usually felt. This night was no exception. By the end of it he was extremely drunk and could barely remember the woman and her friend returning with him to his hotel.

Aleshkovsky said a loose-lipped contractor had alerted the Russians to Ritchie's transfer to the bunker at King's Bay, the nickname given the base's secure building. This was the moment they had been waiting for. A blackmail play was designed centring on framing Ritchie as a paedophile.

The original plan was for the lead recruiter, the woman who had engaged Ritchie in the bar, to arouse Ritchie once back at his hotel. A female minor would then be introduced, brought to the hotel room by a third Soviet operative at a pre-arranged time. The intention was for the woman, the child and Ritchie to engage in sexual foreplay. At some point the woman would declare a preference to watch. In anticipation of Ritchie's urges now having the better of him, his sexual reputation having preceded him, the woman would encourage him to have sex with the child. The non-participating Russian woman, who also doubled as the lead's security guard, would take photographs of Ritchie either penetrating or attempting to penetrate the young girl.

But alcohol consumption beyond a certain point sedated Ritchie. This was the alternative to using prostitutes he occasionally relied on when his private sexual stimulus took hold. On return to his hotel room, the team later reported, Ritchie was too drunk for anything. Incapable of arousal, he had soon fallen back on the bed and passed out. Aleshkovsky would later admit that although the Russians knew Ritchie was a heavy drinker, they had no idea his drinking to excess inhibited his fabled sexual appetite.

When the third Soviet operative arrived at Ritchie's hotel room as planned, he carried a bag containing a Polaroid camera and other items, and had with him a Hispanic girl of thirteen who had been hawked by her drug-addled parents. It was obvious to the Russians it would be impossible to photograph the comatose Ritchie *in flagrante delicto*. Instead they opted for an after the fact approach. This entailed the girl lying naked on the bed alongside Ritchie, whereupon the man inserted dollops of a cream-like substance into her so as to make it look like the remnants of a sexual encounter, so that it seeped out of her onto the bed cover. That done, he picked up Ritchie's shrunken member by its glans – Aleshkovsky was at pains to tell Martin Mumford the man wore surgical gloves throughout – and extended it sufficiently to cover the shaft with theatrical blood. The security guard then took photographs.

Only when the women were satisfied with the quality of the security guard's photographic handiwork was the young girl was allowed to dress. The male operative took her to an appointed drop-off point where he gave her the final instalment of the 1000 dollar fee her parents had demanded. The women returned to their separate hotels, reuniting five hours later to return to Ritchie's hotel.

Aleshkovsky was to explain that the Russians had settled on the paedophile trap because by 1980 community awareness in the United States of child sexual exploitation had progressed to the point where groups had sprung up taking it upon themselves to pursue child sexual predators. Some such groups were little better than the paedophiles themselves, blatantly seeking to manipulate community outrage to advance their own warped agendas. The Russians had assumed, Aleshkovsky said, Ritchie would understand the grief to be visited on him should one of these madhouse outfits get him in their crosshairs. Their zealousness was legendary.

The Russians in fact had again misjudged. Ritchie told the CIA he did not grasp the significance of their threat to feed him to the Child Sanctity Christian Coalition, a malevolent fundamentalist group based in Lafayette, Louisiana. He had never heard of it. Rather, Ritchie said he had agreed to work for the Russians because they mentioned the Lafayette group would almost certainly give the photographs of him to the newspapers. Ritchie said he realized that no matter how much he protested his innocence, some would forever see him as a sexual deviant. All he could think of was the man in Chicago lurking in the shadows, watching and waiting for an unsuspecting victim. He told the CIA the thought of being placed in the same category repulsed and excited him at the same time, and how this feeling distressed him more than words could ever explain. That's why he became a Russian spy. This and the fact the Russians were prepared to pay him two hundred a month. It gave him much satisfaction, Ritchie admitted, to at least extract a measure of revenge against the Navy. Kudermann said Ritchie had howled for a long time after signing the transcript of his confession.

The deal reached with the Russians was for Ritchie to use a miniature camera to photograph documents crossing his desk. He was to give priority to documents classified *Top Secret* and beyond. Each week he would meet a handler who would replenish the camera's film. Aleshkovsky told Martin Mumford that for nearly five years the Soviets had been very pleased with Ritchie's product; the information he provided on American nuclear submarine propulsion systems was of the highest grade.

But by 1986 the creeping introduction of computing meant Ritchie was fast approaching his use-by date. Documents were increasingly distributed electronically and when so an electronic footprint revealed who had accessed them. Moreover, documents captured within a computer could not be photographed satisfactorily; nor could they be printed without creating a record of this. A decision was reached that it was time to sever ties with Ritchie. 'The political people,' Aleshkovsky said, 'didn't want Ritchie in Moscow. But for the sake of any other would-be agent, we at the KGB didn't want to be seen as abandoning him. Shukhov and I reached the same conclusion. He had to be given up.'

Chapter 41 – Epiphany

My apartment in McLean came with two side-by-side car parks. As I had only the one car, it was not uncommon in my early days to arrive home late from the office to find that someone, usually another tenant's visitor, had parked in one of my two spots. I objected to this because when returning home late and tired it suited me to swing into the bays leaving my car straddling both slots. I had complained to building security and the infringement of my parking space had virtually ceased.

I reacted angrily, therefore, on the night of Friday 17 October 1986, arriving home exhausted at 11 pm, when I spied on entering the underground garage a vehicle parked in one of my parking spots. As I drew closer I could see that the car, a sky blue Chevy Camaro, carried diplomatic corps plates. The identification number, however, was not one I knew. I resolved once I found out to which embassy it belonged to make my displeasure abundantly clear.

I pulled in to the vacant slot and to my amazement saw the shapes of two persons sitting in the Camaro's front seats. A tall blond man I had never seen before emerged from the driver's side and opened my passenger-side door. 'You'll have to forgive the diplomatic plates on my car,' he said amiably. 'When you check you'll find they belong to Sao Tome and Principe. They're not genuine. It's just that diplomatic plates were necessary to get past the front security office.' My reaction was to fire-off a rapid volley of questions mixed with aggressive bluster. 'Don't get feisty,' the man said. 'We need to speak and of course my colleague,' indicating with his head to the second man still seated in the Camaro, 'is not here for his good looks.'

The blond man was now seated in my front passenger seat.

'And?' I asked icily.

'My people have certain information the American Government would be pleased to receive and we have decided it would be best if you gave it to them,' he answered calmly. I tried to speak but my incredulity prevented me from finding the right words. 'It concerns a US serviceman, a matelot I believe,' the man went on, 'who for some years has been passing high-grade information to the Soviets. His name is Ritchie Ross and he is currently based at King's Bay in Georgia.'

And who might I say told me this?' I asked acerbically, my voice rasping with tension.

'Whom I represent need not concern you,' the man replied. 'This is because next Friday night you will attend the Austrian Embassy's National Day reception.' He threw back his head in what appeared to be genuine amusement. 'Those lazy schnitzels refuse to work on Sunday, when Austrian Independence Day actually falls this year. But I digress.'

The man was matter of fact again. 'At the function a man called Sukhan Ovezov will approach you. He is attached to the KGB station here in Washington working under political cover. He is from Turkmenistan and because of this doesn't get any of the sexy work. Perhaps that is why the FBI has not identified him as an intelligence officer. But Ovezov has done good work among the Turkmen community in New York City. As a reward, his KGB masters have tasked him to take what he believes is the first step towards recruiting you into a deception operation.

'Please proceed carefully,' the man continued. 'You should not let on you are expecting Ovezov's approach and always remember he thinks the *Ritchie Ross* name is a work name. Ovezov will demand money. The plan so far as Ovezov is concerned is for the first batch of documents he sells you to be high-grade intelligence provided by the source, genuine US Navy documents. He has been told this is to snare you and set you up to be sold bogus information. And the first tranche of documents will be genuine. But they will not reveal a work name as Ovezov thinks; unbeknown to him they will unambiguously identify Ritchie Ross as a traitor.

'You will report the Ovezov contact to London and recommend the obvious – that the Americans be made aware of Ritchie Ross's treachery. In due course Ross will be arrested. Naturally, you will refrain from mentioning Ovezov does not know Ritchie Ross is a real person and if necessary deny any later claims to that effect. You will also recommend the Americans be informed of Ovezov's identity. London is certain to agree. The Americans are always deeply resentful of undetected KGB officers. Mr Ovezov will be expelled, returning to Moscow to an uncertain fate, unfortunately.'

The sheer ruthlessness of the apparent Soviet intention to throw Ovezov to the sharks reminded me of my own vulnerabilities. 'Look,' I said, 'you need to understand I've already had people drop things in my lap and lightning rarely strikes twice.'

'I take it that is a reference to Mr Garrick Cuthberson,' the man said. 'My people have seen no indication the Americans know about him, his WRR minutes and the second Rhodesian matter. If we are correct, your coming across Ovezov will not arouse any American suspicions.' He looked at me questioningly. I stared back, expressionless. Yet, somehow, he still seemed to have detected the truth. 'Perfidious Albion,' he said in mock reproach, smiling broadly. Soberly, he continued. 'Nor should you worry about London's reaction. Your contact with Ovezov will occur during normal diplomatic business and not be seen as out of the ordinary. Added to which, Ovezov's approach to you is not inconsistent with the disaffection often displayed by non-Russian Soviets who feel poorly treated by the Russians. Your head office is always anxious to please the Americans. It will be salivating at the prospect of alerting them to a traitor and providing the name of a previously unidentified Soviet intelligence operative.'

I reached across the man and locked the front passenger door. It was a waste of energy. All he had to do was lift the locking button. But it symbolized how I felt. 'I'm assuming you're from this O'Hare group that wants to pretend it's my fairy godmother,' I said as menacingly as I could. 'I know you've got nothing to do with the IRA. You are not getting out of this car without telling me exactly who you are and why your people want to help me.'

The man showed no alarm. 'My instructions,' he said, 'are to say nothing about our organization. But I do understand your inquisitiveness. Yes, I do act on behalf of the O'Hare group as you choose to call it. We are an international coalition that wants to address global inequity. Our belief is that you, a product of the British working class, being in a position of power in the British Secret Service is a step towards our objective of a fairer world unconstrained by the shackles of left and right ideology.'

'OK,' I said, far from convinced. 'But how do you know what the KGB's Washington station intends to do this time next week and more to the point why is it doing what you say it plans to do?'

'Mr Lambert,' the man said patiently, 'you so underestimate our level of support. We have men and women from all walks of life working for us. Information comes to us all the time. As to why the KGB station proposes to proceed as outlined, I would simply encourage you to accept it has its reasons.'

'Sounds like a load of cobblers to me,' I retorted. The man shrugged and didn't answer. 'Where is your organization based then?' I asked belligerently.

The man looked at his watch. 'I have no more time for questions, I'm afraid. Just do as I ask and I assure you your photograph will soon take pride of place on the mantelpiece at Langley.'

I watched the man and his companion drive away, knowing for certain he'd been selling me a line about the O'Hare group. Slumped at my kitchen table and deeply fatigued, I tried to think this through. Slowly my thoughts crystallized, and when they did the moment of epiphany dawned. The man's knowledge of the internal machinations of the KGB's Washington station was surely the key. Whereas previously the Rhodesian incidents involving Freddie Ladler and Reggie Sullivan offered no inkling of a link to the Soviets, a Soviet connection now existed.

The more I thought about it, the more obvious it became that this O'Hare business was actually a front for a complex Soviet orchestration. Who else had the resources and organizational skills, not to mention the utter ruthlessness? Anthony Delminico's death; Ladler's besmirching; Cuthberson, Reggie and the WRR minutes were all somehow connected. With startling clarity it dawned on me that Agnes's death was not a case of tit for tat revenge. 'It's a part of this Soviet play,' I exclaimed loudly. But in that instant, as my words reverberated around my dark and silent apartment, I also knew this changed nothing. The Soviets had butchered Agnes, whatever their reasons. My resolve to identify Agnes's killer and take retribution had not diminished; even so, it surged anew.

But what was the Soviet play? Why had they previously gone to such lengths to assist me, and why now were they willing to give up a source and an operative all for nothing obvious in return? The answer immediately hit me: the Soviets had a very big fish to fry and for some reason inflating my credentials was central to it. The guaranteed effect of my alerting the Americans to Ross and Ovezov told me that much.

As to the Soviets' end point I had no idea, other than they were prepared to play a long, long game in getting there. But if the Sovs wanted so badly to cosy up to me I would see where it took me, only from here on with my *eyes wide open*. In the interim, if what they were giving me caused the Americans to take me to their hearts I would happily use it. After all, it would probably come down to a race between the Sovs and me to see who got to the finish line first.

The man who drove out of my apartment block garage was Finnish by birth Aleshkovsky later informed us. He had worked for the Russians for a number of years, many of those while living in the United States. Aleshkovsky said that when asked by the KGB Resident how things had gone, the Finn had replied, 'Reasonable but no more. Lambert has seen through the IRA cover and because of that I was forced into giving him the international coalition spiel.'

'The Resident, who knew a little but not the lot, rang on the secure line to warn me of this,' Aleshkovsky told Mumford. 'I alerted Shukhov, telling him that now the Ovezov phase had been introduced, it was only a matter of time before Lambert would work out we were pulling the strings.'

When Mumford asked about Shukhov's response, Aleshkovsky said, 'He was worried, certainly, as I was. But all he said was something to the effect that provided we can get over this step, he was confident Sunlight could do her part.'

Chapter 42 – Ovezov

Friday 24 October 1986. After the usual problems of finding a car park, I entered the front door of the grey sandstone Austrian embassy. A very Germanic-looking Ambassador with brilliantly shined shoes headed the reception line. He shook my hand before quickly losing interest in me. I mingled, chatting to this one and that. Somewhat apprehensive about what was supposed to unfold, I allowed myself a second glass of the dry white wine of the Gruner Veltliner variety the Austrians' so prefer.

The reception was scheduled for two hours. After an hour nothing of note had happened. The mid-point speeches took place, firstly by the Ambassador and then in reply the ranking American, some heavy-hitter from the State Department. Respective national anthems followed each speech. I thought the State mandarin's speech was interesting. He pushed the line that Austria should abandon the neutrality it adopted immediately after World War Two and join the Western Alliance. There he suggested none too tactfully was where Austria's future lay. I found it hard to disagree with him.

Thereafter, a Viennese orchestra was pressed into service and guests invited to dance. I fell into a meaningless conversation with an intense German woman. She asked me if I had ever been to Vienna and did not smile when confirming, in response to my tongue in cheek question, she meant the Austrian capital and not the Northern Virginian town across the river from Washington DC. I affirmed I had but spared her the fact I hadn't gone there as me. The woman asked where I usually stayed. 'The Erdberger Wien,' I lied.

'Ah, well then,' she replied, 'you must go there for your work.'

I took that as a reference to me being an impecunious civil servant unable to lodge at the Erdberger without the assistance of the long-suffering British taxpayer. Inspired by the truth of her insult, and the growing conviction Ovezov was a no-show, I was about to go home. Then I felt a slight tap on my right elbow. A man much shorter than me, swarthy in complexion and wearing rimless spectacles smiled at me.

I gratefully excused myself from my German tormentor and bid the man good evening. 'Mr Lambert,' he said, not bothering to disguise he already knew who I was, 'may I give you my business card?' *Sukhan Ovezov, Second Secretary (political), Embassy of the Soviet Union* it read.

Hiding there in plain sight, amid the hubbub and frivolity going on around us, Ovezov cast his net. 'I am Turkmen,' he said in stilted English, the by-product of rote learning of the language. 'The Russians treat people like me with contempt. I have a proposal. I know of an American serviceman selling secrets to the KGB. For

10,000 US dollars, I will provide you with some of the documents he has passed over. The information I am offering will not reveal the traitor's true identity, only his work name. But what I can provide will facilitate measures to help counteract the damage he has done. Provided you do not reveal me to the Americans as your source, for a suitable fee I can offer you other information on an ongoing basis.'

'Whoa, hang on cowboy, not so fast,' I said. 'How do I know you are telling me the truth? I would need verification there is an American traitor as you claim. I might add that ten grand is a very steep asking price, especially as you don't know the traitor's real name. Money doesn't grow on trees. How about five if you can prove to me you're genuine?'

Spy to spy, I admired the way Ovezov held his nerve. I had fully expected him to meet me halfway on the money. But he knew the key to enticing me into his disinformation sting was not to devalue his product. 'No, 10,000 it is,' he said, 'take it or leave it.' I pretended to think this over but Ovezov coolly feigned impatience. 'Meet me at 4 pm next Thursday at the Air and Space Museum, in front of the lunar landing capsule. I will bring the proof you require, you bring the money.' With that, he disappeared into the crowd. The last I saw of him he was very capably dancing the Viennese waltz with a blonde piece about a foot and half taller than him.

I returned immediately to the embassy. There I cabled a modified report of my encounter to London, one indicating that Ovezov was offering documents identifying a US traitor. I noted the Thursday deadline and the asking price. As a senior station head, I was expected to make recommendations. These were usually acted on unless there was a good reason why not. I made the normally persuasive observation I assessed Ovezov to be genuine and argued that provided his information positively identified the serviceman the substantial expense would be justified. To this, I added the obvious recommendation that the Americans should be informed of the traitor's identity if it was revealed. But I wrote my dispatch already knowing that Ovezov's material would clearly finger Ritchie Ross. I left out the bit about Ovezov, unaware he was poised to shop a real source, preparing to sign his own death warrant.

The question of revealing Ovezov's identity required more nuance. I knew the outcome I wanted but not to come across as too eager. Martin Mumford's wise advice in the aftermath of the Massimov disaster stood me in good stead. I decided to provide two options. One was not to reveal Ovezov to the Americans so long as he gave us good information at a reasonable price. We would then share the intelligence with the CIA in accordance with the standing agreement. The other was to inform the Americans of the likely presence of an undetected KGB officer in their midst, including the word *likely* for the benefit of my readership. The inherent risk, I noted, was Ovezov's expulsion and the loss of his product. I recommended the second option, risk notwithstanding. Alerting the Americans to Ovezov would allow them to decide whether to kick him out or string him along. It was their country after all. I knew Mumford would understand my preference for consultation. He would also be influential in London's decision. For three days I sweated on a response, hoping for the go-ahead on the second option and the deep ingratiation with the Americans it offered.

'Joe, Joe please have another piece of the pecan pie,' Betsy Kudermann, wife of CIA Deputy Director Charles, implored me. 'It's so nice to have you to Sunday lunch. We want you to feel right at home.'

'For God's sake Betsy leave the man be,' Kudermann said. 'He's a big boy. If he's hungry he'll have more pie when he wants it.' Smiling warmly at me he said, 'Let's go into the study, Joe. We can have a glass of bourbon and kick over the traces while we're waiting for Bill to drop by.' Once seated in our floral-patterned lounge chairs Kudermann said, 'It's not every day the Director makes a social call you know, Joe. It's really a gesture to say how grateful we are for your efforts with Ovezov. Turns out this Ross character was really mixed up. A real loner: no friends, no family; just ripe for turning.'

Jesus Christ, I thought, *he could be speaking about me.*

Kudermann then proceeded to give me the CIA's version of the Ritchie Ross story. Hearing him list Ritchie's vulnerabilities prompted me to think about the Service's attitude to loners. Nought had been right about its eventual evolution, to the point today where a person's natural reclusiveness was no longer automatically considered symptomatic of a security risk. I was no doubt a beneficiary of this maturity. Even so, my foundational years were in a less enlightened organization. From that perspective my ill-starred marriage to Kathleen had not been a mistake. And after all, I reasoned, it had served a purpose for both parties.

The recall of my marriage of convenience made me yearn, not for the first time, for Agnes to have been Kathleen. The futility somehow reminded me that since Agnes's death I had reverted to total obsession, not as the dedicated careerist of yore but as her uncompromising avenger. From out of nowhere it struck me how this relentless pursuit had left me unable to differentiate between right and wrong: Delminico's murder; the crucifying of Reggie Sullivan; and Ovezov's recent fate, and the lack of remorse I felt over any of it, signified just how estranged from mainstream society I'd become. A jarring unpleasantness overtook me. Nought's prophecy of moral incompetence, I realized, had come true. I was now the real life equivalent of an outcast wolf solitarily padding across a frozen landscape of death and deception. *Now here I am, I* thought, *The Lone Wolf at Cover, sitting in the CIA's inner sanctum waiting for its Director to come and shake my hand.* I suddenly felt chill. It was the thought there were many twists and turns still to come before the dangerous double game set in train by my visit to Phoenix Investments fully unfolded. How prescient I was.

There is simply no greater indicator of status than a car park, especially a reserved place under the main CIA building. And that's what the CIA gave me: *UK Liaison* the plate on the wall read. I was still unable to walk the corridors of Langley without an escort. But whereas people previously avoided eye contact, those same people were now falling over themselves to greet me as I passed by. My escort on most occasions, more a companion in truth, was usually a senior officer only rarely ever seen accompanying visitors as they transited from one area of the CIA to another. As promised by my tall blond visitor that night in October last year, my photograph was in pride of place on the CIA's mantelpiece.

Robert Sandilands, Director Reception Analysis, the sign on the office door read. Robert was a scholarly man of about fifty. His vague title translated into him having responsibility within the CIA for processing Soviet defectors. We wasted little time on small talk; he wasn't that sort of guy.

'Robert,' I said, 'now that January's over and everyone's back at work, my first project for 1987 is to build up my station's knowledge of current KGB structures. In my opinion we've been tardy on this both here and in London. I've taken it upon myself to address this information gap. We're particularly weak on Soviet clandestine ops against foreign personnel. Wet affairs used to be the province of the First Directorate and psyops, honey traps and naughty pictures, that sort of thing, used to be run by the Third Directorate. I've seen nothing suggesting this has changed, but as to who heads the various sub-directorates and who is coordinating it all we currently have little clarity. I was wondering if you might have someone who has stepped over in the last little while who might have that sort of knowledge?'

My request for information on KGB structures was calculated. I had chosen the topic because the Americans could not assist me with it. They preferred to worry about what they were doing rather than trying to keep track of how the opposition was lined up on any given day. The structures enquiry was also designed to gain access to a defector with knowledge of recent happenings in Moscow Centre and avoid me being saddled with a nonentity who had just jumped the fence at some out of the way Soviet embassy.

Robert reminded me of Petr Klaus, the man whose objectivity spared me from summary dismissal after the Konrad debacle twenty years ago, in that he stared unblinkingly at people while thinking. It had the same unnerving effect. 'We're happy to take requests for additional defector information from the SIS head in Washington,' he said, 'especially from you, Joe,' he added with a smile coming unnaturally to him. 'Let me check if there's anything we can offer you. If there is, we'd be pleased to receive a list of questions.'

'Actually, Robert,' I said, deliberately adopting an unsmiling, businesslike countenance, 'at a luncheon hosted by the deputy late last year, to which I was pleased to be invited, Director Casey spoke of a new era in US–UK intelligence cooperation. In that spirit, as head of SIS station, Washington I will no longer accept the UK being treated as an unequal party when making *ad hoc* requests for defector information. With the commencement of this new era, to use the Director's own words, we will no longer submit questions and accept answers to them filtered through the lens of US perceptions. If you have someone who can help, I expect to be able to speak directly to that person. Check with Kudermann if you feel the need. I am here seeking the level of cooperation to which the Director referred, not asking to be babysat.'

Sandilands considered what I had to say and didn't like it much. His warmth had evaporated and he was now itching to tell me to piss off, albeit in the words of the very reserved man he was. But the mention of the Director had made him cautious. 'I will speak to the deputy as you suggest. If he thinks it appropriate we will consider what might be possible. Good afternoon,' he said, curtly dismissing me. An underling saw me out.

I fretted I had overplayed my hand. Kudermann had witnessed the Director metaphorically slapping me on the back and I wondered in hindsight if he might have been my best bet. That said, I also knew it would have looked odd if I had gone direct to Kudermann without first raising the matter with Sandilands, the officer in charge of the line area. It was a whole week before my assistant advised Kudermann's office had called seeking an appointment with me. I confirmed Wednesday at 2 pm would be fine.

Kudermann and Sandilands were waiting when I was ushered into the former's office. None of the handshaking routine this time, Kudermann got straight to the point. 'It's an irregular request you've made, Joe. And we, Robert and me, are not particularly at ease with it. I hardly need tell you defectors are a very sensitive business. The long-standing practice has been to accept defector information requests from head of SIS, Washington but this has always been conditional upon the incumbent submitting a list of questions. I see no reason to depart from that arrangement.'

'Charles,' I said, using the familiarity of Kudermann's Christian name to remind him of the bonhomie lavished on me at his home, 'you were there when the Director told me my work on Ovezov was the harbinger of a new standard of UK–US intelligence cooperation. You will also recall the Director lauded my proposal to my Service not to run Ovezov until he ran out of goodies but instead to give the US early opportunity to kick him out, which State duly did. Now you seem to be telling me the Director did not mean what he said. Frankly, I am shocked at this development.'

Kudermann was not enjoying the conversation. He wanted desperately to tell me that was precisely the case; that the Director had just been laying it on hoping to encourage similar instances of cooperation. Kudermann also knew that admitting the Director's motive was out of the question. He needed to put the conundrum to bed, once and for all.

Kudermann glanced briefly at Sandilands before speaking. 'You have misinterpreted the Director by some distance. But because of your confusion, and in light of the special relationship between our Services, I am prepared to offer you a single exception to the rule. I do so on the clear understanding that on completion of this exception, or indeed your declining it, the favour you did us henceforth will be fully repaid. The offer is for Robert to arrange for you to speak to someone who came in just under three weeks ago and for whom proper processing has yet to begin. The interview you will be granted is for a maximum of thirty minutes. No notes will be permitted. We will, of course, be listening. And one last thing, with immediate effect we are rescinding your parking rights. You will now have at your disposal the general public parking lot, which I understand offers visitors to the CIA the facility of metered parking.'

I made noises about grave disappointment at the Service's senior-most levels with this tepid interpretation of *a new standard in cooperation* and followed up with a show of indecision and reluctance before accepting the offer on the table. I believe I also uttered the word *petulant* when talking about my ill-fated parking space. But Kudermann had shut down; he wasn't listening. *No more lunches in Georgetown for Joey boy*, I thought grimly as I was escorted from the building, this time in the true sense of the word.

For all that Kudermann was true to his word. On Monday 23 February 1987 in a heavily guarded safe house in Bethesda, Maryland I sat across the table from a tired and nervous yet still alert Major Zamir Umarov, formerly deputy director of the KGB's Third Directorate presently headed by Colonel Dmitri Aleshkovsky. The CIA, of course, was the third party to whom Umarov was to vent his spleen over the disrespectful treatment he had received at the hands of General Shukhov back in January 1985.

Chapter 43 – Umarov

Mumford later told me that Aleshkovsky seemed to bear no grudge against Umarov, despite Umarov's deception of him. 'I suppose by the time I got to debriefing Aleshkovsky,' Martin said, 'they were peas in the same pod by then. When I raised Umarov's defection, Aleshkovsky just gave me the facts without any obvious emotion.'

It seems from what Aleshkovsky had to say that Zamir had taken leave in the second week of January 1987. The family – Zamir, his wife and two children – was planning to ski at a resort in the Ural Mountains. Zamir had provided a hotel telephone number in case of emergency. 'But he did so,' Aleshkovsky had said, 'knowing I rarely bothered my staff while they were on leave and refreshing.

'Two days after Zamir should have returned to the office,' Aleshkovsky said, 'there was no sign of him. I put out a trace. A report was received to the effect that the Umarov family, all four of them, had been allowed to drive across the border into Finland because their passports contained valid exit visas. Further investigations revealed a letter using the forged signature of General Shukhov had authorized the visa issue. I tasked the KGB station in Helsinki to follow-up urgently. It reported that Zamir's car had been found abandoned at Helsinki-Vantaa airport but the Finns could find no record of the Umarovs leaving the country. I knew then Zamir had flown the coop. I had sent him to a security conference in Lyon the preceding November. I remember thinking *I bet that is where whoever it was got to him* once it was obvious he had gone.'

Then, Aleshkovsky told Mumford, a mere forty-eight hours later on an appropriately bleak Friday morning, crisis had turned to catastrophe. 'This took the form,' Aleshkovsky said, 'of a report from Washington station suggesting the CIA's grasp of Lambert to its bosom, triggered by his giving it Ritchie Ross's name and the unearthing of Sukhan Ovezov, had apparently been released without obvious explanation. From dining with the deputy and socializing with the Director late last year, Lambert had last been seen in a convenience store seeking parking meter change before proceeding to Langley for what turned out to be a very short meeting. The report cautioned nothing was definite. But I didn't need to read anymore. As with Umarov, I knew instinctively this was bad news.'

Aleshkovsky said his immediate reaction was to think about how he would break the news of the dual setbacks to Shukhov. 'The General was due back at work the next Monday,' he said. 'He had just spent two weeks ostensibly on leave but in fact at a sanatorium in Sochi where the doctors were trying to remove some of the shit that was clogging up his lungs and slowly suffocating him.'

'This is Mr John Partridge. He is from the British Government. He will ask you a series of questions. Understood?' Umarov nodded.

Thank you, Sergeant,' I said to the marine who had admitted me to the poorly lit, windowless room. I didn't have much time to get to ask the questions I wanted to ask. But I also knew the listening Americans would be expecting me to concentrate on KGB structures where my expressed interest lay. For twenty minutes, I probed Umarov on this subject. He seemed bored, and who could blame him. In all probability he mentioned Shukhov but without a record of the discussions it was impossible to recall all the names he threw up. Now with ten minutes to go I decided to chance my arm.

'Tell me,' I said, 'are you aware of any operations past or present against British civilians; private citizens who are not British Government employees?'

Umarov rubbed the back of his neck. He was not about to tell me much. He needed to amass as many bargaining chips as he could. 'As I told you,' he said, 'I worked only in one of a number of areas covered by the Third Directorate. I have no insights, for example, into political or economic operations designed to influence government policy, usually involving the recruitment of prominent trade union officials or academics.'

I realized then Umarov had misunderstood my intention. He thought it was exactly in these areas where I was focused. That's why he was so openly withholding, signalling he wanted something in return. My pulse quickened a little. Umarov's evasion substantially narrowed the subjects he could talk about. 'Those fields you list, Major Umarov, in which you claim no knowledge, are of major importance to my government. Unfortunately, there is today insufficient time for game playing. I would simply caution you these matters will be revisited and when they are I would encourage you to be more forthcoming if you know what is best for you and your family. For now, however, can you tell me please about any other operations against non-government British citizens of which you have or had visibility, full or partial?'

Umarov's face remained expressionless. But it soon became apparent my question would have pleased him because he proceeded to throw me a bone that involved no burning of capital. 'There was one operation, a recruitment running against a male British person for which I was not indoctrinated. My superior, Colonel Aleshkovsky, had tactical responsibility for it. Strategy was directed by one of the sub-Director Generals of whom I spoke earlier. In this case it was General Sergei Shukhov, who treated the operation as a matter of extreme importance. I have no idea about the target person, what he did or why the matter was so important to Shukhov. What I do know is that one day when expressing his frustration at Shukhov's demands, Colonel Aleshkovsky had let on there had been several operational killings ordered by the General, including the man's girlfriend in a fake car accident. I do not know her nationality or where she was killed, but if the man was British I suppose it is possible the girlfriend might also have been British. The operation was still running when I left. I have no idea as to its current status.'

It was my turn to be impassive. Umarov had just iced the cake that Agnes's driver, Gulam, had baked in his letter to me over three years ago. I stood and without another word rapped on the door. The marine who opened it wore a watch with a large digital display. The stopwatch function had been selected. It showed I had interviewed Umarov for twenty-nine minutes and forty-two seconds.

Aleshkovsky was to tell Martin Mumford of his tenseness as he approached Shukhov's office. 'Shukhov and I had become quite close over the preceding few months,' Aleshkovsky said. 'I hoped this would stand me in good stead. But my worst fears appeared to be realized once I had briefed him. He had been cold and formal, describing the Umarov and Lambert developments as *calamitous*. I wondered if this meant our relationship had now relapsed, or worse.'

But then, according to Aleshkovsky, Shukhov had softened. 'Dmitri,' he said, 'the doctors in Sochi gave me a new type of steroid, a medicine I inhale. Used together with my oxygen mask it helps with my breathing and will hopefully extend the time I have before I get too feeble. I've been warned the reprieve will be temporary and my decline could happen without warning. But the relief I'm currently experiencing is timely. It convinces me that with this apparent downturn in Lambert's fortunes, we can afford to be patient in progressing Citadel. We should not be panicked into revising the operation. The objective for now remains to recruit Lambert while he is in the American inner fold.'

Aleshkovsky told Mumford he was sufficiently encouraged by Shukhov's conciliatory tone to put to him it was impossible to predict when, if ever, I would be restored to the CIA's inner circle.

Shukhov had apparently pondered this for some time before replying. 'As you note, Dmitri, whatever has gone on in Washington has not resulted in Lambert being sent packing, either by the Americans or his own side. My instincts are telling me his position will improve. The unknown is to what extent. I accept we cannot mount another operation to assist him curry favour. That would be far too obvious. But I reiterate we can afford to wait, particularly as that devious Uzbek bastard Umarov cannot compromise Citadel. A small mercy, but one for which we can be grateful. He will bring down the house on a raft of other operations when he finally spills his guts but he has no knowledge of Citadel.'

Dear General, Aleshkovsky said he had thought, *but for you and others like you Zamir would still be here.* 'But I kept that heresy to myself,' he told Mumford with a wry smile.

'The General then proceeded to shuffle his papers,' Aleshkovsky said, 'giving himself time to regain his breath.'

'Let's see if Lambert can recover his status,' Shukhov had said once stable. 'I am prepared to wait up to a year if we have to, unless beforehand this illness of mine completely strips the stripes from the tiger in me. If we become certain the Americans will not rehabilitate Lambert we may be forced to review our plans as regards his recruitment. But let's see. In the meantime sit down and I will tell you about Sunlight. When the time comes we need her to be ready for immediate deployment to Washington. Who knows when Lambert's fortunes might revive?'

I had no option but to report to London on my interview with Umarov. To have not done so would have caused all sorts of problems. The report I compiled was unavoidably a confession, of how I had wasted the priceless collateral we had earned with the Americans without so much as a word of consultation with head office. This admission of unilateralism alone was sufficient for the fifth floor to reach for a large red pen and put a line through my name on its list of potential DDGs, not that I now particularly cared.

I needed to be succinct. A legacy of the root and branch review I did with Freddie Ladler and Brian McGowan years back was that reports were not to exceed three pages. I explained briefly the background: the CIA Director's pat on my back; how I'd taken it upon myself to leverage off this and obtain more direct access to American product; and how the Americans had baulked. I then summarized the circumstances of how I'd come to interview

Umarov on a one-off basis and voice my belief that he knew of several major operations against the UK. I closed with the recommendation the Service press the Americans for early access to Umarov by a specialist interrogation team.

The Americans put me in the freezer for three months. They brought me out in time to allow me to make preparations for the DG's annual visit to Washington in June 1987. There was no formal declaration of the thaw. Rather, they relied on car park diplomacy in that one day in May, out of the blue, an unspeaking official gave me a pass allowing me to park in the area reserved for approved diplomats. It was highly symbolic: parking underneath the CIA was a sure sign of being in the inner circle; parking in the public area, with the accursed parking meters, was an equally sure sign of being on the outer; while parking in the outdoor space reserved for approved diplomats, physically situated as it was between the main CIA building and the public car park, indicated a status somewhere in between. The *status quo ante* had been restored; in as when I arrived I was no longer regarded as on the nose but still someone to be treated cautiously and kept at arm's length.

The DG came alone. His visit went well although he was noticeably cool towards me. It was a living certainty the Americans would have chewed his ear over my conduct, leading me to wonder if I might subsequently be recalled. That did not eventuate, principally I expect because the DG did not want to attract the political attention invited by successive heads of station failing to complete their assignments. Instead the sop he extended to the CIA was a reshuffle of DDGs a month after his return from Washington. The smiling, affable, stab-you-in-the-guts-when-you-were-not-looking Digby Carhiddy became my supervising DDG in place of Martin Mumford. Mumford's becoming the scapegoat for my apparent rashness deeply upset me. He had always supported me. I hoped one day to explain his judgement wasn't astray.

The footnote to discovering Shukhov was responsible for Agnes's death was that my tenuous relations with the Americans and my own Service gave me little leeway to take advantage of the breakthrough. Had I flagged an interest in Shukhov's movements with either, the first thing I would have been asked to explain was why I was seeking this information.

I floated Shukhov's name with my Danish counterpart, a woman with whom I had a good if benign relationship. She wanted to know each and every detail. Rattled, I pleaded secrecy. I knew then I would have to wait until something happened of its own accord, until an opportunity arose. At least my patience had been rewarded in identifying who gave the order to assassinate Agnes. I could only hope for a repeat outcome where coming face to face with Shukhov was concerned.

Chapter 44 – Sunlight

'**J**ust over a year had passed since the Americans disowned Lambert,' Aleshkovsky told Mumford. 'Things other than Operation Citadel had occupied my attention. Then in March 1988, as the winter thaw was beginning, Shukhov called me to a meeting. For one reason or other I hadn't seen him for nearly three months. I was shocked at the deterioration in his health. I saluted. When he looked up at me his eyes were pained and watery. He looked depressed.'

'Yes – Citadel,' Shukhov had said, subdued and speaking slowly. 'A year on since Lambert's setback and still there is no sign of him having access to the CIA any better than that of a third-ranked ally. I know you think I should have acted sooner. But I badly wanted Lambert recruited while ensconced with the Americans so that we might destroy the US–UK intelligence relationship in one fell swoop. I've waited as long as I possibly can. I now have to accept the unhappy fact we must focus on recruiting him in a more limited capacity. Could you activate Sunlight for me, please? Do it under the alternative option we discussed but let her move at her own pace. She needs to be confident that when the time comes her legend is sound.'

' I hurried back to my office,' Aleshkovsky said 'and immediately called in my operations coordinator. I briefed him on the alternative option. It was premised on Lambert having no access to inner American secrets and him being of most value to us as a senior SIS head office source. Sunlight was to form a relationship with Lambert while in Washington and allow it to mature for the remainder of his posting, with a view to them becoming an established couple and Sunlight his emotional bedrock. The plan envisaged Sunlight returning to London with Lambert on those terms. Once he was back in head office, she would begin the task of extracting intelligence from him.'

One by-product of my insularity was I had become a small target outside of the diplomatic and intelligence milieu I inhabited. It was not intentional. It was simply a matter of lifestyle. My erratic hours and a 24-hour supermarket close to my home meant I did not shop for food at regular times; nor did I frequent bars at nights or on weekends; and I had no leisure pursuits, let alone any requiring a routine. My only predictable behaviour was the commute from Virginia to the District, always crossing over the Potomac River via Chain Bridge. In order to avoid the traffic crush, you could set your watch on me traversing the bridge at 7.50 am each workday morning. The security gurus were forever telling me to vary my routine. But I saw no need. As station chief, I did not clear dead letter drops and seldom attended clandestine meetings with agents. I had staff to do this sort of thing. Indeed, I paid no attention at all to possible scrutiny as I moved about. That I talked to the CIA and other intelligence agencies was hardly a state secret. The Soviet watchers were easily able to monitor my movements.

I was at a standstill on Chain Bridge at 7.52 am on Friday 23 September 1988 waiting for the arrow to turn green facilitating my right turn onto Canal Road and entry into the District of Columbia. Suddenly there was a thump and my car lurched forward having been rear-ended. Fortunately, the impact was not severe and I safely avoided cannoning into the car in front. 'Fuck it,' I cursed, as I looked in the rear-view window to see a woman with a look of anguish on her face.

I alighted from my car and the woman from hers. I noted her car had Florida plates. We examined the damage to my bumper, which was slight. 'I'm so sorry,' she had said in accented English. 'My foot slid off the brake onto the accelerator.' I looked directly at her for the first time. She was an attractive young woman of about thirty, quite tall.

The lights had turned green and there was mayhem, with horns blaring and blocked drivers shouting in frustration. I retreated from my navel-gazing. 'Can you give me your name and number and I'll contact you?' I had said in standard traffic accident response. 'We're holding up the traffic and neither of us is injured.' I fished out a notebook from my suit jacket and offered it and a pen to her.

Liliana Leanca she wrote next to her telephone number. 'Can you please do the same for me?' she had asked. 'I am so terribly sorry and want to properly apologize to you.'

By then it had already dawned on me that obtaining quotes to have the woman for pay for the repairs would involve a significant commitment of time. Time I didn't have. Yet the cost of repair would be low. Enforcing my legal rights surely amounted to a case of false economy? I resolved there and then I would have my Service-owned vehicle repaired at official expense.

Why then did I still comply with the woman's request? It was, I later decided, because on looking closely at her I had begun to detect her similarity to Agnes. She was by no means a dead ringer. But Liliana's hair, although darker than Agnes's, was similarly flowing. And despite not having Agnes's high cheekbones, her smile, like Agnes, came from her eyes – black in Liliana's case – and was as just as warm. Even her stance and manner of speech conveyed strength of personality reminiscent of Agnes. Not as direct, certainly, but with the same engaging effect all the same.

Returning home the following day, after spending Saturday in the office, I found a message from Liliana on my answering machine. I rang back with the honourable intention of telling her I would attend to the repairs. I anticipated no further contact. But the sweet lilt of her accented English and ready laugh captivated me.

Liliana told me her family had immigrated to the US from Moldova a decade ago and lived in Miami. Sick of living at home, she had moved to Washington over two months ago and taken a lease on a bed-sit apartment in Arlington, just on the Virginia side of the Potomac. She had recently taken a position at a steakhouse restaurant on Arizona Avenue in the District. Liliana's job was to greet customers on arrival and seat them at their tables. So far she liked the job, even if being a *meeter and greeter* meant she usually did not receive tips. I found myself absorbed by this banality and disappointed when Liliana had to go for fear of being late for work. We agreed to speak again during the next week.

It is a rank understatement to say the spark Liliana ignited surprised me. The combination of past memories, the fact I was on the wrong side of forty-eight and the general lack of interest in me exhibited by females I encountered as I went about my daily business – work, shopping, you name it – had all conspired to sap my emotional confidence. The spark also conflicted me. I had been resolutely faithful to Agnes since her death nearly five years ago, not so much as looking at another woman. I also thought of the bridges I had burned in seeking to avenge Agnes. I couldn't walk away from this even if I wanted to, not least because somehow I was embroiled in a major and as yet unclear Soviet play. The other sobering reality was that even were I interested, Liliana was unlikely to have any romantic notions. I was no longer a handsome young man, if ever I was. Liliana was nearly twenty years my junior. Who was I kidding? I needed to forget about her.

Driving to work the following Monday, however, I discovered that Liliana's place of work on Arizona Avenue was located two blocks before my right turn onto Massachusetts Avenue taking me to the British Embassy. The effect of passing the restaurant was to instil in me a curious sense of pleasurable lightness. Returning home that night, and the following night, I found myself rushing to the answering machine hoping for a message from her. When Liliana did ring on the Wednesday night, I guardedly asked if she would like to have dinner. The safety-net compromise I had reached beforehand, born of Agnes's memory and worry about looking foolish, was to tell myself the invitation would be an act of friendship. Even so, I couldn't deny feeling a rush of adrenalin when she said, 'I would love to.' Liliana did not work Wednesday, Thursday or every second Sunday. We agreed to dine a week later at a restaurant close to her North Oak Street apartment.

I did subsequently declare my relationship with Liliana to the Service. But I was economical with the truth, recording her only as a US citizen, which by her passport she was, but sparing my masters the complicating fact she was originally a native of a Soviet republic. The Service security-meisters would argue, correctly, my intention only to enter into a friendship with Liliana was no defence to this evasiveness.

It is pertinent at this point to address a rather obvious question. Why didn't the interest Liliana displayed in me raise a red flag? After all, I was a experienced intelligence officer, who on the night of discovering the O'Hare group was a Soviet orchestration had sat in his McLean apartment earnestly committing to proceeding with *eyes wide open*. Yet here was a desirable young woman, resembling of Agnes and raised in a Soviet republic of all places, who by some miracle had dropped into my lap out of the clear blue sky. There were marginal factors for my denial: I was an isolated and ageing male reacting naturally to Liliana's attractiveness; and Liliana, directed by Shukhov to activate me only once I was back in head office, showed no interest whatsoever in my work.

But the real reason I blocked out any suspicions about Liliana can be traced back to my introspection that Sunday afternoon in Charles Kudermann's study, when I realized I had become *The Lone Wolf at Cover*. The revelation may have been a shock, but even so it had not tempered my long-professed indifference to living or dying so long as I was able to avenge Agnes. As I came to realize, though, Liliana changed this. Without me recognizing it she had revitalized my instinct to live. All of a sudden I was scared witless by Nought's warning about being *The Lone Wolf at Cover* and spending the rest of my life padding alone across the frozen steppe.

Over the next six months the envisaged plutonic relationship ensued, during which I told Liliana about Agnes and my continuing love for her long after her death in a car accident. For her part, Liliana explained that she grew up in Chisinau, Moldova's capital. After her mother had died unexpectedly, when Liliana was just fifteen, her schoolteacher father had decided on a fresh start for him and his two daughters. Many rejections later, the authorities had relented and the family migrated to the US. Liliana was by now a young adult. She had studied literature at Moldova State University, but once in the US her initially insufficient command of English prevented her working as a journalist as she had hoped. She had drifted into hospitality work, waitressing and the like, and stayed there.

As Liliana and I progressed, though, I found myself thinking more and more that Agnes would want me to move on with life. Little by little my affection for Liliana began to run, until eventually it was freed of restraint. My ability to block out any voice of recrimination, I later reflected, sprang from my fear of *The Lone Wolf at Cover* that spurred by Liliana's enlivening of my want to live. Come month seven Liliana and I had begun petting, leading to us occasionally indulging in greater intimacies.

One Sunday afternoon in early June 1989, just over eight months after Liliana and I first had dinner, we returned to her apartment both buoyed by a glorious day and our walk among the District's fully blooming cherry blossoms. Liliana let our petting explore new

417

frontiers. Soon we were lying on her bed, both naked. To my horror I just couldn't function. Resurgent guilt I expect. Whatever, I was afflicted with some variety of widower's droop. 'Joe,' Liliana whispered, 'I want you to be my big stallion. I want us to make music together.' I took this as encouragement, which did nothing for my performance anxiety.

In fact, Liliana was forewarning me she was going to take control. That she did, not with an exotic sexual technique, but by taking me in her arms and stroking my back, neck and top of head with gentle tenderness. Liliana's touch stimulated my dulled senses. I came to experience a burst of affection emitting from me, literally, the fact of its physically passing to Liliana evident from her sharp, instantly corresponding inhalation. Intimacy overrode misgiving. Liliana kissed me deeply, whereupon her sitting astride me I climaxed away over five years of celibacy.

Whether I actually became Liliana's big, music-making stallion is a matter of conjecture. But from then on we were lovers. It was a slower burn than with Agnes; nonetheless, the steady increase in emotional outlay did in time come to exceed my upper threshold. And when the telltale effusion of calm and emotional surety announced the dowsing of my loner instincts, I recognized that Liliana had become my second *real deal*.

Along the way, as Liliana and I had increasingly immersed, I detected my determination to avenge Agnes start to wane. I made no grand self-declaration formally abandoning Agnes when finally all resolve had gone. Rather, I simply permitted myself to accept that whereas atoning for Agnes's death was once my reason for living, now it was Liliana. Life is for the living I suppose I was thinking.

All I kept from Liliana was my profession, this and the matters of my entanglement with the Russians, their murder of Agnes and my past exploits directed at avenging her. I accepted that one day I would be held to account on any number of these fronts, but committed to deal with them as and when individual reckonings arose, in whatever form they materialized.

Chapter 45 – Transnistria

Liliana was very pessimistic about Moldova's future. 'The Soviet Union,' she said, 'is on the brink of economic and social collapse.' I smiled smugly to myself. Expert assessments I had seen were confidently predicting Gorbachev's reforms of *glasnost* and *perestroika* to graft and the Soviet Union recover to the point of functionality. 'Resulting Russian feebleness,' Liliana told me, 'will eventually cause it to lose control in Moldova.'

'And the problem with this is exactly what?' I queried, screwing up my face with manufactured puzzlement.

Liliana ignored my playacting. 'The problem is,' she said forlornly, 'that in the absence of Russian authority internal divisions within the country will unleash and eventually spiral out of control.'

According to Liliana, the main Moldovan fault line centred on Transnistria in Moldova's east. I knew little about Transnistria, nothing in fact. In 1940 the Russians had apparently incorporated Transnistria, then an autonomous region of Ukraine, and the larger territory of Bessarabia, then part of Romania, into the Moldovan Soviet Socialist Republic. The MSSR was a new entity. Its creation was part of a secret deal made in 1939 by Russia with its then ally Nazi Germany, the so-called Molotov-Ribbentrop Pact, to divide the territories of Eastern Europe between them. Hitler's invasion of Russia in June 1941 put paid to the Pact but the MSSR remained geographically intact.

Russian people relocated by the Soviets after the war to bolster Transnistria's decimated stock of human capital soon became the territory's largest grouping. Concurrently, ethic Moldovans began agitating for the MSSR's reintegration into Romania because Bessarabia, two-thirds of the MSSR land mass, was stolen from Romania as part of Russia's cynical deal with Nazi Germany. Most ethnic Moldovans now viewed Transnistria as an inalienable unit of the MSSR and argued it must also be integrated. As such, when the Soviet Union began to creak and groan under the weight of discontent in its fifteen republics, Russian speakers in Transnistria feared the imminent loss of their culture and way of life. Talk of Transnistria splitting from Moldova began to surface.

'Soviet decline, specifically Russian decline,' Liliana said, 'is already giving impetus to secessionists in Transnistria's capital, Tiraspol. As Russia further weakens, the sentiment will quickly spread to other centres.' Liliana's greatest concern was the stockpile of Soviet weaponry in Moldova, one of the largest in Europe. 'It is widely accepted in Moldova,' she warned, 'that both sides of the Transnistria argument will go to any lengths to obtain these armaments once the Soviet Union implodes, especially things like missiles capable of being fired by a single person with a portable, shoulder-mounted rocket launcher.'

Liliana declared Western apathy to this to be confounding, singling out the UK for particular criticism. So long as the UK sat on its hands, she said, it risked the presence of undisciplined, heavily armed elements in its European backyard. 'You English diplomats should wake up to yourselves,' Liliana admonished me, 'and recognize the serious threat this poses to your country.'

Later, when the Berlin Wall came crashing down in November 1989, I knew Liliana was right about the impending collapse of the Soviet Union and our painted-into-a-corner experts were wrong. Her prognostications about rogue Moldovan actors armed with man portable missile launchers – MANPADS as they were clumsily known – roaming through Europe suddenly took on more sinister dimensions.

In parallel with my blossoming romance with Liliana, my work demands continued unabated. The more entwined I became with her, the more equipped I felt to deal with the rigours of office. In August 1989, working with our people in New York, we landed a mid-level diplomat attached to the Chinese mission to the United Nations. It was quite a coup. But although this won me some kudos, I would have had to recruit the Chinese President to fully repair my relations with headquarters. That much was rammed home to me when shortly after I received advice Freddie Ladler was to replace me immediately my four-year term expired the coming December. The message's subtext was plain to see: *Don't be fooled into thinking the Chinese recruitment means you are forgiven.*

I had heard rumours Freddie had made quite a splash doing his Falklands work. No wonder Digby Carhiddy, my now supervising DDG, genuflected at the mention of his name. The word was also out in secret circles that Britain and Argentina were soon to announce the resumption of diplomatic relations, possibly at a meeting in Madrid a few weeks off in October. With this, Freddie's Falklands commitments would be done, perfect timing for him to take up the posting.

I began to think of life after Washington.

Chapter 46 – Understanding

By now my affection for Liliana ran so deep I had come unquestioningly to accept her feelings for me were the same, even if I did occasionally fret I might not be able to live up to the image of a globetrotting diplomat, which was all she had known me as. One evening in early December, however, about two weeks from my scheduled departure, the warning bell jangled with sufficient volume for reality finally to intrude.

Liliana and I were discussing future plans. The Service's literally telegraphed attitude towards me had been playing on my mind. It would be a bleak existence working in headquarters. A clean break seemed attractive. On the spur of the moment, I told Liliana I could do well to resign. 'We could travel the world,' I said. 'The sale of my London house would finance us. You could even return to journalism, perhaps write a book on our exploits. We'd be fine.' Liliana was wide-eyed. She tried to match my enthusiasm but was noticeably lukewarm. I took her reservation only as surprise, born of the fact she was unaware of the Service's direction I should depart Washington the minute my time was up.

But what did provoke my concern was that shortly after, Liliana became highly agitated. From voicing muted support for my resignation, she switched in an instant to uncharacteristic vehemence, her emotions appearing to boil over. 'Under no circumstances should you resign,' she told me heatedly, before screaming at me, '*You must not resign.*' This alarmed me. Anyone could see that behind her out-of-character outburst there was more than worry I might be making a rushed decision. Her momentary loss of poise gave the impression my proposition had panicked her. This raised more questions than there were answers. I decided for the time being to agree not to resign. With an air of restrained but nonetheless unmistakable relief – I was watching her closely now – Liliana perked up. 'Yes', she said, 'I will join you in London in the New Year after I have visited my father to explain why I intend moving to the UK.' I hoped our disagreement was a misunderstanding and tried to blot out the gnawing sensation it might not be.

London, Friday 22 December 1989. On leaving Washington on 19 December as instructed, the exact fourth anniversary of my arrival, I had returned straight to London and my home in Brent Cross. On the flight back I decided I had to clarify the situation with Liliana, once and for all. She had told me she would be flat out working double shifts in the days following my departure, in the busy lead-up to Christmas. As planned, she would then go to Miami to spend time with her father. Liliana had insisted I should not ring her until 2 January, when she would be back in Washington and able to be contacted at home; it was too difficult otherwise.

My ponderings, however, had taken me to the point where I was no longer prepared to wait. I decided to ring her right then, at the restaurant where the staff would be preparing for the lunchtime crowd. I knew Liliana would not appreciate the call having earlier told me never to ring her at work because the boss did not allow staff private calls. But enough was enough. I was determined that Liliana should tell me what was going on.

The phone connected in the distinctive burr of the American ring. A harassed-sounding male answered after a time. I apologized for the call but said I needed urgently to speak to Liliana Leanca. 'Man,' he said, 'I would like to speak to her too. She left work early on Wednesday night and yesterday morning her husband rang in sick for her, saying she would be off for a couple of days. Said she had bronchitis and couldn't speak. I guess people get sick but she has really let me down. If you are speaking to her, tell her to get her ass in here.'

The husband mention made the hairs on the back of my neck stand up; not because I actually thought Liliana had a husband but because someone had called posing as such. I rang Liliana's apartment – no answer. I sat quietly, thinking. Then on a hunch, I rang a contact in the American customs and immigration service in Washington. It was just after 7 pm in London. The five-hour time difference made it early afternoon in the District. 'Danforth Rickkerts,' I said lightly, 'how are you brother?'

'Joey Lambert, where are you man?' the giant black man replied.

'I'm back in Blighty you bloody reprobate but I have a loose end I need tidy up tonight. If I gave you a passport number could you do a quick check on any known movements in recent days?'

'For you my man anything is possible,' Danforth said, chuckling. I had with me a copy of the contact report I had submitted on Liliana. I read out her passport number. Click, click, click on the lumbering computer at the other end. 'Yep,' Danforth said, 'departed state side at Dulles 2300 local Wednesday 20 December. Turkish Airlines direct flight to Istanbul, ETA 1615 plus one local.'

I wasn't massively surprised. Since the night Liliana had imploded at the thought of me resigning, supposedly from the Foreign Office, I had known something was up – my *eyes wide open* antenna had finally switched on. That Liliana was a KGB plant tasked with recruiting me was high among the possibilities I had considered. Her undisclosed travel coupled with the husband revelation had just confirmed it, of this I was certain, beyond all reasonable doubt as the lawyers like to say.

Liliana, it transpires, did alert General Shukhov that her lapse might have raised my suspicions about her. Shukhov in response had ordered her to attend a crash meeting with him on 22 December in Sofia, Bulgaria. Had the General been in better health they would have met somewhere closer to the US. Liliana had foreseen the possibility of such a meeting, hence her firmness that once I'd left Washington we should forego contact until 2 January.

I learned later that on the night of 20 December, Liliana flew to Istanbul on the American passport the KGB two years earlier had obtained for her and thence onto Sofia on false papers provided by the KGB station in the Soviet consulate in Istanbul. After five hours dead to the world in a Sofia hotel on the night of 21 December, she was roused for her meeting with Shukhov commencing at 6 am sharp on 22 December. The meeting spanned three intense hours, during which she received her updated instructions. Liliana was exhausted but there was no time for sleep. Retracing her steps to Istanbul, she boarded a mid-afternoon Turkish Airlines flight arriving back in Washington on the night of 22 December, some six hours after I had called her apartment.

On 23 December Liliana returned to work apologizing profusely for her unavoidable absence, offering to work extra days for no pay. The boss was grumpy but accepted her offer, while telling her he did not expect her to work for nothing. 'After all,' I understand he had said, 'you do look worn out.'

Armed with all the facts, joining the dots to understand the Soviet intentions didn't take long. Agnes had been killed so as to tear an emotional gap in my life and Liliana had been chosen to fill it. It was no fluke she shared many of Agnes's traits: the tenderness and appealing intelligence; the engaging smile; the mannerisms and the hair. You could bet Liliana had been selected as my recruiter for this very reason. Being Moldovan was no barrier. People from Eastern Europe regularly immigrated to the US. In any event, she couldn't easily disguise her accent and had to be comfortable answering questions, however innocently put, about her background and where she had come from.

Word of my breakdown over Agnes's death had circulated widely in New Delhi. I was sure the KGB's plan predicated on this presuming that once emotionally hooked, the fear of another life-shattering event would open me up to recruitment. Liliana hadn't pitched before I left Washington. It followed that the KGB planned for her to move on me once she was in the UK.

As to the large time gap between Agnes's death and Liliana's approach, some five years, I was less certain. The Soviets had clearly sought to aid my career advancement, indicating an objective to assist me climb the Service's higher rungs before recruiting me. This obviously took time and partially explained the lag. But how could they have been sure I would not have found someone else before Liliana's approach to me?

I decided the answer lay in the fact I was built differently to the average Joe Blow. I thought of it in terms of thresholds of emotional outlay. With Agnes and later Liliana I had identified that above an upper threshold my *Lone Wolf at Cover* persona was suppressed because I was emotionally secure, whereas with Kathleen my experience was an emotional outlay falling below a lower threshold made me indifferent to emotional security, with exactly the same effect. I was positive most men had similar thresholds. But my relationship history had shown the gap between the high and low ends, when my loner instincts were prone to trigger, to be abnormally large. My guess was the Soviets had detected this particularization; they were big on psychoanalysis and other profiling. They had relied on this confident another woman capable of filling the void was unlikely to come into my life.

This analysis assuredly had more than a grain of truth to it. But what I didn't know at the time was that, driven by his own agenda, General Shukhov had delayed the operation well past the deadline for activation recommended by the KGB psychologists.

Chapter 47 – Countering

I mused deeply over the ensuing days, experiencing more a sense of determination than any other emotion. My only rush to anger – real, deep and raw – was when recalling that Liliana's lie, her faked affection for me, had duped me into abandoning Agnes. I cursed my loneliness and my *Lone Wolf at Cover* make-up. 'Could the Soviets have intended I give up on avenging Agnes?' I asked myself. I dismissed the thought. Thanks to deflecting Mrs O'Hare's question all those years ago about my motive for wanting to discredit Freddie Ladler there was not one person on the planet bar me who knew my end game was to kill Shukhov. By the night of 27 December I was clear on what I proposed to do.

Martin Mumford was cool upon opening his front door mid-morning Thursday 28 December. His carrying the can for my indiscretion with the Americans nearly three years ago clearly still rankled. He did not invite me in when I told him I had something important to tell him. Instead we talked for over two hours in the greenhouse in his back garden. He then briefly disappeared inside the house. I stood at the front stomping my feet to stay warm while I waited for Martin to re-emerge. I could hear the faint sound of his wife complaining about his need to go to work. But we didn't go to headquarters. Rather, we drove to Bushwood Road in Kew

Gardens and pulled up outside of the apartment block that was home to the DG.

Martin went in alone and was gone a good hour. When he returned to the car he ushered me forth with a sideways tilt of his head. We rode the lift up to the tenth floor. If Martin had been ambivalent towards me, the now fully briefed DG was downright hostile. We sat in a small anteroom just inside the front entrance of his apartment. Digby arrived shortly after. I was offered nothing in the way of food or beverage over the ensuing two hours. My request for a toilet break was met only with grudging approval.

Late on 31 December Martin rang. 'The DG's just returned from Washington,' he said. 'It's all clear to go. Digby's technically still your supervising DDG but as you came to me in the first place, I'm to take carriage of this phase. You are to take notes throughout the call and at its conclusion. As soon as you're done, come over here. I want a detailed report we can take to the DG.' He hung up, not responding when I wished him Happy New Year.

I didn't try to be light and airy when I rang Liliana as scheduled on 2 January. She initially sought to continue the charade but soon realized that as suspected she had been undone by her mistake. 'I don't appreciate your lot jerking me around,' I said, 'and I know all about your jaunt to Turkey and God knows where. But I suppose business is business. And anyway my deliberate misleading of my employer as to our association puts me in a very vulnerable position. I have no choice but to listen to your proposal.'

'We can have an outline to you tomorrow,' Liliana said. 'Just name the place and time.'

'No,' I replied. 'I want to hear it from you. This was the intention before you fucked up. I'm not starting all over again with some London functionary I've never met before. Let me know your travel plans and I'll pick you up from the airport. You should stay here as planned. My furniture is being delivered tomorrow. You'll have somewhere to sleep.'

'If that's what you want,' she said.

'You betcha,' I replied aggressively.

A pause, possibly to consult someone who was listening. 'Give me a week to make the necessary arrangements,' she said when back on the line. 'I'll take the morning BA flight from Dulles on 10 January.'

'You've really dug yourself into a hole haven't you?' Martin said, as we left the DG's home later that night.

'I have Martin but if we can pull this off maybe it will go some way to atoning for everything.'

'You should be in no doubt the DG has really gone out on a limb here,' Martin retorted heatedly. 'Everything we do from now is ultra-close hold. The full indoctrination list will not be expanded beyond the DG, you and me, and Digby. Not even the Minister's office is to be briefed. Service others may help out but they will be told only what they need to know. All other dealings with the Service are to take their normal course. At least the DG seemed happy with tonight's progress report.' We completed the journey to my home in silence. On arrival, Martin leant over and said softly as I stood at the passenger door, 'OK, see you at the Matilda West Gallery at Kew Gardens, 9 am sharp this coming Saturday, 6 January. The back office past the green curtains. Watch your back. From now on we need to limit your direct contact with the Service to the bare necessity.'

The technical people were at my home first thing the next morning, 3 January. They arrived in a furniture removal van for the benefit of any interested on-looker and actually proceeded to unload the furniture I had consigned to store four years ago. But my second bedroom was the real focus of their attention. Here they quickly built a room within a room just big enough for two people. Its entry was via a heavy door that shut much like watertight doors I'd seen on ships.

After tests and satisfying themselves of the room's integrity, the team leader took me inside. 'This is the only place in the house from now on where you can have a sensitive conversation,' he cautioned. 'The Soviets will try to bug your home in preparation for the arrival of their agent. Your house has an exposed left flank and they have the expertise to attach an encrypted, high fidelity radio microphone under the roof eave on that side. At all times you should act as if they're listening. We're unable to do any sweeping of the house's exterior because of the suspicions that might arouse. Similarly, we're not deploying watchers because out here in the suburbs they would soon become too obvious. But we'll be listening, both inside this safe room and the house generally. Above all else remember that as far as the Soviets are concerned, the Service knows nothing about its agent and will not have wired your home. It is important not to tip them off. When outside this room you must act as if there are no UK ears listening. Should the need arise for a sensitive communication outside the safe room, write a message on a piece of paper and then dispose of it.' He agreed flushing the note down the toilet was probably safe, 'but not foolproof.' The one truly effective method for *ad hoc* disposal of written messages, he told me, was to eat them.

I met Liliana when she arrived in the late afternoon of 10 January. She was nervous. So was I. People were sure to be watching. Fearful my car might be bugged, I said little on the drive from Heathrow to my home. I took her to the second bedroom. Her eyes widened in surprise but she said nothing. We entered the safe room; closing the heavy door electronically shielded us from the outside world. Still standing, I waved my hand at the safe room walls. 'If you so much as hint that my Service has made these preparations, you will be arrested as a Russian spy. Without diplomatic status you can expect a long, long prison term. Do you understand? Say *yes* or *no* out loud please, as the case may be.'

'Yes,' she complied.

'Good,' I said, 'we will talk in here tomorrow.'

I then took Liliana for a Chinese meal. She probably would have preferred something else but this was the arrangement. Mid-meal I went to the bathroom, where I greeted Harry Weideman. Harry would be a staunch ally; he had never forgotten my acceptance of him into the Service at a time when many were resisting it. 'Tell the DG, Martin and Digby I'm confident she validly passed the first test,' I said softly. 'I will introduce the second test tomorrow morning. Look for the signal after 10.15 am, the front sitting room blind. If it's up, I'm confident she's also validly passed this one. If it's down, I'll have detected she's complied for ulterior motive or because of intimidation.' The possibility of Liliana failing the test didn't need to be canvassed; the microphones would tell that story. I gave Harry a minute or so and followed him out of the bathroom.

That night Liliana slept on the couch. The next morning I fed her porridge and fruit. She hated porridge but ate it uncomplainingly. Then I led her into the safe room. 'OK,' I said, 'let's not beat about the bush. The first thing I need tell you is that I've told my Service all about you and me. It's not happy but I'm cooperating with it to try and make amends. Secondly, we are going out to the sitting room shortly, where for the benefit of your listening friends you are going to make the offer you have been sent to make, which I will pretend to consider. When you've finished, we will come back in here and talk about next steps. Let's go.'

Liliana sat in one of my sitting room armchairs, her legs curled beneath her. 'Joe, I know you are angry with me,' she began, 'and I am sorry for my deception. I truly do feel for you and want you by my side. But before then much work needs to be done. All Soviet republics are currently experiencing upheaval. It is fuelled by Western disinformation and temporary economic decline in our homelands. For the sake of Moldova, of Russia and for the West itself this revolution nonsense must stop. Trust me when I say that Soviet patriots will soon put a stop to Gorbachev's reforms and their undermining effect. That is why you must work for us, to make it possible for us to understand the West's tactics and counteract its support for Gorbachev. Stability will eventually return. Then my darling we can be together.' With that, Liliana rose from her seat and kissed me noisily. I decided the racket she made was intended to let the Russian listeners know she was on the job. At the same time, the tenderness picked up by my sensory system told me it wasn't all in the line of duty.

'Well that's all very noble, Liliana,' I said. 'But what about me?' My scorn may have been scripted for Russian ears but it came easily. Bitterness still lingered over Liliana playing me. Her affection reminded me I'd abandoned Agnes because I'd been selfish and weak. I returned to script as the rush of heat subsided. 'If tumbled,' I continued, 'I would assuredly go to prison. My Service would be relentless. It would move heaven and earth to nail me to the cross, a former Washington station head no less.'

Liliana appeared to consider this. 'You would be a vital asset to the Soviet Union,' she replied. 'We would protect you.' Her tone brightened. 'Why don't you come to Moldova, to Chisinau and get a feel for a proud Soviet republic?'

'And just how would I do that?' I asked with a pained voice. 'Service officers can only visit Soviet republics for work reasons.'

'Simple,' she said. 'You are not due to return to work until 30 January. Tell your Service we are taking a holiday to Portugal for a week, leaving say on 19 January. That will give me time to make arrangements for our onwards travel to Moldova.'

I was silent for a time. 'I suppose a trip to Portugal supposedly to catch some sun would not look out of the ordinary at this time of year,' I said. 'Let me sleep on it and I'll make my final decision tomorrow. If I decide to work for your people, I'll consider what you suggest.'

I then walked to the sitting room's front window whereupon I raised the lowered window blind. 'Liliana,' I called out, 'it's just after ten and time for a cuppa. Do you want some tea as well?'

Earlier in the safe room I had handed Liliana a note. *When you pitch at me make the suggestion we travel to Chisinau on 19 January, on the pretext of us taking a week's holiday in Portugal.* I didn't say it out loud despite being in the safe room; I didn't want British ears privy to our discussions to know I'd set Liliana a test.

Liliana had passed her first test the night before, with her silent reaction to the safe room. The safe room note was to gauge her reaction both to the Chisinau request and its secretive raising. I judged she had freely collaborated, signifying her valid passing of this second test. It was a critical step, even if its significance was known only to the indoctrinated few. Together with the first test, it also augured well for Liliana's cooperation where getting to the hugely secret *Main Act* was concerned. But that was for later. Right now the important, if less secret, cover pitch beckoned.

We chatted sporadically while drinking our tea. As soon as we had finished, I motioned we should return to the safe room. 'I'm going to unpack some items still in boxes,' I said, speaking loudly for the Russian listeners. 'You'll have to read or watch television for a while.' The television was blaring as we entered the safe room.

Without ceremony, I asked Liliana why she was working for the Russians. She took a deep breath. 'It's a long story but here goes. My father was a schoolteacher like I told you. But he was also political. He believed the Soviet system held Moldova back. Even if Moldova could not be independent, he still believed it should be more engaged with the West, to access its technological knowhow and trading markets. After Mother died, he began to advocate for change. The Soviets warned him and when he ignored them they threw him in prison. The damp of the prison got on his chest and wouldn't budge. His health quickly began to fail.'

I didn't take notes. Everything Liliana said would be recorded. 'Then Colonel Shukhov was in charge of the KGB in Moldova and Romania. I wrote to him. To my surprise, he was quite a decent man. He called me to his office. I was twenty. Shukhov said if I were prepared to work for the KGB, he would arrange my father's release, subject to him agreeing to refrain from political activities. If I did not agree to his proposal my father would be left to rot. So, I agreed.'

'I take it then your father isn't living in Miami?'

Liliana smiled sadly. 'You are correct, Joe. He is the Russians' insurance. Nowadays, he lives quietly outside of Balti to the north of Chisinau. He tends a small vineyard there.'

'What happened after you agreed to work for Shukhov?'

'I was sent to Moscow for English language and other skills training. I was very good at what I did. I became Shukhov's favourite, especially after he was promoted to General and returned to Moscow. He decided I was to work only on special projects.'

'You told me you live in Chisinau. Is that true? I mean when you're not working on these special projects where are you based?'

'Like I said,' she replied, 'I achieved good results. As a KGB General, Shukhov had a lot of power. He agreed to my request that I be allowed to return to Chisinau where I would be closer to my father. I have had a small apartment there for the last five years.'

'Give me its address.'

Liliana did not hesitate to think. 'Strada Alexei Sciusev 69.'

'And what's a prominent landmark near it?'

She smiled, well aware of the game I was playing. 'It's two blocks from the beautiful Valea Morilor Park.'

I lapsed into silence. The fact that I'd been able to confirm Liliana had an apartment in Chisinau was important, at least so far as the indoctrinated few were concerned.

Liliana interrupted my thinking. 'What does your Service want me to do, Joe?'

'Recent assessments by our people,' I said, 'indicate that rogue Moldovan elements are likely to try and appropriate Soviet MANPADS when the Soviet Union collapses. My government is very concerned at the threat this could pose to British commercial aircraft.' Liliana was only half listening. She knew better about these risks than our analysts ever could. Her face took on the sulky countenance unique to attractive Eastern European women. But as she sensed I was coming to the crux of the matter, she softened and her eyes half closed in concentration. 'We want you to be our eyes and ears on the ground once the Soviets lose control in Moldova. Your job is to forewarn us of any threats, working to a cut-out we'll put in place. The last thing the UK needs is out of control cowboys running loose in Europe with hand-held rocket launchers in their knapsacks capable of bringing down aircraft.'

'And if I decline your offer?' Liliana asked.

'Well *sweetie*,' I said, 'you've made the fatal mistake of coming here. We have you. We'll chuck you in the calaboose and send Shukhov a Christmas card telling him you've fucked up. Goodnight Pop, goodnight everything.' I had meant to threaten Liliana with prison – that was the official line – but I didn't intend to be angrily patronizing in saying it. This spontaneous reaction to Liliana's question no doubt reflected my anxiety that her going to prison would kill-off any opportunity I had to put things right by Agnes. But equally it also underlined just how easily my hostility towards her could surface and – if I was brutally honest – my subliminal hurt that she might refuse me.

I waited for Liliana's response. As I did images of Katya's distraught face at the mention of her family flooded back to me. I felt distinctly uneasy. But Liliana was impassive. Then she shrugged. 'I'd be delighted to help,' she said, the resignation in her voice plucking at my heartstrings. As if of their own volition, I felt my protective instincts ready for launch.

The process to arrange Liliana's cut-out now could now begin. Moldova, of course, hosted no UK embassy. All embassies accredited to the Soviet Union were based in Moscow. That afternoon, Martin Mumford turned into Ladygate Lane in Ruislip. He parked in front of the HOPE office. 'Good afternoon Mr Marks,' Rebecca Normington the HOPE CEO said.

Preliminary tests and cover pitch successfully completed, it was still not time to rest on my laurels. I now had an olive branch to extend. I picked my moment as we readied for bed. My note read, *Why don't you sleep in my bed?* Liliana's eyes fiercely interrogated mine, trying to read my motive. Only after staring at me for a long time did she slowly nod her head in agreement. The night promised to be positively frigid. I had an electric blanket somewhere but didn't look for it – which in hindsight told me what Liliana had concluded in advance. We cuddled for warmth. The feel of her body revived many suppressed memories. And although my antagonism towards Liliana might still have prowled randomly at the time of going to bed, this bank of resentment soon ran dry once Mother Nature raised her benevolent head.

I woke early the next morning worried I had been incautious and nervous about compromise – not involving the Russians but rather on my own side. There was, however, no time for further analysis of the nocturnal developments. I had an appointment.

'I have to get bread and milk,' I yelled, as I left the house. I parked my car at the same Sainsbury's supermarket where years earlier the suave man in the cashmere overcoat had inadvertently told me I was the intended beneficiary of the O'Hare group-cum-Russian activities. I made my way to the dairy section and leant forward to examine the produce. 'Tell the DG and others the olive branch seems to have been accepted,' I whispered to Harry

Weideman's back. 'The last domino has now fallen – the way's clear for me to get to the business end of things this afternoon.'

Liliana asked me over breakfast if I had made up my mind about working for the KGB. 'Don't push me,' I snarled. 'I said I would tell you today and I will. Just give me a bit of space.' Liliana wasn't put off by my response; I had prompted her to ask the question and she knew my anger was pretended. By mid-afternoon I judged the act of indecision had gone on long enough. 'OK,' I said to Liliana, 'I'll do it. I'll work for your people. But first I want to go to Chisinau as you suggest. God knows I'll probably end up having to defect there and I need to know it's somewhere where I could live. I couldn't survive a lengthy prison sentence.'

'You've made a wise decision, Joe,' Liliana said. 'Let me go and pass on the good news. It's best not to make calls from here.' I handed Liliana a piece of paper as she prepared to leave. Reading it literally caused her to flinch. But she went along with it. 'I won't be long,' was all she said. I was too busy eating my message to answer. I did, though, feel a warm glow of affection for her.

Tell them it's essential that Shukhov comes to Chisinau to meet me, my note had read. *Say you think I'm scared stiff and there's a good chance I could still pull out. Emphasize Shukhov must give me his assurance in person I will be looked after at the first hint I am at risk of detection.* There it was, the business end of things, hinging on which was the hugely secret *Main Act*.

I pondered my contrived recruitment while waiting for Liliana to return. The Service strategy intended I string the KGB along until it ceased to exist upon the Soviet Union's imminent collapse. Liliana could then begin her Moldova eyes and ears role safe from KGB reprisal for her part in my, by then voided, recruitment. But there were more balls in the air than our strategists knew, not least the hugely secret *Main Act*, and my private end game attaching to it, of which the indoctrinated few were also unaware.

Plans were made. Liliana and I attended a travel agent on 13 January. We booked British Airways flights to Lisbon departing London at 2.55 pm on 19 January, returning on 27 January.

We weren't the only ones making travel plans that cold Saturday morning. Digby Carhiddy's driver had picked him up at 6.30 am. Digby had a rush visit to Canada to make, to Toronto. It was an early start but he was content; the visit was the perfect opportunity to save the Service from its folly. Digby would later own up to this thinking. He would also admit to high hopes of the Foreign Secretary hailing his enterprise and coming to see the DG and Mumford for the weak-kneed, gullible nellies they were.

Chapter 48 – Rimmington

Close to six years had elapsed since Bill Rimmington, the former policeman and long-time head of the Service's Internal Affairs Branch, had unnerved me in the meeting called by Martin Mumford to discuss Anthony Delminico's death and the so-called Rhodesian disinformation campaign running against the Service. It was well known that Rimmington hated loose ends and annually reviewed all unresolved investigations. For a long time I'd kept my ear to the ground as to any progress he might have made on the Rhodesian matter, certain his suspicions about me had never faded. But after a couple of years, when nothing was unearthed, and on hearing Special Branch had grown weary of his requests for more manpower to be devoted to investigating Delminico's death, I had more or less forgotten about Rimmington.

Rimmington had decided to retire at the end of April 1990. He returned from holidays in mid-January determined to devote his last three months in service to clearing up the Rhodesian mystery. Martin Mumford was later to tell me this and also give me a read-out on the fruits of Rimmington's endeavours. He did so in December 1991 as part of his *Final Briefing*, after Aleshkovsky had come over and been debriefed, and Martin had completed the ancillary interviews he thought necessary, including the one he did with Rimmington.

It turns out by the time Rimmington began his last spurt on the Rhodesian investigation, a new and more amenable person was in the Special Branch Chief Superintendent's chair. I'm told Margaret Otten was a hard-faced and humourless woman but it seems she and Rimmington had hit it off. Otten was happy to oblige when Rimmington suggested on 15 January that apropos of the Rhodesian affair she issue an information request on the Met and regional networks asking for any information to hand which might have an intelligence implication, however minor.

I understand a bright-eyed, young probationary constable in Durham noticed the Special Branch request when sorting messages off the station telex machine. With the blessing of his Sergeant, he contacted Special on 16 January to advise that a man recently arrested by the Durham Constabulary for a supermarket robbery had claimed to have secret information he would share with police in return for leniency. His name was Leslie Stratton.

Rimmington heard about this late afternoon on 16 January. He took the night train to Durham. First thing on the morning of 17 January he interviewed Stratton in the holding cells at Aykley Heads police headquarters. It appears Leslie had fallen on hard times and resorted to armed robbery to pay the bills. He told Rimmington life was so much better when he drove for that crazy Irish outfit.

By late afternoon 17 January Rimmington was back in London. 'The first thing I did,' he said when later interviewed by Mumford, 'was to consult my *A–Z* street directory. Stratton told me that several years ago he had dropped an older Irish woman who called herself Valerie in Claremont Road, Brent Cross and watched her walk towards the roundabout at the bottom of the street. Stratton said he never asked questions, but when he had confirmed the drop-off point the woman had mentioned something about being off to spook the spook. Stratton told me he knew that *spook* meant spies and this made him think the job had something . to do with spying.'

Rimmington told Mumford he thought his bowels were going to move when he had seen just how close the drop was to my house. Martin had readily agreed with me this colourful description reflected Rimmington's deep determination to uncover the extent of my involvement in the Rhodesian matter. Indeed, in the same breath, Martin said, Rimmington had added, 'I have always known Joe Lambert was hiding something. Nearly fifty years of policing was telling me this.'

Stratton had also recounted how after the drop his instructions were to pass by certain locations at ten minutes to the hour for as long as necessary. 'After a couple of no-shows,' Rimmington said, 'the Valerie woman was waiting for Leslie at the 3.50 pm location, the bus stop near Swannell Way. It was also a comfortable walking distance from Lambert's home.'

After the pick up Stratton drove Valerie to a phone box near Cricklewood Station, where she made a short call. From there he drove her to West Hampstead tube station. The last Stratton saw of Valerie was her disappearing into the train station. 'As to the date, or even the year of the job,' Rimmington said, 'Stratton couldn't recall – he was a heavy drug user by now. He could only remember it was a Sunday, the weather was spring-like and it was a nice day for driving.'

It was Brian McGowan who informed Mumford on Rimmington's next step. 'It was quite late on the evening of 17 January 1990,' McGowan said. 'I had been ADDG for about a year by then and seemed always to be stuck late in the office. Rimmington rang on my direct line. He told me he had an urgent request for an internal audit. He wanted to discuss the request with a view to obtaining my signature so that he might get to it first thing the next day.

'I told him to come up in an hour,' Brian said. 'When he did I was surprised to see he wanted to put the cleaners through Joe Lambert. When I told Rimmington the current staff movements advice indicated Lambert would be holidaying for a week in Portugal from 19 to 27 January, I could see him go into overdrive. He had argued strenuously there were sound grounds for preventing Lambert from leaving the country until his investigation was complete.

'Rimmington, however, did not know the entry for Lambert's approved private travel in my copy of the movements advice contained the *Star*. Given this, I told Rimmington that while I agreed the proximity of the woman's drop-off to Lambert's house was curious, I was not prepared to ban his travel without more concrete information. But I would authorize the audit. I signed the approval and noted it to that effect.

'Rimmington was too disciplined to dispute a senior officer's decision,' Brian said. 'Instead he settled for asking what time Lambert's plane left. I told him it was five minutes before three on 19 January. By then it was already 9 pm and I wanted to get away within the next hour. Rimmington had his audit authorization – there was nothing left to discuss. I told him I'd best get on.'

The *Star* was more an asterisk, really. It only ever appeared on the highly classified movement advices issued to the DDGs. Its purpose was to warn the DDGs when private staff travel might have operational implications. The always-unannotated movement advices distributed to the Service's other ranks, the type of document Rimmington might have seen, sat at the other end of the classification spectrum.

Rimmington told Mumford he did not sleep well the night of 17 January. 'I knew I was on the threshold of something major and needed to unearth it before five to three on 19 January. I told my wife the next morning, 18 January, not to expect me home for dinner. I was in the office by 7.30 am and by 8.30 am, as people were arriving at work, I was out on the corridors.'

Rimmington said his first point of call was the weapons registry. There he drew a blank. He then proceeded to the travel documents area but found no record of me having drawn a forged passport since 1976. 'But in the sister registry across the corridor, the domestic documents section,' Rimmington said, 'the now computerized records linked Lambert's name to a bogus driver's licence held under the name of Brian Spinks. The computer entry showed the licence had been issued on branch head authority to a Herbert Muswellbrook on 9 January 1984; he had returned it on 16 January. I requested the old licence issue card be retrieved. On examination, it showed an initialled entry indicating Joe Lambert had possession of the licence from 9–10 January.

'Muswellbrook was on a home posting,' Rimmington said. 'I spoke to him twenty minutes later. All he could say was that Lambert took the licence for an unspecified NTK purpose. On Lambert returning it to him, he had asked a Teresa English in the registry to record Lambert's temporary possession of it. He did so because he'd been taught during induction training that sensitive documents were to be handled responsibly. And he knew Lambert had already used the licence. He calculated this meant asking the registry to update the issue card could not compromise the purpose to which the licence had been put, particularly as registry staff were not permitted to ask about its use.'

Rimmington told Mumford he was informed that Teresa English had left the Service. He requested her personnel file but had to wait until it arrived from the archive. 'When I finally got to see it at 3.30 pm,' he said, 'it showed she'd resigned in April 1988. A forwarding address in Huddersfield had been provided.'

When Rimmington could find no entry for Teresa English in the Huddersfield telephone book, he had enlisted Special Branch's assistance to have the West Yorkshire police obtain her telephone number. This took over two hours. Teresa apparently worked as a music teacher at Huddersfield Grammar School using her married name of Cowan and this had made her difficult to find.

Rimmington was a details man. He was able to provide Mumford with a precise summary of his conversation with Teresa Cowan nee English drawing from the copious notes he took.

'Teresa was initially unconcerned when I rang at 6.30 pm on the night of 18 January,' Rimmington said. 'This told me she had no dark secrets to hide. I asked her to tell me what she knew about the issue card entry indicating Lambert had taken temporary possession of the licence drawn by Muswellbrook in January 1984.

'At first Teresa could not recall anything of note. All she did was repeat what Muswellbrook had said about her not being permitted to ask about the licence's use. She said her job was only to make sure the records were up to date and accurate.

'But suddenly Teresa began to cry. I had seen a lot as a copper and whatnot and was usually unflappable; regrettably, I lost my temper momentarily. "Stop snivelling woman," I demanded, "stop it this instant. Tell me why you are crying."

'She said one word. "Garry."

'I was totally perplexed. I yelled, "What?"

'Then she told me. "I told Garry Bullock that Joe had possession of the licence on 10 January." '

Rimmington told Mumford it had taken a further half hour to clarify who Bullock was and the nature of his enquiry, and another hour to find out he was no longer with the police service. Rimmington again turned to Margaret Otten. 'She moved mountains,' he said. 'By 11 pm I had a phone number in Edinburgh.

'Bullock was not pleased to be dragged out of his warm bed,'
Rimmington said. 'When I asked him the obvious he assumed the
worst. "I'm not speaking to you without my lawyer present," he
said. I tried everything from cajoling to threatening but Bullock
would not be moved. I decided this called for radical action. By
now it was close to midnight. I told Bullock I would be on his
doorstep in six hours and that he should be ready to speak.

'I immediately rang Margaret Otten. She had earlier offered
me the use of the police helicopter. I told her I now had an urgent
need for it. I suggested she come with me in case we needed to
wield a policing power of some sort against Bullock. At 6.40 am on
19 January we rang Bullock's front door bell.'

Brian McGowan again, when interviewed by Mumford. 'My home
phone rang just before 8 am on 19 January. It was Rimmington. He
was ringing from Edinburgh, where he had been up all night. He
told me he now had incontrovertible evidence that a Warsaw Bloc
agent, probably working for the Soviets, had taken an interest in a
bogus Service driver's licence Joe Lambert had in his possession.

'I learned later,' Brian had said, 'that Rimmington had given
Bullock a written guarantee of immunity. We ended up honouring
it, even though Legal wasn't very happy. Anyway, right now
Rimmington was in full flow. He put to me there were compelling
reasons to order Lambert to remain in England until his reason for

having the licence was clear and investigations had been completed into why hostile foreign intelligence elements became involved.'

Brian told Mumford he could tell from the confident tone of Rimmington's voice that he had the evidence of which he spoke – he judged this sufficient to overcome the protection of the *Star*. 'Thank you, Bill, I understand,' Brian had said. 'I will organize for a team to go to Lambert's home immediately and bring him to the office.'

Earlier on 15 January, two days after booking our Portugal flights, I had told Liliana in my sitting room I needed to lodge my travel details with the Service's personnel registry in order to be issued my private passport. This was true. It was standard requirement for officers privately travelling abroad. My visit to headquarters that day was thus an opportunity unrousing of Soviet suspicions for an audience with the DG, Martin and Digby. The DG had wasted no time. 'I'd hoped for a general chat going over Operation Opera,' he had said. 'But there's a headache with the sepop – the separation operation that is.' The DG hated jargon.

He nodded to Digby, who cleared his throat. 'The people arranging the sepop have told me their people don't have the expertise. They'll need to employ sub-contractors on the ground and pay them in US dollars. And they won't pay the subbies from the election money because obtaining hard currency in cash from the Moldovan Central Bank draws the crabs. We've no option but to pay for the sepop COD. That means you'll have to carry the funds. Here's what we propose...'

As I was leaving, the DG told me he had decided to *Star* my travel plans in the movements advice circulated to the DDGs. 'I'm confident the security risk is low,' he had said. 'And you never know, it might help smooth your way in some form or other.'

On my return home, I told Liliana the visit to the Service had really unsettled me. To her, and the listening Russians, I said I was thinking of pulling out of the Moldova visit and possibly my recruitment all together.

'Don't make any rash decisions,' Liliana had cautioned. 'It's only natural that going into headquarters would unnerve you.'

I had voiced my scepticism and pretended to vacillate before grudgingly saying, 'Provided I receive five grand US in cash on arrival in Lisbon, as a gesture of good faith, for now I'll stick with the decision I've made. But make no mistake at the first sign of trouble that's me done.'

'Let me speak to my people,' Liliana had said wearily.

I was now on heightened operational alert. The double-dealing world of espionage was such that even in the best of times a Soviet defector could walk through the door of a largely unindoctrinated Service and give up my plans to visit Moldova. In the contemporary environment, where Soviets of all shapes and sizes were reading the tea leaves and jumping ship, the risk was off the scale. True, I didn't have Rimmington in mind, and I'm sure neither did the DG when during my visit to the Service he had directed now me to act on the Service's time-honoured tenet to take all possible protections against the unexpected. On the following day, 16 January, after I had discreetly booked TAP Portugal flights to Lisbon for Liliana and me departing at 6 am on 19 January, I had Liliana tell her Russian controller the new departure time was a nervy change of mind on my part. Our BA flights at 2.55 pm on 19 January remained in place, just in case of any random check by a Service unindoctrinated.

I met Harry in the supermarket on the evening of 18 January. 'All appears in order,' I said. 'You need now advise Martin and Digby that Santa's on his way.' Harry didn't blink even though, as with all our recent conversations, he had no idea what I was talking about. His loyalty guaranteed he would ask no questions.

Service listeners had of course heard Liliana's seemingly unprompted suggestion she and I go to Moldova and later my supposed demand we visit there as a precursor to my becoming a Soviet spy. These were conversations that unavoidably had to be had for the benefit of the listening Soviets. But the wider Service never got to know about them. The DG, Martin and Digby had first call on the records of conversation the listeners prepared. They had Mavis, the DG's ancient gatekeeper, simply re-type those transcript pages referencing Moldova. The transcripts distributed to Service others, to the unsuspecting unindoctrinated who thought the operation I was running was confined to Liliana's recruitment, thus contained words like *inaudible* and *coughing* where mention of Moldova once existed.

But in the case of our secret early departure on 19 January, it was not dialogue destined for transcription the listeners would encounter but unscripted actions. The fifth floor people were worried a diligent listener monitoring my house could interpret the unexpected change of plan as an indication of something untoward and alert a Service unindoctrinated to the development.

The coded message I passed to Harry, therefore, was a signal to Martin and Digby to brief the specially selected Service listeners who would be on duty from midnight to noon on 19 January. The officers involved would be admitted to a higher category of clearance, one that imposed severe penalties in the breach.

Chapter 49 – Chisinau

By the time the Service security detail dispatched by Brian McGowan had reached my house on the morning of 19 January, Liliana and I had just landed in Lisbon. I didn't need to act nervous; I was petrified. Nonetheless, I managed to put on a convincing show of greedily counting the 5,000 dollars that as agreed the Soviets gave me on arrival. My hand conveniently shook as I signed the receipt and put the money in my backpack where it would be most secure.

And by the time the security detail had discovered our early morning departure from Heathrow, we had just arrived at a Soviet safe house and been issued our false papers for the Air Moldova flight to Chisinau the following day.

Digby rang the DG around lunchtime. It was Saturday 20 January 1990, the day after Liliana and I had travelled to Portugal. 'Flash in from second base advising that Drake drove to location Zebra this morning,' Digby said. 'Seems he has Albatross with him as Gordon predicted.' Digby was conveying an urgent message from the SIS station in Moscow had just advised that Aleshkovsky had driven to Kubinika, the military airbase outside Moscow. His passenger was Shukhov, as the defector Umarov had said he would be.

'Thank you,' the DG said. 'Could you let Martin know?'

'Certainly,' Digby had replied.

The DG's diary entry recorded the exchange.

Digby was later obliged to explain to the Service why he had not contacted Mumford. His answer was to say he was not prepared to be treated as a messenger boy. When asked why Digby had said, 'Because at the time I was convinced I was the only person on the fifth floor with the good sense and balls to prevent the Service from making a rash decision sure to harm its reputation. I considered it disrespectful to be asked to pass on messages.'

The story Service investigators went on to extract from Digby was that exactly a week before telephoning the DG, he had called on a Moldovan priest in the Toronto suburb of New Tecumseth. After handing over 25,000 Canadian dollars for the quite separate matter of electioneering, he had turned his mind to other business. 'I had also been sent to finalize arrangements for the Operation Opera sepop,' Digby had explained. 'This gave me the opening I had been looking for to rectify the DG's *irresponsible* decision to give carriage for a critical UK security interest – early warning of threats from renegade Moldovans equipped with MANPADS weaponry – to a Moldovan *femme fatale* of uncertain quantity over agents I had personally selected and vetted. That's why I introduced an additional element I called the *add-on*.'

Digby said the priest knew that his, Digby's, instructions had to be followed to the letter. Failure to do so would result in election funding being turned off. It was sufficient therefore, Digby argued, where minimizing any risk of interference with Operation Opera was concerned, just to make clear to the priest the sub-contractors should implement the *add-on* only after the sepop's completion. 'On those stipulated terms, and pursuant to successfully completing both tasks,' he said, 'I told the priest 5,000 US would be paid to the sub-contractors by our person on the ground.'

It took a bit of prodding, I understand, but eventually Digby admitted he had let the priest think the sepop and *add-on* were intertwined parts of the same operation, when in fact the *add-on* was not a part of Operation Opera, much less an element sanctioned by the DG. 'I had to do what I had to do – for England,' Digby had claimed, taking the high road with his Service inquisitors. 'Otherwise the entire country, the Service in particular, would be seen by the Americans and others as a laughing stock.'

The investigators were not entirely silly. They pressed Digby hard about his professed motive. Digby ultimately proved to be all hat and no cattle. When the cave in came, his overpowering drive to become the DG and irresistible craving for power were revealed. The *add-on,* the tearfully capitulating Digby had admitted, was directed at contrasting the DG's flawed judgement with his own verve and analytical acumen and bringing this to Whitehall's attention. It was also intended to earn the Service he aspired to lead invaluable American gratitude.

Our departure from Lisbon was uneventful. Liliana and I sat separately in the airport lounge. My forged Zambian passport declared me to be Derek Wallis. To the world at large I was a white Zambian, one of the rare breed who had stayed on after independence, embarking on a solo visit to Moldova to explore business opportunities. Agistment was my specialty. I'm not sure the large sunglasses I donned suited me but they helped disguise my appearance.

It was an era when airline passengers – and their cabin baggage – were only cursorily scrutinized. The Portuguese customs officer at the departure gate certainly asked me no questions. Nonetheless, I kept my backpack close to me at all times. After all it contained five grand US in cash. Oh, and as well, buried under the money safe in its exquisitely embossed leather container was the nine-inch, razor-sharp antique rapier bequeathed to me by Nought as a dying father would his son. With one thrust of this devastating implement into the soft fold of the skin beneath his chin, I would kill Shukhov. The *one-armed wombat* techniques I had learned at Fort Monckton would finally have a role in my life.

Liliana and I arrived in Chisinau in the early afternoon of 20 January, whereupon we dispensed with the separate travel guise. A

KGB officer approached us as we waited for our luggage. He was as nervous as me. 'The situation on the ground in Chisinau is deteriorating rapidly,' he said, anxiously looking around. 'I am tasked with informing you the General will be overnighting in Kiev and arriving here tomorrow morning, accompanied by one other.' He went on to describe how the meeting was to take place at the pre-arranged location – by that he meant Liliana's apartment – at 2 pm the following day and under the agreed terms whereby only the General and the one other would be present. No security detail would be involved. He scurried off, shaking his head as he went as if to say, *What in God's name is the General thinking?*

Liliana and I took a taxi to her apartment before going for a late lunch. I was too nervous to eat much but found comfort in a steadying glass of rich Nistreana red wine. Afterwards we made our way to Valea Morilor Park. The large lake in the middle of the park was frozen solid. We stood in an area perched high above the frozen tundra, surrounded by a small fountain and several large Grecian urns on stone bases. 'This is the first time we've been able to speak freely since you came to the UK,' I said, smiling at Liliana.

But she was in no mood for small talk. 'I know you're up to something,' she said, her eyes ablaze. 'Otherwise why are you walking around hugging that backpack while pretending to safeguard the US dollars you demanded? I know the money means nothing to you. I just hope you know what you're doing.' I could have easily said *Amen* but remained silent. 'Tell me, Joe,' Liliana said, now softer, 'what convinced you I would not alert the Russians to your Service's elaborate plans – the safe room and recruiting me – and I would go along with your private deception to convince Shukhov to come to Chisinau, about which you don't even want your own Service to know?' I could see Liliana wasn't budging until she had some answers.

'There's no question the Service has been slow to focus on Moldova,' I began. 'The Moldova People's Council, the MPC, the ethnic Moldovan political arm, crept onto our radar last year as a result of the mass demonstrations it organized calling for traditional Romanian to replace Russian as Moldova's official language and later the anti-communist riots it instigated. Since then, the Service has cultivated contacts with the MPC.' I knew Digby Carhiddy had been the prime mover but made no mention of it. 'I honestly don't know the exact details,' I continued, 'but there's some tie up between expatriate Moldovans and the MPC, principally through religious groupings in Canada. I know money has been funnelled through these channels to assist the MPC contest the elections early next year the communists have been forced to hold.'

The wind blew off the ice sheet on the lake and I pulled the collar of my jacket higher around my ears. Liliana appeared not to feel the chill. 'Mind you,' I said, understanding she was bidding me to go on, 'when I did tell the Service about you in late

December, it did not immediately accept your value, even after I informed it of your deep-seated understanding of the risk to UK interests in Europe of Moldovan irregulars obtaining abandoned Soviet weaponry. The prevailing view, especially among some senior people, was that sufficient reliance could be placed on MPC contacts.' Again I thought of Digby and again I said nothing.

Liliana scoffed. 'Your senior people are mistaken if they think the MPC will be around forever. It will burn out as soon as the elections are held. It is far too internally fragmented to govern and will have to be replaced by a more stable body.'

I shrugged. 'Whatever, the focus at first was on whether you were worth the trouble. The DG eventually decided that a Soviet agent is a Soviet agent, even if you rejected our approach. So long as you were in the UK, you could be detained. At a minimum, the Service would have a bargaining chip for a future agent exchange.'

'What else did you say about me, Joe? I want to hear it all.'

'My initial approach,' I said, 'was to tell the Service that when we were in Washington I quickly became convinced you are first and foremost a Moldovan patriot. Your anxiety over a possible civil war between ethnic Moldovans and Transnistrian separatists told me you were not someone rusted on to any one side. This convinced me you could be recruited because your heart was with

Moldova, not a discredited socialist ideology. In that vein, I argued the obvious: the MPC is as polarized against the Transnistrians as they are against the ethnic Moldovans. How could we be sure we were ever getting a reliable read-out from either?'

Liliana suddenly changed subjects. 'If your senior people are so enamoured with the MPC, why is it proposed that my controller pose as an employee of a private UK aid organization?'

I wondered if she was testing me, looking for signs of fabrication. 'The cover organization for your cut-out,' I replied, 'is well known to me. It is called HOPE. And, yes, that's precisely the point. I argued that manipulation of elections is one thing and running agents is another. To risk reliance on the MPC was to misread the situation. There is general agreement in the Service that Moldova will eventually attain independence and the UK will have an embassy here. But in the interim, there was a need for a neutral cut-out, not for reliance on one of the obviously biased disputants. It took a little time but eventually one influential deputy and then the DG came around to this proposition. From there on the plan to recruit you came together.'

My explanation transported me back to the discussions that long day of 28 December, when first Martin in his greenhouse and then the DG in his apartment's anteroom had signed on to my thinking. The same could not be said for Digby, who had invested so much personal capital in cultivating the MPC. His smouldering resentment at being overruled by the DG was still on display two weeks later.

'Come on,' I said to Liliana. 'It's too cold to sit here much longer.' On the return walk to her apartment I took her hand. 'Don't worry,' I said, 'the Service will look after you. You'll likely be preventing a bloodbath taking place in Moldova.'

But all Liliana did was to smile wanly. 'You still haven't told me why you want Shukhov in Chisinau,' she said.

Chapter 50 – Secrets

'Liliana,' I said as we lay in her bed that night, 'if you suspect I am up to something with Shukhov why did you assist in arranging his visit here without knowing the reason for it?'

She laughed softly. 'When we were in Washington, Joe, you came to believe I truly loved you. But on discovering who I was you reverted to being a stereotyped Englishman, automatically assuming I could never love you because of our age difference. We in Moldova let our hearts decide everything, not silly prejudices. From the moment I entered your house, when first in the safe room, I knew I was meant to be with you. And when you suggested I sleep in your bed that second night I understood you felt the same way, even though you were still trying to be angry with me and no doubt had your reasons for making the suggestion. This is why I helped you.'

With that, Liliana slept in my arms. I lay there staring at the ceiling wondering if I would be alive this time tomorrow. For years I had schemed to kill Shukhov, even when I didn't know him by name. I never thought the day would come. Questions raced through my mind and fear and self-doubt mounted.

I was too tense to sleep. I replayed over and over the DG's staccato briefing that Saturday morning of 6 January at the Matilda West

Gallery, four days before Liliana's arrival in the UK, when he had detailed the full gamut of Operation Opera, while Martin, Digby and I sat there listening intently. How the American debrief of Umarov had revealed Shukhov was in personal terminal decline. How Umarov had declared Aleshkovsky his certain heir apparent and the man who would be chosen to build Russia's standalone spy agency, the successor to the KGB once the Soviet Union had fragmented in the face of independence sentiment – volatile, rife and rising – in virtually all its republics. But how Aleshkovsky along with his wife and children would be eliminated once his work in building the new Russian spy apparatus was done, simply because he and they were part of the old Soviet regime. And how Umarov, knowing Aleshkovsky and the turmoil and dislocation of his childhood, was prepared to bet that if confronted head-on by this reality, the Colonel would place his family above country. All that was required, Umarov had told his interrogators, was to lure Shukhov out of Moscow. Aleshkovsky would follow as sure as day follows night. And once free of the Kremlin's galvanizing influence on his sense of duty, Umarov had said, leverage could be achieved against Aleshkovsky and a pitch made to him.

The DG had recalled me proposing in his apartment's anteroom that I should demand Liliana come to the UK. 'Once you suggested it, Joe' he had said, 'I immediately identified the possibility of a bolt on to the base operation, one involving Liliana orchestrating Shukhov's use as a decoy to entice Aleshkovsky out of Moscow.

The Americans are confident that Aleshkovsky's defection would cripple Russia's efforts to stand-up a credible successor to the KGB when the Cold War soon ends. After long debate, the CIA green-lighted Opera.' Once Liliana was in London, the DG had directed, I was to persuade her to arrange for me to meet Shukhov as part of my supposed recruitment. Chisinau was the most plausible location. If Liliana had an apartment there that would be ideal. 'Digby,' the DG had explained, 'will organize a side operation to separate Aleshkovsky and Shukhov for about thirty minutes.' Digby had confirmed this was so. Then all that remained, the DG had said with chilling simplicity, was the *Main Act*, or Operation Opera, as my hugely secret planned pitch to Aleshkovsky otherwise was known.

The DG had directed that operational security was paramount. 'Under no circumstances,' he had said, 'can Liliana come to know of the bolt on. This is the opportunity of a lifetime. Liliana is the link to Shukhov. The most she can be allowed to think is luring him to Chisinau is Joe's secret personal initiative. Aleshkovsky must be kept out of it. The risk of detection is too great. For one thing, the Russian voice analysis of her telephone conversations with her controller will reveal stress if she really knows what is at stake.'

The DG's face was grey and creased with strain. 'It is also critical,' he said, 'to keep Operation Opera from the wider Service. Others will be briefed on the base op to recruit Liliana as an eyes and ears asset in Moldova, including the funding offer to be made to this

HOPE outfit. But Joe's travel to Chisinau must be closely guarded. Otherwise, conjecture about our actual objective vis-à-vis Liliana risks leakage of our bolt on designs on Aleshkovsky. If the Russians detected a mere hint of this they would quarantine him.' In the event, the DG had warned with ominous understatement, the Americans would be substantially unimpressed.

I recalled the DG's intense concentration as Mumford detailed the role of my conduit to the Service after Liliana's arrival, first at the Chinese restaurant and then the supermarket. Martin had also outlined how references to my visiting Moldova would be excised from the transcripts of my conversations with Liliana distributed to Service others read in on the base op recruitment. And finally, he had told the DG that those listeners witnessing our secret early departure on 19 January would be specially briefed. Only when satisfied with all three assurances had the DG warily ticked off. 'That Weideman fellow should be the conduit,' he had instructed. 'He is loyal to Joe and can be relied on to keep his mouth shut.'

The DG's closing question was to ask Martin and Digby if they were sure Liliana would cooperate; if she would agree to the base recruitment and subsequently assist me with the critical secret step of arranging Shukhov's visit to Chisinau. Digby had shrugged non-committedly. Martin, however, had said, 'I think so, provided Liliana is wholly devoted to Joe.' We had all stared at him. 'Joe,' he said, 'has castigated Liliana for her deception. Once she has arrived and is in his home, I think he should abandon the wounded lover posture and take steps, shall we say, to extend an olive branch.'

The DG's brow had furrowed. 'I'm more than a little concerned about the optics of Joe romancing Liliana while supposedly running a coercion recruitment revolving around the threat of her long-term imprisonment,' he had said. 'It could create precisely the type of speculation I want to avoid. Her recruitment is not being sold to the wider Service as a lonely hearts entrapment.'

Martin had smiled at the DG in spite of the tension. 'The plan won't work without it, Colin. It's up to Joe to ensure it happens without anyone on our side, listeners included, becoming aware.' Martin wasn't suggesting a fabricated romance. Rather, he had somehow determined in advance of anyone else that Liliana and I still loved each other. It was this he wanted to ignite. He said as much. 'It has to be love,' he had whispered in our ungrasping ears.

I also thought about that day of 28 December when I had confessed the whole ghastly lot to Mumford in his greenhouse – starting with Gulam's letter informing me the Russians had killed Agnes – and repeated the disclosure a matter of hours later to the DG and Digby in the anteroom of the DG's apartment. But there was one key variable. Rather than admit to a plan to kill Shukhov, I depicted my antics as a grief-driven quest to reveal the truth behind Agnes's death. They were not impressed, as I knew they would not be.

The prepared salve I had offered that December day was to propose I recruit Liliana as an early warning, on the ground source in Moldova working to a cut-out under HOPE cover. Mumford and then the DG had agreed that when I rang Liliana on 2 January I should demand the Soviets stick to their evident plan for her to pitch at me in the UK. After all, I was a nervous might-be Soviet agent. Only Digby had abstained. At the time, though, it was not Liliana's recruitment once in London I had in mind, but mine. My private end game turned on convincing Liliana I was serious about spying for the Soviets, but conditional on first meeting Shukhov. I would force Liliana to arrange this. When she did, I would kill him.

My restored resolve to kill Shukhov derived of course from my fury that I had been hoodwinked into abandoning Agnes. This emotional charge still coursed powerfully within me a week and a half later at the Matilda West Gallery. When Operation Opera was unveiled as the near duplicate of my private end game, my intention to kill Shukhov remained the one secret I did not share with the others.

Fortunately Operation Opera, in relying on gentler means for luring Shukhov to Chisinau, diverged from the browbeating of Liliana envisaged in my private end game. Fortunate because my determination to kill Shukhov had persisted after my affection for Liliana was no longer in abeyance, after her second night with me when I no longer had the will to try and force her to do anything.

Chapter 51 – Shakespeare

At 2 pm sharp on Sunday 21 January 1990, there was a short rap on the door of Liliana's apartment. The time had come. For some reason my mind was filled with thoughts of Bootle, particularly the Bootle docks. Try as might, I could not be rid of them. Liliana moved to answer the door. I touched her arm to stop her. She watched, puzzled, as I hung a towel over the small Juliet balcony looking onto Strada Alexei Sciusev. Then I nodded to her.

Greetings were made in Russian, followed by the sound of shuffling footsteps along the short hallway. The door to the living room opened. I held my breath. I had expected two KGB officers in military uniform. Instead I saw a man in loose-fitting casual garments, once obviously large but now white-haired and shrunken. A younger man, ramrod straight and of unmistakable military bearing, also in civilian clothes supported him. The younger man pronounced himself as Aleshkovsky. He held an oxygen cylinder. A plastic lead extended from it curling around the older man's ears so that the lead's two prongs inserted in his nostrils would stay in place. I sat on a small couch. Liliana was to sit next to me to translate if Russian was spoken. Nought's rapier, free from its container, nestled in the inside pocket of my jacket.

'Mr Lambert,' the older man said in English, each word uttered only with considerable effort, 'I have been waiting to meet you for a long, long time.' He gripped Aleshkovsky's arm, releasing it only once he was lowered into a straight back chair he had nominated with his eyes. 'I am close to the end,' he said. 'If I am any judge, the travel of the last two days has just about done for me.'

Looking at Shukhov in person for the first time, my unshakable resolve to kill him – my restored ironclad commitment – instantly evaporated. Dismayed by this and the suddenness of it, flailing and seeking protection from my own condemnation, I willed myself to picture Agnes deferring to Shukhov's state of decay: *Anger's such a counterproductive emotion*, she would say. But thoughts of Bootle, those that were niggling me and would not let go, overrode the obfuscation. I was again a young boy on the Bootle docks learning to talk the talk because I was too scared to fight the fight. My plan to kill General Shukhov would never be fulfilled, in his sickness or health. When the chips were finally down I didn't have the stomach.

Oblivious to my internal turmoil, Shukhov had paused to gather what breath he could. Now he spoke, snapping me from my wallowing. 'Two things quickly, while I can,' he said, his bushy eyebrows rising as he leant forward. 'You want to recruit Dmitri I take it?' Aleshkovsky recoiled at this, vigourously shaking his head. I'm sure I looked stunned too. Shukhov smiled. 'Do you think I am such an old fool as to fall for this nonsense about you wanting personal assurances before we can recruit you? I can smell traps like that from five miles away.' He turned to look at Aleshkovsky, the craning of his neck causing him obvious discomfort. 'You must accept their offer, Dmitri. The socialist dream is over. It's every man for the lifeboats. There will be purges and God knows what before the dust settles. That's the Russian way; it will never change. You're part of the old regime. Your card is marked along with that of your wife and children.'

Turning back to me he ordered me like the General he was. 'Give Dmitri the papers you want him to sign. Give them to him right now so that he can sign them while I'm alive to see it.' Returning his gaze to Aleshkovsky he said, 'You're clever enough to understand, Dmitri, that putting your signature on the forms is not something you can later repudiate. The Presidium will suspect you for signing them, whatever the circumstances, and only execute you and your family quicker than it would have anyway. Sign them now my boy. Sign them so I can die knowing I've given you and those who sustain you a chance at life.'

A moment of hesitation, followed by the flourish of a pen. And with that Colonel Dmitri Aleksandrovich Aleshkovsky embarked on his defection to Her Majesty's Secret Service. 'Go to the Moscow Circus in the Lenin Hills next Friday night,' I told him. 'Someone will contact you there to begin making extraction arrangements.'

'And the second thing, General Shukhov?' I asked, looking up as I returned the signed forms to the hidden pouch inside the lining of my rucksack, my instincts telling me to keep things moving.

Shukhov was exhausted and ghostly pale. I had to lean forward to hear what he was saying. 'Katya Lyubimova Vasilieva, you will know her. She is imprinted on your soul.'

Sensing it was a question I nodded before I realized it wasn't. 'What about her?' I asked, my mouth suddenly dry.

'She was my daughter,' Shukhov said, lifting his watery eyes to mine.

We all looked at him, dumfounded. 'General …,' Aleshkovsky gasped, his mouth agape, unable to find other words to say.

Shukhov appeared not to notice the reaction. 'Not by my lawful wife,' he said looking at me. 'An indiscretion, actually, one I tended to keep quiet. But I loved Katya more than you could imagine. My world changed when I signed her execution papers. I was no longer objective. I wanted to destroy you on finding out it was you who recruited her.' Shukhov was not inventing. He was slipping away and had time for nothing but the truth. I wanted to ask about Katya's mother and understand who had raised her, who it was that Katya so badly wanted to protect when we recruited her. But the questions would not form in my mind. It was all too late. The innocents had already been punished.

No longer with the strength to turn to Aleshkovsky, Shukhov spoke to the floor. 'That's the real reason, Dmitri, why I waited far too long before putting Citadel into operation. My judgement was flawed. I didn't care a fig for the damage we might cause the US–UK intelligence relationship. But I needed the resources of the Soviet state for what I wanted to do and needed a plausible reason for using them, one I had to pretend was a huge secret. I did want Lambert here to betray the Americans from within their privileged inner sanctum but only so I could extract the full measure of revenge. I wasn't satisfied by the thought of him going to prison, even for a long time; I wanted his betrayal to be on a scale where the Americans would run a wet affair against him.'

Shukhov stopped to take several shallow gasps of air before continuing. 'I did toy briefly with executing him ourselves. But issuing orders infringing the gentlemen's agreement was guaranteed to attract political attention and invite discussion. There had to be a better way. The plan I arrived at was to have the Americans do the job for us. That's why I kept waiting and waiting, in the hope of achieving the ultimate revenge. But then Lambert became unloved by the Americans. Some months later, while waiting to see if his situation improved, my illness sharply worsened, without warning as the doctors had said it might. I knew then I was dying. I was spent.

I had no option but to settle for the cold comfort of Lambert's alternative recruitment.'

After all this time, I thought, *all this bloody stress and worry, I finally know it was Shukhov's own agenda driving events.*

I wanted to reflect more, to think about everything that had happened to me. But I couldn't wait. Shukhov was fading. And more than anything I wanted him to tell me the one thing I already knew. 'Agnes?' I said softly.

It was now Shukhov's turn to strain to hear. 'She was to you what Katya was to me' he replied eventually. 'Her death was not a an eye for an eye if that is any consolation; like Katya she was just another operational requirement in this unholy life you and I have chosen.' Shukhov stared at me. We both knew the unpleasant truth. Shukhov's gaze turned to Liliana. 'She was to replace your Agnes,' he said, smiling at Liliana with sad fondness. 'But we were too clever by half; she was too much like Agnes. No doubt Liliana has told you about her visit to Sofia last December?'

'Some, but not the precise detail,' I replied cautiously.

Shukhov continued, wheezing and labouring as he did. 'I strongly suspected what had happened when she reported her mistake in alerting you as to who she was, that she was a Soviet agent. By you, I mean you personally. I know Liliana would never have betrayed me to your Service or the Americans.'

Shukhov began to cough violently, the rattling sound resembling the tearing of plasterboard. With much effort he stilled himself. 'I know Liliana very well,' he rasped. 'She and Katya were so alike. She was like a second daughter to me, particularly after … that … with Katya …' His voice trailed off rich in grief. 'The Sofia meeting confirmed everything I suspected. She is too good to have made such a stupid mistake. The funny thing is I don't think she realized the reason for it. I guessed you would demand she come to the UK. I told my people she should be allowed to do that. I wanted her to understand she had warned you because she had fallen in love with you. My dying gift to my second daughter, my living daughter. Before it was all too late.'

We stared at each other, both reflecting on how alike and intersecting our respective journeys of vengeance had been. 'How were you going to get back at me, Joe?' Shukhov asked after a time. 'What was to be the personal touch you intended in culmination of this clever plan to entice me to Chisinau?' I was taken aback by his forthright familiarity. But he was a man stripped bare and no longer knew formality. I took the rapier from my jacket and showed it to him. Liliana gave a start and Aleshkovsky sat forward in his chair. Shukhov smiled. 'Today certainly, but even a year ago I doubt you would have got me with that.' To my surprise and consternation in equal measure, I found myself laughing with, not at him.

The ensuing quiet was suddenly shattered by the sound of splintering timber. *The fucking sepop*, I thought. I'd been happy to trigger it by placing the towel over the apartment balcony, as called for in Operation Opera. But only because I had calculated that killing Shukhov would be easier without Aleshkovsky present and possibly coming to the General's defence. Now, however, it was an unwelcome interruption that could not be turned off. Two men ran into the room, as if late for an important appointment. They were young, strong and rough-looking. Almost apologetically one blurted, 'The master key did not work.' He spoke Russian. Liliana whispered a translation to me. The others sat transfixed.

'Are you Shukhov?' the other man asked Aleshkovsky.

'No,' yelled Aleshkovsky, rising from his seat in the same instant to confront the intruders as his military training took hold. Both men had handguns. Aleshkovsky stopped. Unarmed, there was little he could do.

'What do you want?' Liliana demanded with fierce indignation.

'We mean no harm,' the man who asked for Shukhov said. He raised his pistol in the air. 'We have these only for our safety.'

The other began an obviously prepared recital. 'We are Transnistrian patriots,' he said. 'We need to speak privately to the General. The MPC is spreading rumours the Russians are guilty of conspiring with the Nazis to defraud Romania of territory in order to incorporate it into Moldova. If true, we must speed up our timetable for independence, before these wretched Moldovans wanting to suckle from the Romanian teat have their way and there is a Romanian flag flying over Tiraspol. We need to consult General Shukhov on this now, right now, this moment.'

Shukhov appeared to be sleeping, his head inclined to one side as though he was straining to hear a bird sing. Yellowy-tinged fluid seeped from his mouth, trickling down his neck and onto his shirt collar. We waited for Shukhov to respond, we and the intruders alike. But the General did not. Indeed, he could not. For the Great Russian Bear was dead.

There was a moment of confusion. Aleshkovsky was first to recover. He took Shukhov gently in his arms while mouthing something in Russian, a religious liturgy I assumed, and laid the body on the hearthrug before lightly kissing Shukhov's snow-white forehead. The MPC sub-contractors looked at one another. One turned to Liliana and spoke in the Romanian language of Moldova's heritage. I didn't understand him but his tone was questioning and I detected he said, 'Liliana Leanca?' Liliana nodded in confirmation. He then raised the arm in which he held his pistol.

I immediately sensed what he was about to do. The rapier still in my hand, I lunged forward as he fired two rapid shots into Liliana's upper torso. The recoil of the discharging gun pushed him slightly backwards, resulting in my rapier contacting only his arm. My forward momentum caused me to fall to the floor. The shooter yelled in pain and his companion in alarm. The injured man's gun fell to the timber floor of the apartment and slid over its smooth surface in the direction of Shukhov's body over which Aleshkovsky crouched. The two men stood still exchanging bewildered looks. One looked down at me and said in English, 'Money?' That was the last word he ever spoke. Aleshkovsky, having picked up the fallen firearm, shot him and his companion dead, both with perfect headshots delivered from a kneeling position.

As if in slow motion, I crawled to Liliana and took her in my arms. The flow of blood from her chest told me the worst. It was the scene of a Shakespearean tragedy. The two men dead off to one side, Aleshkovsky sitting in vigil over the dead body of Shukhov, and me cradling the lifeless second love of my life, unable to think of anything other than my preordained destiny to be *The Lone Wolf at Cover*.

Chapter 52 – Stilled

I later told my people in London how Aleshkovsky took control. He had called his office before instructing me to change into clean cloths. Initially I couldn't react and stood there rooted to the spot. He had slapped me hard across the face to get me moving. The bodies of Shukhov and Liliana had been removed by a Russian military ambulance by the time I left for the airport in an unmarked car and my onwards journey on the night flight to Rome. A windowless van arrived just as I was leaving, its job to dispose of the men's bodies. I was barely functioning. But once in Rome I was able to draw on the 5,000 dollars in my rucksack to buy myself a hotel room. Only when in the room did I discover I had managed to return Nought's rapier to its embossed presentation box and bury it in my carry bag. I had no recollection of doing so. It took a whole day before I was able to make any impression on the British Embassy. Eventually, however, travelling under a temporary travel document issued in my own name I returned to London into the waiting, if decidedly untender, arms of the Service.

The DG deigned not to see me. 'You're too much of a political hot potato,' Brian McGowan said genially as he spread a raft of papers before me. As ADDG, he was to manage my exit. 'Under the SIS Act, Joe, we could have thrown the book at you on any number of fronts; criminal charges aplenty. But the Minister decided to exercise the discretion the law affords him. He judged you had made an important contribution to the recent recruitment of a high-ranking Soviet source and that overall it was best to avoid the hoo-ha of a trial and be rid of you quietly.' I nodded. 'But you haven't got off scot-free,' Brian cautioned. 'There's a financial penalty involved in the form of us withholding your pension and payment of all leave credits, as the Act also entitles us to do in cases of gross indiscipline.' I didn't respond; my spirit was too sapped for further bureaucratic battle. 'Sign here, here and here,' Brian said perfunctorily. 'And date it as of today, 7 February 1990.'

I did. 'That's it?' I asked.

'That's it,' he confirmed. Brian stood to leave. 'One last thing, Joe,' he said softly, 'even though technically it's now none of your business. I thought I'd let you know that Digby's also resigned. Not on the DG's Christmas card list at the moment, not by a long shot. A Service investigative team is shortly to interview him. He will likely face charges for arranging Liliana's death.' I raised my eyebrows but said nothing. 'Looks like Rupert Heneshaw will get the nod to replace him as DDG. Seems he's had his son in therapy with positive results. Rupert's been freed up to do some good work over the last couple of years. He's fully recovered from any career setback associated with his inglorious retreat from Washington.'

'I see,' I said. 'I'm sure that will disappoint my old friend Freddie, even though he's close to Heneshaw.'

Brian laughed, recalling the enmity between Ladler and me he had first witnessed long ago when we did the root and branch review. 'A submission's currently with the Minister to upgrade Washington head of station to a DDG position,' he said. 'The relationship just continues to grow and with that so do the station's responsibilities. I expect we'll get the tick very shortly. We'll need to advertise the vacancy but Ladler's a dead certainty to get it.' Brian snapped his briefcase closed. 'If you say a word about what I've just told you about Digby, Heneshaw or Ladler, I'll garrotte you.' He was smiling because he knew I wouldn't. 'Just treat it as my parting gift to you.' He closed the door behind him as he left.

Martin Mumford saw me out. We walked in silence initially. 'On hearing your story,' he said as we approached the janitors' desk at the front entrance, 'I admit I wasn't very happy with you. But I now accept any advantage you took of me was incidental to your plan to kill Shukhov. Anyway, life's too short for grudges.'

Martin reflected for a moment. 'Our friend you just signed up will in due course give us the full story of your saga from the other side's perspective. Come back to London, say towards the end of 1991. You know where I live. I should be done with debriefing Aleshkovsky by then and have completed all the other interviews I need do. I'll let you read what I might and where I can't give you papers, I'll tell you what I can.' That promise, of course, became in its honouring Martin's *Final Briefing*.

We exited the front of the building. I held out my hand. Martin shook it firmly. 'Joe,' Martin called out as I walked away, 'you had all the makings of a first-rate officer. Pity you wasted it.' I watched him turn and re-enter the Service.

I returned to Brent Cross, not directly to my home but to the local real estate office to put my house on the market. The next day I travelled to Hungerford, to the Memorial Wall in Saint Saviour's Cemetery. In conversation with Agnes, I explained about Liliana and how fate had led me to love two women. I told Agnes I now needed to return to Moldova to find Liliana's body, contact her father and arrange for her proper burial. I asked for understanding, telling Agnes I had chosen the means for fulfilling my obligations to Liliana specifically because it would also bring us closer together.

Finally, I told Agnes of my shame on discovering I had no stomach for my perceived duty to avenge her. I said I always knew she would have regarded my plan to kill Shukhov as a retrograde step at odds with her forward-looking philosophy of forgiveness. But full of guilt and negative energy I had ignored this. When I found to my surprise I liked Shukhov, my shame in not killing him was replaced by relief. I told Agnes how this came to tell me the revenge I had sought was only for myself. I realized then that all she would ever want of me would be to ensure we were always together. I could guarantee this. No matter where I went or what I did the vial of her ashes her mother gave me would be by my side.

Returning to London late at night, I was up early the next morning for my trip to the HOPE office in Ruislip. Rebecca Normington the CEO greeted me on arrival. 'We're pleased to have you on board, Joe,' she said. 'To be honest, I was relieved when Mr Marks rang to say the Foreign Office was now unable to fund the proposed HOPE office in Chisinau.' She smiled. 'We pride ourselves on our low pay and poor conditions. When I told Mr Marks we were still keen on opening an office in Moldova, he mentioned your name and that you had resigned from the FO. We were thrilled to receive your letter of interest. It's also timely that the FO intends to relax its rules on former employees visiting Moldova, subject to free and fair elections at the end of this month. Your diplomatic experience on the ground will be invaluable.'

I arrived in Moldova on 14 March 1990. My arrival coincided with my fiftieth birthday. That was by design. I wanted my new decade to mark my new beginning. Alone – certainly. But not as *The Lone Wolf at Cover* of which Nought had warned. In one way or another, I was now with both my loves. It was as if I were a bobbing cork in the ocean that had taken half a century to still.

Glossary

Secret Intelligence Service (SIS) hierarchy

DG: Director General answering to the Foreign Secretary

DDG: Deputy Director General with operational responsibility
ADDG: Administrative Deputy Director General

FADG: First Assistant Director General – division head
Washington/Brussels/Bonn station heads: FADG-level positions
Personnel: FADG-equivalent subordinate to the ADDG

Branch head: Head of operational branch answering to a
FADG/**Director**: Section head answering to a branch head

Service divisions/branches/sections

CIB: Counter Intelligence Branch/**CIS**: Counter Intelligence Section
FIU: Falklands Intelligence Unit – headed by Freddie Ladler
INS: Indonesia Section
SID: Southern and Central Europe and Iberia Division
SPB: Soviet Political Branch – comprising **MAS**: Moscow Affairs
Section/**SSS**: Soviet Satellites Section

General

DGSE/GID/RAW/SIMSI: Service counterpart organizations in
France, Egypt, India, and Italy respectively
FO: Foreign Office
HOPE: Agnes's employer – London-based aid organization
MANPADS: Portable, shoulder-mounted missiles launchers
MPC: Moldovan People's Council – ethnic Moldovan political arm
NTK: *Need to know* – the Service's key secrecy principle
TDC: Thames Development Company – aid delivery contractor
PA: Positive Action resources – specialist staff based in CIS
UDI: Unilateral Declaration of Independence
WRR: White Rule for Rhodesia – London-based activist group

30697067R00290

Printed in Great Britain
by Amazon